A SCRIBE DIES IN BROOKLYN

ALSO BY MARVIN J. WOLF

For Whom the Shofar Blows
Abandoned in Hell: The Fight for Vietnam's Firebase Kate
Where White Men Fear to Tread
Rotten Apples
Family Blood
Fallen Angels
Perfect Crimes
Buddha's Child

A SCRIBE DIES IN BROOKLYN

A RABBI BEN MYSTERY

MARVIN J. WOLF

RAMBAM PRESS

Published 2017
ISBN: 978-0-9899600-2-1

Book design by Stacey Aaronson

Antenna Books eBook edition © 2016 by Marvin J. Wolf
Rambam Press Paperback Edition Copyright © December 2016

Printed in the United States of America

"Ye shall not swear by My name falsely, so that thou profane
the name of thy God: I am the LORD."
—Leviticus 19:12

Acknowledgments

While this is a work of fiction, and its component characters and story are entirely my creation, it was my intention to present such material as relates to Judaism and to other religions, and to actual places, historical figures and world events as accurately as possible. To this end, my efforts have been greatly aided by the assistance of Rabbi Daniel Shevitz of Congregation Mishkon Tephilo, a Conservative synagogue in Venice, California. In addition, the story and its verisimilitude have been materially enhanced by the insights, suggestions and factual corrections provided by Rabbi David Stein and by Ms. Catharine Nelson. Dr. Cynthia Goldstein proofread my manuscripts and corrected numerous errors of fact and usage.

I am also indebted to my daughter, Tomi, for her forbearance and emotional support while I struggled over this story. Most of all, I am indebted to my literary agent, Douglas Grad, whose expressions of support and belief in my work and in this mystery series in particular have been and will be very important to my writing.

—Marvin J. Wolf, Asheville, NC, 2016

PROLOGUE

June 2007

BORED OUT OF HIS MIND, BARRY "THE BEAST" Laudermilk, Major, USAF, yawned, stretching his six foot, six inch, 240-pound body. A guy with more than 800 hours in F16 cockpits. A guy with three confirmed Iraqi MIG kills. A guy flying a TV screen an hour up the road from Las Vegas? No way in hell is this the path to a squadron command, he thought. No chance now of retiring with stars on his collar. Not for a guy half a world removed from the real action. Not for pushing a slow, defenseless drone around the skies. Any computer geek with an hour on Flight Simulator could do this work.

The Beast blinked and peered at one of the six big monitors before him, watching a line of Army Humvees pick its way across a trackless expanse of Iraq's Western Desert. Three miles above, an MQ-1B Predator described lazy circles in the hot, turbulent air, transmitting data and pictures through a satellite link to Laudermilk's cubicle at Creech Air Force Base.

The Humvees were a recon platoon moving to ambush positions near the Syrian border. After dark, they'd deploy ground radar and look for jihadi infiltrators. Laudermilk's job was to watch their flanks, ensure that they didn't stray into Syria, and support them with Hellfire missiles if they ran into more than they could handle.

As if anyone but a fool dogface would be running around under a desert sun with air temps upward of 130 degrees. Five more hours of this, he thought, and I can drive home and catch the Yankees-Red Sox game on TiVo.

"Sloppy Boxcar, this is Bitter Pumpkin Six, over," said an unmistakably New York voice in Laudermilk's ear. With a jolt, The Beast rejoined reality.

"Sloppy Boxcar, go," Laudermilk replied.

"Is that what I think it is, up high on our Sierra Echo?"

"I'll have a look. Wait."

Laudermilk banked the drone until its nose camera framed the southeastern horizon — and a galloping gray-yellow wall of billowing sand. A haboob, and huge.

"Crap!"

He punched buttons on his console, and then eyed the monitor showing a weather satellite feed from 22,300 miles above the Indian Ocean. A vast ochre mass swirling northeast out of the Arabian Peninsula was heading straight for Iraq.

"Bitter Pumpkin Six, Sloppy Boxcar, over."

"Six, go."

"Yup, that's a ginormous sandstorm. You got maybe three-zero to find cover."

"Copy, a big haboob inbound."

"Stand by, and I'll have a look around for you."

Laudermilk leveled the Predator, watching the nose camera feed. Three kilometers to the northwest, along the Syrian border, the narrow mouth of a wadi yawned. He zoomed the camera for a close-up.

"Bitter Pumpkin, Sloppy Boxcar."

"Six, go."

"Steer two-niner zero about three clicks, and find the wadi. About a click in, it angles left, then goes under a road. Stay clear of the road; that's in Abu Kamal, Syria."

"What do I need to know about Abu... what's it called again?"

"Abu Kamal. Farm town—all you gotta know is that it's full of Syrian border police and we don't need any international incidents. Stay well clear."

"Copy two-niner-zero degrees, three clicks, avoid the road."

"Roger. I've got to get up top of that weather, so it's adios for now. Check back on this freq when the storm clears. Hey—you from Brooklyn?"

"Hell, yes. You know Bensonhurst?"

"Believe it! Grew up in Canarsie."

"Small world. Thanks, Canarsie."

"Good luck, Bensonhurst. Out."

In the right front seat of his Humvee, Platoon Sergeant Scott MacPherson, in headset and helmet, reached down to the radio and flipped over to platoon frequency.

"This is Six Actual. Big sandstorm inbound. We're moving to cover on azimuth two-niner-zero. Roger in turn, and join up on my flanks, over.""Roger One, over."

"Roger Two, over."

"Roger Three, over."

"Roger Four, two-niner zero and moving."

The five vehicles turned, spread out abreast and bumped across the broken, rock-strewn desert floor as fast as MacPherson thought was safe. After about ten minutes, as they approached the base of a sandstone ridge, the wadi mouth opened before them.

"Bitter Pumpkin, let's slow it down. Let some air out of those tires."

MacPherson watched the gauge as PFC Paul Franklyn, his

driver, flipped a switch and bled pressure from all four tires simultaneously.

"That's good, Frankie. Right there."

One by one, MacPherson in the lead, the vehicles entered the wadi, negotiating a sandy floor cut with shallow gullies.

Five minutes in, the walls rose and closed to little more than the width of two vehicles. The wadi angled left. Ahead, MacPherson saw the silhouette of a suspension bridge. That had to be the road that Canarsie, the Predator pilot, had warned him about.

"Hold it right here."

MacPherson jumped out, feeling the approaching storm, the charged air, the acrid taste and smell of ozone evoking a memory of his grandfather's old Lionel electric train.

Tall and lean, with skin the color of a mocha frappuccino, MacPherson was 30, young to be a platoon sergeant with more than twelve years' service. He gestured with his arms for his men to dismount and gather around him.

"Listen up. In ten minutes, give or take, this bitch is all over us. The wadi walls should help with the wind, but sand is gonna blow into everything. If you gotta pee, take a dump, smoke, eat something, now's the time. Bring the water cans and MREs inside, get out of your web gear, get comfortable, then back in the vehicles and button up. Goggles and face scarves. Kill your radios and save the batteries. And easy on the water. It's gonna last all day. We might could even be here for days.

"Do it."

The men scurried around under MacPherson's gaze. He watched Torres, one of his best men, climb atop a Humvee bumper to grab a water can lashed to the roof.

"Sergeant Mac! There's a cave up there," called Torres, pointing to the wadi wall.

"Don't see it."

"Gotta come up here with me, Sarge."

MacPherson leapt onto a bumper. Scanning the sandstone, he saw a dark slit.

"Got it. You looking for privacy so you can—"

"Could be some of them hajjis hiding in there."

MacPherson looked at the bridge. Torres was right. A cave like that was the perfect place for a border crosser to hole up during the heat of a desert day.

"Okay, Torres, get up there and look. Sergeant Jonas, go with him," MacPherson added, pointing to a short, thin, buck sergeant. "Side arms and flashlights."

Minutes later, Jonas appeared on a ledge above and whistled. "No hajjis, Sarge, but you gonna wanna see this!"

MacPherson turned to his troops. "Everybody in the vehicles and button up—now! I'm going up. Frankie, let us know when we gotta get out."

"Roger that, Sergeant Mac."

By the time MacPherson had climbed the wadi wall to the cave's mouth, he could see the storm front, well within rifle shot and greedily eating the horizon. A hot breeze, building by the minute, stung his face and hands with grit scented like exotic incense. Little eddies of swirling sand materialized to dance down the wadi, then vanished.

MacPherson's throat went sandpaper dry. His eyes itched.

Jonas handed him a flashlight and pointed into the cave.

"All the way back."

Bent almost double, MacPherson pushed into the darkness, his light playing across the cave floor to a pair of mummified corpses smiling though blackened teeth, one smaller and clad in the remains of a dress. Nearby were blackened lumps of dried leather—maybe water bags, he thought—and an old-fashioned suitcase. Mac knelt to open it: clothing, books with

Spanish titles, a big, rectangular object wrapped in waxed fabric. Mac grabbed a leather pouch that crumbled at his touch, its contents tumbling into the suitcase. His flashlight beam caught the sheen of metal. He reached down—

A cacophony of Humvee horns sounded from below.

The cave filled with talcum-fine dust.

"Sergeant Mac, we gotta go NOW!" Jonas yelled.

CHAPTER ONE

A BOY OF ABOUT FOUR OR FIVE OPENED THE DOOR. Freckles danced across his cheeks, shrouded in coppery curls. Ben caught his breath, recalling his own childhood photos; the resemblance was striking.

"Mom is busy," said the boy, slowly and distinctly, trying hard to be grown up.

The child of a single parent, Rabbi Ben Maimon thought. Too much responsibility for his age. He smiled at the boy. "Please close the door, and then go get her. I'll wait here."

The boy ran off, leaving the door open. Ben turned to look up the street, taking in new cars at the curbs and manicured lawns behind them. He'd known this corner of the San Fernando Valley only as terra incognita, a spot on a map. Now he saw that it was a prosperous, upper-middle-class community.

He looked at the doorpost and frowned. No klaf, the tiny scroll of parchment, usually encased in a more-or-less ornate container, or mezuzah, upon which was inscribed the instruction from Deuteronomy, "Hear, O Israel: The Lord our God, the Lord is one. Love the Lord your God with all your heart and with all your soul and with all your strength. These commandments that I give you today are to be upon your hearts. Write them on the door frames of your houses and on your gates."

Such scrolls had been displayed on Jewish houses at least back to the time of the Dead Sea Scrolls and probably long before; Ben had never seen a Jewish home without one. And although he hadn't expected to find one, neither had he expected the contrary. But maybe this wasn't the person he was looking for.

"Can I help you?" said a pleasant female voice, and Ben turned to find a petite, pretty woman in her late 20s, barefoot in jeans and an oversized man's dress shirt, sleeves rolled above the elbow. Her skin was fair with a burst of freckles, and the long hair pinned atop her head was the burnt orange of copper wire, perhaps a half shade lighter than his own.

"Hello—" Ben began, stopping because the woman had gasped audibly and taken an involuntary step backward. She forced a smile, peering at him for a long moment, taking in his red hair, the piercing blue eyes that matched her own, his slim, athletic carriage, expensive, stylish clothing—a nice-looking man in his late 30s, a bit on the short side.

"Sorry. It's just that you reminded me of someone."

"Was that someone your father?"

The woman blanched. "How did you know that?" she whispered.

"Was your father's name Mark Thompson Glass?"

Again, she emitted the gasping sound.

"No! I mean, yes, it was. Who are you?"

"I'm not sure, but I could be your brother."

She cocked her head, regarding him. It was exactly the involuntary gesture that Ben made while thinking.

"And I'm pretty sure I don't have an adult brother."

"Until this minute, I was pretty sure you didn't have one, either. And now, I think, maybe you do."

She frowned, uncertain. "What's your name?"

"The name on my birth certificate is Mark Thompson Glass."

"This is soooo creepy. You can come in, but I warn you, I have a black belt in taekwondo—fourth dan. Don't try anything funny."

Ben threw back his head and laughed.

"Why is that funny?"

"Because I, too, wear the dan—sixth degree."

The woman wrinkled her face. Too much information, coming too fast. She needed time to make sense of things.

Ben followed her inside, noting the big corrugated boxes stacked along one wall.

"Moving out?"

"Moving in. This was my father's house— had it rented out. He died a year ago last April, and when his estate cleared probate—did you know that he died?"

"I came across his tombstone at Shabbat Tamid, the cemetery in Burbank."

Ben failed to mention that a few days earlier he'd been kidnapped, and then almost buried in that cemetery. Buried alive.

"Show me some I.D."

Ben took out his wallet and handed her his Massachusetts driver's license.

"You really are Mark Thompson Glass!"

"Everyone calls me Ben."

"Ben?"

"My Hebrew name is Moshe Benyamin. I've been called Ben all my life."

"I'm Marcia Bender."

"And your son?"

"Actually, Mort is my brother. He's almost six."

Ben looked interested, waited for Marcia to continue.

"Look, Mr. Glass, you might be my brother. Or not. You seem like a nice enough man, but I don't know anything about you. What do you do? Why are you here?"

"I'm here because, until about a month ago, I believed, as my mother and grandparents told me, that my father died when I was a baby, in an overseas plane crash—"

Again, Marcia gasped. She looked at Ben, measuring him. "That's not funny. Who sent you? What do you want?"

Ben shook his head. "Obviously, I said something that upset you. I'm sorry for that, but I'm not sure what it was."

"My husband's plane disappeared over Afghanistan. They never found the wreckage, much less the crew."

"I'm very sorry for your loss. Was he in the military?"

"It's been two years. I've missed him every day."

Ben blinked away a real tear as he made a mental note that Marcia had ducked his question.

Marcia lifted her chin. "Tell me why you're here."

"My mother died when I was 12. I was raised by my grandparents. And until about a month ago, I knew nothing about my father. Not even what he looked like. Then quite by chance, a couple of Burbank police detectives I'd met read me excerpts from the rap sheet of one Mark Thompson Glass. And that was because I have the same name."

"Rap sheet? What are you talking about?"

"His arrest record. My father, and I think yours, was a career swindler who used a variety of aliases to rip off thousands of people from coast to coast. He was arrested many times but never convicted."

"Maybe your father was a crook, but mine was a very successful investor and real-estate developer. He wasn't a con man."

"If you say so. In any event, when I found his tombstone, I suspected that whoever had buried him, perhaps his family might live in this area. In the Valley. And if that was true, if he had a family, then I might have a sibling or two that I never knew about. I found this address in an old phone book. The phone number didn't belong to my father anymore, so I

A SCRIBE DIES IN BROOKLYN | 11

came out to have a look around and see if, maybe, the present occupants of the house might know anything about him or his family."

"So that's it?"

"Yes."

"I took care of his funeral. And don't you even think about laying claim to his estate unless you can provide a DNA sample proving that he was your father. Which I doubt you'll be willing to submit."

Ben's stomach did flip-flops. I shouldn't have come, he told himself. He looked at Marcia. "We should both get DNA tests. But I don't want his money. I don't want anything from him or from you. I just wanted—

"This was a mistake. I'm sorry that I bothered you."

Ben turned toward the door.

"Wait! You never told me what you do for a living."

"I'm a rabbi."

"Really? A rabbi? Where's your temple? Massachusetts?"

Ben's iPhone rang, and he pulled it from his belt and eyed the screen. "I have to take this. It's my doctor."

"Okay, but you're staying for dinner, right?"

CHAPTER TWO

BERT EPSTEIN, M.D., PhD, HUNG UP THE PHONE AND sighed, absent-mindedly looking through his window at the sandstone chimneys and weathered red brick of the Harvard campus.

Short, bulky, his bulging forehead rising into a mop of unruly dark curls, at 39 Epstein was approaching the apex of his career. Among the world's leading authorities on viruses, he sought to understand the multitude of issues these mysterious microscopic life forms raised while having their parasitic ways with humans.

Sometimes, however, he thought that viruses were easier to understand than humans. Today was one of those times. Barbara, his wife, adored Ben. She had asked him to call Ben and tell him something that he knew to be a lie. She had promised that no harm would come to Ben, but that she couldn't tell him anything more except that there were some things in life more important than family and friendship. Epstein was both Ben's close friend and his personal physician. So what he had asked him to do—and what he had just told Ben—caused him, not for the first time, to ponder the meaning of friendship, and the ethical complexities of competing loyalties.

BEN GOT OUT OF A cab at the corner of Fifth Avenue and 93rd Street, paid the driver, and looked around. It was a sunny, hot Manhattan day in early summer, and he paused to take in the blossoming splendor of Central Park and the dark waters of the Jacqueline Kennedy Onassis Reservoir, familiar ground. He'd grown up a few miles away, across the East River, in Brooklyn, and in his early 20s, he had spent four years at JTS, the Jewish Theological Seminary, twenty blocks north and on the other side of the park. Somewhere around here, he recalled, was the white stone mansion that housed The Jewish Museum.

Pulling a slip of paper from his shirt pocket, he checked the address, and then made his way down the sidewalk. The address was oh-so-posh Fifth Avenue, but the building faced 93rd Street. Ben rounded the corner and went down the sidewalk until he came to the entrance. Inside was a locked foyer, the walls on either side lined with buttons and brass nameplates. He rang the one under Dr. Dana Emanuel's name.

Bert Epstein had been unusually mysterious. All he'd said was that he'd made an appointment for him with a certain Dr. Dana Emanuel that could not be rescheduled, and it was vital that he arrive on time.

A little worried, Ben had asked his friend to tell him why Dr. Emanuel was seeing him, but all Epstein would say was that it was important. "Don't worry; you're not going to die. At least, no time soon," he'd added.

So Ben had caught the red-eye from Burbank back home to Cambridge, slept a few hours and early this morning boarded an Amtrak coach at Boston's South Station. He got off at Penn Station in Midtown, caught a cab, and here he was.

A tinny woman's voice issued from a hidden speaker above his head. "Dr. Emanuel's office. Who is calling?"

"This is Rabbi Ben Maimon."

"Straight ahead through the door, then take the staircase down."

Before Ben could reply, the buzzer sounded, and he hurried through the door into a spotless chamber with gray marble floors. To his right was an elevator, and to his left an open door leading to stairs.

The stairs ended two flights down at a door with faded gold lettering: Dana Emanuel, M.D. Inside, Ben found a Spartan waiting room: two chairs, an empty magazine rack and a water cooler. As the door closed behind him, another opened to his right. He turned to find an attractive, middle-aged woman in a stylish business suit.

"Rabbi Ben Maimon?"

"Yes."

"I'm Dana," she said, pronouncing it "Dan-nah." She sounded more London than New York, but she was not from London, Ben was certain. Probably an Israeli, he thought. And if she was Dr. Emanuel, then he was a cocker spaniel.

Ben said, "Pleased to meet you, Doctor Emanuel."

"This way, please."

Ben followed her down a short corridor and into an office with a desk and a pair of overstuffed chairs.

In each chair sat a muscular, dark-haired young man clad, uncomfortably, in business attire. Both rose to their feet.

"I'm sorry," said the woman. "But it can't be helped. You'll understand everything in a minute. Please don't be alarmed, but these men are going to search you."

Ben took a step back. "What the hell is going on?"

The two men got to their feet. One spoke in Hebrew.

"Don't get excited. There's no reason to be afraid."

Emanuel smiled. "Really, it's all right. I'm sorry for the deception. Bert Epstein is my cousin. You can trust me."

Ben pulled out a cell phone. "I'll just call Bert—"

The man nearest Ben snatched the phone away.

Emanuel said, "Give it back, please. There's no cell reception in this basement."

Smiling, the man handed Ben's phone back.

Emanuel said, "Rabbi, please, you must trust me."

Ben said, "Bert's parents were both Holocaust survivors. They lost their entire families, everyone. Bert is an only child and has no uncles or aunts. No cousins. So who are you, and why should I trust such a bad liar?"

Emanuel smiled. "Actually, I'm his wife's cousin. Barbara Epstein's father is my mother's older brother."

Ben grimaced. "Maybe. But the only licensed M.D. in the city named Dana—'Day-na' not 'Dan-nah'—Emanuel is almost 70, a hematologist and adjunct professor at Weill Cornell."

"You have to trust—"

Ben shoved her aside and sprinted through the door, turning down the corridor and then into the outer office.

Two more dark, muscular men barred his way. One leveled a pistol at him. Ben recognized it as a Jericho 941, standard Israeli Defense Forces issue. Therefore, he realized, the man must belong to Aman, Israeli Military Intelligence. He relaxed, no longer afraid of being abducted. Probably a case of mistaken identity, he told himself. Or perhaps they thought he might know something that he didn't.

"Turn around, please," said the gunman, in pleasant, matter-of-fact Hebrew.

Ben raised his hands and turned, facing the wall.

As the second man approached Ben, the first moved to the side, keeping the Jericho leveled at Ben's chest. The door opened, and the two men from the inner office entered. One blocked the door leading to the corridor; the other remained in the doorway.

Quickly and efficiently, Ben was patted down and the contents of his pockets examined, then returned.

The guns disappeared.

"Please come with me," said the woman who was not Dr. Epstein.

One of the Aman men opened the outer office door, and another went through into the corridor, glanced around, then moved into a dark space below the staircase, where he tugged open a steel door that lay flush with the floor, to reveal a steep stairway. Taking a small flashlight from his pocket, the guard descended. After a moment, a light came on below. Trailed by the woman and the other guards, Ben descended into a claustrophobic space that soon became a tunnel sloping downward into darkness.

"Dr. Emanuel is visiting his family in Israel," explained the woman as they moved down the tunnel. "About 90 years ago, during Prohibition, his grandfather, a bootlegger, bought this building and had a tunnel dug."

"An escape route?"

"Perhaps more to move product and customers in and out without attracting attention to this building."

The floor leveled, and the man leading the way came to a door secured by a huge, ancient brass padlock. He produced a key, unlocked the padlock and stood aside as the others passed. He closed the door behind him and locked it from the far side.

The party moved in silence through a warm, damp, low-ceilinged basement with thick, low-hanging pipes. Soon they came to an elevator.

As though in response to a signal, the elevator door opened to reveal a tall, heavy man with a full head of white hair. He smiled at Ben.

"Shalom, Rabbi Ben Maimon, and welcome to the Jewish Museum of New York," said Yossi Bar Tzvi, president of the State of Israel.

CHAPTER THREE

EN SAID, "GENERAL BAR TZVI?"

"It's good to see you again," Bar Tzvi replied. "And I'm happy to say that you look so well now. Please accept my apologies for the cloak-and-dagger routine, Rabbi. In a few minutes, I hope, you'll understand why it was necessary. Please, get in."

Ben entered the elevator, followed by the others. "What is this about, General?"

"First, don't be angry with Mrs. Shapiro. She's my chief of staff, and those men are her security detail. They follow my instructions."

The elevator stopped and its door opened. The guards and the woman, now revealed as "Mrs. Shapiro," exited, followed by Ben and Yossi. Ben trailed Yossi across a broad corridor and into a large, bright office with an expansive view of the park.

Shapiro and the guards remained in the corridor as Yossi closed the door and gestured toward a pair of easy chairs. He took the near one and waited for Ben to sit.

"You must have many questions, Rabbi."

"I do. If those men are her guard detail, where is yours?"

"At the consulate, guarding Dov Sokol—my security double. In about two hours, Dov will get into my car and be driven here for a formal dinner. Before the cocktail reception, Dov will need to visit a private restroom, where I will be waiting. While I'm at dinner, he'll remove his wig, change clothes, and catch a cab. He's got tickets for 'The Book of Mormon!' He'll come back and switch places with me for the return ride to the consulate. And I'll catch a cab and enjoy a quiet night at a small hotel, for a change."

"Wait. Mrs. Shapiro's security is Aman—military intelligence—but yours is Shin Bet?"

"What makes you think that?"

"Shin Bet, which is like our FBI and Secret Service, is equipped with the Glock pistol. Those men carried the Jericho 941, IDF issue."

"That's good, Rabbi. You don't miss much. Here's how it is. I am the Head of State, elected to a single, seven-year term by the Knesset. It is, of course, a great honor to be chosen. But I am a figurehead. I have no political power at all. My budget, including that for my security detail, comes from the Knesset, which means, in the real world of Israeli politics, that I can't hire a secretary—actually, I can't even order a box of pencils—unless the prime minister's office approves. Mrs. Shapiro isn't authorized a security detail; it isn't in Shabak's budget. By the way, we Israelis call Shin Bet 'Shabak.' Shabak's director doesn't like spending shekels on personal protection details. He prefers to use his funds for operational matters.

"But it happens that Mrs. Shapiro's husband, Yaakov, is Aman's deputy director of operations and will likely be so until he dies or decides to retire, which will be never. Aman, as you correctly noted, is part of the IDF. So when I decided that Mrs. Shapiro needed a security detail, her husband provided it. It comes out of his budget, which is a state secret. Except for a few members of the Arab parties, nobody in the Knesset ever questions details of the IDF budget."

Ben said, "You retired from the IDF some years ago, so you

still have friends—maybe that's why you don't care if Aman knows we're meeting. But why not Shabak?"

"Shabak reports are available to the prime minister."

"And?"

"And it might be that, maybe, Mrs. Shapiro encourages my Shabak detail to think that she and I are engaged in a romantic affair. This never fails to amuse her husband, Yaakov, who is also my wife's brother."

"That is interesting, but you haven't said why you want to conceal our meeting from the prime minister. What is this all about, Mr. President?"

The office door opened, and Mrs. Shapiro, carrying a tray with a silver thermos and two elegant teacups on equally elegant saucers, backed into the room.

"I thought you could use a little pick-me-up," Shapiro said, putting the tray on a table between the chairs, and then closing the door behind her.

Ben took a sip of what turned out to be surprisingly good coffee, then looked at Yossi Bar Tzvi and smiled.

"Now I remember! You came to my hospital room."

"Nine years ago. You were sedated."

"You were ... thinner."

"I was still Minister of Defense."

Flashing back to a night in Jerusalem, Ben shuddered. He was in Israel for his third year of rabbinical training; his wife, Rachel, pregnant with their first child, had flown in to spend the Passover break with him. On the day after the weeklong observance had ended and Jewish law again permitted eating *chametz*, bread and fermented beverages, they had gone out to dinner. The café was busy; there was a long wait to be seated. Before their meal was served, Ben drained two glasses of Goldstar lager. He was emptying his bladder in the men's room when a suicide bomber blew herself and the café to bloody pieces. Rachel was killed. Their son, delivered by Caesarian by an emergency medical technician, died the next day. Fourteen other people died in the bombing; many others were injured.

Ben suffered dozens of mostly superficial wounds and was drenched in blood spurted from the dying and maimed. At least one of these victims was infected with human immunodeficiency virus, HIV. Virus-laden blood had thereby gained access to Ben's bloodstream and infected him.

That was how he came to be treated by Bert Epstein. Under a rigorous regimen of daily antiretrovirals, Ben remained outwardly healthy. Outside a small circle of close friends, he avoided discussing his condition and tried to keep it secret.

"President Bar Tzvi—"

"Call me Yossi. Everybody does."

"Then call me Ben."

Yossi said, "By the way, that young man in the café, the one you saved from choking to death? He's now a psychiatrist specializing in post-traumatic stress disorder. He's pioneered a number of early-intervention techniques that the IDF and the emergency services find very promising."

Ben thought about his own recurrent nightmares, the nights he had cried out in his sleep while re-experiencing the bombing and its aftermath. Early intervention was no longer relevant, but maybe there was another approach, anything that would bring him even a measure of relief.

"I should go see him, but I never knew his name."

"Lev Bronstein."

Ben exploded with laughter. "You've got to be kidding! Is he related?"

Yossi shook his head. "His grandparents were Russian communists. When Trotsky was purged, they left the Party and became Zionists. Lev's father named him for his own father's idol,"

"Amazing!"

"Ben, this is a secure room; we can speak freely. But we have only an hour, so ... have you heard of the Keter Aram Tzova?"

"The Aleppo Codex? Of course, the oldest known Hebrew copy of the complete *Tanakh*, all twenty-four books of the Hebrew Bible, including The Five Books of Moses."

"What do you know about it?"

"About what any rabbi would. It's the work of the famous scribe Rabbi Aaron Ben Asher and it's the foundation for all modern copies of the Masoretic text, that which distinguishes the Hebrew Bible from versions derived from the Greek Septuagint."

Yossi smile. "Correct. The Codex was used by Maimonides, your namesake. And for a thousand years, it was Judaism's most authoritative text."

Ben said, "I know that it was made near Tiberius in 920 CE, that it was kept in Jerusalem and later ransomed from the Crusaders, remained in Egypt for centuries and then, about 600 years ago, a descendant of Maimonides took it to Aleppo, Syria."

"And then?"

"And then, in 1947, when the United Nations voted to allow the establishment of the State of Israel, an Arab mob sacked and burned the Great Synagogue of Aleppo. The Codex disappeared. Ten years later, it surfaced. Now it's in Israel."

"All of it?"

"Most of the Five Books are missing. Yossi, what is all this to me?"

"A few weeks ago, a Jewish woman here in New York, discovered—or, at least, thinks she did—the missing pages, or perhaps only some of them. They were hidden in the home of her beloved great uncle, who had just passed away at age 97."

"That's wonderful news!"

Bar Tzvi shook his head. "Not so wonderful. Two days later, someone broke into the uncle's house and stole it."

"Who else knew that she'd found it?"

"An excellent question! You should ask her that."

"The State of Israel wants me to find the missing Codex pages? Mossad is too busy? Shabak can't be bothered? What about Aman, since you have so much influence?"

"The State of Israel asks nothing of you. Were you to accept any task for us in this country, you would be obliged to register as a foreign agent. Mossad and Shabak would know immediately. I would be unhappy if either agency—if anyone in the Israeli government—hears anything about you or the Codex."

"Why is that?"

"You probably know that we have many political parties in Israel. Too many, really. No party ever wins enough seats in the Knesset to form a government on its own.

"So every election is followed by a few days of back-room horse-trading—perhaps necessary, but very unseemly. The small parties are single-issue parties; to get enough seats to govern, the ruling coalition always includes a few of them."

"You're talking about the religious parties?"

"I am. And their issue is ensuring that the haredim, the ultra-Orthodox, get what they want: power."

"You mean their leaders? Not individual voters but the politicians representing them?"

"Precisely. And as Lord Acton put it—"

"'Power tends to corrupt, and absolute power corrupts absolutely.'"

"The haredim now provide Lord Acton's proof. They have become powerful; the most powerful are the most corrupt. Their political power—and opportunities for graft—stems from being able to say who is a Jew and who is not."

"In my limited experience, few Israelis are very observant. Why do they care?"

"The haredim have made it impossible to avoid their influence. We have no civil marriage in Israel; you can't get married unless a religious service is performed by a rabbi who meets haredim approval. No Conservative, Reform or Reconstructionist need apply. Even most American Orthodox rabbis don't meet their standards. A haredim rabbi decides which brides and grooms are Jewish enough to merit marriage.

"No immigrants can become Israeli citizens unless they are Jewish, and the haredim decide that. Converted to Judaism by a Diaspora rabbi? Forget about marrying another Jew or becoming a citizen by right. Your baby boy can't have a *brit milah*, a ritual circumcision, unless the haredim allow it. You can't even be buried in a Jewish cemetery unless the haredim say so.

"Before long, if they get their way, the haredim can summon anyone in Israel before their Bet Din, their rabbinical court, and find a pretext to revoke their Jewish identity and citizenship. Already, they have decreed that certain women weren't sufficiently observant—and refused to let them marry."

"Can they really do that?"

"It doesn't matter what documents or witnesses you might produce; there is no way to prove that you are a Jew unless they say you are."

Ben sighed. "And they call themselves rabbis! You know, the Diaspora began with Rome's sacking of Jerusalem and the Second Temple in 70 CE. And our sages tell us that this was hastened by the *sinat khinam*, causeless hatred, of the Zealots."

"I live in Jerusalem, Ben. To us, there is no such thing as ancient history. So yes, I fear that our Zealots, the haredim, will repeat that 2,000-year-old mistake."

"What can be done?"

"The haredim terrify most Israeli politicians. What if, for

example, they decided that the prime minister's mother, dead so many years, wasn't actually Jewish?"

"Oh, come on. They can't do that."

"But when they feel strong enough to dare such a thing, they might try.

"Here's something you might not know. In 1958, when the Aleppo Codex was still missing, the Sephardic Chief Rabbi of Israel commanded any Jew who knew where it was to produce it. Very soon, the Codex, except those still-missing pages, mysteriously re-appeared—in Syria!—and was smuggled into Israel.

"Which leads me to the reason for this conversation."

Ben cocked his head, thinking. "Let me guess. You don't want the haredim to get their hands on the missing portion of the Codex. And this is because ... because ... if American Jews, the Jews of the Diaspora, take possession of it, they have a bargaining chip. They can demand, perhaps, that the haredim recognize Diaspora conversions, marriages, etc. And this is vital for Israel; in the long run, Israel cannot survive without the support of Diaspora Jews."

Yossi nodded. "Exactly. And I can see that you are just the man to do this."

Ben shook his head. "I'm not the right man for this."

Yossi grinned. "You are much too modest. My brother-in-law, Yaakov, tells me that Mossad has an open file on you. Perhaps Shabak keeps one, as well."

"That's ridiculous! Why?"

"A man who brought down a multimillion-dollar organized-crime scheme? Working alone, without a support team? Why indeed?"

"Not alone. With the police and the DEA."

"The police of a small city, who were of little help. And the DEA came in only to make arrests. Let's not quibble. You are a man who knows how to get things done."

"But I know very little about ancient texts. I can't tell if a Torah page is a hundred years old or a thousand."

"If that's your only problem, it's easily solved."

"It's not my only problem. I have an appointment for Lasik surgery in two weeks. In California."

"You might be finished by then. And if not, I'll personally buy you a roundtrip ticket to Israel and pay for your surgery. We have wonderful doctors, you know."

"That's very generous. But even so, I'm not a wealthy man. I must earn a living."

"An American organization has volunteered to pay your fee."

Ben sighed. "You're making this very hard. Yossi, I haven't had even a few days off in more than a year. Since my wife died, I've been alone in the world. No family at all. It's a hard life, to be utterly alone in the world."

"My parents were Holocaust survivors. I understand."

"But wait! Two days ago, I discovered that I have a sister and brother in California. I'd like to get to know them, spend some time with them before the High Holy Days."

"And what will become of your sister, Marcia—Malka bat Mikel—and your brother, Mort—Mordechai ben Mikel—if the power of the haredim is not checked? Their mothers were Jews by choice, their conversions supervised by rabbis that the haredim don't recognize. Will they be allowed to visit the Wailing Wall? Will your sister, a Reform rabbinical student, be allowed even to touch a sefer Torah? Not long ago, a Conservative woman, a rabbi, was arrested at the Wall merely for carrying a Torah!"

"Marcia is a rabbinical student? How is it possible that you know more about my family than I do?"

"Mossad keeps an eye on certain people. People like you. And your father, *alev hashalom*, may he rest in peace."

"They watched him because he was a remorseless swindler who preyed on synagogues and Jewish institutions?"

"I wouldn't say remorseless. Not entirely. In the last few years of his life, he gave a lot of money to Jewish causes: hospitals, medical research, homeless shelters, and Legal Aid societies. Maybe he was trying to make amends for his earlier life."

Ben's head swam against this rush of new information. He took several deep breaths, trying to focus.

"Yossi, I appreciate all that you've told me. But you haven't given me a single reason why I, of all people, would have a chance of finding the Codex."

"So. I will now provide that reason."

Yossi touched a button on the phone. Seconds later, the door opened to admit the most beautiful woman Ben had ever seen: a face to make Da Vinci weep; tall and graceful, like his dear Rachel, with glowing, flawless skin and dazzling teeth; a modest business suit that displayed magnificent legs while failing to hide a lush but perfectly proportioned body.

"Rabbi Ben Maimon, this is Dr. Chana Kaplan of the Jewish Philanthropy Institute."

Chana smiled, filling the room with light and warmth. The faint scent of her perfume seemed to evoke the gardens of Paradise. Ben felt her dark eyes penetrating deep into his soul. As though from a great distance, he heard Yossi speaking, and forced himself to listen.

"So we can count on you, Rabbi? You'll work with Dr. Kaplan to help find the Codex?"

Unable even to summon his voice, Ben nodded, yes.

Yossi said, "Doctor Kaplan?"

She snorted. "This is your fearless genius? Your troubleshooting rabbi? This shrimp? I thought he'd be much taller."

CHAPTER FOUR

B EN OPENED HIS MOUTH, A TAUNTING RETORT ON HIS LIPS. But looking deep into Chana's eyes, noticing her dilated pupils—often an unconscious response to intense sexual attraction—he realized that she was protecting herself, testing him. If he uttered the words that he'd first intended, he might never see her again.

He threw back his head and roared, joined by Yossi and a moment later by Chana.

Ben said, "It's so refreshing to find a beautiful, accomplished woman with a sense of humor."

Chana said, "I'll bet you say that to every girl you meet."

Ben laughed again, enjoying the moment.

Yossi said, "You two should get a room. But first, you need to talk about the Codex. Chana, would you please tell Ben about Jewish Philanthropy International?

"That might be easier to explain in my own office."

Ben said, "And where is that?"

"On the other side of the park. It's a ten-minute walk."

"And if we walk very, very, very slow?"

Yossi put his coffee cup down, climbed to his feet, found his briefcase and said, "It was good seeing you again, Rabbi."

But by then the office was empty.

CHAPTER FIVE

TROLLING CLOSE ENOUGH THAT THEIR SHOULDERS occasionally touched, Chana and Ben moved through the park, saying little, pausing from time to time to glance at each other, as if to assure themselves that the other was still there.

Abruptly, Chana stopped, sighed, and turned to face Ben.

Ben said, "Something wrong?"

Chana sighed again. "I'm married."

Ben laughed. "So that's why you're wearing half of Tiffany's inventory on the third finger of your left hand!"

"You knew and still flirted with me?"

"If Yossi knows that my sister, whom I met yesterday for the first time, is a rabbinical student, then surely he must know that you have a husband. And yet he said nothing as we flirted. That tells me that either you're getting a divorce or that Yossi thinks I'm gay."

"My God! You're gay?"

Ben laughed so hard that after a moment Chana joined in.

"So you're not gay?"

"It's possible—just maybe possible—that, during second grade, I might have felt homoerotic urges for Noa Rosenzweig. Then I discovered that she was not a boy with long hair, and lost all interest."

"You're pulling my leg, right?"

"Not until your divorce is final."

Chana said, "We should get moving. We have a lot to cover."

They headed west along the curving walkway, admiring the greenery and scores of boisterous children engaged in sports and games under the watchful eyes of parents and teachers.

Chana said, "What do you mean, 'half of Tiffany's inventory'? It's only sixteen carats, including the smaller stones."

"I meant it's a dazzling ring that must have cost a fortune. The one I gave my wife, my grandmother's ring, wasn't half as valuable."

"You're married?"

"Widowed. We met in college, married in grad school and she died in a suicide bombing in Jerusalem nine years ago."

Chana took Ben's arm as they strolled in silence.

"I'm so sorry, Ben. Yossi didn't tell me that."

"So, sixteen carats. Your husband is what? A hedge fund manager?"

Chana gasped. Then she chuckled.

"Yossi told you, didn't he?"

"You're close to him?"

"I majored in Hebrew, took my senior year in Israel, then stayed on and served a year in the IDF."

"You were a soldier?"

"Barely. After basic training, I became a glorified secretary. Aviva Shapiro was Yossi's executive secretary, and for a few months, I was one of her assistants."

"This is when he was Minister of Defense?"

"Before. When he was Ramatkal, chief of the General Staff."

"So that's the connection."

"Not entirely. My husband is also Aviva's second cousin."

"You met your husband while you were both serving in the IDF?"

Chana shook her head. "Morris had a residency at Hadassah Medical Center."

"He's a ... cosmetic surgeon?"

Chana giggled. "He's a doctor who can't stand the sight of blood."

"A psychiatrist?"

"While I worked and finished my dissertation on Semitic languages, he started a practice in lower Manhattan. Many of his patients worked on Wall Street."

Ben said, "He learned their secrets, then started a hedge fund?"

"Pretty much. According to Morris, analysts and computer programmers do the heavy lifting. The rest is market psychology and getting people to trust you. And, I suspect, having a network of industry insiders on your payroll doesn't hurt."

"He gave you the ring when he made his first billion?'

Chana shook her head. "His net worth is probably only half that. It's hard to know because he's got money stashed all over the world."

She stopped, turned to face Ben. "He gave me the ring when I found out about his mistress."

"No! What man would cheat on you?"

"I left him when I found out about the masseuse and her office visits. Then I found about the girl he kept in Bridgehampton just for occasional weekends, and another mistress that he cheated on with the girlfriend of the week."

"I can only imagine the pain this has caused you."

"I filed for divorce two years ago. His lawyer got continuances, then he got a new lawyer, then it was motions for this or that, one after another—every legal trick in the book—stalling."

"He's worried about a settlement?"

"The money I saved from working two jobs, plus what I borrowed from my parents for a down payment on a house—he took that to start his fund. My lawyers argue that whatever that grew into should be as much mine as his."

"And the longer he can stall, the easier it is to hide assets."

"So my lawyers tell me. But here's the thing: They—my lawyers—are much more interested in winning a big settlement than I am."

Ben said, "Makes sense. Lawyers are about winners and losers. If they don't bring their clients big paydays, their own professional reputations are tarnished."

"Of course. But you know what? I don't need hundreds of millions of dollars. All I want is enough to start over, get a decent place to live, make sure my mother is taken care of and provide for my retirement."

"That sounds like a few percent of half a billion."

"Exactly."

"You've told Morris that?"

"In so many words."

"Then maybe this isn't about money at all. It's about power. He wants to possess you, and if he can't, he will keep you from enjoying your life."

"That's what my mother thinks."

"A wise woman. No children, Chana?"

She shook her head. "The office is in there," Chana said, indicating a building near the corner of 84th and Central Park West.

"An apartment?'

"JPI has the top floor."

"How long do you think this will take?"

"Now you're in a hurry?"

They left the park, waited at the curb for the light to change before crossing.

Ben said, "I came down from Boston expecting to be home for dinner. If I don't make the 8:15 from Penn Station, I'll need a hotel room. Then I've got to buy a few personal things."

"You can stay here tonight."

"Here?"

"JPI keeps several guest apartments. And a kosher kitchen."

"That's very kind of you. But before I get into all this, the Codex, I'll need to return to my apartment and pick up some clothes and stuff."

"We can send someone, if you like."

Ben thought about the drawer full of antiretrovirals that he required for a daily regimen that had for nine years staved off the onset of AIDS. He was outwardly healthy and aimed to remain that way. But his medical condition was a secret. He wouldn't bet, not now, that Yossi didn't know, but unless and until things progressed much further with Chana, he wanted to keep that part of his life private.

Ben said, "I really should do that myself."

"But every day that we delay will make it harder to find the Codex."

"Then someone should have told me what was going on, instead of luring me to New York with a cock-and-bull story."

"You're right, of course. Still, time is of the essence."

"The Codex was lost sixty years ago. One more day won't make a difference."

A burly young man in livery held the door for them.

Chana said, "If you say so."

As she stepped inside, Ben could feel her moving away from him. He had known her less than an hour, but the thought of losing her felt like a crushing weight.

CHAPTER SIX

R ABBI BEN MAIMON, DR. EZRA STEINSHAFFNER, THE executive director," Chana said.

A hunched, gaunt, pale, graying man somewhere past 60 rose behind a modest desk to grasp Ben's hand and shake it with surprising energy.

"I knew your grandfather, of blessed memory."

"You went to JTS?"

"I've always worked in the nonprofit sector. But it would be difficult for any Jew of my generation living in New York to avoid Rabbi Salomen Maimon. He taught, he lectured, he consulted, he twisted arms—"

Ben said, "Excuse me?"

"A very effective fundraiser. Always very quietly. He'd find out whom to see and go see them, even fellows who had been approached many times in the past and who never donated more than a pittance of what they could afford to give, the sort of men who bristled when someone suggested naming a building after them if they would open their checkbook. Your grandfather always came away with what was needed. There are schools and hospitals all over the country that would not exist without him."

Chana said, "You didn't know this?"

Ben shook his head. "He was my *zaideh*, my grandfather. Everyone seemed to love him, but all I knew was that he studied and taught, studied and taught. Once in awhile, he'd put on his good suit and give a talk. But fundraising? This is news to me."

Steinshaffner said, "I suppose if you're going to crack tough nuts, it is better that they don't know you carry a hammer."

Ben said, "I'm sorry to be so abrupt, but Chana made me understand that time is of the essence. How can we help each other?"

Steinshaffner nodded. "Well said. If the Codex hasn't left the country, we have a chance of finding it. It might take days or weeks to arrange a sale, particularly an overseas sale—whatever the thieves have in mind—so perhaps it's still in the city."

Chana said, "I should remind you, Dr. Steinshaffner, that we don't know for certain that it was the Aleppo Codex. Many ancient Torahs and other scrolls were taken from the Aleppo Synagogue and remain missing. It might be anything at all."

"Of course. In fact, that's probably the case. So let's assume that your first task, Rabbi, is to learn what she found and why it might be the Codex. Then, proceed as you judge most prudent and locate it."

Ben said, "Of course. But first, who am I working for? What is JPI? What happens to the Codex if I do find it? What do you propose to pay me?"

Steinshaffner smiled, nodding. "Yes, the business first."

He sat back down behind his desk, opened a drawer and withdrew an envelope, which he handed to Ben. Ben lifted the open flap and glanced at the check within. His eyebrows flew skyward at the sight of the six digits preceding the decimal.

"That is very generous. Perhaps too generous."

"I made inquiries, Rabbi, and I know the sort of fee you command. No one complains that you are overpaid. If you, however, feel that you are, I'm sure you can find a worthy cause for the excess."

Ben nodded. "Where did this money come from?"

"From some of our frequent benefactors, who wish to remain anonymous. Chana can fill you in on JPI's mission, and our books are open on our Web site."

Chana said, "Jewish hyphen philanthropy dot org."

"And what happens to the Codex if it is found?"

"If you can locate any part of it, the Jewish Museum here will keep it safe, undertake restoration efforts, and allow scholarly access until it can be reunited with the rest of its pages in Jerusalem."

"On mutually agreeable terms with the Sephardic Chief Rabbi of Israel."

"I should think so. By the way, as far as anyone outside of the three of us is to know, you are working for the museum."

"It was a pleasure meeting you, Dr. Steinshaffner."

"Call me Ezra, please."

"It's Ben."

"You are in capable hands with Dr. Kaplan. Good luck with your treasure hunt."

Ben followed Chana down a corridor past several private offices and into a large, windowless room filled with low wooden tables. In one corner were a desk and a row of wide filing cabinets.

She sat behind the desk, gesturing for Ben to take a guest chair to one side.

Ben said, "Dr. Steinshaffner—Ezra—seems like a pleasant sort."

Chana's lovely features arranged themselves into a Mona Lisa smile. "Don't be fooled by Ezra's physical appearance. I've heard that he spent many years as a spy."

Ben said, "Mossad?"

Chana shrugged her shoulders. "Doubtful. Even before he left the military, Yossi was very suspicious of them. More likely, Ezra didn't spy for Israel, but who knows?"

"But espionage? That's what he meant by the nonprofit sector?"

"Exactly."

"Why is a former spy running a philanthropic organization? And what exactly does JPI do?"

"Last question first: JPI was founded three years ago to coordinate fundraising for Jewish institutions around the world. Raising funds for nonprofits is very competitive, often almost cutthroat, because the very existence of many organizations depends on finding funding, while the pool of donors and dollars is very shallow. I'm sure not everyone would agree, but there are probably too many agencies."

Ben said, "Too many? Those that I'm familiar with are overwhelmed with demand for services."

"A surplus of organizations but a scarcity of services. If some merged, even some of the larger ones, if they consolidated administration and facilities, more funds could go to services and less to overhead."

"Why don't they?"

"The first priority of most agencies is maintaining their own existence."

"The bureaucratic imperative: The organization must survive at any cost."

"Exactly. So JPI was founded, in part, as a way to encourage and facilitate mergers where they make sense, while maintaining essential services."

"And this happens how?"

"Major donors often overlook smaller organizations. So JPI engages in a kind of reverse-bundling, where one donor writes a check that is distributed to, say, six or ten organizations. This puts JPI in a position to influence mergers and such."

"How much of a rake-off does JPI take?"

"Not a sou, nor a pfennig nor yet a farthing. None. Institutional overhead is covered by an endowment, and JPI separately raises funds for special projects and for its other principal mission, which is philanthropic intelligence."

"Spying?"

"Most nonprofits guard donor identities; they spend a lot of time and effort cultivating donors and worry that someone else might poach them. Some employ fundraising professionals, and good ones don't come cheap. JPI tries to help them all, but especially the smaller organizations, by developing data on who has money, who is capable of giving, who is likely to give, what sort of donations they are likely to favor, how they might best be approached.

"JPI then shares this data with Jewish philanthropic centers and social service agencies and encourages them to share their own sources."

"Hence, Ezra, skilled in gathering and analyzing data, runs the show."

"Exactly."

"I'm betting that Steinshaffner isn't his real name."

"Rumor has it that on his first visit to Chicago, he stayed in a hotel across the street from a clothing store called Hart Schaffner Marx. Down the block was Stein's Delicatessen."

Ben chuckled. "You keep saying, 'JPI does this or that,' not 'we do this.'"

Chana smiled. "I'm the Malka Potash Professor in Semitic Languages at Fordham University. JPI brings me in from time to time to translate documents and to assist in authenticating ancient manuscripts."

"How does that fit into the mission you just described?"

"My first job for JPI was authenticating a scroll for a possible donor, a Dutch Jew who thought he had a pre-Inquisition-era copy of the Megillat Ester, the Scroll of Esther. It had been in his family for generations, and he was considering donating it in exchange for a big tax write-off. I found that it was an authentic Megillah but only about 150 years old and in bad condition. Not worthless, but not what he'd hoped for.

"Sometimes, individuals and institutions want to sell or donate an ancient manuscript. In my experience, most are forgeries. Before expensive, time-consuming testing of paper, parchment or ink, I'll just read it to see if the calligraphy is what one would expect in such a document, if a text is a copy of a known document or by a known scribe. Sometimes, it takes five minutes to spot a fake, but it can also take much longer. If it seems genuine, then other tests are applied. And from time to time, I translate documents dealing with property ownership. And special projects, like this one."

"Besides Hebrew, you speak—"

"—three Arabic dialects, Farsi and a little Turkish. My more important skill is reading those languages, along with Aramaic, Akkadian, Amharic, Ge'ez, Phoenician and Maltese."

"Wow. I've never heard of Ge'ez, and I didn't know the Maltese spoke anything besides Italian and English."

"The Beyta Israel, the Jews of Ethiopia, speak Ge'ez. Maltese is written in Roman characters and is a mixture of Arabic, Italian, Sicilian and English.

"And Malta is important to Judaism because it's the home of the oldest Jewish community outside Israel itself."

"That is astonishing."

"It goes back to the time of the Phoenicians."

Ben got to his feet, stretched, and yawned.

"Chana, you are the most amazing and fascinating woman I've ever met. I could sit here and talk to you all day and all night. But we need to find the Codex, and I also need to get some of my things. So I have an idea."

"Yes?"

"Now that I'm rich, why don't I buy us two roundtrip tickets to Boston and you can brief me on the way? If we leave right now, we can be back by nine tonight, and if I can't arrange a hotel online, I'll accept your offer of a room here at JPI."

"Do we have time for me to tell Ezra and use the ladies' room?"

"I'll go downstairs and get a cab."

CHAPTER SEVEN

BREATHLESS FROM THEIR SPRINT FROM CAB TO TRAIN platform, Chana and Ben found seats in a half-empty car as the Acela Express pulled out of Pennsylvania Station.

Chana said, "We don't have tickets!"

Ben pulled out his iPhone. "I logged on to Amtrak's Web site while I was waiting for you to come down. I have an account, so ..."

She smiled. "Now I'm impressed."

Ben smiled back. Their eyes met for a long moment, and Ben found himself sinking into a slow fantasy about undressing Chana.

Get a hold of yourself, he thought. This is a married woman. Act like a rabbi. Act like a Jew. Act like a man.

Ben said, "Chana, what can you tell me about the Codex?"

Chana reached in her bag and pulled out an iPad Mini, thumbed through a couple of menus and consulted the screen. "Six days ago, in Brooklyn, Shemuel Benkamal died after a short illness. He was 97 and was born in Aleppo, part of a large, well-known family that was influential in the affairs of Joab's Synagogue. He came to the U.S. in the early Fifties and within a few years became a leader in the Syrian-Jewish community. He was quite wealthy. His only living heir is his niece, Miryam."

Ben said, "She found the Codex?"

"Yes. She took it to Rabbi Zeev—"

"Malachi Zeev?"

"You know him?"

"He came to my grandfather's home several times when I was a child. I'm surprised that he's still alive."

"He's quite old. Well, Rabbi Zeev looked at the pages and told Miryam that it might be the Codex and that she should put it in a safe place."

"So she hid it in the basement, right?"

"Locked it in a safe in her uncle's home office."

"Someone broke into the house and cracked the safe?"

"They took the safe, which weighed about 600 pounds."

"And nobody saw them?"

"Apparently, it happened during the funeral. Benkamal's funeral. All the neighbors were there, along with hundreds of other Syrian Jews. When she returned, the kitchen door was off its hinges, and the safe was gone."

Ben said, "What else do we know about this?"

"Not much. Miryam is an only child. Her parents died when she was young, and she was raised by her great uncle. She now lives in California, teaches part time in a synagogue-affiliated preschool, and is pursuing a master's in early child education. She came back when her uncle was hospitalized. She was with him when he died."

"Then I guess we go see her and Rabbi Zeev tomorrow."

"You go see them. I've got a full day: two lectures, a meeting with my post-docs and office hours for my undergrads. When—if—you find some pages, I'll try to determine, first, if they have the correct script, punctuation and cantillation notes. Then, I'll compare them with photocopies of the rest of the Codex, which we know was written by Solomon ben Buya'a and corrected by Aaron Ben Moses Ben Asher, who added punctuation and cantillation. If the style matches, I'll arrange carbon dating of the parchment and micro-spectro-photometry to confirm the ink age."

"That's all you know? You could have told me that in the cab!"

"But then I wouldn't get a free trip to Boston and dinner."

"You're so devious!"

"Thank you."

She inched close to Ben and laid her head on his shoulder. "I'm going to take a nap. Tell me a bedtime story?"

"Once upon a time, there was a beautiful princess who spoke Maltese ..."

CHAPTER EIGHT

B OSTON WAS QUICK AND EASY: AS RUSH HOUR ENDED and the roads cleared, Ben retrieved his car from the Amtrak lot at Boston South. En route to his Cambridge apartment, he detoured to Brookline for kosher Chinese take-out. After a quick meal, Chana helped Ben pack a large suitcase while he went into the bathroom to slip a thirty-day supply of anti-retrovirals into his ready-to-go travel toiletries kit.

He even had time to retrieve his mail before a cab returned them to Boston South, where they boarded the last south-bound express of the day with minutes to spare.

As Chana caught up on her own phone messages and email, Ben went through his mail, depositing JPI's check by scanning it with his iPhone app, paying bills by phone, then returning emails. Finally, he opened a cushioned envelope to discover a tiny circuit board and a software CD, a Mac Book Pro add-in that he'd agreed to help test for a friend and former M.I.T. classmate. Ten minutes later, it was installed and working.

Just before midnight, Chana and Ben emerged from Penn Station.

At the curb, they hugged for a long moment, then Ben held a cab door for her; Chana was headed uptown, while he would spend the night in Brooklyn.

As Ben turned for the next cab, someone grabbed his arm and spun him around.

A tall, well-dressed man in his 50s with dark, curly hair and a short, salt-and-pepper beard released his arm and moved closer. From the corner of his eye, Ben saw two younger men in leather jackets hanging back.

The older man said, "Who are you? What's the nature of your relationship with Mrs. Kaplan?"

Ben said, "Who are you, and why do you need to know?"

"Not your concern. I'm asking the questions."

"I'm leaving now. Try to stop me, and I promise that you will regret it."

Gripping Ben's left forearm, the older man pointed his chin at the two younger ones, and they moved behind Ben, blocking his escape.

Ben dropped his bags and pivoted on his left toe, swinging his outstretched right leg in a short swift arc that dropped the man on the sidewalk, his nose bleeding profusely.

Whirling, Ben flew at the nearer of the jacket-clad men, stepping aside at the last moment to seize his sleeve, then planting both legs and hurling him headlong into a lamppost. The man crumpled to the pavement, groaning.

The third man took a step backward and produced a pistol. "Stop!"

Ben looked over his shoulder to find Chana.

CHAPTER NINE

CHANA SAID, "PUT THAT THING AWAY!"

After a long moment, the gun disappeared inside the leather jacket.

Chana turned to the older man, who was trying to get to his feet.

"Are you all right, Mr. Klein?"

"I think my nose is broken."

Ben said, "I warned you."

Chana said, "I'm very sorry for your injury, Mr. Klein. Please tell my husband that my attorneys will make him explain to a judge the kind of games he has you play. I hope it costs him a lot of money."

Klein pointed his chin at the man who had held the gun, who stood frozen.

"What are you waiting for, moron? Go help your friend."

Chana said, "Mr. Klein, this is my colleague Rabbi Ben Maimon. If anything happens to him, anything at all, I'll have you arrested."

Ben said, "What's going on here?"

Chana said, "Get your bags. You're coming with me."

AS THE TAXI EASED INTO traffic, Ben said, "What was that about?"

Chana said, "Are you all right? Did they hurt you?"

Ben suppressed a smile. "I'm fine. Thanks for coming to my rescue."

"As soon as I saw Klein ..."

The driver said, "Where to, Miss?"

"Beekman Place and 50th."

Ben said, "They couldn't have followed us all the way to Boston and back?"

Chana said, "I'm sure at least one of them did. Probably the one with the gun."

"Chana, has this happened before?"

"A few times. Klein just shows up out of nowhere, usually when I happen to be out with a man, no matter his age or the nature of our relationship."

"And who is Klein?"

"Chief of security for my husband's firm. What did he say to you?"

"He asked me who I was and what was I doing with you."

"And you told him what?"

"That it was none of his business. If he tried to detain me, he'd regret it."

She took his arm. "And it seems you are a man of his word."

"I try, Chana. Did you think that goon of his would have shot me?"

"Yes."

"Then I thank you for my life."

"You're welcome. Although now, on reflection, I'm not so sure who I saved: you or the goon."

"I will always believe that you saved me."

"Ben, you're coming home with me."

"You know I booked a room online at the Hotel Le Jolie in Williamsburg."

"Let it go. I have a guest room."

"It doesn't look right, Chana. You're a married woman."

"I don't care what it looks like. Klein and his thugs have beaten or driven away four of my friends, but he won't harm you as long as you're under my roof. And if that makes my husband angry, so much the better."

Ben sighed. "It's late. I'll stay tonight, and we'll see how it goes in Brooklyn tomorrow. Maybe we'll know something definitive about the Codex by then."

"Thank you."

"Beekman Place?"

"It was our pied-à-terre. We own homes in Greenwich and East Hampton. When I moved out—"

"Say no more."

Chana sat back, leaned her head against Ben's shoulder.

"Just one thing, Ben."

"No hanky-panky?"

"Absolutely no hanky-panky."

"Farthest thing from my mind."

"You're such a bad liar."

CHAPTER TEN

———

CHANA UNLOCKED THE DOOR, AND BEN FOLLOWED her into a living room with just enough expensive Danish Modern furnishings. An enormous picture window framed a glowing panorama of the Manhattan skyline.

Ben said, "Wow. Some pied-à-terre."

"Thank you. Mo—that's what his pals call my husband—hired a decorator. He complained about the size—it's 1,500 square feet—but Mo complains about everything. I think there's plenty of room, more than enough for two people, and if I wind up owning it after the settlement, I'll send all this furniture to a thrift shop and do my own decorating. But for now, your room is at the end of the hall."

Ben carried his suitcases down the hall and came back. "I just had a thought."

"We agreed there would be no hanky-panky."

Ben threw back his head and roared.

"Okay, so now I had another thought: Maybe Klein doesn't have to follow you in order to know where you are."

"Go on."

"Check your purse, your jewelry. Maybe there's some kind of transmitter, a tracking device."

"I don't see how that's possible."

"If you have a lot of money, almost anything is possible."

"Will you help me find it? I don't know what I'm looking for."

———

"In the morning?"

"No. It's late, and we both need to sleep, but in the morning, we'll be rushed."

"You're right. Let's go in the kitchen. Bring your purse."

Ben dumped the contents of a Chloe Paddington bag on the empty counter and quickly went through each item: lipstick and other makeup, tissues, a handkerchief, a coin purse, wallet, key chain, gum wrappers, a few scraps of paper with scribbled notes.

"Nothing obvious," Ben said.

"It would have to be something I wear or carry every day," Chana mused.

"Your cell phone."

"My phone?"

"What kind?"

"An iPhone."

Ben nodded. "Let me see it."

Chana retrieved the phone from the hallway table and handed it to Ben. "I have the same one, and it has a built-in GPS device."

Chana stared at the phone.

"So then Klein—or my husband—buys some hardware to track the signal, or pays someone, maybe someone who works for the phone company? Is that legal?"

Ben shrugged his shoulders. "Technology always runs before law. Right now, I'd say it is legal. But I'm a mere rabbi. Ask your lawyers."

"What should I do?"

"Hold on. Your husband doesn't need to rent the phone company; there's a much simpler way to track the signal. Let me see the phone."

Ben fidgeted with the instrument, scrolling through menus and folders.

"There!"

"What?"

"It's a GPS tracking app. Sends your location in real time to a satellite, and that's accessed from a Web site. All you need is the site or account password."

"How did it get in my phone?"

Ben shrugged. "A dozen ways. Maybe he paid someone to borrow your phone for five minutes and download it. But probably it was delivered in a Trojan horse."

"Haven't met any Greeks bearing gifts. Not lately."

"A Trojan is something like a virus except it doesn't replicate itself. It hides inside an innocent-looking email attachment, a link, even a picture. Open the attachment, and it's activated. It takes over the phone for a few seconds and installs that ap. Easy, no risk, very effective. That's how I'd do it."

"You wouldn't do something that sleazy."

"Talk to your lawyer."

"It will take me a few days to set up a meeting. What if I handle this myself?"

"First thing I'd do is get a new phone and a new number. Don't give the number out to anyone except your most trusted friends and family. In fact, don't give the number to anyone. Set the old phone to automatically forward all calls to the new one. Then leave the old phone at home or in your office. Or if you want to blow Klein's mind, overnight it to somebody out of town, tell them to turn it on and keep it charged. After a few days, they ship it back to you. Then send it to someone else in another part of the country."

Chana smiled. She liked this game.

"Or I could get one of my girlfriends to carry it around for a day or two. Then give it to a different friend. And then another and another."

"I love it when you're really devious."

"Thank you, Ben. Now I really need to sleep."

Ben handed the phone back to Chana and turned away.

"Ben. There's something else."

"If you changed your mind about the hanky-panky, I'm really tired."

Chana giggled, shaking her head. "Ben, where did you learn to fight like that?"

"I took self-defense classes at the local YMHA."

"Come on."

"And at M.I.T., and again at the yeshiva, I joined a couple different dojos and learned a little of the martial arts. And then there were a couple of IDF self-defense classes during my third year of rabbinical school in Jerusalem."

"What if I hadn't come back when I did? Would he have shot you?"

Ben shook his head. "First rule for carrying a gun is, don't, unless you're prepared to use it. Second rule, if you point it at someone, you have to shoot him. Third rule, if you shoot, shoot to kill. But Klein's man? He was scared. Didn't know what he was doing."

Chana said, "Explain that."

"No confidence in his own abilities. When I took the other two out of the fight, he got scared. The gun was in a pocket, not a holster, and the safety was still on. His finger was on the trigger, but I'm very sure he didn't have a round in the chamber."

"How long before he could have shot you?"

"At least three seconds. And by then I'd have the gun."

"You'd bet your life on that?"

"A better bet than waiting while he put a round in the chamber."

"Why not run away?"

"Carrying two bags?"

"Leave the bags."

"Then I'd have to negotiate for their return."

"Why not just abandon them?"

"Because Klein—your husband—would use the bags to punish you. It was cleaner if I make them go away and then go on about my business."

"So you really didn't need my help."

Ben thought for a long moment. "I was actually overwhelmed with affection and gratitude that you came back to protect me. That's worth much more to me than the macho thrill of whipping some big bonehead's butt and taking his gun away."

"Affection? Macho thrill? Who talks like that?"

"Me. Sometimes."

"I'm really sorry, Ben."

"Sorry?"

"Sorry that there's not going to be any hanky-panky tonight."

"I'm sorry, too. But I'm also very glad to know you, Chana Kaplan."

"Chana Sarah Siegler is the name on my diplomas. And will be again when my divorce is final."

"Sleep well, Chana Sarah."

CHAPTER ELEVEN

A LITTLE BEFORE SIX THE NEXT MORNING, BEN emerged from the basement entrance at the rear of Chana's apartment building into a leafy inner courtyard. He wore white running shoes with blue stripes, a Mets cap and a dark blue jogging suit. His wallet, with cash and credit cards, was in a money belt under the loose shirt. His iPhone was strapped to his left arm and linked to a Bluetooth headset.

After ten minutes of slow stretching, Ben slipped through a narrow passage between buildings leading north to 51st Street, turned right, then slowly jogged south on Beekman Place. He saw an old white Corolla double-parked facing south near the entrance to Chana's building. Behind the wheel was the leather-jacketed man whom he'd slammed into the lamppost the night before. His nose and forehead were bandaged.

Ben suspected that this was the guy whom he was meant to see. He picked up his pace slightly, head forward, eyes scanning back and forth, looking for the other one, the one he wasn't supposed to know was lurking somewhere near.

He found the man who'd pulled a gun half-hidden behind a corner lamppost on 50th. Ben waved. The man ignored him, so Ben circled back, jogging in place.

"Hey, moron!"

The man looked up.

"Still got that gun?"

With a shout, the man lunged forward. Ben took off, heading west, loping just fast enough to support his pursuer's illusion of catching him. As Ben approached First Avenue, the man slowed to a walk, breathing hard. The Corolla roared around the corner and braked to a halt beside him. The man jumped in.

As Ben reached the corner of First Avenue, he heard a short blast of a siren. An NYPD squad car blocked the Corolla's way. Two patrolmen got out, guns drawn.

Ben suppressed a giggle. Fiftieth is one-way going east and one short block from the United Nations complex, an upscale district chockablock with foreign embassies and consulates. Any car going the wrong way on that street, Ben knew, was a beacon to the dozens of officers patrolling the district. He hoped his pursuer was still carrying a gun.

Ben switched on his headset and said, "Call Chana."

When she answered, Ben told her that she was free to leave her home without fear of being followed.

After ending the call, Chana removed the battery from her phone, making GPS tracking impossible. While she headed for the gym and then a working breakfast, Ben ran south on First Avenue toward Delancey Street and the approach to the Williamsburg Bridge, just under three miles south. He ran five miles nearly every morning; today, he would go six, crossing the East River to Williamsburg and then to the hotel where he'd made an online reservation before sleeping the previous night.

By 7:00, he was enjoying an omelet and a bagel in a Flushing Avenue deli. Ninety minutes later, he had bought new underwear and socks, checked into his hotel and showered. By 9:30, he'd returned to Beekman Place by subway. And less than an hour after that, wearing what he thought of as his summer rabbi outfit, a Panama hat and lightweight blue suit, Ben strolled up a Bensonhurst street toward Rabbi Zeev's home.

"Awesome hat!"

Ben turned to see a tall, pretty girl in her late teens, with skin the color of a mocha cappuccino. She smiled, displaying dazzling teeth.

Ben said, "Thank you, Miss."

"My brother Scott would love a hat like that. What kind is it?"

"It's a Panama hat. How old is your brother?"

"About your age—he's the youngest sergeant-major in the whole U.S. Army!"

"That's very impressive. He must be a great soldier."

The girl beamed. "Do you have to go to Panama to get one of those hats?"

"Actually, they're made in Ecuador. But you can find them in some of the better haberdasheries. Or on the Internet."

"Haba—what? Dashiki?"

"Haberdashery, a mens clothing store."

"Are they like, real expensive?"

"About eighty or a hundred dollars. That's a lot for a young person."

"I start Hunter College in the fall. And I have a job. A hundred doesn't even buy a really good pair of shoes."

"I suppose not."

"Are you a rabbi?"

"I am," Ben said, hiding his surprise.

"If you're going to see Rabbi Zeev, he's usually okay in the morning, but after lunch, he gets tired and forgetful and has to take a nap."

"And how do you know that, Miss?"

"My mother is his housekeeper."

"Then maybe you can tell me which house he lives in?"

She pointed. "Next to last one on the left."

"Thank you, Miss...?"

"I'm Cindy MacPherson."

"I'm Rabbi Ben," he said, and they shook hands. Cindy giggled again.

Ben turned to leave.

Cindy said, "If they're made in Ecuador, why are they called Panama hats?"

"I'll bet if you Googled 'Panama hat' or 'sombrero de Jipijapa,' you could learn a lot about these hats."

"Hippy hopper?"

Ben spelled the word, the name of a town famous for its woven straw headgear.

"That's way cool. Thank you, Rabbi Ben."

"Curiosity will take you very far in this world, Cindy."

Ben turned away, then back again. He handed his hat to Cindy.

Ben said, "Don't move your head, but is there a guy across the street, near the corner?"

"Uh huh. Kind of skinny, one of them Hasid guys in a black coat?"

"I think he's following me."

"He just ducked back around the corner."

"Cindy, do you have a cell phone with you?"

"Always."

"With a camera?"

"Uh huh."

"If you can get a picture of this guy's face and email it to me, I'll buy your brother a hat like mine."

"Deal. How do I get it to you?"

"Rabbi Ben at Gmail.com."

"Got it."

"I'll need to know your brother's head size."

"Uh huh."

"Okay, now point at Rabbi Zeev's house again. I'll cross to the other side and head that way. He'll come over to this side, and you can get a picture as he walks by."

"What if I can't see his face too good?"

"Do the best you can, but don't take any chances."

"Why's he following you? Is he some kind of cop?"

Ben shrugged, then took his hat back and set it on his head.

"I don't know, Cindy. But a picture might help me find out."

CHAPTER TWELVE

A TALL, FLESHY LIGHT-SKINNED BLACK WOMAN IN LATE middle age, who bore a pronounced resemblance to Cindy, opened the door to Rabbi Zeev's house.

She said, "Help you?"

Ben said, "May I speak with Rabbi Zeev, please?"

"Expecting you?"

"I believe that he is. Or that he should be—Rabbi Maimon."

"Tell what is about?"

"The Keter Aram Tzova."

"Keter Aram Tzova. Is right?"

Ben nodded, and the woman escorted him to a small, dim parlor filled with faded, overstuffed furniture that smelled faintly of camphor. The sofa and chair tops were covered with crocheted antimacassars, reminders of the long-ago era when men groomed their hair with Macassar oil. Diffused sunlight streamed through lace curtains.

"I'll see he can do it," she said and vanished down a long, murky hallway.

The room seemed faintly familiar to Ben. Had he been in this house as a child? He had a good memory for faces and places, but the street outside, lined with buildings upward of 60 years old, evoked no memory. Had his mother, perhaps, brought him here? And if she did, why?

The woman reappeared. "Rabbi will see you. He takes lunch at noon. Then he needs the nap. Please give respect."

"Of course. I shouldn't need more than a few minutes."

"This way," she said, and led Ben down the hallway and to an expansive room, its walls lined with books. Seated at a small desk near a large, curtained window, Rabbi Zeev, with his carefully trimmed white goatee, translucent skin like ancient parchment and clothing a century out of fashion shrouding his shrunken frame, seemed like a figure from a Velasquez painting. But his eyes sparkled with intelligence as he stood, slowly and carefully, a welcoming smile on his lips.

"Shlomo! It's been much too long," he said, his speech faintly colored with the clipped accents of a small, distant British colony.

"Shalom, Rabbi Zeev."

"But you haven't changed! You look just the same …" Confusion clouded his aristocratic features. He stared at Ben, then drew back in fear.

"I went to your funeral," he gasped.

"Rabbi Zeev, it's me, Benny."

The older man hesitated, then seemed to focus. He smiled again. "Benny! You look just like your Saba Shlomo, your Grandpa Salomen."

A question bloomed in Ben's mind, but he shoved it aside. Stay focused, he told himself. The Codex. Find the Codex, if it's really here in Brooklyn.

Ben took the older man's hand, smiling. "Are you well, Rabbi?"

Zeev cocked his head, as though considering. "Well enough. I can walk without a cane, if it's not too far. I can drive a car, but it's too much trouble, and they won't give me insurance. My eyes were always weak, and now they're worse. I get tired. But... I will be 94 next month, God willing. And

you, Benny? How are you? Your wife is well? You have children?"

Ben's eyes filled. "I'm sorry to say that my wife died nine
years ago in Jerusalem. A suicide bomber."

The old man sighed, shaking his head. Slowly he sat, gesturing to an empty chair near the table. Ben sat. A long moment of silence passed between them.

"It's a vale of tears, Benny. Our people ..."

Abruptly, he seemed to lose his train of thought.

"Esperanza, my Dominican woman, said something about
the Keter? The Aleppo Codex? You have news?"

"A few days ago, I am told, Miryam, the niece of Shemuel
Benkamal, may he rest in peace, came to see you."

"Yes, yes. She showed me some parchment pages from *Bereshit*, from Genesis."

"What did you make of them?"

"It might be the Keter. It was very old. Two-sided—not a
scroll but a codex. I didn't recognize the hand of the sopher,
the scribe. The scribal style was like none that I've seen. It
might have been the work of Solomon ben Buya'a, in which
case that would indeed have been the Codex. But it was too
much for these old eyes. It would take an expert to confirm it."

"So it could have been something else, some other old
Tanakh?"

Zeev pondered this a long moment. "Of course. But I—
many in our community—have long suspected that Benkamal
had some pages from the Keter, perhaps even all the missing
books, or most of them, hidden away. Maybe in his house."

"That is very strange, Rabbi."

"He was a strange man. Not a bad man, not at all. Yiddish
speakers—your grandfather, of blessed memory—would have
called him *tzadik im peltz*."

"A saint in furs. Like our father, Noah?"

Zeev nodded. "Shemuel was like that, righteous for his time. He gave money to our *beit midrash*, our house of study, but could easily have given much more. He sent a few boys to Israel to study but could have sent many. Once or twice, he paid someone's hospital bill, but he could easily have endowed that hospital. He loaned small sums to a few people and then forgave their debts, but he could have assisted many, many more. And you had to ask him. He never came forward, never tried to learn who needed help.

"Also, he was very private. Came to services but sat alone in a corner. Declined honors, would not read from the Torah, or even carry it. Wouldn't even open the ark."

"Maybe he was only modest."

"Perhaps. He honored the dead, but went only to the shiva, the mourning service, at a home and never to the cemetery. If you asked him to serve on a committee, he'd find someone for the job, but he wouldn't do it himself. Always in the background."

"But why would he have had the Aleppo Codex?"

The old man peered at Ben through shrewd eyes. "This is what you do now? Hunt for old Torahs?"

Ben shook his head. "No. I help synagogues, charities, hospitals—Jewish institutions—when they have a problem. The Jewish Museum would like to recover the Aleppo Codex and restore it, and they asked me to find it."

Comprehension dawned in Zeev's face. "Yes, yes, I recall now. I've heard that you do wonderful things. Almost miraculous."

"Not so miraculous. But I try to help."

"A great mitzvah, Benny, to serve God in this way."

"It is a privilege. What about Benkamal? Why would he have the Codex?"

"The Benkamals were very important in Syria, not only to

Jews but to the country: merchants, traders and bankers, a wealthy and cultured family. For centuries, they were among the leaders of Joab's Synagogue, the Great Synagogue of Aleppo. "

"Where the Codex was kept."

"Until the Arab mobs sacked the Great Synagogue, and stole or destroyed hundreds of ancient books and scrolls."

Ben said, "Yet, some were recovered?"

"Yes. The mob tore the temple apart and burned many scrolls, but the Great Synagogue's *shammash*, the caretaker, secretly braved the flames and saved many valuable parchments. Aleppo's leading Jewish families quietly hid these ancient texts."

Ben said, "The Benkamals were part of that effort?"

Zeev said, "One must assume so. There was never a definitive inventory of what was saved or who saved what. But years later, one by one, dozens of individuals smuggled parchments and scrolls out of Syria. We know that some families took many parchments, some only a few. So why not Shemuel, as well?"

Ben said, "Except that he came here, instead of going to Israel."

Zeev nodded, yes. "Or to Argentina, where most of the Benkamals went when they fled Syria. And there's one thing more."

"Excuse me, Rabbi Zeev."

Ben turned to see Esperanza in the doorway.

"Your lunch will be ready."

Ben said, "Of course. I'll be leaving in a minute."

Zeev said, "I'd invite you to join me, but she didn't prepare enough for two."

"It's fine, Rabbi. What was the other thing you were going to say?"

Zeev appeared confused.

"About Benkamal?"

"Oh. Wait. It was ... just on the tip of my tongue."

"I'll come back tomorrow."

"No, not tomorrow. I have a bet din, a rabbinical court."

"Even now they ask you?"

"We must all serve God."

"Rabbi, did you make a copy of the document that you saw?"

Zeev shook his head. "She promised to make some, but then it was stolen."

"How can I reach Miryam, Benkamal's niece?"

"Esperanza will help you."

Ben assisted Rabbi Zeev to a bright and airy kitchen at the rear of his home, where a green salad, a soup of red lentils with sesame muffins and a tiny bowl of Muhammara dip—red pepper, olive oil and walnuts—awaited.

Ben said, "Shalom, rabbi. I'll come back the day after tomorrow."

Esperanza said, "Before ten, Rabbi. Or earlier."

Zeev said, "Show Benny out, and tell him how to reach Shemuel Benkamal."

Esperanza shrugged. "He died, Rabbi."

As they moved down the hallway, Ben said, "He meant the niece."

"She stays at the old house?"

It was Ben's turn to shrug. "I hope so."

"Then a phone book, I think."

"Rabbi Zeev doesn't keep a list, a roster?"

"I don't go in his office."

"*Muchas gracias por todo*, Señora Esperanza."

"*Vaya con Dios, Rabbi*," she said, and shut the door firmly.

CHAPTER THIRTEEN

———————

THE AIR SHIMMERED IN THE MIDDAY HEAT AS BEN emerged from Rabbi Zeev's home. There was no sign of Cindy; the street was quiet and empty except for a bulky woman with a headscarf slowly pushing a baby carriage on the opposite side.

There was something peculiar about the woman, Ben decided, but he couldn't quite say what. He turned toward her and ambled back the way he had come, watching her and thinking about what he would like to have for lunch. The woman turned the corner; a minute later, when Ben reached the corner, she had vanished.

That's strange, he thought. And then a moment later, he wondered whether he was paranoid. Maybe she's just a woman with a baby, and she went home.

A few blocks up was Coney Island Avenue, where Ben strolled until he found a small neighborhood restaurant. The tables were full of men in working clothes. A discreet window sign in modern Hebrew announced that the kitchen was certified kosher by a certain Rabbi Armut. Good enough, Ben decided.

The menu was disappointingly ordinary: sandwiches, burgers, salads, fried potatoes, eggs, meatloaf, fried fish, macaroni and cheese, fried chicken. Except for the substitution of soy analogs for milk products like cheese, it could have been any truck stop or greasy spoon in America. But it was clean and bright, and Ben was hungry, so he ordered a turkey burger with soy cheese, a green salad and a scoop of strawberry sorbet for dessert.

Exactly when the waitress brought his food, a man came into restaurant and took a corner booth. He was clean-shaven and wearing worn jeans, a Hawaiian shirt and a new Yankees cap, but Ben thought he looked like the same Hasid who followed him to Rabbi Zeev's house from the 79th Street subway station. Out of the corner of his eye, Ben saw the man unfold a newspaper and lay it on the table. He put his head down to read it.

Ben was considering his next move when his cell phone vibrated against his leg.

It was a text message from Chana with her new number and asking whether they could meet for dinner or whether he had anything to share now. Thumbs flying, he suggested a sushi bar in Yorkville, a mile or so north of her house.

Ben then checked his email, which included a short message of apology from Bert Epstein, his doctor, asking him to call. There was also a missive from Cindy, forwarded from his Gmail account: The man that he'd wanted a picture of had never returned.

Maybe, Ben thought, because he was busy shaving his beard.

Ben put his phone away and, without moving his head, scanned the room. The ex-Hasid was still reading his paper. A half-eaten sandwich lay before him.

Maybe, Ben thought, he was only imagining the resemblance. Maybe no one followed him.

Ben sat back in his chair, staring, sure that the man would look up.

Five minutes ticked by. Ten.

The man looked up. Their eyes met, and he quickly returned to his paper.

Ben still couldn't be sure.

Dropping two dollars on the table, he went to the cashier and pushed the check and a fifty across the counter to a plump, graying woman in an apron.

"I'm going out the back way, through the kitchen."

The woman opened her mouth to speak, and Ben put his hand over the fifty.

"The change is yours if you don't say anything or look at me."

The woman closed her mouth and moved her eyes sideways toward the rest room.

Ben headed toward the rest room, and then ducked into the kitchen. He was through it in five strides and blew out the back door at full speed.

The woman with a headscarf and a baby carriage, her back turned, blocked the alley mouth.

Gripping his hat in his left hand, Ben ran as fast as he could in the other direction. As he neared the residential street, he heard a man's shout behind him.

The subway station was about three blocks, east on Avenue M.

Ben was there in under a minute.

It was the middle of a summer day, and the platform was almost empty. Ben waited, his back against a wall, near the exit. But the only other riders were an older woman and her three frisky grandchildren, a young Japanese couple, and a black youth in baggy trousers and a muscle shirt carrying a bass violin in a case.

Ben took the first train south and got off in Coney Island, where he walked aimlessly for half an hour until he was certain that no one had followed him. In the men's room of a coffee shop, he pulled out his iPhone and dialed Information, but no Benkamal was listed in Brooklyn.

So he found the Coney Island branch of the Brooklyn Public Library and asked the motherly woman at the information desk for a 20-year-old Brooklyn telephone directory. The only Benkamals were Aida and Isaac, both at the same address.

As he rode the Q train back to Manhattan, Ben began formulating a plan for visiting the house and interviewing Miryam Benkamal. The first thing he'd do is get out of his rabbi clothes. He'd change trains at Union Square, and he was pretty sure there was a costume shop near there. And then maybe he'd try to find a thrift store.

But there was something else, something that Rabbi Zeev said. Something personal, a question that had arisen in his mind and that he had put aside to concentrate on the more important matter at hand. He couldn't remember what that was, and it bothered him.

CHAPTER FOURTEEN

HANA SAID, "WHY ISN'T AN EEL KOSHER? DOESN'T it have fins and scales?"

Ben smiled, glad to be back on familiar ground. "Fins, yes, but eel scales—they're tiny, raised ridges, part of the skin. Bumps. They don't scrape off."

"How do you keep all this in your head?"

"It's not all that much to memorize. The rules are laid out in the Torah. And there's tons of rabbinical literature on the subject. The hard part is when you come across an animal that wasn't known to the ancient world, like a turkey."

"Come on! Turkey is kosher."

"But in the 15th century, Rabbi Isaiah ben Avraham haLevi Horowitz—"

"I'm sure that's a fascinating story, but I'm hungry."

Ben worked his chopsticks to grab a small slice of fish the color of raw beef, which he dipped in a tiny bowl with a mixture of soy and wasabi, Japanese horseradish mustard. "Try this," he said, extending the morsel to Chana, who recoiled.

"At least the eel is grilled. I told you I wasn't wild about raw fish."

Ben smiled. "Do you trust me?"

"Of course."

"Then close your eyes and open your mouth."

"And then what?"

"I'm going to put a bit of tuna on your tongue. Give it a few seconds before you decide. Then, if you don't want it, I'll give you a napkin, and we'll go find a deli."

"Okay. But I'm going to spit it out."

Ben gently laid the tuna on Chana's extended tongue. She flinched.

"Give it three seconds. One, two—"

Chana's eyes flew open, her mouth closed and she smiled. Then she swallowed.

"That's ..."

"I believe 'yummy' is the correct scientific description."

"Can I have another piece?"

Ben pushed the plate of sashimi toward her. "I'll order another plate."

"Ben! This is so good!"

"I can't believe you live in New York and never had sushi or sashimi."

"I grew up in Ann Arbor, Michigan! By the time I moved to New York, I was married."

"That's no excuse. You should try the yellowtail."

"What else?"

"Oh, there's lots of kosher sushi. Mackerel, halibut, salmon—"

"Let's have some salmon. Do they have whitefish?"

"I doubt it. But they have herring, snapper—"

"Let's try them all."

Ben burst out laughing, and Chana turned bright red. "I'm just saying ..."

Ben caught the chef's eye, and then asked for another plate of tuna sashimi and three more orders of sushi.

While the chef worked at his art, Ben leaned closer to

Chana and in a low voice told her about the men who had followed him to and from Rabbi Zeev's house.

"I'm going to call my husband and give him hell. He's way out of line."

Ben shook his head. "I don't think this has anything to do with you."

"Then who followed you?"

"Mossad, maybe. If they have an open file on me, as Yossi says, then they might keep tabs, in some fashion, of my comings and goings. Maybe monitor my plane and train reservations."

"Mossad has ... what? Spies? In Brooklyn? Why? And why would they follow you?"

"Good questions. I'd assume that Mossad has assets in every major Jewish community."

"Assets?"

"A few people, not formally members of the organization, not full time, probably not Israelis but undoubtedly Jewish, that they rely on for small tasks from time to time."

"Like following you?"

"Or delivering a message, providing a safe house for an agent, introductions, local muscle, obtaining equipment, whatever might be required. Including just keeping an ear to the ground for interesting gossip or rumors. They probably heard that the Codex surfaced. And then I turn up. It's two plus two. So if they are indeed in Brooklyn, they'd like me to lead them to the pages. But that's mere speculation."

"But Yossi said—"

"He said he wanted to keep them out of it. But now we have to assume that they are at least aware and consider me a person of interest."

"Are you in danger?"

"Not from them. Your husband's little band of hooligans is another matter."

Chana pursed her full lips and looked down at the counter. "I'm really sorry about this. I didn't think Mo would act this crazy."

"Has he harassed any other men that you were involved with?"

She looked up, peered deep into Ben's eyes.

"Are we involved?"

"I don't know about we. I am involved."

"What does that mean, Ben?"

Ben lifted a piece of sushi with his chopsticks, deftly dipped it in sauce, and then popped it in his mouth. He chewed, thoughtfully, considering his answer.

"Chana, do you know the difference between ham and eggs?"

She smiled. "An odd question, from a rabbi. No. What's the difference?"

"When breakfast is served, the chicken is involved, but the pig is committed."

"So you think we're involved but not committed."

"We could be. It's kind of your move."

She lay down her chopsticks and took Ben's free hand in both of hers.

"I'm still a married woman."

"So no hanky-panky."

"Not yet. Maybe not ever. Is this going to work?"

"I'm comfortable with limits. For now. Let me help with your divorce, if I can."

"I don't think there's anything you can do, Ben. But that's still the sweetest thing anyone's said to me in a long time."

CHAPTER FIFTEEN

B EN SAT ON THE EDGE OF HIS NARROW HOTEL BED,
hunched over the screen on his MacBook Pro, using
Google Maps' satellite feature to recon the neighborhood around the Benkamal home. Google showed him slightly
soft images of a tree-lined street of blocky, modest, two-story
private homes and apartments.

Ben stared at the picture, puzzling over the men that had
followed him. If they had meant him harm, he concluded, they
would have attacked when he left Rabbi Zeev's home. And if
they were indeed Mossad, Ben reasoned, someone would now
be watching the Benkamal home. And someone, or several
someones, would probably be waiting near every subway stop
in Bensonhurst. Unless by now they knew where he was staying, in which case they would stake out the hotel.

But to what purpose? he wondered. To intimidate him? To
have him lead them to the Codex? Was something else going
on? Ben didn't know, and he didn't want to risk calling the
Benkamal home—the line could easily be tapped—until he'd
met Miryam and could explain the situation. He needed a way
into the house without alerting watchers.

He peered again at his computer. Four houses down from
Benkamal's was the concrete playground of a Catholic school.

A fence about seven feet high guarded adjacent backyards. A mature tree extended a green-clad limb over the fence.

A parochial school presented problems. He'd need a plan.

BY 7:00 THE NEXT MORNING, Ben had run a five-mile circuit around Williamsburg and environs and returned to his hotel for a shower and a quick breakfast of coffee, juice and toast. Wearing old jeans, a T-shirt and black training shoes and carrying a small bag, he hailed a cab and left it near Brooklyn's Borough Hall, where he walked around until he was satisfied that no one was tailing him.

In Borough Hall's marble corridors, he found a restroom with a vacant stall, where he changed into the clothes that he'd rented the previous afternoon. He rode the subway into Manhattan, surfaced at Lexington and 59th, and walked to the Cardinal Terence Cook Building at 56th and First Avenue.

A black Lincoln with darkened passenger windows picked him up there. Ben had the livery driver take him to back to Bensonhurst, then circle the residential streets surrounding St. Hermione's Catholic School. Down the block from the Benkamal home, he saw two men in a battered old Mazda with a clear view of the house.

The same two men who had tailed him the previous day.

Ben had the driver stop in front of St. Hermione's.

The driver said, "Shall I wait, Father?"

Ben handed him a hundred dollar bill. "What's your cell phone number?"

The driver wrote it on a scrap of paper. Ben said, "Wait right here for half an hour. Then go have coffee, and I'll tell you where to pick me up."

"Standing in a school zone is a two hundred dollar fine!"

"It's exactly a hundred and fifteen, but if you get a ticket,

I'll pay it. And another hundred if you stay right here the full thirty minutes."

"You got it, Father."

Wearing black summer-weight trousers and a white shirt with a Roman collar, Ben stepped out of the air-conditioned Lincoln and into the heat and humidity of a Brooklyn summer. He marched into St. Hermione's and hailed the first nun he saw.

"Sister," he said, in excellent mimic of what one of his college professors had called a Belfast brogue. "Where might I find Sister Agatha?"

The nun was in her 50s, a handsome arrangement of lines and angles in summery street clothing. She smiled warmly at the handsome Irish priest.

"Third floor, street side. Shall I show you, Father ...?"

"Horace. Father Horace Cole."

"I'm Sister Ignatia. This way, please, Father Horace."

Sister Agatha was pushing 60, as plump and as plain as Sister Ignatia was slender and aristocratic. She smiled at the young priest through shrewd hazel eyes.

"And to what do we owe the honor?" she trilled.

"A small honor indeed, when a humble servant of God visits one of the Church's finest schools," Ben said, still pushing the pseudo brogue.

"Humble servants don't usually travel in such grand style, Father."

"Nothing eludes you, Sister Agatha."

"What can I do for the Archdiocese today?"

"It's what you've already done," Ben replied, a smile playing on his lips. "Your fifth-grade girls have shown every Catholic in New York the value of a good education."

And, glory to God, that's all over the Internet, Ben thought.

Sister Agatha flushed with pleasure. "It's kind of you to say so."

"It's His Eminence who says so."

"His Eminence himself? Cardinal Dolan?"

"He's very high on your school, Sister Agatha."

"I'm so tempted to be flattered and prideful."

"He's considering a visit."

"The Cardinal's coming here? When?"

"You can't tell anyone, Sister."

"And why is that?"

"It's the reason I'm here."

"Where are my manners! Would you like a cup of coffee, Father?"

"Thank you, but I allow myself but one cup, and that's now ancient history."

"Something stronger, then?"

"Sister, I stand with Thomas Aquinas on the virtue of temperance."

Sister Agatha looked contrite.

"Then again, if we could both swear that the sun had set on the Hudson and you had a wee drap of the Jamie, I'd happily do my penance with the others."

Sister Agatha burst into laughter. "Tell me what you need from St. Hermione's."

"Thomas Aquinas, no less than His Eminence, ranks prudence first of the cardinal virtues. Sad to say, but the day when a man like Timothy Michael Dolan could go anywhere in this city without fear—that day has passed."

Sister Agatha bowed her head.

"His Eminence has enemies, Sister, but also many friends. And some right here."

"The Jews, you mean?"

"Indeed. They may be stiff-necked, they may refuse to see the errors of their beliefs, but they remain our elder brothers, our family in faith."

"Of course. As the Holy Father in Rome has instructed us—"

"Exactly. And they have observed some suspicious foreigners in this area."

"Not the ones in black that never shave their whiskers? The Hassids?"

"Some of those Jews are very close to His Eminence. I refer to strangers, possibly from the Middle East."

"Terrorists?"

"I pray that they are not. In any event, my superior, Monsignor Pierce—"

Sister Agatha raised a plump palm. "A tall, heavy man with deep blue eyes?"

Ben shook his head. "Neither tall nor short, heavy nor thin. And as for his eyes, blue or brown, he misses nothing. One of my junior colleagues calls him 'Hawkeye.' He serves his Eminence as, shall we say, secretary of prudence. He asks that I have a look around the grounds, if that's not inconvenient."

Sister Agatha's frown was enough to turn any 10-year-old's knees to jelly. "Summer classes are in session. What are you looking for?"

"Entrances and exits. Places to hide explosives or weapons."

"You must think me a fool."

Ben's heart sank. She was on to him! Somehow he mustered a smile. "Not at all."

Sister Agatha said, "These children are more precious than all the bishops in Christendom. And yet they are safe here. Do you suppose that is mere accident?"

"Certainly not. But no physical security is foolproof. And your resources are limited. More to the point, the Church has many schools but few princes. I commend you for keeping our children safe, but I need a look around just the same."

Sister Agatha sighed. She'd made her point but gained nothing. "But how is it that you just materialize on my doorstep like a David Copperfield, without so much as a phone call to introduce you, with the courtesy of an hour's notice?" she inquired.

"A fair question, Sister. At one time, not so long ago, if you picked up a phone in Manhattan to call Brooklyn, there was wire all the way from one instrument to the next."

"So what?" Sister Agatha snapped.

"And now it's all digital, it's all radio waves, and anyone with a hundred dollars can buy a little black box and listen to anyone else. Do you suppose nobody's tuned in to the Cook Building, listening to every word that goes out into the ether?"

Sister Agatha sighed. "Of course not, Father. Where shall we start?"

"No need to disturb your students. Let's begin in the basement."

FORTY MINUTES LATER, HAVING DESCENDED and climbed every flight of steps in the school and ascertained to Ben's satisfaction that there was no hidden passage, unguarded door, or secret entrance, Ben allowed Sister Agatha, panting and damp from her exertions, to return to her office while he inspected the playground.

He found no holes in the fence. Ready to abandon his masquerade, he slowly paced the wall between the schoolyard and the two adjacent homes, one facing 82nd Street and one 83rd and separated by small yards. He paused near the tree, eying the overhanging limb, measuring its height and thickness. He backed away, a step, two, three. He crouched. Then in one fluid motion, Ben flew forward, bounding skyward with his third stride to seize the limb, extending his legs before his body, letting his momentum carry him up and over the fence and out of sight in the blink of an eye.

He landed with bent knees and let himself roll forward on the grass.

An enormous mastiff bounded into the yard, fangs bared, then crouched, growling, 150 pounds of terror ready to spring at his throat.

CHAPTER SIXTEEN

———————

BEN PULLED HIMSELF UPRIGHT AND KNELT, REMOVING his smashed hat and calling to the dog in a low voice. If the mastiff attacked, Ben decided, he'd feed him the fedora. He fished in a jacket pocket for a strip of turkey bacon, tore it in half and held one piece aloft. Still growling, the mastiff edged forward, then stopped to scratch at a flea just out of reach on its massive underside. It turned its head, salivating.

Ben said, "Sit!"

And the huge dog sat.

"Good boy. Shake."

The dog lifted his paw for Ben to shake.

Ben dropped the hat and squeezed the dog's outstretched paw. Then he extended his other hand, palm up, with half the treat, and the dog licked it up.

Ben said, "Good dog." He climbed to his feet. "Sit."

The dog sat again, and Ben looked around. A flat-roofed storage shed about six feet high offered a step for the next wall.

He turned to the dog, held the treat high.

"Stay."

In three strides, he was at the shed and in one quick motion pulled himself up to the roof. His cheap black fedora lay forgotten on the grass behind him.

———

The dog inched forward. Ben tossed the treat into a far corner, then grasped the top of the wooden fence and lowered himself into the adjacent yard.

He looked around. No grass here, just swept concrete, a gas barbecue and a pair of old lawn chairs. The far wall, however, was only shoulder high, and Ben pulled himself over it without effort into another concrete-covered yard. This, too, had a shoulder-high fence. He crossed to the other side and peered into the Benkamal yard.

And froze. Petite and lovely, a dark-haired young woman whose shapely, olive-skinned body was bursting from a tiny bikini watered a small vegetable garden. Against all intentions, an almost irresistible surge of desire pulsed through his loins.

This won't do at all, he thought. His cell phone vibrated against his leg, making things much worse. He ducked down out of sight, considering his next move.

A female voice said, "Is someone there?"

Ben stood and looked over the wall at the bikini-clad beauty. Her eyes widened.

"Who are you? How did you get in that yard?"

"I mean you no harm, Miss. Are you Miryam Benkamal?"

"How did you get in that yard?"

Ben half-turned, gesturing back over his shoulder. "From that one."

"And how did you get into that one?"

"This is embarrassing! My name is Ben Maimon, Rabbi Ben Maimon, and I need to speak with you."

"You're a rabbi? Then why are you dressed as a priest?"

Ben laughed. "I feel very foolish. Someone is following me, and someone is watching your house and, I suspect, tapping your uncle's phone. In order to—"

"You haven't told me how you got into that yard."

"Went to St. Hermione's dressed as a priest, convinced Sister Agatha to let me do a security inspection, and then jumped over the wall into the first yard."

"You jumped over the wall?"

"With help from the tree. It sticks out over the fence."

"And what did you find in that yard?"

"A huge mastiff that likes turkey bacon and wouldn't hurt a flea."

"Samson wouldn't hurt a flea? Every kid in the neighborhood is terrified of him."

"I imagine so. But they're not fleas."

"Your story is so outrageous that I'm inclined to believe it. Except the part where you're a rabbi."

"Try me."

"First, let me see you jump over this fence. And don't step on my tomatoes."

Ben backed away from the fence, and then ran forward, seizing the top plank with both hands and swinging his body up over the fence and into the far yard.

The woman said, "Very impressive, but I was expecting a high jump."

Ben shrugged.

"And you blew your landing. No Olympics this year for you, Father."

"It's Rabbi. Rabbi Ben Maimon."

"Convince me that you're a rabbi."

"Certainly. But first, would you please put on some clothes?"

Smiling, Miryam dropped the hose and retreated into the house.

Ben used the interval to peer at the doorframe, which was newly painted.

Miryam returned wearing a bulky man's coat that was far too large for her.

"That was a very good start. But a priest might say exactly the same thing."

"You're enjoying this!"

"Why shouldn't I have a little fun? It's not every summer morning that a priest claiming to be a rabbi tames the neighborhood terror and jumps into my yard with a weird story about being followed and tapped phones."

"Actually, I'm not sure about the phone. I'm just assuming."

"Convince me that you're a rabbi!"

Ben switched to Hebrew. "Do you speak Hebrew?"

Miryam nodded. "I spent two years at the Technion," she said in Hebrew.

Still in Hebrew, Ben said, "My undergraduate degree is from M.I.T."

Still in Hebrew, Miryam said, "Any priest can learn Hebrew! Let's pray *Shacharit*, the morning service. That would convince me."

Ben said, "My grandfather was Rabbi Salomen Maimon, of blessed memory, a friend of Rabbi Zeev. He was born in Poland; I was raised in the Ashkenazi tradition, so I'm not too familiar with the Sephardic service. But I believe the parts are the same. Shall we go inside?"

"Let's do it out here. Do you need a book?"

"Not really. But I didn't bring my *tephillin* or my *tallit*."

"Skip that part. Girls don't use *tephillin*."

"They do in most Conservative and Reform congregations."

Miryam looked thoughtful. "Really? That's very interesting. Now let's pray."

Ben reached into his back pocket and extracted a tiny yarmulke, which he placed on his head, then turned to face east. Feeling faintly ridiculous and struggling not to think about what was under Miryam's coat, he began by reciting morning blessings.

After a few minutes, Miryam interrupted him.

"Skip ahead. Do Rabbi's Kaddish, then Mourner's Kaddish, then *Aleinu*."

"You're letting me off very easy."

"Pray for me."

"And pray for me, as well!"

Still in Hebrew, Ben recited the two versions of Kaddish, which were similar but not identical, the former used to conclude one part of the service and the latter for elevating the souls of the departed. Finally, Ben did the full version of Aleinu, a hymn praising God that dates to the Talmudic era. In most synagogues, it's the closing prayer.

Miryam said, "Why don't you come into the house, Father Ben."

Ben laughed.

"I think I passed."

"I'm still going to call you Father Ben."

CHAPTER SEVENTEEN

IRYAM LED BEN TO A DIMLY LIT PARLOR THAT AT first glance looked like Rabbi Zeev's: worn carpet, ancient overstuffed chairs, antimacassars, lace curtains. But the windows were open, and the curtains billowed in a faint breeze.

Miryam said, "Make yourself at home. I'm going to change."

Ben sat in the nearest armchair and turned to look at the room again. And blinked.

The mantle over a fireplace, the end tables flanking the sofa, the coffee table, a rocking chair, the sofa cushions and three uncomfortable-looking chairs—every flat surface except the chair he was in was covered with small paper bags stuffed with money.

Miryam reappeared, barefoot, in a sundress that displayed a lot of cleavage above and her sensational legs below, leaving Ben to wonder whether she had any idea of the effect her body had on men.

She unceremoniously swept the bags from a chair onto the rug and sat down.

Ben said, "What's all this?"

Miryam shrugged. "It's all over the house, in almost every drawer, in the freezer, in the panty, in the oven, for Chrissakes. And that's just the first floor, so far."

Ben's mouth fell open in surprise.

"'Scuse me, Father Ben. Didn't mean to curse."

Ben laughed in spite of himself. There was something addictive about this girl, her rough-honed New Yorker's sense of humor, her utter lack of self-consciousness.

"Your uncle was a drug dealer?"

It was Miryam's turn to laugh. "Tío Shemuel, cartel kingpin!"

Abruptly, her smile faded, and her lovely, darkly Semitic face turned thoughtful. "Actually, that might make sense. He gave my parents money, he gave me money, and it was always cash. Twenties, mostly. Sometimes hundreds. And I never really knew what he did for a living. He had some kind of business, but nobody talked about it. He was just always there here, in this house—and if we needed something... And then Mommy and Daddy died, and I moved in, and when I needed money, he just gave it to me. I paid my college tuition in cash, bought my plane ticket to Israel in cash, and it never occurred to me to wonder where it came from."

Miryam began to weep.

Ben pulled a new handkerchief from his pocket and handed it to her.

He waited until she had dried her eyes.

She gestured around the room, and then shook her head. "Synagogues always need money. Take some. Help yourself."

Ben shook his head. "I don't want your money. And you shouldn't do anything with it yet, make any big decisions, until you've had plenty of time to think things through. Anyway, I don't have a congregation. I'm not that kind of rabbi."

"What kind of rabbi are you, Father Ben? The red-headed, wild beast-charming, wall-jumping, heart-stealing kind?"

Ben blushed from the tips of his toes to the roots of his hair.

Miryam said, "Wow. Got you that time."

Ben shook his head, not knowing how to respond.

"No, really, what kind of rabbi are you, if you don't have your own *beit Midrash*, synagogue?"

"I guess you could say I'm a kind of Jewish paladin."

"A rabbi knight errant! You came to rescue me from this horrible house, and you fought your way through the Crusaders on the corner, past the beast that guards the castle walls, then you breached the walls and—"

"And then we *davenned Shacharit*. Sort of."

"Why are you here, Father Ben?"

"You showed Rabbi Zeev something that might have been the Aleppo Codex. It belongs in a museum."

"While I was burying Tío Shemuel, who I don't really think was a drug dealer, they—somebody—cut the lock on the side gate, took the hinges off the back door and the office door, and hauled his safe off. The Codex, or whatever it is, was in that safe."

"How closely did you examine it?"

Miryam shrugged. "It was on brownish parchment. Really old. Very elaborate Hebrew calligraphy, but faded. I think it was a Torah but not on a scroll. Just a pile of pages." She held up her hands about ten inches apart. "Maybe that thick."

"Did you notice if there was writing on both sides of each page, or just one?"

Miryam closed her eyes, as though trying to visualize the pages.

"I'm not sure. I don't think I turned the pages over. Why would that make a difference?"

"Because the Keter, the Aleppo Codex, is not a sefer Torah. It's a *Tanakh*. There was writing on both sides, which you won't find in a sefer Torah."

Miryam closed her eyes again, and something leaped in

Ben's heart. She was so lovely that he wanted to reach out and touch her face.

She opened her eyes and looked directly into his. "I just can't remember."

Ben said, "It's okay. We only do what we can do. Where did you find it?"

"In Tío Shemuel's office. It was in a little red suitcase, very old-fashioned."

"The kind of suitcase you might carry a big old typewriter in?"

"Father Ben! I was born in 1989. I've never seen a big old typewriter."

Ben held his hands about eighteen inches apart. "About this big?"

She nodded. "And covered with some kind of fake plastic leather."

"Flat on one side and rounded on the other, like a circle with one side cut off?"

She nodded. "I think so. Something like that, anyway."

"A makeup case. Probably from the '50s."

"How old are you, Father Ben?"

"Why don't you give 'Father Ben' a rest. Call me Ben."

"How old are you, Ben?"

"Why does that matter?"

"I told you my age."

"How old would you like me to be?"

"Either a whole lot older or about 30. But you're what? 35?"

"Thirty-seven. Almost 38."

"Married? I don't see a ring."

"We priests don't marry."

Miryam giggled. It gave Ben goose bumps, and he struggled to picture Chana.

Ben said, "Why did you think those pages were the Codex?"

"I didn't. I'd never even heard of it until Rabbi Zeev said it might be."

"Think back to what you remember when you looked at the pages. Why did you think it might be a Torah?"

"I read a few lines, and it reminded me of Torah readings."

"Were there vowels and cantillation marks, do you recall?"

"Don't know what that means, cantillation."

"In Hebrew, *taamey ha-miqra.* It's for the trope, for chanting it aloud."

"I've never seen a Torah scroll up close, never touched one. I'm a girl."

"I forgot that you come from the Sephardic tradition—"

"Women and girls are 'impure' at certain times and not allowed to touch the Torah or to read it aloud if men are listening. Ever."

Ben nodded. "It's an ancient tradition. But in fact, nothing in *Halakah,* Jewish law, prohibits a woman from touching a Torah, or reading from one aloud."

Miryam's face was a sea of conflicting emotion that made him think of his own struggles, years earlier, to come to terms with injustice masquerading as tradition.

"I'm sorry that you had to put up with that. It makes no sense in this day and age."

"These people, Tío Shemuel's people, don't live in this age," Miryam said, almost spitting out the words. "They don't live in this world. They live in Syria before the State of Israel was proclaimed, which is just like Syria 500 years ago."

"Or like Jewish Spain before the Inquisition."

"Exactly. So why aren't you married? Are you gay? Do the Conservatives have gay rabbis now?"

Ben laughed. "I think we do have a few gay rabbis. And many female rabbis."

"So you're gay?"

Ben laughed again. This was getting out of hand. "No, Miryam, not gay. I'm a widower. Nine years ago, my wife and unborn son were killed by a bomb in Jerusalem."

Miryam's eye's filled, and she felt for the handkerchief in her lap.

"You must think that I'm a total jerk."

"Please don't cry. And I understand: You lost your parents as a child. Now your uncle is gone, and you're alone, adrift, without anything or anyone to anchor you."

She dried her eyes again. "Not exactly. I have a job that I love. I'm in a master's program. I know what I want to do with my life. And I have a fiancé who loves me. Sort of, I think. Except he didn't want to come here with me."

"Then why all the questions about my age and marital status? What's going on?"

"I don't know, Father Ben."

"Come on, stop that."

"Can you handle the truth?"

"Of course."

"Okay. Here it is: When you vaulted over that fence, I realized that David, my fiancé, is a wuss. He's a sweet guy, very smart, very industrious. He's going to make a million dollars some day, but he'll never rock my socks the way that you just did."

"That's very unfair to David."

"I know. Maybe he could vault that wall, too. He's six-one and goes to the gym every day. And he's very handsome; he could be a movie star. But he's not like you."

"I know. I'm not handsome."

"Oh, but you are very, very cute, in a short, red-haired sort of way. And you're soooo confident. David would never jump into a yard with a monster dog. He'd never disguise himself as a priest to con a whole school full of nuns."

"Miryam. You don't even know me."

"I know enough. I bet you do stuff like that almost every day, right?"

Ben thought, I can't encourage this girl. She's clearly falling apart.

"Not even most days."

"But sometimes. And then you just do it, right? Because you have to, because it's important, whatever. You just do it, and you know you can."

"Miryam, where is this going?"

She burst into tears. "I don't know!"

And she ran from the room, just as Ben's phone vibrated against his leg.

CHAPTER EIGHTEEN

BEN PULLED OUT HIS PHONE AND THUMBED IT ON.

"Hello?"

"Ben, it's Bert Epstein."

"Bert, it's okay, you don't have to apologize."

"I'm calling about something else. Something wonderful."

"Go on."

"There's been a breakthrough. I should say, probably."

"We spoke a few weeks ago about bone marrow transplants."

"That's still a way off. As I told you then, under the best of circumstances, bone-marrow replacement therapy is hard on the body. But it might not be necessary. Some of my colleagues are on to something that might be better. And less risky."

"A vaccine?"

"DNA replacement. The animal studies are remarkable. A hundred percent efficacy in preventing reproduction of the virus in virtually all subject macaque monkeys. I've reviewed the data personally, and it's very, very solid. And I know the researchers: first-class guys, very careful, very thorough."

"So there's to be a clinical trial?"

"As soon as CDC approves the protocols. And they've been fast-tracked. They're hoping to begin selecting subjects for the initial study by early fall."

"Thanks for keeping up with this for me. Please let me know when I can apply."

"Three things, Ben: There's always some risk in trials. And at this point, even the primary investigators don't know what kinds of subjects they'll want: otherwise-healthy people or those with acute AIDS symptoms, or some mixture. Finally, you'd have to live in Pittsburgh for a year and be monitored with weekly blood tests."

"If there's even one kosher restaurant in Pittsburgh, I'm there."

"Stay healthy; this is important for many reasons now."

"Always. And Bert, thanks for the introduction. Does your wife really have a cousin named Shapiro?"

"She does. Aviva is a terrific woman, and her husband is a great man."

"Talk to you soon, Bert."

Ben clicked off, and then dug out the scrap of paper with the livery driver's number.

He answered on the first ring. "You ready to go now, Father?"

"Not yet. Have you had lunch?"

"Just coffee."

"Get yourself something nice, on me. I'll call you in about an hour."

"You got it, Padre."

Ben clicked off and looked up to find Miryam staring at him.

"Was that your girlfriend?"

"My livery car driver."

"Oh. Do you have a girlfriend?"

"Miryam. Please, don't come on to me. It doesn't feel right. You're a beautiful, intelligent young woman, and you're going to have a wonderful life if you'll just let it happen. Anyway, I'm not that special. There are plenty of wonderful men who would love to marry someone like you. And right now, I've got a job to do."

"Yes, the Codex. Why is that so important? Because it's old?"

"Tell me, if someone stole the only original parchment of the Magna Carta, and you had a chance to recover it, would you think that's important?"

"Of course. So the Aleppo Codex is like our Magna Carta?"

"In regard to its historical importance. Now, what you saw might not be the Codex. It might be some other old Torah or maybe not a Torah at all but something else. But until I can figure that out, I don't have time for anything like a romance."

"But after that? Then you might?"

"I should tell you: I just met someone, two days ago."

"And you're sleeping with her, is that it?"

"No. It's not like that at all. She's a wonderful, beautiful woman, and we're sort of interested in each other, but we're both super busy now and... and it's complicated."

"She's married."

"In the middle of a divorce."

"So that's my competition."

"It's not a competition! Listen, there's a lot to like about you. But I also have to tell you, I'm probably too old for you, and you already know that."

"My father was almost twenty years older than my mother. They had a beautiful life together, a wonderful marriage."

"Tell me about them," Ben said, hoping that talking about her family would help Miryam see her own life in better proportion.

"Daddy was born in 1945 and came here with Tío Shemuel from Aleppo when he was six."

"You call him Tío because he spoke Ladino?"

"And Arabic. And English, too, of course, but not as well. Usually Ladino and Arabic with his older friends."

"Okay, go on."

"My mother was born in Jerusalem in 1964. By the time they met, she was 21, and my father had been married and divorced."

"No children?"

"No. Maybe that's why they divorced. Anyway, my father had a fellowship in oncology at Sloan-Kettering when he met my mother. They were married in six months, and I was born eight months after that."

"Wow."

"Yeah. They were like totally hot for each other. Then when I was nine, they went on a vacation in Turkey, kind of a second honeymoon, and they took a ferry across the Bosporus, and it turned over and sank, and they both drowned."

Ben shook his head. "Unbelievable."

"It still seems like a bad dream. Tío Shemuel took me in, hired a nanny to help me through adolescence, and sent me to college. He was a very strange dude in so many ways, but he took good care of me, and I know he loved me very much."

"What about Shemuel's wife?"

"Tía Hadassah. She died before I was born."

"Miryam, where do you think all this money came from?"

"I've been thinking about that for days. It's in all kinds of different bags. But there are two that I think I know where they came from.

"One is from a bakery that we used to go to. The owner was a friend of Tío Shemuel, and then he died a few years ago. His son used to come over sometimes, and I think he brought a bag like that one time."

"They might have had bread or pastries in them."

"Of course. But once I thought I saw the baker's son give my uncle one of those bags. He put it in his coat pocket."

"Okay. Where else?"

"There was another man who came sometimes. I don't think I ever knew his name, but his bags have a logo. It's a shop where they sell leather goods: gloves, hats, belts, coats and jackets."

Ben said, "That's interesting. So maybe they were some kind of payoffs? Could your uncle have been blackmailing them or something?"

"That's hard to believe. Then he'd have to be blackmailing dozens of businesses."

"Maybe he had something on them."

"I don't think so. These were my father's friends. Everybody liked Tío Shemuel. Respected him. It has to be something else."

"Okay. We'll look into that. Together, if that's okay?"

"Yeah. I'd like that."

"Miryam, there's something I'd like you to do right now."

"What's that, Father Ben?" She was back to her playful self.

"Take all these bags, all the money, put them in a big plastic bag or a big suitcase and get it out of this room. Find a place for it. But it shouldn't be here."

"Why don't I go to the bank and open an account?"

"Because banks are required to report cash deposits of $10,000 or more to the government. And that's probably why your uncle didn't put this in the bank."

"But he has bank accounts. Two or three, at least."

"Did he leave a will?"

"An old one. He was going to make some changes, but now that the safe is gone, I don't even know where to look."

"You need a good estate lawyer."

"I don't know any lawyers. Will you help me find one?"

"Of course."

Ben got to his feet. "When does your mail get delivered?"

"Before noon. Maybe it already came."

"I want you to go outside and check. While you're out there, look down the street, to your right, and see if there's an old blue Mazda with two men in it."

"This is a joke, right?"

Ben shook his head. "No joke. They were out there two hours ago. I want to see if they're still watching the house so I can figure out how to leave."

"You're leaving now?"

"Not yet. But pretty soon."

"There's a door in our basement that goes into the house behind us. The coal chute opens into their side yard. It's never locked."

"How do you know about this?"

"When I was a girl, I used to play with the kids next door. When it was raining or snowing, we'd go back and forth that way. And I liked to slide down the coal chute."

"Can you go check the mail now?"

Miryam stood. "Don't go yet, Father Ben. I haven't even started working my feminine wiles on you."

Ben tried not to laugh but couldn't stop himself. Damn, she's cute, he thought.

CHAPTER NINETEEN

———————

BEN WAS FAIRLY CERTAIN THAT THE HOUSE WAS STILL under surveillance, but he wanted to impress Miryam with the seriousness of his cause. And of the danger she might be in.

Miryam returned, clutching a handful of mail and looking thoughtful.

"Tell me, Father Ben, how do you know that they're watching this house and not one of my neighbors? Or that they're not doing something perfectly innocent in that car?"

"Because yesterday the one behind the wheel was dressed as a woman and pushing a baby carriage up and down Rabbi Zeev's street. And later, when I went to lunch, he was watching the alley behind the restaurant."

Miryam drilled Ben with a look that mixed fright with something else, something he guessed was excitement.

Ben said, "This excites you?"

"Kind of. Yeah, I guess it does. Like water-skiing or sky-diving."

"You sky-dive?"

"I don't even water-ski. But I sort of can imagine what they feel like."

"Don't get too comfortable with it. This isn't a game to those guys."

"But you'll protect me, right?"

"I'm not a superhero. And this isn't a comic book or a movie!"

"So you won't protect me?"

She was playing with him again, Ben realized. He smiled to show he got it.

"Can we talk about the Codex? Did you ever hear your uncle or his friends mention 'The Crown of Aleppo?'"

"How 'bout just 'The Crown'?"

Ben nodded.

"My Ladino isn't too good, and I know only a little Arabic. But I think once or twice one of his friends said something that sounded like 'para la coronar.'"

Ben nodded. "'Coronar' means crown?"

Miryam said, "Yeah, like what a king or queen wears. So what does it mean?"

"It's a respectful nickname for the Codex. How is it that you remember that?"

"Because the only times it happened, Tío Shemuel looked at me in a strange way, and the other man immediately changed the subject."

"What did you think at the time? When it happened? Do you remember?"

Miryam shrugged. "My uncle had so many secrets; all sorts of things that he wouldn't talk about in front of me. So this was just another one. No big deal."

"I was raised by my grandparents. They spoke Yiddish when they wanted to tell each other something that was unfit for my young ears."

"It was probably about sex."

Ben blushed. He'd been thinking the same thing.

Miryam said, "Gotcha again."

To change the subject, Ben pointed at the bags of cash strewn around the room.

"Do you have a big trash bag? Can I help you do this?"

"Let's look in the kitchen."

Ben followed her the length of the house and into the kitchen. She started opening drawers and stopped, sighing.

"More money but no trash bags. This is ridiculous."

"Do you have a New York driver's license?"

"California. Why?"

"Because I'm thinking now that this isn't a safe place to keep money. If they broke in once ..."

"So I should get a safe deposit box?"

"A big one. But you'll need something to prove you're a New York resident."

"I still have my New York I.D. card."

"Why didn't you say so?"

Miryam stuck out her tongue. Suddenly, irrationally, Ben felt hungry.

"Do you have any food in the house?"

"Peanut butter but no bread. Stale cereal but no milk. Canned soup. Three-year-old matzoh in its original shrink-wrap. But no butter or margarine. I threw out all the moldy vegetables when I came back from California. I need to shop."

"How about this: We find something to put the money in—"

"There are about four jillion shopping bags behind the fridge."

"Good. We pack up the money, I call my driver, and we go through the tunnel and out the coal chute and drive to a bank and you rent a box."

"Good. And then I'll buy you lunch, and we'll go grocery shopping. It'll be like a date with David, except that you won't flirt with the waitresses and grocery checkers."

"Your fiancé flirts with other women in front of you?"

"He can't help himself. Women just throw themselves at him. But he's faithful to me. I'm pretty sure he is, anyway."

"You don't have to buy me lunch."

"But I've got all this cash, and you charmed Samson the monster dog and conned a coven of nuns and warned me about the guy who dresses like a woman."

"Things sound so much more dramatic when you describe them. Wait a minute—a coven of nuns? That's not funny."

"It would be if you grew up on this block. Some of my best friends were convinced that they were being schooled by witches."

"If it makes you feel better. But this isn't a date, Miryam. It's business."

"Sure. When you buy lunch, that's a date. Now, Father Ben, even though you have a livery car, I know that you've taken a vow of poverty. But I really hope you didn't sign up for the whole chastity thing."

Shaking his head, Ben grabbed a stack of shopping bags.

CHAPTER TWENTY

C HANA WAS NOT HAVING A GOOD DAY. AFTER HER first class, an 8:00 a.m. graduate seminar in Sumerian cuneiform, she tried to call her husband, Morris, only to learn that he was out of the country. Then she met with Selim Hussein, Avril LaRoche and Yehuda ben Levi, the trio of post-docs she supervised, but instead of reviewing the research proposal they'd worked on for several weeks, she was forced to act as referee to the three stubborn scholars, each convinced that his or her approach was right. Exasperated, she told them each to submit a proposal; she would pick one, and the other two would have to live with it. Half an hour later, while she was trying to catch up on correspondence, all three crowded into her tiny office to beg for another chance to submit a joint proposal.

After lunch at her desk—a hardboiled egg and a yogurt cup—Chana tried to call her divorce lawyers. She was told that one was in court, another was with a client and the senior partner, usually the most responsive, was vacationing in Yellowstone.

With an hour to kill before her three o'clock undergraduate class in Semitic alphabets, Chana went for a walk in Central Park, where she turned an ankle while dodging a teenage boy skating in the wrong direction on the Lower Loop.

She was resting on a park bench when Ben phoned.

Ben said, "I've been meeting with Miryam Benkamal."

Chana said, "Did she have the Codex?"

Ben said, "No way to tell. She's very bright and had a good Jewish education, but she's never seen a sefer Torah close up—"

"She's Sephardic?"

"Exactly. Said it looked like a pile of Torah pages, no rollers. Very old, brownish parchment, faded ink. Elaborate—her word—calligraphy."

"That certainly fits the Codex. But it could also be a hundred other old Torahs."

"Until Rabbi Zeev said that it might be the Codex, she'd never even heard of it."

"Ben, what about the Mossad? Are those guys still following you?"

"They staked out the Benkamal house. I found a way in without them seeing me."

"How?"

"Kind of a long story. I'll tell you all about it when we get together."

"Dinner?"

"Not tonight, Chana. Benkamal's house is full of stuff that I want to look at. I'm hoping that if I can find out who he was, what his life was about, I might get some idea if it was possible that he had ever had the Codex. And if so, then who might have taken it. Right now, I'm about to have a late lunch. Then I'm going back to the house. And tomorrow I've got an early appointment with Rabbi Zeev. By the way, how are you?"

"I'm in the park, and I just turned my ankle."

"Are you okay? Do you need me to take you to the hospital? I'll postpone—"

"It's not that bad. I'll be fine. I was just ... hoping to see you tonight."

"If I get back to my hotel at a decent hour, I'll call you."

"Okay."

"Something else is wrong? You sound a little ... down."

"It's just been a really rotten day, Ben. That's why I was hoping—"

"I'll grab a cab and come over."

"No, no. Time is of the essence. We both know that."

"Are you sure?"

"I'm sure. And Ben?"

"Yes?"

"I'm very glad that you're in my life. I just thought I'd tell you that."

"Cloud Nine, Chana. That's where you'll find me."

"Goodbye, Ben. Please, be careful."

"Depend on it. But you be careful, too."

———

BEN CLICKED OFF AND LAID his phone on the hotel bed. Then he shucked off his priestly garb and began changing clothes.

An hour earlier, he had emerged from the coal chute, followed by Miryam, onto the street behind the Benkamal house. The street on which, a hundred yards north, in front of St. Hermione's, were parked two NYPD squad cars. One bristled with antennas, announcing that it served as a rolling command post for a very senior officer.

Ben and Miryam waited out of sight behind the porch, until the livery car stopped.

Between them they carried eight shopping bags filled with cash. They casually stowed them in the trunk of the town car, then got in and drove away. When they turned onto 15th Avenue, Miryam and Ben, sitting at opposite corners of the back seat, looked at each other and burst into laughter.

Ben said, "The Dime Bank in Williamsburg: Do you know where that is?"

"Fifth Street, near the BQE?"

"That's it."

Ben had the driver wait around the corner while he went into the bank with Miryam. After renting two of the largest safe deposit boxes, they were escorted to the vault with their bags. Ben left Miryam to fill her boxes in privacy; the livery driver waited outside the bank while Ben hailed a cab to take him to his hotel.

Ben emerged from his room wearing a polo shirt, khaki slacks and his best running shoes. Downstairs, he ducked into a coffee shop for a pair of tuna sandwiches to go, then hailed a cab and returned to the bank, where Miryam directed the driver to a Bensonhurst supermarket. As they left the store with a cart full of groceries, Ben drew Miryam aside. "Can we get back into your house the same way we left it?"

"With all these groceries? The Cabassos, my uncle's neighbors, are at their cabin in Crown Point for the summer. Their housekeeper will let us in, and we'll go down into the basement like grownups."

"Crown Point?"

"In the Adirondacks."

"Let's get a taxi. I don't want to drive past St. Hermione's in that car again."

"Good idea."

Ben paid the livery driver, tipping him lavishly. Waiting for the cab, he spied a Radio Shack store across the street.

"I'll be right back," he said, and dashed away.

He returned to find Miryam watching the taxi driver, a middle-aged black woman, putting her groceries in the taxi.

Miryam said, "What was that about?"

Ben handed her a cheap cell phone and an instant battery

charger shaped like an elongated egg, and then pulled their twins from his pocket. "If I have to call you, we'll use these. I bought fifty dollars worth of calling time."

"But I already have a Samsung Galaxy."

"Yes, but if somebody is tapping your phone, they may know about your cell. They won't know about these."

"You think of everything, Father Jason."

"Jason?"

"Father Jason Bourne, of course."

"You never give up, do you?"

"Never. And neither did Tío Shemuel, you know. He was relentless."

"And one more thing. I'm kind of tired of sneaking around. You know those two bozos watching your house? I think I'm going to make them leave."

Miryam said, "And then me and my groceries slip into the house through the front door, and they're none the wiser. Very good, Father Jason. But how will you do that?"

"Watch me," he said, and got into the cab.

CHAPTER TWENTY-ONE

———————

B EN HAD THE TAXI STOP A LONG BLOCK NORTH OF THE Benkamal house.

"Wait here until I call you."

"Be careful, Father Ben. You don't have anything to prove."

With a sad smile, Ben climbed out of the taxi and trotted down the sidewalk, looking down the block for the blue Mazda and scanning the other parked cars. He passed Miryam's house without seeing his quarry, then continued to the end of the block and to the cross street.

The car, and its watchers, was gone.

He dug out his new phone and called Miryam.

"They're gone. I'll meet you in front of the house."

The taxi beat him by half a minute; by the time he reached the house, he could see that something was very wrong.

Miryam stared at the house, and then pointed. "The door!"

Ben turned to look and after a moment realized that the front door, an ornate, old-fashioned wooden portal, was propped against the porch wall. Its hinge pins were gone.

Ben vaulted the fence and flew up the steps.

He found the house protected by an inner door of steel bars and heavy mesh.

Its hinges protected, the lock and double deadbolt of this

security door bore fresh scratches but were otherwise-undamaged.

Carrying bags of groceries, Miryam joined Ben on the porch.

Ben said, "In back, that's a new door?"

Miryam nodded, fighting tears.

"Give me your keys; I'm going around to check it."

Miryam gave Ben her key ring and showed him the correct key. "Right back," he said, and hopped off the porch, went through an unlocked side gate and ran to the back.

Fresh scratches adorned the back door's locks, but its internal hinges were secure, and the door remained closed.

Ben let himself in, locking the door behind him, and then went room to room on the first floor. To his eyes, at least, nothing seemed disturbed.

He opened the front door to find Miryam and the groceries. The taxi was gone.

They carried the bags into the kitchen in silence and put them on counters.

Miryam turned to Ben and fell against him, sobbing.

"I feel so ... violated," she gasped.

Ben wrapped her in his arms, felt her heart beating fast against his chest, held her tight. He felt himself becoming aroused and fought the impulse to fondle her. When her sobs at last subsided, he held her for another long moment.

Miryam said, "Thanks, Father Jason. I'm okay now."

Gently, he released her. "We should put this stuff away before it spoils," he said.

Five minutes later, they sat facing each other across the kitchen table, slowly eating tuna sandwiches while silently eyeing each other.

Ben had never wanted to make love to anyone more than he did at that moment.

Miryam finished her food, wiped her lips on a napkin.

"Should I call the police, Father Ben?"

"They might get some fingerprints off the door."

"They didn't the last time."

"I think we might have a better idea now of who tried to break in this time."

"Do you think it was the same people who took the safe?"

"Same M.O., as they say on TV. They went for the hinges."

"And you know what they look like."

"I know what the guys watching the house look like. We don't know for sure they tried to break in. They could have been lookouts."

"Are we going to make love tonight?"

"I don't think I'm going to be here tonight, Miryam."

"Then how about right now?"

"Right now, you're going to call the police, and I'm going to look for bugs."

"I saw the bill. An exterminator came just a month before Tío Shemuel died."

"Not those kinds of bugs."

Miryam stared at him, wide-eyed, vulnerable. "Why would you—"

"They seemed to know the house was empty. But we went out the back way."

"Maybe they left some kind of listening device?"

"We'll see. Call the police."

"Yes, Father Ben."

"If you call me that in front of the cops, they'll probably take me with them."

Miryam got out of her chair and sat down next to Ben. "What name did you use with the wicked nuns of St. Hermione's?" she whispered.

"Father Horace Cole," he whispered back, and they both giggled.

"You just made that up?"

"A hundred years ago, there was a guy named William Horace de Vere Cole, an Irish practical joker who once passed himself off as the emperor of Abyssinia and inspected HMS Dreadnaught, pride of His Majesty's Navy. Among many other stunts."

They both giggled again. Then stared into each other's eyes for a long moment.

Abruptly Ben stood up. "Call the cops. I'm going to look around."

"I know you want me," she said, just above a soft whisper. "I can feel it."

"You also know this is not the right time or place. Call the cops!"

By the time a pair of plainclothes officers arrived, Ben had found transmitting devices concealed in lamps or chandeliers in the living and dining rooms and the office. A fourth device was hidden inside the mouthpiece of the office telephone. Ben turned all four over to the officers.

The lead cop, a thin, dark man in his 30s, asked Ben to come with him into the kitchen, where he produced a fingerprint card and an inkpad. "We need your prints so we can rule them out if we find them on the door," he said. Ben allowed himself to be fingerprinted, meanwhile trying to recall whether he'd touched anything at St. Hermione's.

"We gonna find your prints in the system?"

"I have a Massachusetts driver's license, and I used to teach high school."

"What subjects?"

"Introduction to the Talmud."

"You some kind of rabbi?"

"Exactly."

"You live in Massachusetts. What are you doing in Brooklyn?"

"I was born and raised here. I came to see Rabbi Zeev, a friend of my late grandfather, and he told me that Miryam had lost her uncle and needed help getting his affairs in order."

"You sleeping with that girl, Rabbi?"

Ben shook his head. "That would be very unprofessional."

"But you might force yourself."

"That's really none of your business, officer."

"Don't get your back up. Just doing my job."

"I hope you're equally thorough with the fingerprints and the listening devices."

"Did you know this house was burgled last week?"

"Miryam told me."

"Where were you last week?"

"I was scholar-in-residence at Congregation Beit Joseph in Burbank, California."

"How'd you happen to find those devices, Rabbi?"

"I looked in obvious places. It seemed like too big a coincidence that someone tried to break in precisely when Miryam and I left the house to go grocery shopping."

"You're living here now?"

Ben shook his head. "I have a hotel room in Williamsburg."

"How much longer you gonna be around, Rabbi?"

"Hard to say. Probably not more than a week or so."

"You ever dress up like a priest?"

Ben's heart stopped for an instant.

"Excuse me? A priest?"

"A Roman Catholic priest. Like over at St. Hermione's."

"I can't say that I've ever even dreamed of dressing like a priest. Why?"

"Just routine, Rabbi."

"Whenever you meet a rabbi, you ask if he dresses like a priest?"

"Somebody matching your general description and pretending to be a priest infiltrated St. Hermione's today."

"Infiltrated? He stole something? Swindled them? Baptized a baby?"

"We don't know what he was after. Roamed around the school for half an hour and disappeared. One minute he was on the playground, and the next he was gone."

"Very weird. And he looked like me?"

"Five-seven or eight, red hair, Irish accent."

"I assure you that no rabbi that I've ever met would do a thing like that."

"No offense. Just routine."

"Okay. Anything else?"

The officer handed Ben a business card. Ben read it aloud: "Officer Donal Novello, Brooklyn South, Anti Crime.

"Irish mother, Italian father?"

"That's Brooklyn, ain't it? Call us if you find any more of those devices."

"I will, Officer Novello, and thanks for coming out."

Ben followed him to the front door, where Miryam and the other cop waited.

They stood side by side, watching as the police drove away.

Miriam put her arm around Ben's waist.

"Ever dress up like a priest, Father Ben?" she said, and they both giggled.

CHAPTER TWENTY-TWO

B EN SAID, "MIRYAM, WHERE DID YOU FIND THAT CASE with the old Torah pages?
Miryam said, "Under the desk in the office."

He followed her down a dim hallway to the office, which was dominated by a huge roll top desk almost half the length of the small room. A narrow, barred window looked out on the vegetable garden; it had an old-fashioned pull-down shade. Ben had been in the room earlier and recalled stacks of books and papers piled everywhere. Now he flipped a wall switch, but the ceiling light didn't work, so he switched on the floor lamp from which he had earlier removed a listening device. It cast a weak, yellow light. Even with the window shade up, the room was dim.

Ben put his head close to Miryam's and whispered, "Do you have a step ladder?"

"There's a closet off the kitchen," she replied in a whisper.

Ben left the room, returning a few minutes later with the ladder and a new light bulb. With Miryam's help, he cleared a space in the center of the room to open the ladder, and ascended until he could reach the fixture, a small square of frosted glass with raised edges that reminded him of a candy dish. With difficulty, Ben removed an ornate brass nut and handed the grimy fixture to Miryam. The light socket was empty. Miryam handed Ben the new bulb, and he screwed it into the socket. But when Miryam flipped the wall switch, nothing happened. Ben left the bulb, replaced the fixture and climbed down.

"What's in the room above?" he said in a normal voice.

"Tío Shemuel's bedroom. Why did we have to whisper before?"

"Because I couldn't be sure there wasn't another bug in that fixture."

"And now you are?"

"Reasonably. But it bothers me that this room is so dim."

"And such a mess."

"Oh? I thought maybe you made that, looking through your uncle's papers."

"Everything is pretty much the way it was when I got here last week. I sat down at the desk and tried to open it. It's stuck or locked. Then I felt something under the desk, and it turned out to be that case with the old Torah."

"When you put it in the safe, what else did you see?"

Miryam shrugged. "Papers, some gold coins. An old gun. I was going to go through the papers, but I never got a chance."

"What about your uncle's new will?"

"I haven't found it yet. He gave me a copy when I first went to Israel. Then last year, he told me on the phone that he was making a new one and he'd give me a copy the next time I was home."

"So you don't know what's in it?"

Miryam shrugged. "I was his only living relation. He had a life insurance policy, and I'm the only beneficiary."

"Would you mind if I asked how much that was for?"

"Twenty thousand dollars."

"You should file a claim as soon as you get your uncle's death certificate."

Miryam nodded. "Will you help me find his will?"

"Sure. Where have you looked?"

"The desk is locked so I started to go through the other papers. I've looked at everything on the chair, but it's mostly in Arabic. Do you read Arabic?"

Ben shook his head. "A few words. But the people I'm working with—"

"The museum?"

"They have someone who can translate Arabic or Ladino."

"If it's just personal stuff, I don't need to know details. Just if it's something I need to deal with his estate, wind up his business. Whatever that was."

"I can have someone take a look at them."

"Thanks. I wish I could get that desk open."

Ben walked around behind the desk and peered at it. He stepped back, thinking.

"Did I see a china cabinet in your dining room?"

Miryam nodded. "And there's another, a breakfront, in the living room."

"Let's go look at them."

Ben followed Miryam into a long, spacious dining room. Along one wall was a massive cabinet of wood and glass. All of its doors were locked. Miryam squatted on the floor and with her right hand probed the floor under the cabinet, affording Ben a view of her spectacular bare breasts. She rose, holding an ornate brass key.

"So, Father Ben, did you like what you saw?"

Ben turned crimson.

"Gotcha again!"

Ben held out a hand for the key.

Miryam said, "You wouldn't have this problem if we went upstairs for a nap or something."

"I thought you wanted the desk opened?"

"That could wait."

"Miryam, if you don't cut that out, I'll have to leave."

"I thought you were trying to find that Codex thing."

"You're making it unnecessarily hard."

"A hard man is good to find."

Despite his best intentions, Ben guffawed. She was a handful. He only wished—

Stop that, he told himself. Focus on the job.

He snatched the key from her hand and returned to the office. The key was a little small for the lock, but a minute or so of working it produced an audible click. He pushed the roller up into its storage space, and then used the same key to unlock a master drawer.

"It's all yours."

"Wow. Father Jason strikes again. You're amazing."

Ben doffed an imaginary hat. And suddenly remembered that he'd left his rented black fedora in Samson's yard next to St. Hermione's. He hadn't planned on returning the costume—his deposit would more than cover it—but now he worried that the police might track the hat back to the costume shop.

He'd used a nom de guerre. Paid cash. But if the shop had a security camera...

"Where are you, Father Ben? Father Ben, come in please!"

Ben turned, smiling, to Miryam, who had begun to pull folders and papers from the drawers and stack them on the desktop.

"Sorry. I just recalled that I left my rented priest hat in Samson's yard."

"That dog chewed a combat boot to shreds in half an hour. How much of your hat do you think is still recognizable?"

"Maybe just the rental label."

Miryam paled. "The police could trace that, couldn't they?"

"If they care to spend the time. But there was no crime. No

one lost anything. No one was harmed. If anything, New York Catholic schools will be a bit more secure because teachers and principals realize how easily they can be penetrated."

"You penetrated all those nuns, but you won't penetrate me?"

Ben laughed. "You really are relentless. Do you and David have a lot of sex?"

"Okay! Now we're discussing our sex lives. Father Ben, David's always busy working on his dissertation or flirting with waitresses or undergrads. When we see each other, it's usually just five minutes of frenzied groping until he's satisfied. Now it's your turn. How's your sex life?"

Ben smiled. "Would you like to know how many women I've slept with?"

"Will I be shocked?"

"Not you. The answer is, two before I married my wife, and none after."

Miryam stared. "So you haven't had sex in..."

"About nine years."

"Because you spend all your energy jumping over fences and charming nuns?"

"Because self-control is part of living a Jewish life. Sex is a beautiful and wholesome expression of mutual love. It's not like eating a nice steak or drinking a fine wine. For an observant Jew, sex is a glorious part of a mutual, life-long commitment to another person."

"So you wouldn't ever have sex just to have sex?"

"If I did, I'd have been all over you hours ago."

"Now we're getting somewhere! Go on."

"I can't kid myself that lust is the same as love. If a woman is not prepared to stand with me under a chuppah, a wedding canopy..."

"Wow. I'm horny as hell, and I meet the last moral man."

"I'm sure there are plenty of men, Jewish and not, who believe this."

"Could you marry someone like me?"

"There's a lot to like about you, Miryam. But we don't know each other well enough to speak of such things. We met just today!"

"What about your girlfriend?"

"I've known Chana two whole days. We share a mutual interest in finding a spouse. But she's still married, so we haven't even considered making love yet."

"But until then, you'd give me a chance, wouldn't you?"

Ben had to smile. Such an earnest and innocent plea from the lips of this self-styled sexpot.

"In almost any other circumstances, we wouldn't need to have this conversation. But Miryam, I'm here on a very important task. I need to concentrate on that, and you're starting to be a distraction, a very beautiful, funny, nice distraction, but a distraction nonetheless. Can you cool the sex talk, please?"

"When this is over, when you find that Codex—"

"I'm not sure if it was the Codex."

"—before you go back to wherever you're from, can we go on a date? Like regular people?"

"I can't promise. But I would like that. Once my work is finished, I will try. But you should also understand that, before this is over, I may have to leave New York."

"And go where?"

It was Ben's turn to shrug. "I have no idea where or even if. But I will try."

"Even if it means coming out to California?"

"What will David think? Your fiancé?"

"My ex-fiancé."

"Come on. That's not fair to David, and it's not fair to you."

"Father Ben, marriage and relationship counselor?"

Ben shook his head. "Miryam, listen to yourself. You've known me for a few hours, and now you're rearranging your whole life? Is that really wise?"

She frowned. "I guess not. But now that I have met you, I know that I could never marry anyone like David. And I also know that he won't shed many tears when I tell him. He'll just move on. He's so gorgeous; he'll find another girlfriend in a day or two."

Ben threw up his hands in defeat. "It's not really my business. But don't start making plans that include me."

"Except we'll go on a date. One date."

"I'll make every effort. But no more sex talk, okay?"

"I will also make every effort, Father Ben. But after nine years, it's getting pretty hard, right?"

"Miryam!"

Miryam took a stack of photographs from the desktop and handed them to Ben.

Ben said, "There's no light in here. Let's take everything into the dining room."

CHAPTER TWENTY-THREE

BEN SPREAD THE PHOTOS OUT ON THE LONG DINING room table, peering at each in turn.

Miryam said, "Most of these were on his office wall for years and years. When I came back home after graduation from Berkeley, he'd put them away."

She pushed a framed photo of a tall, lean young man with a hawk's nose and chiseled Semitic features next to a boy of eight or nine. "My father and Shemuel in Aleppo," she said.

Ben studied the image. It had been taken in front of a studio backdrop that was a painting of a stone fortress that Ben supposed was the famous Aleppo Citadel. He felt that there was something strange about the photo, a little off, but Ben couldn't identify what it was.

Next was an older, somewhat faded photo of a petite bride and her equally compact groom in wedding finery. The bride wore a large, unusually shaped Hamsa, a raised hand with a center eye sometimes called the Hand of Miriam that the superstitious wore as a defense against the "evil eye." She bore a striking resemblance to Miryam.

Ben said, "Your grandmother?"

"Naomi. Taken in 1942, I think."

"Do you know what became of her?"

Miryam's lovely face looked pinched. "Tío Shemuel always said that my grandparents probably died in the Farhud after the sacking of the Aleppo synagogue."

"Farhud?"

"Like a pogrom. An Arab mob killing Jews."

"But your father survived?"

"My grandfather was a cheese merchant. He imported cheese from all over Syria, and from Lebanon, Iraq and Turkey. And he was very wealthy. The mob looted his house, and then set it afire. But one of his Arab competitors, a neighbor, hid my father, and dozens of other Jewish children, in his own home."

"Blessed be his name."

"I wish I knew it. Anyway, after things calmed down, Tío Shemuel and his wife came out of hiding, found my father, and took him out of the country. The rest you know."

I wish I did know, Ben thought.

The next photo was a youth clad in white and wearing an oversized *tallit,* or prayer shawl, surrounded by bearded men. Behind them, slightly out of focus, his face in shadow, was Shemuel, a head taller than the next tallest adult.

Ben said, "Now I can see how tall he was!"

Miryam said, "About six-three, I think. But he shrank as he got older."

Next Miryam passed Ben a faded color photo of a short, powerfully built man in a white tuxedo with a longhaired, petite beauty that could only be Miryam's mother.

"She was so lovely, as was your paternal grandmother. You come from a family of beauty queens, Miryam."

"I do have good genes. My Mom's name was Aida. She was very, very smart, too. Graduated from Columbia at 20. She was going to be an obstetrician until she met my father."

There were more pictures of family gatherings with

Miryam as a tiny tot, as a first-grader, at an all-girls summer camp. Shemuel was in a few of them, but in every case, his face was turned away, or in shadow, or partially obscured by something.

This is a man who does not want his picture taken, Ben thought, wondering why.

Finally Miryam held up a color snapshot of an adolescent girl, an older woman and a much older man, Shemuel, now hardly recognizable as the handsome young Syrian in an Aleppo photo studio.

"That's you?"

"I was about 12. That's Beneficia, our housekeeper."

"I'd like to talk to her, too."

Miryam shuddered. "One morning, last February, she opened the front door to bring in the newspaper. The porch was icy, and she fell and fractured her skull."

Miryam wiped a tear from one eye.

Ben said, "You were close?"

"She was like my grandma. Took care of Tío and me and did everything for us."

"I'm sorry to bring up such painful memories."

Miryam shook her lovely head. "Not your fault. Some jerk kid, probably, threw a Coke over the fence. It landed on the porch and froze solid."

Ben stared at the picture.

"How do you know that?"

"Tío Shemuel found a paper cup and a food wrapper on the porch. From McDonald's"

"So what did he do after that? Get another housekeeper?"

"Some woman. Kitzy, Kizzy, Kitty, something like that. I never met her."

"And where is she now?"

Miryam shrugged. "Tío Shemuel found her in his office,

which he always kept locked. She said he probably forgot to lock it and he said, 'Go and don't come back.'"

"So he was still mentally sharp right up to the end of his life?"

"Oh, yes. I offered to come back and take care of him, but he said he would find someone else. But he never did."

"What did he die of?"

"Every morning, for as long as I can remember, after he had his coffee, he'd get dressed up in a suit and tie and go for a walk around the block. Sometimes, he'd go up around the corner on 13th Avenue to schmooze with his pals. Every Friday, he went to the library to read Arabic newspapers. So some stupid kid skateboarding on the sidewalk ran into him. Broken hip, fractured collarbone and a serious concussion."

"That's when you came back?"

"Yes. He was in and out of consciousness for four days, and then he died."

"What about the skateboarder?"

"It was just down the block from the library, and six or seven people saw it. He just kept going."

"The police are looking for him?"

"They said they didn't have enough of a description, that it could be anyone."

Ben sighed, not wanting to share what he was thinking. He decided to hold off, chew on it some more before broaching the subject.

Ben was all but certain that the tall, mysterious Shemuel Benkamal had been murdered, as had the Benkamals' housekeeper, Beneficia. Now he needed to learn why and whether it had anything to do with the Aleppo Codex.

CHAPTER TWENTY-FOUR

B EN KICKED OFF HIS SHOES AND STRETCHED OUT ON
his hotel bed.

Miryam had retrieved dozens of Arabic and Ladino documents from the roll-top desk that required translation. Ben had borrowed the one clear photo of Shemuel as a young man, and while he took it and the documents to a nearby FedEx store, Miryam had prepared a simple but tasty meal of red snapper, brown rice and salad.

By the time he had dispatched the documents to Chana, joined Miryam for dinner and ridden the subway to Williamsburg, it was 10:30, and he was very tired. Nevertheless, he punched in the numbers for Chana's new phone. For several minutes, they exchanged the minutia of their days; mindful of eavesdroppers, Ben omitted any mention of the elaborate ruse he used to reach Miryam's home unobserved. Nor did he mention his suspicions that Benkamal had been murdered: That would have to wait until they were wide awake and face to face.

Chana yawned. "What did you send me?"

"A lot of handwritten stuff, mostly correspondence, I think. Plus several documents with letterheads or official seals. And a photo that I'd like you to have an expert check out. It's

Shemuel, about 1950 or so, and a kid that Miryam says was her dad. But there's something odd about the photo. I'm not sure what, exactly."

"The museum has somebody that will know if it's hinky," Chana said.

"Great. I'm going back to Rabbi Zeev in the morning. Early, so I can spend a few hours with him."

"Okay. Sorry, but I'm very sleepy. Is there anything else?"

"Yeah, but it will wait. Dinner tomorrow night?"

"I'm all yours."

"Don't make offers you can't fulfill."

Chana laughed. "You know what I mean. Good night."

"Sleep well."

Ben broke the circuit, and then prepared for bed, starting with his evening dose of anti-retrovirals. After brushing and flossing, he climbed into bed and turned off the light.

As was his habit, he prepared a mental checklist, things he needed to do in the morning: exercise, shower, eat, anti-retrovirals, subway, walk to Rabbi Zeev's. Then, more important, the questions he intended to ask: What was there about Benkamal that had made him suspect that the pages Miryam showed him were from the Codex? Who else might have known what Miryam had showed him? If Benkamal had the Codex, who might have known about it? If he did actually have it, why had he kept it hidden away?

And finally, the one question that had been a shadow on his mind since Zeev first greeted him, a personal question, if only he could recall. It was about his resemblance to his grandfather Salomen ...

Ben rolled over on his side and, as he had long ago trained himself to do, fell into deep sleep in seconds.

THE RADIO SHACK PHONE RANG.

Ben sat up in bed, momentarily disoriented. The phone rang again. It could only be Miryam. He grabbed the phone.

"Miryam, it's very late—"

Miryam's voice was edged with panic, "They're trying to break in!"

Ben said, "Who? How?"

"Someone! They put a ladder against the building! They're cutting the bars off a window!"

"Calm down. Call 911, then turn on all the lights and make all the noise you can."

"Will you come?"

"Hang up and call 911. I'm on my way."

Ben put on his glasses and looked at the hotel's digital clock-radio: 3:22 a.m.

He dialed the car service he'd used the previous day and got a recording. He dug out the driver's cell phone number and punched it in, but the call went to voice mail.

He dialed Yellow Cab; a sleepy dispatcher promised a cab at his door in twenty minutes.

Ben said, "Twenty? For sure?"

The dispatcher said, "Twenty-five, tops."

Ben hung up. Thinking furiously, he slipped into jeans, a T-shirt and a hooded sweat shirt. He pulled on socks, laced on running shoes, slipped his wallet and both phones into assorted pockets and ran out of the room.

He took the stairs, dashed past a dozing desk man and into the street.

At this hour, he knew, the subway ran infrequently. And he'd have to change trains twice. Bus lines offered even less frequent service.

He could outrun a bus that had to slow or stop every few blocks.

With no direct route from Williamsburg to Bensonhurst, he ran south, pacing himself to run the entire distance if need be, but veering west toward downtown Brooklyn, where there were several big hotels. Maybe he'd get lucky and find a cab there.

The Radio Shack phone rang again, and without slowing his pace, he pulled it from the hoodie pouch.

"Miryam?"

"The police said they were coming, but that was almost ten minutes ago."

"What about the guy on the ladder?"

"He's sawing through one of the bars."

"Do you have a baseball bat or a shovel or something?"

"In the basement."

"Go down into the basement and lock yourself in."

"Are you coming?"

"I'm on my way. Get behind some locked doors, now!"

"Hurry!"

Ben tucked the phone away and picked up his pace as he turned into Myrtle Avenue. Ahead, he saw an intersection; beyond it loomed the bulk of the Sheraton Hotel.

As he approached the intersection, headlights appeared behind him, and he moved to the right of the street. He turned the corner to see another set of headlights coming straight at him. The car jerked to a stop so close that he almost ran into it. As he dodged to the left, a siren sounded, and the car behind him skidded to a stop. Spotlights front and rear bathed him in a blinding glare, and he stopped.

"HALT!" commanded an amplified male voice.

"Police! Freeze! Show us your hands!"

Ben stopped, slowly raised his hands.

A man's silhouette appeared in front of him. Ben saw the gun pointed at him just as someone grabbed his arms from behind, kicked his feet from under him and shoved him face first into the pavement.

"Gotcha, douche bag!"

The cop patted him down, none too gently, taking Ben's wallet, hotel key and both phones, and then dragging him to his feet.

Another voice said, "Name?"

"Mark Glass," Ben replied, using his legal name instead of the usual Hebrew Moshe Benyamin Maimon, by which he had been known familiarly since childhood.

"What are you doing running the streets at this time of night?"

"Trying to get to the Sheraton so I could get a cab to take me to Bensonhurst."

"You live in Bensonhurst?"

"I live in Cambridge, Mass. I have a hotel room in Williamsburg. A friend lives in Bensonhurst, and she called to say someone was trying to break into her house."

"She called you? Why not dial 911?"

"She did. Waiting for the police to arrive. It's been about 20 minutes now."

"Why do you have two phones?"

"One is for business."

As if on cue, the Radio Shack phone rang.

The cop held the phone to his ear and said, "Hello."

Miryam said, "Who is this?"

"This is Detective Matthew Marko, NYPD. Who is this?"

"Miryam Benkamal. Where is Rabbi Ben?"

The cop looked at Ben. "She's asking for some rabbi."

"My Hebrew name is Moshe Benyamin Maimon. People call me Rabbi Ben."

The cop put the phone back to his ear. "What does this Rabbi Ben look like?"

"He's got red hair and freckles. He's not too tall, and he's in very good shape."

"Is he actually a rabbi?"

"Of course he's a rabbi! Is he okay?"

"He's fine. Miss, did you call 911 to report a break-in?"

"The other officers just got here. A minute ago. I was calling to tell Rabbi Ben."

"I'll tell him you called."

"Why can't I speak to him?"

"Because he's under arrest."

"Arrest? For what?"

"Your friend Rabbi Ben is the Running Rapist."

CHAPTER TWENTY-FIVE

B EN SAT AT A BARE WOODEN TABLE SCARRED BY cigarette burns, squinting into bright lights. Across the table, their faces shadowed, sat two men in rumpled suits. In the mirror behind them, Ben could see the backs of two balding heads, one sandy, the other dark. On the other side of that glass, he knew, at least one officer watched and listened.

Ben said, "I'm not the Running Rapist. I'm not a rapist at all."

Detective Marko, the larger man, said, "Shut up until we ask you a question."

"If you want to waste your time haranguing me, fine. But I'm telling you now, you have the wrong man. I am not a rapist."

"We got you dead to rights, Glass. Running flat out a mile from the scene of the crime. You're gonna stand in a lineup, and then you're going to Central Booking."

Ben sighed. "What time did the victim's call come in, please?"

Marko set his face. "See, the way it works is, we ask the questions."

"If you passed fifth-grade math, you'll eventually figure out that, if the call came in more than seven minutes before you grabbed me, I'd be more than a mile from the crime scene, wherever that was."

Marko looked at the other detective, a wiry man with a saturnine face, who thumbed through a dog-eared notebook, then shoved it in front of Marko.

Marko glanced down, and then looked at Ben. "It takes you how long to run a mile?"

"My best time is four minutes, forty seconds. I was looking for a cab, but I was prepared to run to Bensonhurst if necessary. So I paced myself at about six minutes."

Marko looked thoughtful. "It's what? Eight miles from Borough Hall?"

"It's about eight from Williamsburg. As the crow flies. Close to ten on the street."

"You telling us you were gonna run ten miles? At 3:30 a.m.?"

"I'm telling you that I was hoping to find a cab at the Sheraton. But I would have run all the way if I had to."

"You run that far before?"

Ben nodded. "Sure. Could have made it in about an hour."

"Okay, say you didn't do this one. Maybe you raped somebody else, and they haven't reported it yet."

Ben sighed. "Or maybe I was merely sleeping in my hotel room."

"Look, Glass. We got you dead to rights. We're gonna make a DNA match, we're gonna find your body hair in the victim's bed or on her person. You should be trying to help yourself here."

"I've never raped anyone. And telling the truth does help me. But tell me, when did these other rapes, the Running Rapist's crimes, when did they take place?"

"You know when. You did them."

"Did any of the rapes that you're looking at occur in the last sixty days?"

"Keep talking."

"Call Detectives Mendoza or Harris, or Captain Henderson, Burbank PD. That's California. They'll tell you I worked with them almost daily for the last two months."

"That so?"

"Or you can ignore that and waste your time and the taxpayers' money."

Marko turned to his partner. "Detective Wise, would you want to go check that out while I listen to more of this jerkoff's bullshit?"

Wise pushed back the chair and wearily climbed to his feet. "That's Mendoza, Harris or Henderson, Burbank, California PD?"

Ben said, "Yes. And remember, it's the middle of the night there."

Marko said. "I think we got ourselves a smart-ass here."

Wise shuffled out of the tiny room, a picture of resigned exhaustion, and Marko turned back to Ben.

"What were you doing in Burbank?"

"Assisting Mendoza and Harris in a murder and money-laundering investigation."

"I thought you said you were a rabbi?"

"I did. I am."

"Why would you be working with a PD on a major case?"

"That's confidential. Let's just say that I was able to offer some insights that might have taken the police a while longer to arrive at."

"You're all over the map here, Glass. You live in Mass, you were just in California, and now you're in Brooklyn. What kind of rabbi are you?"

"The inquisitive kind."

"So you're like some private investigator?"

Ben shook his head. "Not exactly. Our sages tell us that the role of the Jewish people is to work toward perfecting God's creation. We call this *tikkun olam*, healing the world. That's what I do. From time to time, people or organizations with problems call on me to help them. Mostly, these are Jewish people, but not always."

Marko pulled a rumpled pack of Winstons from a pocket, then a book of matches. He offered the pack to Ben, who shook his head.

Marko lit up, exhaling smoke over Ben's head.

"You're totally full of shit, you know. But I gotta say, this is quite a show. I've never seen a calmer perp. I mean, you're looking at life in the slam, and you're all cool dude spinning wild-ass stories just like you actually believed them. Maybe you're some kind of psycho. That's gonna be your defense? That you're nuts?"

"My defense is that I'm innocent. My demeanor is understandable because I know there's no evidence that I'm a rapist. In fact, it's a laughable accusation."

"Rape is nothing to laugh at."

"We agree on that. The joke is your accusation."

"We're gonna run your prints. What are we gonna find, Glass? You in any sex crimes databases? You a suspect in serial rapes in Mass or California?"

"Those databases public? Anyone with a computer can just log in and browse?"

Marko shook his head, no. "You gotta be law enforcement to have access."

"Then how would I know what databases I'm in?"

"You'd know because you were arrested or questioned. Maybe the Burbank goddamn PD gave you access. Or because you committed those rapes."

"Well, I don't know what's in those databases. I fact, I don't even know that there are such things as rape databases. I've never seen one. I've never read about one. Maybe that's something you just made up?"

"You know, when we drop you off at Rikers, we can let people know that you're a serial rapist. There's a lot of guys in there, very scary guys, who don't like rapists."

"Talk like that helps buy you early retirement without a pension."

Marko jumped to his feet. "You're threatening me?"

The door opened, and Wise shuffled in. "Lieutenant says cut him loose," he said.

"He say why?"

"Talked to this guy, Mendoza. Burbank homicide. Said Glass was out there with them the last few months and he's a straight arrow that runs five miles every morning. And, the Lieutenant had the file. All the vics pretty much agree the Running Rapist's dark-complected, around six feet tall and totally shaved, no body hair. Puts on a wig—all different ones—before he runs off from the vic's home."

Marko stood up and walked around behind Ben. He grabbed his hair and tugged on it, hard, satisfying himself that it wasn't a wig.

Ben said, "Someone was raped tonight?"

Wise said, "Call came in at 3:11."

Ben stood up. "If I can get my stuff back, I'd like to call a cab."

Marko shook his head. "Not yet."

He pulled a digital camera from an inside pocket and took a flash picture of Ben, then copied information from Ben's license to a yellow card.

A uniformed officer opened the door to hand Wise a plastic bag with Ben's property. Wise handed it to Ben, who stood up.

Marko said, "We'll give you a ride."

"So that's it?"

"Yeah, that's it. You're free to go. Or maybe you were expecting an apology?"

Ben shook his head, no. "Your job is eating you alive. You should get help."

Marko cocked his head, opened his mouth to speak, shut it. Looked at Ben, a hard, searching look.

"Girls and women raped in their own beds, scared to sleep for the rest of their lives. People stabbed or shot or beaten to death. Kids with cigarette burns. Sure, it eats me."

"There are plenty of mental health professionals. Find someone you like, someone you can trust. I'm sure your health insurance will cover it."

"You know, I'm thinking now you might actually be a rabbi."

A second uniformed officer appeared.

Marko said, "Take this guy wherever he needs to go."

When the door had closed behind Ben, Marko turned to Wise.

"There's something weird about that guy. Maybe he's not a rapist, but there's something hinky going on in with him. We should keep an eye on him."

Wise nodded. "I was thinking the same thing. So I dropped a tracking algorithm into both his phones. His GPS will tell us where he is and was, in real time."

Marko smiled. "I'm a little behind in my geek-speak lessons, so I'm not sure what you just said, but you got my attention at 'tracking.' Don't we need a warrant for that?"

Wise looked even more tired than usual. "Who's gonna know?"

CHAPTER TWENTY-SIX

EN UNLOCKED HIS HOTEL DOOR AND LOOKED AROUND. Nothing seemed to be out of place. When traveling, he usually left tiny paper markers in suitcase zippers and in the doorframe; if someone had opened them, the markers would be moved or missing. But this time he had left in such a hurry that he hadn't bothered.

Very tired, he kicked his shoes off, left his trousers and hoodie in a heap on the floor and climbed into bed. Then he remembered his phones needed charging, so he got out of bed and retrieved them from his hoodie pouch. Both were turned off. But, Ben recalled, they had been on when he was arrested. Suddenly wide awake, he connected his iPhone to his laptop and scanned its folders for new additions. In minutes, he found Wise's tracker, a small string of code in the same folder as his GPS program.

Ben copied the code onto his MacBook, accessed it with a program he'd written as an M.I.T. undergraduate and refined periodically afterward. It allowed him to view any program's code line by line. What he saw produced a chuckle: It was an archaic instruction set filled with amateurish touches such as repeated lines and lines intentionally rendered inoperative. A kid's work, he decided. He thought for a few seconds, and then changed four lines. He copied the altered code back into his phone, replacing the original version. Leaving the phone off, he plugged in its charger. The next time it was turned on, the phone would report itself 1,818 miles west and 72 miles north of Ben's actual location. Every eighteen hours and 18 minutes, the offsets would change by a random number of miles between 36 and 180. Let them figure that out, he thought. He left the Radio Shack phone off, got into bed and in minutes was fast asleep.

CHAPTER TWENTY-SEVEN

———

THE NEXT MORNING, BEN TOOK THE SUBWAY TO BOR-
ough Hall and went to a nearby Radio Shack store. He
bought another cheap phone, identical to the one in his
pocket.

He called Miryam on the new phone. She told Ben that
police had remained at her home throughout the night and
that workmen were even now replacing the sawed-through
window bar and installing wire mesh security windows behind
the bars.

Ben said, "Are you all right?"

Miryam said, "A little tired. But what about you, Running
Rapist Ben? Or is it Jail Break Ben now?"

Ben had to laugh. "Mistaken identity. Apparently, there's
some guy raping women, then running away, very fast, to escape. I had the bad luck to be running nearby about half an
hour after the report came in."

"You were running to come rescue me?"

"Actually, I was hoping that I'd only have to run as far as
the Sheraton. There's usually a few cabs waiting at the biggest
hotels."

"Fleet Foot Ben! You charm wild beasts, escape from

prison, and penetrate nuns, even joust with the police to rescue me. It's the most romantic thing I ever heard!"

"Come on, Miryam."

"A little joke, Father Ben. A little joke."

"Listen: I'll come by later, around noon, if that's okay. Notice that I'm calling from a different phone. When I see you, I'll explain."

"I can hardly wait!"

Ben rang off, and then hailed a cab. Before getting out in front of Rabbi Zeev's home, he turned on the old Radio Shack phone and shoved it deep into the backseat cushion. It might be days before anyone found it. In the meantime, the police would be treated to a continuous data track of a taxi cab's meanderings.

As before, Esperanza answered Rabbi Zeev's bell, this time granting Ben a brief smile of recognition, then silently leading him through the house to the rabbi's study.

Ben said, "Shalom, Rabbi Zeev!"

The old man's face lit up with happiness.

"Benny! Please, sit down."

Esperanza vanished, only to reappear within seconds bearing a silver tray with two cups of tea and a plate of tiny sesame muffins.

Both rabbis watched in silence as she poured, then left.

"Benny, I've been thinking about this Shemuel. I made some notes when I got up this morning."

Ben said, "Thank you, Rabbi, for your help."

"I can't say it is help, not yet. But now I can recall why I thought those pages might be, could be, from the Crown of Aleppo."

"Please, share your thoughts."

"It has always been a puzzle to me, Benny. We are the People of the Book. And Torah teaches us that we draw closer to

God through holy thoughts and good deeds. Yet some of us, too many, really, have long sought the comfort of slavery to superstitions.

"You've seen the women and girls, with those things around their necks to ward off the evil eye? The hand?"

Ben said, "The Hamsa, yes."

"Magic! Superstition. And what, Rabbi Moshe Benyamin Maimon, what is superstition?"

Rabbi Zeev was in rare form this morning, thought Ben. "Superstition aims to circumvent God, go around Him, with magic: incantations, potions, rituals."

"You are your grandfather's student! Exactly. To be a Jew is to demand a direct relationship with God, which requires both intellectual and moral excellence. For the lazy, for the coward, there is superstition, a way to bypass God, to manipulate God."

"Benkamal was a superstitious man?"

"Now that is the curious thing. I don't believe that he was. But when I first came to Brooklyn, still a young man, not yet sure what I would do to support my wife, *aleha hashalom*, she should rest in peace, and our children, people told me to go see him."

"Told you to go see Shemuel Benkamal?"

"Exactly."

"But why?"

"They never said, exactly. But I asked around. It had to do with starting a business, I think. People went to him, and he gave them advice."

"Just advice?"

"No, there was something else, and now, all these years later, I think I know what it was. We were speaking of superstition."

"Yes, Rabbi."

"Amulets—do you know of those?"

"A little. In the Middle Ages, especially."

"Even from Talmudic times, Benny. From maybe 300 years before the end of the Second Temple, many of our people looked to amulets. Even rabbis."

"And these were written by a sopher, a scribe. A prayer, or part of a Torah verse."

"Yes, those were very popular. But tell me, if the word of God can keep you safe from the evil eye, if a verse from the Torah can bring you prosperity, help you find a good wife, keep your children safe, what would be the best verse, the best prayer?"

Ben shrugged. He had never thought about this.

"I suppose if you're looking for an amulet, you tell the sopher what kind of protection or help you want, and he writes something appropriate to your problem?"

"Yes, that would be good. But what would be better?"

"Better, you should study the Torah every day, keep it close to your heart, and speak of it to your children daily."

"You're not lazy. You would never wear an amulet."

"I guess not, Rabbi. Where are you taking me with this?"

"What if you could have a whole Torah as your amulet?"

"Even with tiny writing, that's a very big amulet."

"Then what about a page? One page? With your favorite verse? Or a verse that you believe will help you in some particular way?"

Ben's head swam. Turning a thousand-year-old treasure into amulets for the protection of the superstitious! What audacity! What selfishness!

Ben said, "Rabbi, are you telling me that Shemuel Benkamal sold pages from the Keter as amulets?"

Zeev spread his hands wide, palms facing Ben. Then he took a tiny sesame cake, popped it in his mouth and slowly chewed, swallowed, then took a sip of tea. Another.

Ben waited.

"Benny, there was talk. For a time. A few years, I think."

"That's all, talk?"

"Yes. Until about a year ago, it was just talk."

"What happened a year ago?"

"Yosaif Aharoni died. He was my age, almost. His house-keeper found him—died in his own bed. A good end, I think. He was never sick, that I knew of."

"Who was this Aharoni?"

"Men's wear. If you wanted a good suit, Yosaif would take good care of you. A good hat—no, go elsewhere—but a suit, he was your man. And he did very well. He had three sons and two daughters, and he set each one of them up in a store. Queens, then New Jersey, then White Plains, I think. They do well, even now."

"He had an amulet?"

"Forgive an old man, Benny. I tend to wander these days. Yes, his sons found it around his neck, sealed in a leather pouch, with beeswax, I think. And they opened it up, and it was a page from *Va Yikra*, the first chapter of Leviticus, '*Lo talin peulat sachir itcha ad boker*, Don't withhold a day-laborer's wages until the morning.'"

"You saw this amulet?"

"No, not myself. But one of the daughters-in-law came to see me. She was upset, her husband was arguing with his brothers about this. What to do with it, who should keep it, should they keep it at all."

"You told her the best thing was to bury it with Yosaif."

Zeev looked startled. Then he laughed. "Yes, yes, of course. Exactly. Bury it. Keeping peace in the family is always best. Your grandfather always said that you had a good Jewish head on you."

A Jewish head. It was his beloved grandfather's highest

praise, and remembering him say it about others, about great scholars, Ben fought to keep from tears from his eyes.

Ben said, "But why do you think this was from the Keter? It could have been any old Torah page."

Zeev nodded. "Of course. But the daughter-in-law—Zipporah, her name was—said the brothers, men in their 60s, mind you, kept talking about going to see Benkamal. So she thought he had given it to Yosaif, and that fits with the rumors of fifty years ago, that Benkamal had some of the missing pages.

"But there is something else, too. Do you recall the story of Nadav and Avihu?"

"The sons of Aaron?"

Rabbi Zeev nodded. "Yes. Go on."

"They approached the altar with a sacrifice, and a strange fire consumed them."

"Exactly. Now, the sages offered many different explanations for why they were punished. The sons were drunk, they considered themselves the equal of Moses and Aaron, they were improperly respectful, it was an improper sacrifice, and so on."

"What do you think the reason was, Rabbi Zeev?"

Zeev shook his head impatiently. "It's not important. My point is that from that moment on, the Ark of the Covenant, the box that housed the tablets of the Law that Moses brought down from Mt. Sinai, had what we would call magical powers."

"I hadn't thought of it that way before, Rabbi."

"The Keter was the same."

"Excuse me? Magical powers?"

Zeev nodded. "In Aleppo, for centuries, bar mitzvah boys were brought before the vault where the Codex was stored and told that if they had any disrespectful thoughts, any evil inclinations, even looking at the Codex would bring a curse on them."

"No! Really?"

Zeev nodded again. "It is a fact. Men brought barren wives to stand before the Keter and pray for children. Legend has it they became pregnant almost immediately."

"You're saying that an object made by men—ink on parchment—became imbued with magical powers. They made a book into an idol and worshipped it."

Zeev smiled. "Exactly. Over and over, the very words written in the Keter, and in every Torah scroll and *Tanakh* volume, tell us that an object created by man is not to be worshipped. And yet for centuries, those who were the Keter's guardians—rabbis who surely knew better—stood that prohibition on its head."

"You're saying, then, that for anyone who believed in the Keter's magic, a single page was powerful magic, imbued with God-like power?"

Zeev nodded, and then stared off into space. Seconds passed. A minute.

Ben said, "Are you all right, Rabbi Zeev?"

"What? Oh. I was thinking about those years, when my Leah was alive, and my children were in school. Hard times, but good times, too."

Ben sensed that Zeev was beginning to tire.

As if tuned to his thoughts, Esperanza appeared in the doorway, shot Ben a reproving look, then hoisted the tray with the empty dishes.

"It will soon be lunch time," she said, and left.

"Rabbi Zeev, I have reason to believe that Shemuel Benkamal was murdered. I think his housekeeper was, too. Who would want to kill him?"

Zeev studied Ben for a long moment.

"Murdered? I heard it was an accident?"

Ben pulled a face. "First, someone throws a cup with a soft drink on his front steps at night in the dead of winter, and the next morning, the housekeeper slips on the ice and fractures her skull. It might just as well have been Shemuel himself.

"He hires a new housekeeper but catches her in his study, which is always locked, so he fires her. Then, a few weeks later on his regular weekly walk to the library, he's knocked down by a hit-and-run skateboarder who doesn't even stop to see what he did."

"Very bad luck, Benny. But murder?"

"I think so. Rabbi Zeev, who steals Torahs?"

"Do you know the Romani?"

"Gypsies?"

"They call themselves Rom, or Romani. In Spain, they are known as Gitanos. In Syria, the Arabs treated them like dogs. Worse than dogs, even."

"The Romani are here, in Brooklyn?"

"Of course. But they are not murderers. They are thieves. For many years, they stole our Torahs, Benny. For ransom, of course. Any synagogue would pay to get their Torahs back. But now we mark each Torah, in a kosher way."

"Yes, I know about this. Tiny pinholes in a unique pattern. They can't be sold."

"If Benkamal had the Keter, or any old parchment, that they would steal. But murder? I do not believe so. The Romani are proudly thieves, but they shun murderers."

At that moment, Esperanza returned. "Lunchtime, Rabbi."

Zeev struggled to his feet. "Come again. And soon. I find this most enjoyable."

"I will. One more thing, Rabbi. It's personal."

"Yes?"

"When I came last time, you said that I resembled my grandfather."

"You look very much like him at the age when we first met, here in this house."

"When I was in California, I discovered that I had a sister and a brother."

"Surely not, Benny."

"My father had another wife. In fact, two other wives. And when I met this sister for the first time, she was in shock, because she said I looked just like her father. And we have the same name, me and my father: Mark Thompson Glass."

"This is confusing, Benny. You had no sister or brother. And your father died in a plane crash, overseas. In Lebanon, I heard."

"If I look just like my mother's father, how could I also look just like my father?"

Zeev's eyes clouded. "It was a long time ago, Benny. Ask me next time."

They shook hands formally, and Ben made his way toward the front door. Then, he doubled back and surprised Esperanza as she placed a dish in front of Rabbi Zeev.

"He needs to eat!" she snapped.

"If you don't mind, I'll go out this way," Ben replied, and stepped out onto a shaded porch above a grassy yard.

CHAPTER TWENTY-EIGHT

BEN PULLED OUT HIS IPHONE, SWITCHED IT ON, AND waited for it to boot up. As he watched his voicemail and text messages queuing, he suppressed a chuckle. His GPS now reported to police that he was in a suburb of Laramie, Wyoming.

It had been just about long enough since the police tuned up his phone for him to get to an airport and fly to Laramie. So if anybody was watching the GPS output, and he felt certain that this was the case, they would now be pulling up airline schedules.

He scanned his text and email messages: a note from Chana that she had received the FedEx box with the Benkamal documents and a second suggesting that they meet in Chinatown at Buddha Bodai, a Mott Street eatery that offered vegetarian fare.

He texted confirmation: 7:00, with XXXs and OOOs and an emoticon smiley face.

There was a voice mail from Mendoza, which he had expected; everything else could wait.

He slipped the phone into his pocket, and then let himself out of the yard into a narrow alley. There was no one in sight as he made his way south toward 13th Avenue, where he sat in a bus shelter and called Miryam on the new Radio Shack phone.

"On-The-Lam Ben!" she answered.

"As you will," he replied.

"I'm making lunch for everybody. Are you coming?"

"Who's everybody?"

"I told you, there's three guys here fixing my doors and windows."

"If it's kosher, I'm in."

"My special tuna salad sandwiches."

"Can I bring anything?"

"How 'bout some cold beer for the hard-working boys?"

"You got it. I'll be ten or fifteen minutes."

"Perfect!"

Ben clicked off and looked around. A convenience store down the street had a Brooklyn Brewery sign. Beer is almost always kosher, and Ben was partial to Brooklyn Brewery's Summer Ale, so he bought a dozen bottles, hopeful that he'd get to save at least one for later.

Back in the bus shelter, he called Mendoza, who picked up on the first ring.

"The 'Running Rapist'? Really, Rabbi, how do you manage to get yourself in such deep shit so often?"

"Nothing to it, Detective. Just try running down a major thoroughfare in Brooklyn around four in the morning. Works every time."

"So you're now hot in Brooklyn. Did you make bail?"

"No bail. The guy they want is six feet, dark complexion, and no body hair."

"I told them that you're a master of disguise."

"I was moving pretty fast. We all look alike in the dark, I guess."

"I'm glad you're okay."

"Thanks for verifying my alibi. Got one thing to ask you: What do you know about Gypsies? The New York kind."

"Not a lot. But they're like ants. You never find just one. It's always a family, all the way out to second or third cousins. Some are only tangentially involved, others at the center of things. They work long cons, and they can be very, very patient. And they're clever about making things look like accidents."

"Whoa! Explain that a little more. What things?"

"Insurance scams, like supermarket slip-and-falls or car collisions."

"Would they deliberately put someone into a situation where he'd probably fracture his collarbone, say, or his hip?"

"Depends. If it was part of something else, something likely to have a big payday, yeah, sure they would."

"That's all useful information. Anything else?"

"Yeah, they don't all look like movie Gypsies: dark hair, dark skin, big brown eyes. Some are blonds or redheads. They can be tall or short, heavy or skinny or anything in between. They can look like any kind of person you ever met. Ever heard of 'Irish Travellers'?"

"Outside of the Dublin airport, no."

"East Coast and Midwest, they're Scots-Irish Gypsies, basically. They run all sorts of scams, but they specialize in home repairs."

Every hair on Ben's body stood at attention. Home repairs. Like those under way at the Benkamal home right now.

"Tell me more about that."

"Unlicensed contractors. They offer to put a new roof on your house for next to nothing. Then they do a crappy job, leave in the middle of it and you find out that they've ripped off your stamp collection, your silver, your wife's jewelry and anything else laying around."

"Very good to know. Thanks, Mendoza."

"One more thing. Nothing happens in a Gypsy family, a

real Gypsy family, without the alpha male—who they call their king—without his okay. He gets a piece of everything, so he always knows what's cooking."

"You're a pal, Mendoza."

"Hey, just keep it in your pants, Rabbi!"

Chuckling, Ben ended the call. He remained on the bench for a long moment, thinking about everything Mendoza had told him, sorting through its implications. What had happened to Shemuel and his housekeeper now seemed more sinister, more deliberate, than it had only an hour previously. More urgently: Who were these guys putting in new doors and bars on Miryam's windows? Could they be Travellers?

He grabbed the beer and ran for Miryam's home.

He saw the truck as he rounded the corner. "Five Star Locksmiths" was painted on the side with a Flatbush address and a phone number. He called the number.

"Hey, is that your truck over here blocking my driveway on 83rd in Bensonhurst?"

"Hold on," said a woman's harried voice. After a long interval, she returned. "We'll call him and tell him to move it. Sorry."

From down the block, Ben waited until an older man came down Miryam's steps, looked at the truck, walked all the way around it, and then pulled out a cell phone.

So they're probably legit, he told himself, and walked swiftly to Miryam's door. In spite of his reservations, he realized, he was looking forward to being with her.

CHAPTER TWENTY-NINE

B EN STEPPED THROUGH THE OPEN DOOR AND GLANCED to his right, into the living room, where two burly men in their 20s were installing a hinged apparatus of steel bars. He looked again. The men were clearly brothers, if not twins.

"Ben! Darling!"

He turned just in time to drop the bag of beer and throw up his arms to receive Miryam, who wrapped herself around him, smooched his cheek, whispered in his ear.

"Play along. I'll explain later."

Then she kissed him again, a more leisurely and passionate kiss. Ben found himself enjoying it and hating himself for that. Releasing him to step back and put an arm around his waist, she turned to the workmen, including the older man that he had seen outside. One look told Ben that he was father to the other two.

"Mr. Hedaya, this is my fiancé, Rabbi Ben Maimon."

The older man's face lit up with pleasure. "Congratulations!"

All three men crowded around to shake Ben's hand.

Clad in a loose man's work shirt and knee-length cutoffs that showcased her sensational legs, with her long tresses pulled into a tight bun, Miryam wore only a trace of lipstick and still managed to look like a movie star on vacation. Ben was struck by her sense of style; she was dressed perfectly for the occasion.

"Lunch is ready," she said, turning toward the dining room, where a giant salad bowl and a platter stacked high with sandwiches waited.

Ben stooped to retrieve the beer; by the time he had it, the senior Hedaya, with an easy familiarity that surprised Ben, had opened the dining room cabinet. He came away with a tall, blue bottle in one massive hand and five tiny shot glasses in the other.

"A *shehecheyanu* to celebrate your engagement!" he cried.

Hedaya poured splashes of a clear liquor all around. Glasses raised, he recited, "*Barukh atta Adonai, Eloheinu melech ha'olam, she-hecha yanu v'qiyy'manu, v'higiy'anu lazz'man hazzeh!* Blessed are You, O Lord, our God, Ruler of the Universe, who has granted us life, sustained us, and enabled us to reach this occasion."

"Amen!" said the others, including Ben, whose head swam with the ramifications of what had just happened: He would henceforth be known as the fiancé of a member of one of the community's most distinguished families. And he couldn't say a thing about it.

With the others, he tossed back the clear liquor, a fiery concoction that brought tears to his eyes. Ben said, "What is this?" in a voice so hoarse that everyone laughed.

Hedaya said, "Arak, not my first choice for a *shehecheyanu*, but Tío Shemuel, *alev hashalom*, always liked it. Our Arab cousins can drink it because it's made from dates."

Ben nodded to show that he understood. "Not grapes, not from the fruit of the vine, and therefore, to some, halal. But I thought I tasted a little—what is it, licorice?"

"Anise," Hedaya explained. "Rabbi, let me introduce my sons, Ethan and Chaim."

Ben smiled. "Named for Revolutionary War heroes?"

Hedaya ducked his head, smiling. "I came here as a baby. Our family had nothing in Syria. We made a wonderful life here. This country, America, this is the best country on earth, thanks be to God, and so I named my sons."

"And both good Jewish names, as well," Ben replied. "*Mazel tov.*"

Miryam put a basin of water, a large, two-handed cup, and a hand towel on the table. They went around the table, each person reciting a silent blessing, then pouring water over one hand, then the other, then drying their hands on the towel.

As Miryam took the basin into the kitchen, Ben turned to Chaim and nodded.

Chaim smiled. In a distinctive Aleppo dialect of Hebrew, he recited the prayer for bread: "Blessed art Thou, O Lord, our God, ruler of the Universe, who brings forth bread from the earth."

"Amen!" said everyone and pulled out chairs. Ben took a seat next to Miryam; as salad bowls were filled and sandwiches were passed around, Miryam took Ben's hand.

"Mr. Hedaya is like family, Ben. Tío Shemuel had him change the locks every year for as long as I can remember."

Ben almost choked. Change locks every year? Who did that?

Hedaya said, "Tío Shemuel was a very good friend to my father, of blessed memory," he said. "He used to send me over every month, remember?"

Miryam looked blank.

"With the ... bag?"

"Oh yes, of course. But that was grownup stuff. I just liked to watch you change the locks. I remember when you first put the bars on."

"Oh, that's gotta be fifteen, twenty years. Right after—"
Hedaya hesitated.

"Right after my parents died, Mr. Hedaya. It's okay. You can talk about it."

"My parents, you know, may they rest in peace, they were a little superstitious. Certain things they would never talk about, like it was inviting trouble to mention them."

Ben said, "I understand. My grandmother, of blessed memory, was like that sometimes."

Hedaya said, "Rabbi, you're a very lucky man. Half the boys in this neighborhood wanted to marry Miryam."

Ethan said, "More than half!" and Chaim, his mouth full, nodded vigorously.

Blushing, Miryam said, "I can't understand why. I'm not that special."

Ben was trapped, and he knew it. "Modesty is the least of her virtues. She cooks better than Julia Child and looks better than Julia Roberts—way better— but she does have faults. Her biggest one is that she's convinced that I'll make the perfect husband."

Miryam stroked his face. "Not perfect. But trainable, I think."

As the Hedayas cracked up, Ben took a sandwich and some salad, pulled the top off a beer. If he was henceforth to labor as a condemned man, he told himself, he might as well eat something.

Chewing and swallowing, his mind churning furiously, Ben tried to make sense out of what he had seen and heard in the last few minutes. When he had eaten and finished his beer, he looked at Hedaya.

"Mr. Hedaya, have you ever heard of a bunch of people called 'Travellers'?"

The older man's face darkened with anger. "Thieves, you

mean. Irish Gypsies. Pretend to do home repairs, then steal everything in sight. You saw that truck this morning, too?"

"I was interviewing Rabbi Zeev this morning."

Miryam said, "For the book he's writing."

Hedaya looked interested. "So you're that kind of rabbi? You don't have a congregation of your own?"

Ben shook his head, no. "What truck was that, Mr. Hedaya?"

"This morning, when I was parking in front, this pickup came by. New Jersey plates. Lots of Travellers in Jersey. Back was filled with junk. Big sign on the door, something home repairs, but it was a magnet, know what I mean? You can put anything on the truck, be anybody, then you take the sign off, and you can be somebody else."

"I understand. So the truck just came by?"

"They were looking at this house, going real slow, kind of like they were going to park. Then they saw us and sped up and drove off."

"And you think they were Travellers?"

"Could be. I got a good look at the driver. Kind of reddish-blonde hair, getting bald, white skin. An Irishman, he looked like."

Ethan said, "Excuse me, Rabbi, but why did you ask?"

Ben said, "I was thinking about last night. Somebody tried to break in by sawing through the bars. And before that, they ripped the front door off its hinges."

Chaim said, "That ain't gonna happen again. We put new hinges on the inside. And the new bars are all tungsten steel and twice as thick."

Miryam said, "Ben, do you think Travellers wanted to come here and offer to fix the doors and windows?"

"I wondered about that. But somebody thinks there's something in this house that's very valuable. Besides Miryam, I mean."

That drew grins from the Hedayas. As they returned to their work, Ben drew the older man aside. "Excuse me for asking, Mr. Hedaya, but when did your parents die?"

"Let's see, my father, *alev hashalom*, about seven years ago. Mom went right after that, a few months. Why do you ask?"

"As Miryam said, I'm doing research for a book, if I can find the right theme."

"You mean, about Syrian Jews?"

"In a few years, the first generation here will be gone. No one will remember firsthand what life was like in Syria, what it took to start over in America."

"Yeah, that's a good point."

"You mentioned that your parents were a little superstitious?"

"My dad more than my mother. But both of them, yes."

"Did either of them ever wear an amulet of some kind? A charm?"

"Like a little leather bag with some kind of Hebrew writing in it?"

"Something like that, yeah. But there are many different kinds."

"Dad used to wear one sometimes. I think one of my sisters has it."

"I'd love to look that at that, if she won't be upset."

"She lives over in Red Bank now. I'll give her a call. Hey, my wife was born in Aleppo. She's a great cook. Why don't you and Miryam come tomorrow, for Shabbat?"

"Are you walking distance from here?"

"We're in Coney Island, off Avenue P. I guess you could walk it."

"I'll check with Miryam, and we'll call you. And thanks, it was great meeting you and your sons."

Ben found Miryam in the tiny office where new window

bars had been installed; they swung out of the way in case of fire. In the shadowed room, light reflected by the shiny bars made her face a Rembrandt masterpiece, and Ben thought that he had never seen anything quite so beautiful.

Ben closed the door behind him and looked at Miryam, trying to be angry but failing: Their announced engagement was a farce, but contemplating it, for a long moment he felt imprisoned by loneliness. He had filled the years following the death of his beloved Rachel with work and study and travel and, if he was honest, with exciting adventure. Now he felt an enormous void in his life. He had been alone for more than nine years and yearned to have someone like Miryam in his life, if not as a wife then as a best friend, a confidante, a lover.

But that was impossible for him.

CHAPTER THIRTY

M IRYAM SAID, "DON'T BE MAD AT ME."

Ben said, "I'll get over it. What was that all about?"

"Mr. Hedaya has known me since I was baby. What would he think if he found you here, hanging out, coming and going?"

"That I might be your boyfriend. So what?"

"But Tío Shemuel told him that I was engaged. The first thing Mr. Hedaya said when he got here this morning was that he wanted to see a picture of my fiancé."

"You don't carry a photo of David?"

"David's no longer in my picture. I called him last night and ended it."

"How did he take that?"

"It doesn't matter. He was never the one. Never my beshert, my soul mate."

"Beshert is what you get from years of hard work, of give-and-take, of struggle and failure and success and joy. From spending years of pain and effort together, good times and hard times, compromise and sacrifice. Beshert doesn't walk in the front door."

"Father Ben, marriage counselor! Please, the heart wants what the heart wants."

"You're quoting Woody Allen to me?"

"I guess. Although to be honest, Father Ben, I didn't know I was quoting anyone."

"He was talking about his relationship with Soon-Yi."

"So there! A dirty old man and a sweet young thing, and that could never last, right? Except they've been together, what? Twenty years?"

"Give or take."

"Ben, listen to me: Maybe David didn't know it, but he didn't really want me, except as an accessory, an adornment, maybe some kind of trophy. And by the way, you didn't just walk in my door. You leaped into my yard. After vanquishing Samson and penetrating all those nuns."

Ben favored her with a wan smile. "You make it sound so much more interesting than it really was.

"But why didn't you tell Hedaya that you were no longer engaged? Why not just introduce me as a friend of Rabbi Zeev who's helping you settle your uncle's estate?"

"Because Jake Cassin called last night."

"And who is that?"

"The boy Tío Shemuel wanted me to marry. A few years ago, he spoke with Jake's parents. I think they came to him. Maybe he promised them some money, like a dowry. My uncle called me into this room and told me that I was going to marry Jake."

"And you said no?"

"I told him that I was capable of supporting myself, and that if I ever decided to marry, I would choose my own husband. That I was not going to live as a medieval Jewess. Not in so many words, of course. Respectfully. While professing eternal gratitude for all that he had done for my parents and for me."

"And that must have gone down pretty hard for both of you."

"He didn't speak to me for almost a year. But it all worked out; I left for school in Israel. When I came back on vacation, things were fine. He never mentioned it again."

"So why did this guy ..."

"Jake. He called to ask me out. I told him that I was engaged. He said I was engaged to him, that it was all agreed, a dowry had been pledged—his word, pledged—and that he expected me to honor Tío Shemuel's wishes."

"And?"

"And I told him to go stick it where the sun doesn't shine."

"So who is he? What does he do?"

"I haven't seen him in four or five years. I remember him as a very good-looking guy. Very popular in high school: senior class president. He was on the football team. Baseball, too, I think. He had lots of girlfriends, but I was never one of them."

"And now?"

"He dropped out of college. After his father died, Jake ran his business into the ground. Then there was a fire. Now he sells insurance."

"He doesn't sound that bad."

"I think he set the fire."

"Oh."

"Jake sells insurance to small businesses. If they pay, nothing bad happens. If they don't, lots of funny things happen. Stink bombs. Fires. Rats. Broken windows. People slip and break their legs in stores. Employees go on lunch break and never come back."

"A protection racket. You're saying he's a thug."

"He is a thug. He also sells weed and meth, if I what I hear is true."

Ben sighed. "So you're thinking, you're only going to be here a few weeks, let me be your flesh-and-blood fiancé, and maybe he won't bother you."

"Not just my fiancé. A fiancé who isn't afraid of guys like him."

"Miryam, I'm glad to help you. But the only reason that I'm here is the Codex."

"Yeah, the Codex. I've been thinking about that. And I think that any guy who stole it out of this house has to live in the neighborhood. So you need to talk to people, ask lots of questions. And guess what, Father Ben: They won't tell you anything."

"Because I'm an outsider?"

"This is Little Syria, Ben. It's Aleppo on Gravesend Bay. But, if you were my fiancé, and you were helping me recover Tío Shemuel's Torah, people would talk to you. They'd open their doors, invite us in, they'd ask their friends and relatives. Somebody's got to know something, but you'll never find out much on your own."

Ben thought for a long moment, his face a mask. Then he smiled. "You're just about as smart as you look. It might take me years to get your neighbors to open up."

Miryam smiled. "So, partners?

Ben said, "Deal."

Miryam said, "First thing tomorrow, we'll go buy a ring."

"Whoa! You don't have a ring?"

"I'm gonna send David's ring back to him. Anyway, it's too small for a guy like you. But that's not important. If we go to a certain jeweler in Manhattan and buy a ring tomorrow, by Saturday morning everyone in the community will know about it. So it's not the ring that's important; it's buying the ring."

"How much are we spending?"

"Two bags."

"You found more money?"

"In the upstairs bathroom."

"That reminds me. You put those Torah pages in your uncle's safe, and then you locked it. Do you have the combination?"

Miryam frowned. "No. The safe was open; in fact, it was never locked. But Tío Shemuel bought it from Mr. Hedaya, so he might have the combination."

It was Ben's turn to frown. Hedaya knew where the safe was, he thought. He's a locksmith; surely he could open a home safe. He certainly knew how to get into the house. Could this family friend have snatched the safe while Miryam was at the cemetery burying her uncle?

Ben said, "I hate to ask, but did Mr. Hedaya come to the funeral?"

"Of course he did."

"And his sons?"

The door behind Ben, the door that he had locked on entering, opened with a click, and Chaim Hedaya took two steps into the room and stopped.

Chaim said, "Sorry! Didn't know anybody was in here."

Miryam said, "What do you want, Chaim?"

He pointed at the floor next to the window. "I left my drill."

The burly Chaim retrieved the electric drill, apologized again, and hurriedly left.

Ben and Miryam exchanged shocked glances.

Ben said, "Miryam, how well do you know Chaim?"

"Chaim and Ethan came over to pray with us on the last night of my shiva."

"But not any of the first six days?"

"And they weren't at the funeral. Mr. Hedaya told me that they were fishing in the Adirondacks, in an area with no cell service."

CHAPTER THIRTY-ONE

B EN SAID, "HOW'S YOUR ANKLE?"
Chana said, "I'd almost forgotten about that. It's fine, now."

They studied each other across the tiny table, oblivious to the noise of two dozen conversations and the crash and rattle of crockery in the crowded Chinese restaurant.

Ben felt uneasy, as if Chana sensed that something had changed. Or maybe, Ben thought, it was only that he felt guilty; he had done nothing wrong, but that he had even entertained fantasies about Miryam weighed heavily on his conscience. Maybe, he thought, he was projecting his own inner turmoil onto his perception of Chana.

"What's going on, Chana?"

She pursed her lips, wrinkled her nose. "Let's not get into it. It's just more of Mo's B.S., and there's nothing I can do except let the lawyers handle it. So tell me about Bensonhurst. How did that go?"

Ben leaned forward and in a low voice described his foray into St. Hermione's.

Chana listened intently, and then burst into laughter when he mentioned Samson, the mastiff. "You make it sound almost fun," Chana said.

"After the fact, maybe. But surrounded by nuns and walking around wearing a Roman collar, masquerading as a priest, I was a little scared."

"But you pulled it off. So, tell me about the Benkamal girl."

"Early 20s and quite beautiful, in some ways very worldly and in others surprisingly naïve. She's in over her head trying to pull her uncle's estate together. I promised to help her find a good estate lawyer. Any suggestions?"

"I'm sure my attorneys will know someone. I'll ask when I see them Monday."

"Thanks, Chana. Did you get a chance to look at those papers? And the picture?"

"It's mostly correspondence, rambling texts, not written by scholars. But Arabic is often imprecise by design, and it can be verbose and quite flowery, as are Benkamal's letters. From what I read, the late Mr. Benkamal had business dealings with Arabic-speaking people in many countries, including Argentina and Brazil, but I can't tell what his business was."

"Could the letters be in code?"

Miryam looked reflective. "I hadn't considered that. I'll have another look. And by the way, I haven't heard back from my imaging expert, but I'm sure you're right about that picture. When you look very closely, it seems a little off."

"There's something else going on, Chana. Two days ago, in mid-afternoon, while Miryam was out, somebody removed the front door of her house. Pulled it off its hinges."

"Isn't that how they got in to steal the Codex? I mean, if it was the Codex."

"Exactly. But now there's a security door in back and another behind the front door. Then last night, somebody tried to saw through the bars on a second-floor window."

"What?"

"She called me about three in the morning. Miryam. She

also called the police, but it took them a long time to get there. So I got dressed and went looking for a cab. I was running down Myrtle Avenue when the police grabbed me."

Ben paused while a waitress set before them plates of steaming vegetables that resembled and tasted like meat. Ben and Chana began filling their plates.

Chana said, "The suspense is killing me. The police grabbed you?"

Ben said, "They thought I was the guy who's been terrorizing Brooklyn for the last several months, raping women, and then jogging away before the police can respond."

Chana nodded. "I've heard about that guy."

"Anyway, they let me go. Meanwhile, other police came to Benkamal's house, and yesterday Miryam had locksmiths, old friends of her family, in to change the doors, put new bars on the windows and so forth."

"Clearly, there's something in that house that someone wants."

"And one more thing: I'm pretty sure old Mr. Benkamal was murdered."

"What?"

Ben was hungry. Between bites, he sketched out his theory of how Benkamal and his elderly housekeeper had been killed, then a digest of Rabbi Zeev's observations about Benkamal, the old rumors, and Zeev's suspicions.

Chana listened in wide-eyed silence until Ben had finished. As he went back to his food, she picked up the thread.

"So, based on what Rabbi Zeev told you, you suspect that Benkamal sold ... pages from the Codex? As amulets?"

His mouth full, Ben nodded vigorously. Sighing, he pushed the plate away. His eyes wanted more, but he knew that he'd had enough.

Ben said, "There's one more thing: the money." He described the scene that had greeted him when he first sat in the Benkamal parlor, the paper sacks of money everywhere. "What do you make of that, Chana?"

Chana shook her head. "Was he selling drugs? Importing hashish from Syria?"

Ben scowled. "Not likely. Miryam said some of the bags had store names on them. One was from a neighborhood bakery, and another from a leather goods shop."

He stopped, cocked his head, thinking. "Wait a minute. Miryam told me about this neighborhood boy, Jake somebody. A few years ago, her uncle and his parents spoke. She thinks some money changed hands. Then he tried to force her to marry Jake."

"Relevance, please?"

"Yeah, I forgot something. Jake's a college dropout, a thug who now runs a protection racket on small neighborhood businesses."

"Maybe that was Benkamal's business? He sold it to Jake, along with his niece?"

"That's what I'm thinking. And since Jake maybe doesn't have startup capital, he gets in for nothing down and a percentage of collections. Then maybe he gets tired of waiting for the old man to die and finds a way speed that up."

"Are you sure about all that?"

"I'm not sure of anything. Too many loose ends. Someone breaks in, steals the safe, and then leaves all those bags of money sitting around the house? Really? And then there's the locksmith. He sometimes brought a bag. He or his sons could have gotten into the house, taken the safe. And what does all this have to do with selling Codex pages for amulets?"

"Mark Thompson Glass, a.k.a. Rabbi Moshe Benyamin Maimon?"

Ben and Chana looked up to find a chubby, middle-aged

man in a rumpled seersucker suit and a forgettable tie. In one hand, he held a leather case open to show an NYPD detective's badge. Behind him stood two officers in dark blue summer uniforms.

Ben tried to get to his feet, but the detective roughly shoved him back down.

"You Glass? Or is it Maimon?"

"Glass. Maimon is part of my Hebrew name. What's this about?"

Ben reached into his pocket for his wallet, but the man tugged his arm free.

"Keep your hands on the table where I can see them."

"Who are you?"

"Damon Little, Detective second. You know a man named Michael Klein?"

"I'm not sure if I do."

Chana said, "He works for my husband. Officer, this is all a big mistake."

Ben said, "Now I recall having met Mr. Klein. Once."

"What about Pytor Moskovich?"

Pulling out her cell phone, Chana said, "One of Klein's goons."

Ben said, "I think that I've met him. I'd have to see him."

"On your feet. We're going outside."

"Am I under arrest?"

"Not yet. But you're coming with me."

Ben pushed his chair back and stood up. A cop immediately grabbed his arms and cuffed him from behind as Chana spoke urgently into her phone.

By the time she'd dropped money on the table and reached the sidewalk, Ben was being placed in a squad car. On the sidewalk, she found Little with Klein and Moskowitz, the man Ben had shoved into a light pole. Each man's nose was adorned with a huge bandage. Hovering nearby was the third man, the one who'd pulled a gun.

Chana ran to Detective Little. "Where are you taking him? What's the charge?"

"One Hundred Centre—Central Booking. Charge is aggravated assault."

"That's nonsense. These men attacked him."

"Tell it to the judge."

"Wait, I'm going with you."

"Call a cab."

"Why can't I ride with you?"

"Because you're maybe a witness, not a suspect. I'd have to place you under arrest before I could put you in that car."

Chana whirled and ran a few steps to Klein. "You son of a bitch," she cried, and clubbed his face with her purse. The white bandage on his nose turned red.

A cop grabbed her and pinned her arms at her sides. Little shook his head, disappointed. "You're under arrest, Missus."

Klein said, "I won't press charges against Mrs. Kaplan."

Chana said, "It's Doctor Kaplan."

Little sighed. "You can tell that to the judge, Mr. Klein. Now turn around, Doctor, I gotta handcuff you."

CHAPTER THIRTY-TWO

S TILL IN HANDCUFFS, BEN WAS LED TOWARD A COURT-
room for arraignment, where a judge would hear the evidence against him and decide whether he should be tried
or freed and, if the former, whether he would be allowed bail.
As an out-of-state resident, Ben knew there was a good chance
that, if bail was granted, it would be high enough to require a
bondsman, and that would keep him confined for several hours
at least. Three hours had passed since his arrest, time spent
going through the stations of the cross that turned a free man
into a prisoner of the state. He was a little worried: Ben carried
a plastic bottle with pills enough for one of his twice-daily
anti-retroviral regimen. It was impounded with all his other
possessions. Missing even one course of drugs invited the
dormant virus lurking in his marrow to awaken and blossom
into AIDS, compromising his immune system until every microbe he encountered was potentially lethal to him.

His hope was the phone call that Chana had made before
being arrested. Punching Klein was very brave of her, he decided, but also foolish; free, she could easily arrange his bail.
Now, she was presumably somewhere in the NYPD's booking
system.

But as he entered the corridor leading to the courtroom,

there she was, smiling, apparently not in confinement, and accompanied by a tall, gray-haired man in an open-necked white shirt and sports jacket.

Ben's escort, a bailiff, indicated an empty bench. "Your attorney is here. You have five minutes," he said, and stepped back out of earshot.

"Ben, this is Archie Paradise. Don't worry about a thing."

Ben said, "Thank you for coming, sir."

Paradise said, "Ordinarily, it would be at least a day before your arraignment. I petitioned for an expedited hearing. To my surprise, the district attorney didn't object."

Ben said, "So what happens now, sir?"

"Now we go into court, and I get the judge to drop the charges."

"What about Chana?"

Chana said, "Klein refused to sign the complaint, and that detective, Little, claims he can't recall if I actually hit Klein or if I stumbled and fell against him."

Ben said, "So they let you go."

"This is all Mo's doing. He's calling the shots."

The bailiff stepped forward, and Ben got to his feet. Trailed by Chana and Paradise, he was led before a high bench, behind which sat an attractive woman with milk-chocolate skin and salt-and-pepper hair. Her head was down, scanning the papers before her. A simple nameplate announced that she was The Honorable Yvonne Scott.

A tall, handsome man in his middle years and attired in a splendid suit appeared and stood near Ben.

"People v. Mark Thompson Glass, a.k.a. Moshe Benyamin Maimon," said the bailiff. "Aggravated assault, two counts."

The man in the splendid suit spoke. "David Middleton for the People."

"Archibald Paradise for Rabbi Glass."

The judge looked up, surprise flooding her face. "The Manhattan chief deputy district attorney, the president of Fordham Law and—" she peered at Ben—"who are you, sir? Bernie Madoff's bagman? A Guantanamo escapee?"

That drew chuckles from everyone except Ben and Chana.

Ben said, "Rabbi Moshe Benyamin Maimon, Your Honor."

Middleton said, "Alias Mark Thompson Glass, Your Honor."

Ben said, "Excuse me, Judge Scott, but I don't use an alias. Like all American Jews, I have a legal name and a Hebrew name. In the context of my work, I use the latter."

Scott studied him. "What's that about, the Hebrew name? Is it just a custom?"

"The Torah tells us that long ago our father, Jacob, and his sons, and their wives and their children—seventy souls in all—went down to Egypt to join Joseph. And although they lived there for 210 years, Your Honor, they never became Egyptians. They retained their Jewish names, they learned to speak Egyptian but kept their Hebrew as well, and they wore distinctive dress. And so, when they departed from Egypt, they were still Jews. We follow their example, Your Honor. We are neither better nor worse than others, but we are a people, and we retain our distinctive ways."

"So you speak Hebrew, you have a Hebrew name and that little skullcap is your distinctive dress?"

"Yes, Your Honor, as well as the fringed garments some of us wear."

"Got it. So we have a rabbi and two of New York's best legal minds in my courtroom. What's going on here? You first, Mr. Middleton."

Middleton said, "The defendant savagely beat these two men, Your Honor."

He pointed to Klein, now sporting a freshly bandaged nose, and to Moskovich.

Judge Scott looked at Klein, then Moskovich, then Ben.

"Mr. Middleton, have those two victims—"

Paradise said, "Objection. Alleged victims, Your Honor."

Judge Scott scowled. She did not like being interrupted. "Yeah. You two, with the nose bandages, go stand next to the rabbi."

They stood next to Ben, both towering over him. The judge eyed all three.

"Mr. Middleton, you said that the defendant beat these two. Savagely, you said."

"That is the charge, Your Honor."

Scott said, "Rabbi, hold up your hands. Let me see them, both sides."

Ben held up both hands, turning them to show both sides.

"Mr. Middleton, do the People allege that the defendant used anything except his hands to 'savagely beat' these two? His hands, which bear no bruises or scabs?"

Middleton said, "No, Your Honor."

Scott said, "Your turn, Dr. Paradise."

Paradise said, "These two men, the alleged victims, and a third man"—he pointed across the courtroom at the one who had pulled a gun—confronted Rabbi Maimon near Penn Station around midnight three days ago. All three men are employed by the estranged husband of Dr. Chana Kaplan, who was with Rabbi Maimon and is his professional colleague. She witnessed their attack on him. The one who's not wearing a bandage had a gun. Rabbi Maimon defended himself. End of story.

"Move for dismissal of both counts and for sanctions on Mr. Middleton, who clearly knows that the Rabbi, all five-feet seven inches of him, did not attack these two men, each of whom is a head taller and outweighs him by forty pounds."

Scott peered at Ben again. "Rabbi, did you punch these guys out?"

Ben said, "No, Your Honor."

"How did they get their noses broken?"

"When I was a rabbinical student, I took a self-defense class at the 92nd Street Y."

"Elaborate on that for me, Rabbi."

"I learned to turn an attacker's strength, size and momentum against him."

"Momentum, you said? I hope you got an 'A' in that class."

Ben shrugged. "It was a long time ago, Your Honor."

Scott looked at Middleton. "Will the People withdraw charges, or do I dismiss with prejudice and enrich the court by, say, a thousand dollars in sanctions from your pocket, Mr. Chief Deputy?"

Middleton frowned. "This is outrageous! I have three witnesses to the assault, Your Honor."

"And all three are employed by the estranged husband of the woman who was with the defendant. Would you now care to go for two thousand dollars?"

"The People withdraw charges, Your Honor."

"Rabbi, you're free to go. And Mr. Middleton, I don't know what kind of game you're playing tonight, but I'll expect your check by morning, and if you pull something like this in my courtroom again, I'll have you explain yourself before the Bar."

"I apologize, Your Honor."

Judge Scott rewarded Middleton with a hard, appraising look.

"And if I learn that you're running for Congress or mayor or some such, and this little charade was for the benefit of one of your deep pockets, I intend to revisit this matter. You got me, Counselor?"

"I understand, Your Honor."

She turned to Ben. "Bailiff, get those cuffs off that man! And, Rabbi, the court apologizes for this dreadful waste of taxpayer money. Dr. Paradise can advise you on seeking redress from the city for false arrest. And if you ever want to talk more about your people's customs, or anything at all, you just come see me in chambers."

Smiling, Ben bowed his head. "I might do that, Your Honor."

CHAPTER THIRTY-THREE

A LITTLE BEFORE 10:00 THE NEXT MORNING, BEN LEFT the subway at Rockefeller Center, then walked west several blocks to find Miryam perched on a fireplug near the mouth of Cutter Lane, a dim, narrow street of store-fronts overshadowed by skyscrapers.

Miryam hurried to Ben, and they embraced. Ben felt awkward; a few hours earlier and only a few miles away, he had hugged Chana before leaving for his Brooklyn room.

But Miryam didn't seem to notice Ben's ambivalence.

"We can spend $6,000," she said, handing Ben an envelope bulging with cash.

Ben said, "There was that much in two bags?"

Miriam shook her head. "Last night, I went through the whole house and found more. And I think there's a secret room in the basement."

"We'll look at that when we get back. Now, where is this jewelry store?"

"Mr. Beyda used to come to our house, but I've never been here. I called this morning, and his son said to bring you to Cutter Lane and he'd give us his best price."

"He didn't give you an address?"

"He said that any good rabbi could find his store in no time."

"Ah ha. Let's go look."

They moved slowly down the street. Peering into shop windows, they found no trace of anything resembling jewelry or diamonds. Few displayed signs of any kind; some lacked even a street number. Halfway down the block, they found a shop whose small, murky window held only a pair of dusty clocks.

Ben said, "This is it."

Miryam scoffed. "How can you tell?"

"These clocks remind me of a story that my grandfather used to tell. He was born in a little shtetl, a Jewish village, in the Carpathian Mountains near the Czech border. The village mohel, one who performs circumcisions in accordance with Jewish ritual, kept a stopped clock in his window with its hands pointing to 1:17. Understand?"

"No, but I think I heard a joke about a mohel and a clock."

"Everyone's heard that joke. But this is Poland, before the Shoah, the Holocaust, and this was a real mohel. He set a window clock to 1:17, referring to the first book of the Torah, Bereshit or Genesis, Chapter 17."

"Is that where God tells Abraham that he must be circumcised?"

"Exactly."

"What about these clocks? One says 3:21, the other 3:15. What do they mean?"

Ben pulled out his iPhone. "I'm pretty sure 3:15 refers to Proverbs, the line about a good wife being 'more precious than rubies.'"

He thumbed in a word search of a digital version of the *Tanakh*, the Hebrew Bible. "Let's try Isaiah 3:21."

He held the phone so that Miryam could see it.

Miryam said, "'Rings, jewels'."

Ben chuckled. "So the two clocks tell us that what this

place sells is 'More precious than rubies, rings and jewels.' Very clever."

Miryam wrinkled her nose. "Why not just put up a sign?"

"He's a wholesaler. Probably stocks a king's ransom in diamonds. His customers are retailers; they know where he is. Anyone else is a bother they don't need, or a thief."

"You're so smart!"

Ben shook his head, no. "Jews have done business in quiet ways for centuries."

Miryam reached for the doorbell, but Ben put his arm out. "We need to talk."

"I know you're not really my fiancé, Father Ben. Although I'm still hoping."

"Listen: We'll pick out a ring, and then you find an excuse to step away while I work out the price."

"It doesn't matter how much it costs."

"If I don't bargain, he'll lose respect for me. He might not give a penny, but to everyone in the jewelry business, a guy who doesn't press for a better price is a schnook. A sucker. Not the kind of guy he'd want you to marry. So this is for your benefit."

"Is there anything that you don't know about?"

"I'm continually amazed at how much there is to know and how little of it I understand. It's just that I've lived longer than you. In ten or fifteen years, you'll know much more than you do now. If you're even half as bright as I think you are, you'll know more about many things than I ever will."

Miryam reached for the bell again, but before she could press it, the door opened, revealing a compact, balding man in his early 50s.

Miryam said, "Shalom, Mr. Beyda."

"Miryam! You're more beautiful than ever! Please come in," said the man.

Ben said, "I'm Ben Maimon."

"I'm Yakov Beyda," said the man. "That's Rabbi Ben Maimon, correct?"

"Correct."

"This way, please. My father is anxious to see you both."

Yakov led them through a series of three steel doors, each heavier than the one before and spaced about six feet apart. He closed and locked each door behind them before opening the next. They emerged into a brightly lit corridor leading to a suite of three offices. In the doorway of the last stood a wizened man, tieless in a white shirt and black suit, with a tiny *kippah* covering a head bald but for a crown of wispy white hair. His face lit up with pleasure when he saw Miryam.

"Shalom, my beautiful child!" Miryam stepped forward to embrace the man, who kissed her on both cheeks, then released her and with a quick wink to Ben, took her hand.

"And what honor brings you to my door, Marita?"

"Señor Beyda, I'm getting married!"

Again Beyda winked at Ben. "And who is the lucky man? A rich businessman? Or perhaps a great scholar?"

"Señor Beyda, may I present, Rabbi Moshe Benyamin Maimon, my fiancé."

The old man cocked his head. "Moshe Benyamin Maimon?"

Ben nodded, smiling. "It is a pleasure to meet you, Rav Beyda," he said, using the Hebrew for a man of great learning.

"Your father was Salomen Maimon? The great master of Talmud?"

"My grandfather, sir, of blessed memory."

"I knew Salomen well, a great man. But Moshe Benyamin, you cannot marry our Marita. You already have a wife, do you not? Or maybe you recently divorced?"

"My wife died in a bombing in Jerusalem, nine years ago, Rav Beyda."

The old man's eyes filled, and he looked away. "I didn't know. But Moshe Benyamin, what became of her ring? Her engagement ring?"

Ben pursed his lips. "I don't know. When I left the hospital a few days later, her body had already gone to Chicago for burial. What was left of her clothing and her purse were given to me, but no rings. Her parents asked about the rings, too."

"Stolen?"

"Possibly. I prefer to believe that, if the ZAKA men, those who search for body parts after these tragedies, found the ring, they didn't find the finger or the hand it went on. Rachel, of blessed memory, was seven months pregnant. Her hands were often swollen. I was in the men's room when the bomb went off. Rachel may have taken the rings off for a moment. If they were found, maybe they went to someone else whose wife or mother was killed. More likely, they were simply lost in the rubble."

Miryam said, "Señor Beyda, why do you ask about this?

"Some years ago, Salomen brought me a ring to be cleaned and resized."

Ben said, "It belonged to my mother, of blessed memory. My grandfather gave it to me when I asked his permission to marry Rachel."

Miryam said, "You needed his permission?"

"I was a student. He supported me financially. It was the right thing to do."

Beyda nodded in sympathy. "Nowadays, no boy would ask his parents or his grandparents. This is a very good man, your rabbi here."

Ben said, "But why do you ask about the ring?"

The old man gestured to a pair of chairs in his cramped office, and then seated himself behind the small desk. He pushed a button on his phone, and a minute later a plump, grandmotherly woman appeared with a tray bearing teacups and tiny almond cakes.

"Please," said Beyda, and waited for tea to be poured and the woman to depart.

"The stone in the ring that your grandfather brought me was cut in Amsterdam by Joseph Asscher, the most famous and successful cutter of his time. He was the one who cut the Cullinan, the so-called Star of Africa, for Edward VII of England.

"That ring, your mother's ring, was made for Salomen's mother-in-law, your great-grandmother. It is of the original Asscher cut, 58 facets, just over five carats. An extraordinary Indian diamond, as nearly flawless as any stone can be, and with a brilliant blue fluorescence."

Ben said, "How do you know all this?"

Beyda swiveled in his chair, and then leaned forward to twist the knob of a small safe. When it was open, he took a key from his pocket and unlocked an inner drawer, from which he took a velvet pouch with a drawstring. He opened the pouch and removed a clump of cotton batting, which he parted to reveal a large square-cut diamond in a graceful platinum setting. The stone beamed brilliant blue highlights.

Ben's head swam. He was again in the smoldering ruins of a bombed-out café. The smell of blood and bodily waste and burning flesh—the stench of death—assaulted his nose. His ears filled with hideous screams. Blood and ruin lay all around him. His heart raced; his body temperature soared until he was covered in sweat. He blacked out.

Miryam said, "Ben! Are you all right?"

Ben fought his way up from the darkness, willing his heart and breathing to slow.

After a long moment, he made the effort to open his eyes and smile. "Just a flashback," he whispered, his voice hoarse. "I still get them once in awhile."

Miryam took his hand.

Beyda displayed the ring in the palm of a gnarled hand. "This was your wife's ring," he said. It wasn't a question.

"How?" Ben croaked.

"One of my customers has a pawnshop in Dutchess County. Upstate. A Satmar Hassid brought it in; they have a colony near there. You know the Satmar? They hate the idea of the State of Israel. That's for the *Moshiach*, the Messiah, to establish, as they believe. Most of them are very poor. Anyway, the pawnbroker asked the Satmar where he got the ring, and the man said that it had been in his family for a long time.

"This pawnbroker told me that he didn't think he could sell such a ring for enough; people come to pawnshops looking for bargains. That's true enough, but I thought then that he was more worried that the police might come around and then he'd find out it was stolen. So he decided to take a quick profit; he thought I might want to re-cut the stone—Asscher is now considered very old-fashioned—and make two smaller marquise stones from it, each worth far more, wholesale, than he asked. But I remembered this diamond. No cutter could ever forget it. I bought it just last week."

Beyda stood and beckoned to Miryam. He slid the ring onto the third finger of her left hand, twisted it, slowly, left and right. It fit perfectly

Miryam said, "This is so amazing!"

She handed it back to Beyda, who returned it to the pouch.

Ben said, "Please, tell me how much you want for it."

The old man sat back in his chair and sighed. "The ring is not for sale."

CHAPTER THIRTY-FOUR

B EN SAID, "HOW IS IT, RAV BEYDA, THAT YOU KNOW so much about this ring? The history, I mean. About who cut it and for whom it was made?"

Beyda sighed. "The setting has Asscher's mark and the 58-facet, square-cut was his patented design. Salomen told me that his wife inherited it from her mother, Klara Pinto. When I heard the name, I knew the rest: Klara Pinto saddened her family by marrying a Pole. To them, a Jewish Pole was still an ignorant Pole. And Klara Pinto was my maternal grandmother's sister."

Miryam said, "So you and Ben are cousins, sort of, by marriage."

Beyda smiled. "There must be a Yiddish word for that."

Ben said, "Rav Beyda, why won't you sell me the ring?"

Beyda said, "Patience, *boychik*," using the Yiddish term of endearment for a young son.

Ben's face was a mixture or amusement and surprise.

Beyda continued, "To be a Jew and a diamond cutter is to know Yiddish. You understand, this isn't the usual thing for a boy whose parents spoke Arabic and Ladino at home and Hebrew or English otherwise."

Ben said, "It is a little curious, even for New York."

"The Jews of Aleppo—do you know their history, Rabbi?"

"Not so much."

"According to Bereshit, Exodus, on his way to the Land of Israel, our father Abraham watered his flocks in what is now Aleppo. A village grew up near the well, then a town. Jews have lived there since Biblical times. When Rome began to colonize Iberia, there were hundreds, perhaps thousands, of Jews in Aleppo. Some saw opportunity—the way our people have always seen it—and followed the legions to Spain. A thousand years later, in 1492, comes the Inquisition and the Expulsion. Many Spanish and Portuguese families returned to Aleppo, where they had kinsmen. For a long time, for centuries, there were two Jewish cultures in Aleppo, Ladino speakers and Arabic speakers. Each had its synagogues, its prayer books. It was only about a hundred years ago that the Spanish Aleppo families and the Syrian Aleppo families began to intermarry, to become a single community.

"My family left Syria about that time. Many Syrians—Jews, Christians, Muslims—settled in lower Manhattan, near where the World Trade Center would be built. Did you know that there was once a mosque just where the Twin Towers went up?"

Ben and Miryam shook their heads, no.

"I was born here, in 1926," Beyda continued. "When construction for the Twin Towers began in 1966, the City of New York bought all our homes. Eminent domain, they said. We moved to Brooklyn.

"At that time, I had a little factory that manufactured television antennas. It was doing very well. I finally had time to study Talmud, so I looked around for a teacher.

"The Talmudists whom I met were Sephardic. They liked Isaac Luria and the Kabbalists. They liked the Zohar. They favored the mystical over the historical. I was looking for something else, and that is how I met Salomen. He used to have a

Tuesday night Talmud study group, for anyone interested, at the Bensonhurst library. I was the only Ladino speaker. Many of the others, at least the ones who remained, week after week, month after month, were diamond cutters. Yiddish speakers.

"About 1970 or 1971, Congress passed a law, and the first cable television came to New York. I knew immediately that I should find a new business. I sold my factory. One of my friends from Talmud class needed capital. He was looking for a partner. He taught me diamonds, and I taught him to manage money, hire good people, to run a business. When he died, I bought his widow out."

Ben said, "Why are you telling us all this, Rav Beyda?"

"So that you will understand how it is that a Sephardi like me, a Sephardi with Mizrahi uncles yet, speaks Yiddish."

"I see."

"Yiddish has a most wonderful word: Beshert. You know what is Beshert?"

"Destiny."

"From nowhere, you two turn up, and I learn how the ring left your family. I put your wife's ring, your grandmother and great-grandmother's ring, on this beautiful little girl, on our Marita. In Ladino, we say, little Miryam, or Marita. That's a large stone, and it's tricky to adjust the setting so it won't slip around a small finger. But you saw: It fit her hand perfectly. It can only be Beshert. You, Miryam and this ring belong together."

Miryam's mouth flew open.

Ben felt a pressure in his head, a ringing in his ears.

Beyda handed Ben the pouch with the ring. "There is no price I could sell this for that would please me more than giving it to you, to both of you. Now put it in your pocket, because I don't want my son Yaakov to know, not until I can talk to him privately."

Ben said, "Rav Beyda, I can't—"

"I insist, Rabbi. You wouldn't deprive an old man of a chance to perform a mitzvah, a commandment?"

Miryam said, "Of course not, but—"

Beyda said, "Good. Finish your tea, and Yaakov will find you a nice platinum band, ten or 12 stones, Princess cut, about a carat and a half, total, the very best quality. Whatever he asks, you offer half."

Ben said, "Rav Beyda, we are both forever in your debt."

Miryam squeezed Ben's hand.

Beyda said, "Then perhaps some day you will repay me, if not in this world, then in the world to come."

Ben didn't know whether to laugh or cry. Trapped in a beautiful lie, with each step he took he felt its bonds tighten. Escape seemed more and more impossible. And the bonds felt more and more inviting.

CHAPTER THIRTY-FIVE

BEN AND MIRYAM STEPPED INTO CUTTER LANE AND
heard the door lock behind them.

Miryam said, "Don't be angry, Father Ben."

"I'm not angry. It's a lot to process. I'm just feeling—"

"—like me wearing your wife's ring is a little creepy?"

Ben said, "Uh, I was going to say, I was feeling a little hungry."

Miryam said, "Oh. Maybe we could get some coffee and a
munchie? Then I'll make lunch when we get home."

They emerged onto 49th Street and ambled east in silence
for most of a block until Ben stopped short. "Miryam, I'm also
feeling awkward about our fake engagement."

"I know. Me, too."

"Let me be a rabbi for a minute, okay?"

"Okay."

"According to Maimonides, my namesake, if a couple pretends to be engaged, then they are in fact engaged. And there's
a good reason for that."

"Go on."

"Jewish law treats an engaged woman as if she were already
married. That's for the woman's protection; in our ancient patriarchal society, men, even married men, weren't bound by

many restrictions. They could have consensual sex outside of marriage, and while the community might frown on, it was lawful. But once a woman's betrothal, her engagement, was announced, men were forbidden to approach her. That's why, even now, very observant Orthodox men won't shake hands with a married woman."

"Ben, I wanted a pretend engagement so Jake Cassin would leave me alone."

"You told me that. But now this is all much more complicated."

"I didn't have any idea that Señor Beyda would—"

"Of course not. We had no idea about the ring. But it happened. Your community will now understand that we're getting married."

"But Ben, that's what we wanted, right? So people will talk to you about Tío Shemuel and the Codex?"

"I guess I hadn't thought this through far enough. What happens to you when I leave? When you go back to California?"

"I'll just say we called it off. Or maybe I won't say anything. I don't plan on living here, anyway."

"When do you finish school?"

"I've got just one class next quarter, and I have to finish my thesis."

"And then what?"

Before she could answer, Ben's phone rang; it was Chana.

"My boss," he said, and put the phone to his ear.

"Hey, Chana!"

"You okay?"

"I guess so. I'll say it again: That was very brave of you last night."

"I don't know what I was thinking. I wasn't thinking. I'm really sorry that you had to go through all that because my husband is an ass."

"Not your fault. But it all worked out. What's up?"

"Can you meet me at the museum this afternoon? Their forensic photo guy wants to present his findings."

"I'm with Miryam Benkamal, and we're over near Rocke-feller Center."

"Do you feel comfortable bringing her with you?"

"Sure. But we were going to stop for lunch."

"There's a nice cafeteria on the second floor. Why don't I meet you there?"

"Half an hour?"

"See you there. Bye, sweetie."

"Bye, Chana."

Ben clicked off, wondering whether he'd just screwed up again. Now he'd have to tell Miryam about his arrest. And why he'd broken a couple of men's noses. How would Chana and Miryam react to each other?

There was only one way to find out.

Ben said, "Ever been to the Jewish Museum?"

CHAPTER THIRTY-SIX

D ETECTIVE WISE SAID, "THERE'S SOMETHING WEIRD with that hinky rabbi, Glass."

Detective Marko looked up from the pile of paperwork on his desk, hoping for something, anything, that would take him away from it. "What's going on?"

"Well, first he sends his one phone, the burn phone, all over the city until we figure out he stashed it in a taxi. Then he diddles with my boy's program, and for about two days it looks like he's in Montana or Colorado someplace. Then my kid says to just ping his phone, which gives us his nearest cell tower, and he's here in New York."

"And now?"

"He was picked up for aggravated assault yesterday."

"Here in the Seven-Two?"

"Couple of guys from One Police Plaza collared him, believe it or not."

"Major Case? Musta beat up some big-shot's wife."

"It was two guys. Big guys. They work security for some hedge fund manager, and they both have sheets: a weapons charge, assault and battery, suspicion of jury tampering. No angels, those two."

Marko chewed his lip, thinking. "Glass is the little guy, says he's a rabbi?"

Wise nodded, looking even sadder than usual. "Yeah. Witness says he flew around like some martial-arts freak and kicked their asses. That seem right? A rabbi beating up on guys?"

"What if they deserved to get beaten up?"

"He's got something hinky going. I can smell it."

"We should go see him. He's in Rikers?"

Wise shook his head. "He comes into court last night with an A-list lawyer, and the judge has the D.A. drop charges."

"You're right. This gets stranger and stranger."

"I'm following him with this pinging thing. He's up on Park Avenue. Manhattan."

"And?"

"And he's got a hotel room in Williamsburg. We could have a quick look-see."

Marko frowned, "We'll never get a warrant."

Wise smiled. "So we don't ask for one. It's a hotel. We just poke around, see what we see. In and out. Five minutes. Maybe find something, maybe not. You never know."

"One of these days, you're gonna lose me my pension, Wise."

"You think so?"

"Sooner or later."

"Then what's wrong with today?"

CHAPTER THIRTY-SEVEN

T HE DOOR TO THE MUSEUM DIRECTOR'S OFFICE OPENED, and a tall, silver-haired, white-coated man, Central Casting's idea of a brilliant-but-heartless brain surgeon, entered.

Chana said, "This is Dr. Wilson, the museum's imaging expert. Dr. Wilson, this is Rabbi Ben Maimon and Ms. Miryam Benkamal."

Wilson granted Chana a perfunctory smile. Then without preamble, he turned to Ben. "I approached this image with a methodology and protocol of my own devising."

Ben bent forward slightly to show that he was listening.

"This involved a primary scan sequence at variable source angles with visible light in the spectrum from 3400 to 6200 Kelvin, which is—"

Chana said, "I'm very sorry to interrupt, Doctor, but perhaps we could save some of your very valuable time if you just skipped ahead to your conclusions."

"Excuse me?"

"Just tell us what you found, please."

Wilson did not seem like a happy camper. "Dr. Kaplan, I appreciate your regard for my time, but please appreciate that, in the imaging disciplines, specifically in the application of forensic techniques, methodology is everything."

Ben swallowed a grin. Wilson was telling Chana that linguistics was a squishy science where conclusions could be challenged, especially over methodology.

Chana smiled back. "Of course, Dr. Wilson. It's just that Ms. Benkamal, the owner of the image, is a layperson. The brilliance of your protocol and the expertise that you demonstrated in following it would be utterly lost on her."

Miryam smiled, filling the room with sunshine. "I'm not an idiot. I'm a grad student at UC Berkeley."

Wilson favored Miryam with a searching look. "And your field of study, Miss?"

"Early childhood education," she replied with another smile.

Wilson favored Chana with the tiniest of nods. He produced an iPad from his briefcase and swiveled it so that his audience could see the screen, then tapped. An image of Miryam's family photo appeared. "The image in question was made on an Agfa paper manufactured in Germany before 1939, consistent with products in use in Syria during the early postwar period. The image is the product of the exposures of two negatives made from dissimilar film stock and exposed onto the same photo-sensitive paper sequentially, then airbrushed. Excellent workmanship, considering the state of imaging technology prior to the introduction of microprocessor-aided devices."

Miryam looked pale. "Excuse me, Doctor. Are you saying it's a fake?"

Wilson nodded. "Precisely."

"That's not my father and his uncle?"

Wilson removed a pair of expensive eyeglasses and wiped them, considering his words carefully. "I have no opinion as to the identity of the subjects. I'm saying that they were not in the same place at the same time when this image was made. It was made in a darkroom, not in a studio, from two images created some time earlier in different places."

"But how do you know that?"

Wilson shot Chana a tiny look of triumph. For him, science was process. The results were secondary, whatever process yielded. And now he would get to explain his protocol. But he was a civilized man. He would not gloat, at least not very much.

"I began my protocol with destructive analysis of the photo paper," he began.

Miryam said, "Wait! You destroyed my picture?"

"No. Using a laser cutter, we removed a slice sample less than a third of a millimeter wide, and about two centimeters long, from a corner of the photo. When we replaced the original in its frame, this was not visible."

Miryam nodded. She didn't like the idea of someone cutting the photo, but it was done. "Go on."

Wilson tapped the iPad screen again, and a page of text appeared. "From analysis of residual traces of sodium thiosulfate, which is employed during darkroom processing to remove residual silver halides, we ascertained that it was of a type consistent with German manufacture in the 1930s. In fact, it's only slightly different from what is currently manufactured.

"The paper was also consistent with German manufacture prior to 1939."

Ben said, "Why don't we skip ahead to show us how two images are on one piece of paper."

Wilson shot Ben a withering glance but said nothing. Instead, he tapped the iPad again, and a close-up of young Shemuel appeared on the screen. "A highly magnified view of this part of the photo reveals the grain pattern of the original film stock."

Wilson tapped the screen twice, and the screen was filled with part of Benkamal's eye. "Are you with me, Miss Benkamal?"

Miryam shook her head. "No, you lost me."

Now in his full glory, Wilson directed his attention to his small but rapt audience.

"These images were captured on film. This was then 'developed' in a darkroom, using a two-step chemical process that yielded a negative. When dried, this negative was projected through a lens and onto a photo-sensitive medium, in this case, coated paper. By magnifying the image sufficiently, we can view the grain pattern of that film."

Wilson tapped the screen again and zoomed in still more. Using thumb and forefinger, he made the image smaller while retaining its magnification. Then he tapped the bottom of the screen, and another image appeared side by side with the original. "By comparing this part of the photo with a known type of film, I conclude that it is consistent with the Isopan F emulsion manufactured by the German company Agfa prior to 1947."

Wilson tapped both images, which disappeared. He tapped again, twice, and two more images shared the screen. "On the left is a magnified portion of the image from your photo, taken from the area occupied by the young boy. On the right is a sample of Selo Fine Grain Panchromatic, a film emulsion manufactured in the United Kingdom before 1939. They are, in my professional opinion, virtually identical in grain structure.

"From this, I conclude that the two individuals pictured in this photo were placed on the paper sequentially from negatives of two different manufacture."

Ben said, "You mentioned airbrushing?"

Wilson actually smiled. "Yes, of course." He tapped the screen several more times, bringing up the original scan of the entire photo, zooming in on an area between the two people, then zooming in still further. Then he cropped the image on the screen and tapped some more until a second image appeared next to the first.

Wilson said, "An air brush is a very fine aerosol used to paint a surface. When we look at this area, we can see the magnified pattern of individual droplets.

"The right-hand picture shows the same pattern, made by an airbrush artist, on a photographic image from my database. It is nearly identical with that on the left-hand image. There can be no doubt that this area was airbrushed to provide the appearance of natural gradation of light and shadow. As I said earlier, taken in its totality, this is a highly professional job. I would be surprised if it was done by anyone but an accomplished forger or a graphic artist. As Syria had no advertising industry until very recent times, you may draw your own conclusions as to who did the work."

Miryam blinked away a tear. She turned to Ben. "But why would he do that?"

Ben wanted to hold Miryam and comfort her. Instead, he shook his head. "That's the mystery." Then he had another thought.

"Doctor Wilson. What about the photo's backdrop: the painting of the citadel?"

"Ah! Yes, I looked at that, as well. As it happens, we were able to find upward of a dozen period photos in various archives that were taken in front of that or a similar painting. So far as we can tell without further investigation, all of the photos were taken in Aleppo prior to 1950."

Ben cocked his head, thinking. "That would suggest, would it not, that if the grain of the backdrop matches that of either of the two people, the boy or the man, we could tell which one was in front of the backdrop when the photo was taken?"

Wilson nodded. "Yes! It would. And we can check that right now."

After several more taps on the screen, Wilson pushed it forward to show the others. "On the left is a section of the boy. On the right is the backdrop. They match."

He tapped the screen again a few times. "And here is the grain on the gentleman's face, compared to the grain of the backdrop. I conclude, with the rabbi's assistance, that the boy was in the photo with the backdrop and the man's image was put into that scene."

Fighting tears, Miryam took a tissue from Chana and daubed her eyes.

Chana said, "Ben, can you think of any reason why her uncle might do this?"

Ben shrugged. He could think of many reasons, good and evil. "All we can tell from this is that Shemuel wasn't in the picture when it was taken. Before we jump to any conclusion, let's remember that he was a surrogate father to this boy, to Miryam's father, for many years. He provided him with a loving home and a good education. And remember that the picture was created during a turbulent, dangerous time for Jews. During the war, when Syria was controlled by Vichy France, which collaborated with the Nazis, and then the years before the birth of the State of Israel. There was violence against Jews. Houses were sacked and possessions seized. Documents were hard to come by. Maybe Shemuel simply needed something to show kinship so that he and his nephew would be allowed to leave Syria and then to enter this country. It could be as simple and as honorable as that."

Miryam dried her eyes. "I'm sure you're right, Rabbi. Something like that."

Ben was worried about Miryam; this revelation could undermine notions of her own identity. Her apparent acceptance of his surmise cheered him, but only momentarily. Deep down, he didn't believe that as a young man Shemuel Benkamal had found a costly, expert forger merely to convince Syrian authorities that he was his nephew's uncle. There was something else, and his gut mumbled that, whatever it was, it probably wasn't good.

CHAPTER THIRTY-EIGHT

WHILE MIRYAM BROWSED THE COLLECTION OF paintings and Judaica decorating the director's office, Ben and Chana held a quick, quiet meeting in the hallway outside. He sketched his most recent conversation with Rabbi Zeev, including what he'd said about Aleppo Jews and their superstitious desires for such things as amulets. Without mentioning the encounter with Beyda, the diamond cutter, Ben explained how he had been roped into posing as Miryam's fiancé.

Chana said, "That's brilliant! Now you'll be welcomed into people's homes. Her friends and their families will talk to you."

"All credit goes to Miryam. She's worried about some guy she knew in high school. A few years ago, her uncle tried to arrange a marriage between them, but Miryam refused. She doesn't want to give the guy any reason to come around."

"I understand. And she's a really beautiful girl."

"She is that. And very bright. Now, what's going on with your husband?"

"My attorneys are preparing a lawsuit. Incidentally, Dr. Paradise—Archie—is prepared to draft a complaint for false arrest against the NYPD on your behalf."

"One of the secrets of my success, however you care to define that, is keeping a low profile. So I'll think it over, but I'm inclined to just let that whole episode go."

"Can you come over later for Shabbat dinner?"

"I'd love to, but unfortunately, now that I'm 'engaged' to Miryam, we're invited to dinner at one of her friend's home. And not incidentally, this is a family that might have an amulet made with one of the Codex's missing pages. Might have."

"Wonderful."

Ben glanced at his wristwatch. It was almost 4:00. Sundown and the start of Shabbat, the Sabbath, were three hours off, but he had first to go by his hotel for medicine and to change clothes before going to the Hedaya's home. It would be tight.

Ben said, "We better get moving if we're going to make Bensonhurst before Shabbat."

Chana opened her arms, and they embraced for a long moment. She tilted her head back, looking deep into Ben's eyes, and he felt the beginnings of a now-familiar ache in his loins. It had been so long …

"Excuse me!"

Ben and Chana moved apart and turned to Miryam. "Sorry, but it's getting late, Rabbi, and I need to go home and get ready for Shabbat."

Chana said, "Why don't you use the museum's car, Ben? It won't save time over the subway, but at least you'll arrive in better shape."

Ben said, "That's very kind of you."

Chana extended a hand to Miryam, and they shook, meanwhile exchanging quick, appraising glances. "Thanks for helping Rabbi Ben, Miryam. We appreciate it."

"Oh, he's been a big help to me, too, Chana. You've got no idea."

AS THE ELEVATOR DOOR CLOSED, Miryam leaned against Ben. "So, Father Ben, that's your girlfriend, huh?"

Ben grinned. "I've known her a day longer than I've known you. And I've spent more time with you."

"She's drop-dead gorgeous, Father Ben."

"I've got eyes, Miryam."

"She wants to sleep with you."

"She told you that?"

"Just the way she looks at you. A minute ago, she wanted you to kiss her."

"So you can see the bind that you've put me in."

The elevator stopped, and they got out to find their driver waiting.

BEN PRESSED A BUTTON IN the armrest, and the privacy window went down.

Ben said, "Driver, stop up there, across from the hotel."

The driver steered the town car through the busy intersection, then gently braked to a stop.

Ben said, "Wait here. If you get hassled, go around the block and come back. Miryam, do you have your phone?"

Miryam said, "I do, Father Ben."

Ben shot her a look that said, Don't push it.

"I'll be back in five."

As he got out on the traffic side, a blur of motion caught his eye, a man in a rumpled suit moving laterally at the edge of his field of vision.

Ben swiveled his head and caught a flash of the man ducking into the doorway of a shop whose window displayed a variety of medical prostheses.

That's odd, Ben thought. He walked around behind the car, and then stepped onto the sidewalk. Staying close to the wall, he moved swiftly toward the shop to find the rumpled man, his back turned, pressing a cell phone against his ear.

Ben waited, listening but hearing no conversation above the traffic noise. After a few minutes, the man turned to face Ben. Detective Matt Marko of the Brooklyn Sex Crimes Task Force smiled lamely.

"Good afternoon, Rabbi."

"Don't tell me that you're following me? No, wait, you're the lookout! Your partner is inside, searching my room, isn't he?"

Marko spread his palms as if to say, You got me. "He's not answering his phone."

Ben said, "Why don't we see if he found anything interesting."

Reluctantly, Marko pocketed the phone and followed Ben to the crosswalk, where they waited for the light to change. Just before it turned green, the door to the hotel opened, and a short, burly, man came out. Despite the midsummer afternoon heat, a green hoodie obscured most of his face. But there was something familiar about his gate, the way he moved quickly away down the street. Suddenly, Ben realized that it was the guy who was dressed as a woman while pushing a baby carriage on Rabbi Zeev's street.

Ben said, "Detective, I know that guy. He's been following me for days."

The light changed, and Ben streaked across the road, followed at a growing distance by Marko. The green hoodie disappeared around a corner; Ben looked every way, but the man had vanished as quickly as an August sun shower.

Ben trotted back to find Marko waiting at the hotel. Ben looked across the street and waved to Miryam, who lowered a darkened window and mouthed, "Hurry up!"

Marko said, "It was the limo that crossed me up. Couldn't see inside."

Ben said. "There's something strange going on. Let's go up to my room."

The lobby was vacant. Not even a desk clerk.

Ben said, "Something's wrong. There's always a desk clerk on duty here."

Marko said, "What does he do when he has to take a dump?'

"Calls the bellman or the concierge."

They rode the elevator in silence. It stopped on the fourth floor, and as the door opened, a man fell into the car. He was covered with blood.

Ben said, "That's the desk clerk. I'm calling 911."

He pulled out his phone, but Marko clamped one big hand on the phone and put the other over Ben's mouth.

"Stay behind me and be quiet," he whispered, releasing the phone and pulling a Glock from a shoulder holster.

Ben looked past Marko and saw bloody footprints leading from an open door to the elevator. From the door to his room. He touched Marko's shoulder and pointed. Marko nodded and moved down the hallway on tiptoe, Ben creeping behind him.

Ben's Radio Shack phone rang. He shut it off and followed Marko into the room.

Detective Leonard Wise lay face up on the carpet between the bed and the dresser. With each beat of his heart, a ribbon of blood spurted from his neck.

As Marko pushed into the room and checked the bathroom, Ben knelt next to the stricken man, forced his index finger into the hole, probed for the artery, found it, inserted his thumb, squeezed the pulsing fountain and cut its flow to a trickle.

Marko said, "What the hell are you doing?"

Ben said, "Trying to save his life."

"I'll call the paramedics."

"No time, Detective! Go downstairs and get me four or five strong men. If anybody says, 'But it's almost Shabbat,' tell them 'to save one life is to save the world.'

"Send them up, then call 911, and have the ER at Brooklyn Hospital Center get ready for him. We'll put him in your car."

Ben's iPhone rang. He let it go to voice mail.

Marko said, "Are you sure you know what you're doing?"

"He'll die if we don't get him to a trauma center and put some blood in him."

Marko left, and Ben slowly shifted his body, trying to maintain a grip on the slippery blood vessel while finding a position that wouldn't cramp his own muscles.

Two minutes later, behind him, Miryam screamed in fright.

"OmyGod, OmyGod, OmyGod!"

Ben turned his head until he could see her at the edge of his vision.

"Miryam! Calm down. Get hold of yourself."

"Ben! Are you hurt?"

"It's not my blood. This man will die if I let go of his artery."

"Ben, there's another man in the elevator."

"He's dead. Miryam, listen to me carefully. Take a deep breath."

He heard Miryam gulp air, then exhale.

"I need you to be very strong and do exactly as I say. Can you do that?"

"Are you sure you're not hurt?"

"I'm sure. There's no time, so just listen: Go into the bathroom, find the large brown shaving kit."

"The shaving kit. What's in it?"

"Take it, use the back stairs, and go to the car. Have the driver take you home."

"What's going on?"

"Miryam, do you trust me?"

"Yes."

"Then just do it. Bathroom, shaving kit, back stairs, car, home."

"Okay."

"Go now!"

Ben concentrated on keeping his fingers on the artery. He heard Miryam whisper a soft "I love you" and felt rather than saw her leave.

When he turned his head a minute later, a big man in work clothes filled the doorway. "What the hell?"

Ben said, "Where are the others?"

"Coming up the stairs."

"We'll wait for everyone, and then I'll tell you what to do."

"Who's that guy?"

"A police officer."

"Who're you?"

"Call me Rabbi Ben."

Three more brawny men crowded into the room, and Ben explained what must be done. Squeezing the pulsing artery, Ben slowly shifted until he faced the top of Wise's head. Two men slid their arms under Wise's head and shoulders. With one hand, they cradled his head and with the other grasped each other's outstretched hand beneath Wise's shoulders. The other pair slid arms under Wise's hips and grasped hands: a chair of arms.

On Ben's command, they slowly rose, keeping Wise's head a little higher than his body. They carried him into the corridor, into the elevator, down into the lobby and out into the street. Ben backed into the rear seat of Marko's car and put the detective's head and shoulders in his lap.

One of the men jumped into the front seat with Marko.

Ben said, "Steady's better than fast. Try not to toss us around back here."

Siren blaring, the car pulled away from the curb, threading the rush hour traffic and heading south toward the hospital.

In the back seat of the museum's limousine, Miryam watched them go, shocked, but filled with awe and admiration for Ben, and worried: Who was the dead man in the elevator? Who was the bleeding man, and what was he doing in Ben's hotel room?

And what was so important about his shaving kit?

CHAPTER THIRTY-NINE

B EN SLUMPED IN A CHAIR AS THE ER WAITING ROOM filled with sick or injured people and those who had brought them. The small patch of sky visible through a window slowly faded to black. Oblivious to such temporal events, Ben's mind was elsewhere, in a place where he held his breath against the sickening miasma of gore, an aerosol of blood, plastic explosives, burnt flesh and burning tablecloths that filled the air in a ruined Jerusalem café. When he could stand it no longer, he drew a breath, choking on the acrid smoke. Something hit his leg, and he looked down to find a young man writhing in the wreckage. Ben knelt beside him, shoved his hand in the man's throat, felt for his tongue, pulled it out of the airway and was bitten for his efforts. A uniformed figure materialized out of the smoke and flame, a voice shouted past the crashing in his ears. He followed this man, this doctor, to a bloody lump, obeyed the command to put two fingers into its wound, to hold a torn, pulsing artery while the doctor pulled a long metal clamp from his kit and replaced Ben's aching fingers with it.

Suddenly, he was back in Brooklyn, and Detective Marko stood before him with a haggard-looking young doctor in blood-stained scrubs. Ben struggled to his feet.

Marko said, "Doc here thinks Wise is probably gonna be okay."

Ben said, "Thank God!"

The doctor said, "Thank you. You saved his life. You're a paramedic?"

Ben shook his head, no. "A rabbi."

"How did you know to pinch that artery?"

Ben looked at Marko and made up his mind. "Detective Marko told me exactly what to do, and I just did it."

Marko coughed, turned his back, coughed again, and then recovered his composure. He said, "It was something I saw on TV once. I didn't know what else to do, so I just threw a kind of a Hail Mary. If it worked, great."

The doctor rewarded them with a searching look of disbelief. "Great work, both of you." He turned to Ben. "We should check you out before you leave."

"I'm just awfully tired. But if you want to help, let me use a shower. And then lend me some clean clothes. Anything, until I can get back to my hotel room."

Marko pulled a face. "Uh, that's a crime scene. It'll be awhile before you can get back in there. Sorry."

Ben frowned. He'd known this would happen. "I can buy more clothes. But I can't go around looking like this."

The doctor said, "Come with me."

Marko said, "After that, you need to come back to the precinct with me."

Ben said, "I'm wiped. Can't this wait until tomorrow?"

"We need your statement."

"You're gonna look for the guy I saw on the street? A sketch artist is standing by? In a pig's eye. You're going to sleep and start fresh in the morning. Am I right?"

Marko favored Ben with a lopsided grin. "I guess. Tomorrow, first thing?"

BEN GOT OUT OF THE squad car, wearily climbed the steps and pounded on the front door. Seconds stretched into minutes, and Ben began to fear that he'd collapse.

Then the door opened, and Miryam appeared, barefoot and clad in a teenager's modest pajamas replete with a pattern of tiny penguins.

"It's Doctor Ben!"

Ben wore surgical scrubs, a gift of the ER doctors. Spent as he was, he smiled.

"My clothes were ruined."

Miryam wrapped her arms around him, held him for a long moment.

When she had closed and locked the door behind him, Miryam took his arm. "I was worried about you. Are you okay, Doctor Ben?"

"I need the shaving kit. And some water."

"Right now?"

"Yes, now. Please."

"If you're going to shave, use the bathroom."

It took an effort to grin, but Ben managed. "The kit, and a glass of water," he said, his voice falling to a hoarse whisper. She released him, and then ran to the kitchen.

He lurched into the parlor, landed heavily on the sofa, waited until Miryam returned with the bag. He dumped the contents on the coffee table: disposable razors, a small canister of shaving cream, a tube of toothpaste, a tooth brush in a protective case, dental floss, a nail clipper, comb, hair brush. He reached into the empty bag and lifted the seam, revealing a false bottom. A velvet sack held small plastic bags of pills.

Ben ripped open a bag and one by one put nine pills in his mouth. Miryam handed him the glass, and he emptied it in one long gulp.

Miryam said, "Ben, what's going on with you? Can we talk a minute?"

Ben shook his head, no. "In the morning."

Exhausted and emotionally spent, he began to weep.

Miryam went for a towel, and then carefully mopped his face. She sat beside him in silence, wrapped both arms around him, lay her head against his chest.

AWAKENED BY MORNING LIGHT STREAMING through filmy curtains, Ben opened his eyes to find himself on the couch, a pillow under his head and Miryam nestled in his arms. Ben spent several minutes watching her until he drifted off to sleep again.

The odor of fresh coffee pried Ben's eyes open. The living room was dark, lit only by the glow of a street light through the window. He threw off a blanket, climbed to his feet, stiff, sore and disoriented, and followed his nose to the kitchen, where Detective Marko and a uniformed police officer sat drinking coffee.

Marko turned to his companion. "Foster, call the precinct and cancel that All Points. Our fugitive has turned himself in."

CHAPTER FORTY

B EN SAID, "WHERE'S MIRYAM?"
Marko said, "She went for takeout. Sit down and have some coffee."

He turned to Foster. "I think I left my notebook in the glove compartment. If it's not there, it might be under the seat or in the trunk. Could you find it, please?"

The cop drained his coffee cup and got to his feet. "I can take a hint," he said.

When the front door had closed, Marko leaned in to Ben. "Why'd you tell that ER doc it was all my doing?"

Ben said, "Wise doesn't need to have to explain why he was in my hotel room. I don't need to be a hero, but I can always use a friend. So here's what happened: I called you and said I had a tip on the Running Rapist guy, and we made an appointment at my hotel. Wise went up to my room while you parked, but I was delayed in rush-hour traffic. Wise found the desk clerk dead in the elevator and followed his bloody footprints to my room, where he was stabbed by an unknown suspect.

"When I arrived, we spent a minute across the street talking, and then I saw that guy come out of hotel and chased him. Then we went inside, and the rest happened pretty much as we know. Except that it was your idea to have me plug the leak that way while you rounded up some men to help, you told me what to do, and all the rest of it."

Marko nodded approvingly. "I was dead wrong about you. You're a stand-up guy, Glass."

"Now that we're pals, call me Ben, or Rabbi Ben."

"Rabbi Ben it is. And listen, don't take our first meeting too personal. We were just doing our job."

Ben nodded, swallowed some coffee. "I get it. And in the interests of justice and all that, I've even forgotten that somebody carrying a gold shield monkeyed with my phones. Now, tell me about Wise. Is he awake?"

"Sedated. No visitors. I'll get him on board, and I'll have your statement typed up. You can come in tomorrow and sign it. And you'll need to look at some mug books, see if you recognize anyone."

"Mid-morning, if that's okay?"

"That'll work."

"What about my stuff? From the hotel room?"

"I called in a favor and got it released. Your girlfriend carried it all upstairs."

"That's great. These scrubs are getting a little ripe."

"You know, it used to be that people in this town looked up to doctors. Now, to get a decent table in a decent restaurant in New York, you gotta pretend you're a judge."

Ben chuckled. "In this neighborhood, being a rabbi is almost as good."

Marko said, "By the way, we have to think that the guy who stabbed Wise and the desk clerk was after you. He might be back. I got my captain to put a detail on this. A couple of plainclothes guys are in the house across the street, and a couple more are staked out on the cross streets at either end of the block. Anybody suspicious goes in or out, they'll be watching."

"That's very good of you, Detective."

"Aside from me and Wise and maybe our lieutenant, the NYPD doesn't care that much about you or your girlfriend. It's just that, if you try to off a cop in this town, we're gonna hunt you down."

"Thanks for your candor. By the way, when you brought my clothes, you didn't happen to bring my computer, too?"

"There was no computer in the room, Rabbi."

"A MacBook Pro?"

"Nuh, uh. The evidence team inventoried everything. No computer."

"Could somebody other than the guy who stabbed Wise have taken it?"

"Well, sure. The doer might have had a pal with him. An accomplice. He might have gone out the back while the guy you saw went out the front."

"How long was the room unguarded?"

"Ten minutes, more or less, until a patrol unit secured the scene."

"So some other guest might have taken it?"

"Or a hotel employee. Or one of the guys who helped carry Wise out might have seen it and gone back. I'll get someone on that right now."

Marko pulled out his phone, called the station, spent a few minutes talking to someone, and then clicked off. "The watch commander's sending a unit to the hotel to do a room-to-room canvas for your computer. If it's there, we'll find it."

Ben finished the dregs of his coffee, thinking.

"Let's hope that my computer was taken by whomever it was that stabbed Wise."

"Why is that?"

"Because my Mac has an internal 4G wireless modem—a prototype. Before I went to rabbinical school, I got a degree in computer science at MIT. I'm in a Beta group testing that hardware. I installed it the other day, on the train coming down here. When my computer is turned on, I can access it and, maybe, determine its location."

"How? You have a special computer gizmo?"

"On my iPhone. Which is wherever Miryam put it when I passed out last night."

Marko pulled a face. "Yeah, about that. I gotta talk to you, man to man."

Ben said, "About my PTSD?"

"So you know about that?"

"Flashbacks, night sweats, panic attacks, sudden loud noises that freak me out. Of course I know."

"I was an MP in Saudi Arabia. The first Gulf War. And I was lucky; all I ever did was direct traffic. But I've got pals didn't get off so easy. When I saw you in the ER, shaking, sweating, talking to yourself, I could see what was up. Were you in Iraq?"

Ben shook his head, no. "Jerusalem. A suicide bomber blew up a café, killed my wife, a bunch of others. I was taking a leak when the bomb went off so I was cut some, bleeding, but mostly superficial stuff. An IDF doctor was having dinner down the block when he heard the blast. He was first on the scene. Had me help him with a guy who was bleeding out. Showed me how to stick my finger in and close the artery off."

"You save that guy?"

Ben shrugged. "No idea. Never saw him or the doctor again. Sometimes I wonder if it was all a hallucination, part of my PTSD."

"Had to be real. The way you stuck your fingers into Wise's neck, held on to that artery, stayed so cool, I thought you might actually be a doctor or at least a paramedic."

"I've done that thing with the artery at least fifty times, but only in flashbacks."

"You think finding Wise stabbed and all triggered your PTSD?"

Ben shrugged. "All that blood, I think. And a bloody body falling into our elevator."

Miryam opened the back door and stepped into the kitchen, looking lovelier than Ben had ever imagined a woman could look. She held up a large paper sack.

"Anybody hungry for Kosher Chinese?"

Marko climbed to his feet. "I was just leaving," he said.

CHAPTER FORTY-ONE

MIRYAM FILLED A GLASS OF WATER AT THE SINK AND put it in front of Ben. From her purse, she took a plastic bag of pills. Ben ripped open the bag, swallowed the nine pills and washed them down with water.

"Thank you," he said. "How did you know?"

"When you woke me up this morning on the couch, you told me that you had to take them twice a day or you'll die."

"I don't remember that."

"You also called me Rachel. Who is Rachel?"

"Rachel was my wife."

"The one who died?"

"Yes. Oh, Miryam, you've been so patient with me. Please, sit down, and I'll tell you whatever you want to know."

Miryam slipped into a chair opposite Ben. She began to sob. "You're going to die! I knew it was too good to be true."

Ben took her hands and held them.

"Everyone dies. But if I take my pills regularly, if I eat right and get enough rest, enough exercise, I'll probably live a long, long time."

"What's wrong with you?"

Ben sketched the events in the Jerusalem bombing, how he had been cut by flying glass, how there was blood everywhere, that somehow his wounds had become infected with the human immunodeficiency virus, H.I.V.

Miryam was in shock. "You have AIDS?" she whispered.

Ben shook his head. "No. I have the H.I.V. virus. These drugs almost completely suppress its ability to invade human cells and reproduce. Almost completely. There's no measurable amount of virus in my blood. So I'm healthy. If I catch cold, my body handles it. If I cut myself or catch some bug, some disease-causing microbe enters my body, my defenses are robust. I recover quickly.

"But the virus is still in my body, dormant, hiding in my bone marrow. As long as I stick to my drug regimen, I'm safe. If I miss even a day, I run the risk of the virus awakening. If that happens, it can and probably will mutate. Then drugs that were once effective against it don't work well. Or don't work at all. That will cripple my immune system, opening me to all sorts of infections and diseases, which is what we call AIDS."

Miryam blinked away tears. "Wow. Wow. And even with all that going on, you're not afraid of anything. I saw you on the floor, covered with blood, but I didn't know what had happened. That police detective told me that his partner had been stabbed and you stuck your fingers in his neck and closed his torn artery."

"An ambulance would have taken too long. It was the only thing I could imagine that might save him."

"Doctor Ben. Father Ben. Rabbi Ben. You are the most amazing man."

Ben reached across the table and stroked her cheek. "You are amazing. To put up with all this *mishegas*, craziness, to be such a good friend to someone you hardly know."

"Tío Shemuel trained me well."

Miryam got up and opened a kitchen cabinet, removed a pair of plates and put them on the table. "Chopsticks or fork?"

"Chopsticks."

They ate in silence for several minutes, periodically looking at each other, peering deep into each other's eyes, enjoying the quiet.

Miryam spoke first. "Okay, I have more questions."

"Shoot."

"Remember when we were at Señor Beyda's place, and he took out the diamond, Rachel's diamond, and you kind of freaked out for a few seconds?"

"I had a flashback. To the bombing."

"And then last night when you came home, you were like totally out of it, and after you took your pills, you kind of passed out. And then you were babbling all night."

"I'm sorry you had to hear that. I have post-traumatic stress disorder."

"You mean, like soldiers get?"

"Exactly. Anybody who's suffered a severe mental trauma—a rape victim, a car crash survivor, anything that kind of rips away the illusion that we are safe in this world—they can get PTSD. Most do. Mine comes and goes. I have nightmares, sometimes. Yesterday, with all that blood, and the dead man in the elevator..."

"I get it. What was all that about an illusion of being safe?"

"We grow up, most of us, in a family that looks after us through childhood. Protects us. So we grow up thinking that we'll always be fine. Many teenagers, for example, seem to think that they're indestructible. Some psychologists use the metaphor of constructing a mental safety net. We believe that we will be safe. Then you got shot by a robber, or witness a plane crash, something horrible like that. The net is torn, and we realize that we could be killed or that our loved ones could die at any moment, that we're not safe, that the world's full of danger and we are vulnerable."

"A mental safety net. I've taken many psych classes, but I never heard that."

"Ever had a cat?"

Miryam shook her lovely tresses. "Tío Shemuel didn't like cats."

"Cats don't have that mental safety net. They're jumpy. They flee from loud noises, hide from any apparent danger, even when it isn't actually much of a threat."

"That's where 'fraidy cat' comes from? And 'scaredy cat?'"

"Exactly right. And if we didn't have that safety net, we'd be more like cats: unable to concentrate, to reflect, control our emotions, free ourselves to think of things that transcend the moment. We might never have been able to create an advanced society, let alone advanced technology."

"Is there a cure for P.T.S.D.?"

"Yes and no. The mistake most people make is that they refuse to admit they have a problem—that it's somehow un-manly or weak. So they self-medicate—alcohol, drugs, sex—and that soon makes things worse. I see a good friend of mine, a psychiatrist—and, not incidentally, also a rabbi—three or four times a year. It helps."

"What about tranquilizers?"

"I'm one of a small number of people who find that their side effects are worse than whatever we suffer from P.T.S.D. My tranquilizer is exercise. That's why I try to run five miles every morning. It calms me, sets me up for the rest of the day."

"One more thing, Doctor Ben."

"Anything. Go ahead."

"It's about you having the H.I.V. virus. Is that why you're not, like, a regular rabbi? With your own synagogue?"

"In the years after my ordination, after Rachel died and I learned that I was infected, I went looking for that kind of job. I was offered synagogue pulpits and teaching jobs in several different parts of the country. And each time, when I told the search committee about my medical condition, they withdrew their offer."

"Really? But why?"

"Because they believed—and I understand this—that their members would freak out if they hired an H.I.V.-positive person to teach their children and interact with them on a daily basis. It's an irrational fear, and maybe, over time, people will become more enlightened. But I'm a realist. It probably won't happen until a cure for H.I.V. is found."

"And the virus? That's why you won't sleep with me?"

Ben nodded. "Partly the reason. The last thing I want is to infect you. Or anyone. Now, it's possible to have safe sex. But that requires both parties being knowledgeable and consenting. Also, and just as important, it would be wrong to take advantage of someone in an emotionally fragile state. You just lost your uncle, your only family. Somebody broke into your house. You're not thinking as clearly as you do otherwise.

"And then there's Rachel. She was my life. I don't think I can ever forget her."

"She's gone, Ben. I'm so, so, sorry, but she is just not coming back."

"I know. But in the few years of our marriage, I learned a lot. About giving and taking and about compromise and cooperation. So at this point in my life, I'd never sleep with a woman unless she was ready to step under a chuppah, a wedding canopy, with me. To share my life as I share hers. That's a big step, a life-changing event. And, Miryam, you are lovely and sweet and sexy, and I see that you are not only a good woman but a wonderful person, but we've only known each other a few days."

"What about Chana?"

"She's very beautiful, as you saw. And so bright, so accomplished, so very much together—a wonderful, wonderful woman. But Chana is in the middle of a nasty divorce. She isn't ready to marry again, and as a matter of personal principle, not to mention Jewish law, I'm not about to sleep with a married woman. But I must confess that I was very, very interested in her."

"Was?"

"Was."

"Go on."

"For a short time, while I was still interested in Chana and right after I sort of dropped in on you, I fantasized about what it would be like with two wives. One who could support us, tend the sheep and goats, plant and sow the wheat and barley, look after the vegetable garden, do the cooking and the housekeeping, and the other to bear, oh, maybe ten or eleven children. All sons, of course."

Miryam giggled. "But what if that wife didn't want to have ten kids? Or couldn't?"

"Well then, I could get a couple of their housemaids—with that many kids, we'd need housemaids—and maybe get them pregnant, too."

Miryam's mouth flew open, and her color rose.

"But then I got to thinking, no, that wouldn't work out so well. First of all, sheep stink quite a bit. And I really don't want to have to move to Egypt when I'm old."

Miryam giggled again, then punched Ben, hard, on his right shoulder.

"So you see yourself as a modern Jacob, with two wives and two concubines?"

"It was just a fantasy. Lasted maybe half an hour, tops."

She giggled again.

"And then what?"

"And then I decided that, if I were ever to remarry, I couldn't find a better woman than you."

"Ben!" Miryam shrieked.

"IF I were ever to remarry. IF."

Miryam took Ben's hands. "Tell me straight out, Rabbi."

"Against my better judgment, against everything I've believed after Rachel died, I'm struggling against falling in love with you. And I'm getting tired of that struggle."

Miryam's face lit up like Coney Island on a summer night. "Go on," she whispered.

"I've given this a lot of thought lately. And I understand now that what I felt for Chana was never more than lust, sexual longing. It's been nine years! Self-denial isn't much fun—it can be agonizing. Chana is a beautiful, poised, intelligent woman, my intellectual peer in every respect; I instantly connected with her own feral hungers."

"Wait, you said that you never slept with her?"

"Never. But I wanted to. Immediately. But after I met you, after getting to know you a little, seeing you in action, I realized that whatever might eventually have been between me and Chana, there would always be one thing missing: I was never ready to surrender myself entirely to her."

Miryam frowned. "What does that mean, surrender yourself?"

"What I feel for you is all my accumulated lust and desire, but something more. Something that engages my mind, brings out my protective feelings, makes me want to be worthy of your trust. Worthy of you. You've made your feelings plain from the start."

"Yes."

"Well, this has just made me helpless to deny you anything."

"Helpless? Really?"

Ben's eyes filled. "It's an emotion I have felt before only once. For Rachel. For my wife. Just like her, you have awakened feelings in me that go way beyond the sexual and the intellectual. I don't know how to describe it better than that."

"The day we met, you had me at Aleinu. But keep talking, Ben."

Ben said, "It's exhilarating and terrifying at the same time. And that makes me as nervous and fearful as I've ever been as an adult."

"I don't understand."

"You have some idea, by now, that I sometimes engage in risky behavior."

"I think I have a pretty good idea about that, Father Ben. Doctor Ben."

"And if I'm honest with myself, I have to admit that I kind of enjoy what I do. And I'm good at it. I'm not rich, but I make a good living this way. I take assignments only from people or institutions that I believe in, and I won't take a job for a bad cause or out of greedy motives. And still, I've had some close calls, my dear Miryam, some very close calls."

"And yet here you are."

"Here I am, and here I am, having trouble concentrating, because I keep thinking about what it would be like to be with you."

"Oh. That's good, I think."

"But bad, if I need all the concentration I can muster for my job. For example, right this minute I should be on the phone with a guy in Cambridge trying to get his help finding the guy who killed the hotel desk clerk. But I'm talking to you. And Miryam, dear Miryam, beautiful Miryam of so many feminine wiles–"

Miryam jumped up. "I'll get your phone!"

Ben said, "Let's finish this. A few minutes now won't make any difference."

Miryam said, "But next time, they might?"

"They might. And that worries me. It worries me even more that this time or next time or some time, someone might come after you in order to harm me, to stop me."

Miryam looked glum. "I think I know where this is going."

"You don't know. Because I don't know. I'm going to finish my job here. I'm going to do what I can to learn whether your Tío Shemuel once had part of the Aleppo Codex, and if so, I'll try to find it. And then I'm going to take a long, hard look at whether I should find another line of work."

"Oh. Oh! Moshe Benyamin, I think you should kiss me now."

So he did.

CHAPTER FORTY-TWO

I T WAS A LITTLE BEFORE 10 P.M. WHEN BEN'S IPHONE, neglected until its battery was depleted, had been recharged enough to use.

He sent a text to Howard Hopper, the M.I.T. classmate who'd given him the MacBook modem to test. Ben told Hopper that his computer had been stolen and that the likely thief was wanted in connection with a murder. Was there a way to track the computer's location using the modem?

It was early Saturday evening in California; Ben supposed that Howard was probably awake and near his phone. On the other hand, as head of a Silicon Valley startup, he might be anywhere in the world, so Ben didn't expect an immediate answer.

Next, he opened an iPhone app called Remote Jr. and attempted to contact his computer. The call went to a voicemail box that Ben didn't remember from his cursory look at the modem's manual. The manual was stored, naturally, on his computer.

Only then did he check his own voice mail, to find a message from Marko: Two officers had combed the hotel but found no trace of his computer. Wise was awake, cogent but not talking: His vocal chords had been nicked by his assailant's blade.

"Ben! Paging Doctor Ben!" shouted Miryam from upstairs. "Ben, hurry!"

Ben flew up the stairs two at a time and found himself in a gloomy corridor lit only by light coming through an open door. Inside, he found Miryam on her bed, watching TV.

"Look!" she said.

Ben turned to the screen and watched a fuzzy, jerky cell phone video of four large men carrying Wise out of a hotel and down the street to a squad car. At Wise's head, walking backward, was Ben. After a cut, a second video, shot from much closer and with better video quality, followed Ben down the street, showing his fingers inside the detective's bloody neck and how he controlled the pace of the other men with voice commands, then, cradling Wise's head in his lap, folded himself into the back of Marko's unmarked police cruiser.

After an establishing shot of Brooklyn Hospital's ER, a male talking head appeared on the screen, describing what had just been shown. Then came brief interviews with two of the men who had helped carry Wise to the car. The reporter came back to wrap things up while behind him the video of the rescue repeated, out of focus, on a screen. Ben heard his name mentioned four times, and the story's tag line was something about a "heroic rabbi."

Lord save me, Ben thought. Just what he had so fervently hoped to avoid.

Miryam's cell phone rang. Down the hall, another phone rang. Ben's phone rang.

Chana said, "My God, Ben! What happened? Why didn't you tell me about this?"

As Ben explained about the stabbing and its aftermath, he heard Miryam talking into her phone.

"Yes, yes, my Ben. Yes, isn't he wonderful?"

Chana said, "Ben, where are you?"

Ben said, "At Miryam's. I couldn't go back to that hotel, and the police think I might still be a target, so they put some officers here to protect us."

"You've been spending a lot of time with that girl, Ben."

"I have. And since yesterday, which I spent at the ER or sleeping on her couch, all of it has been about finding the Codex."

"You sound a little defensive."

"I'm a little overwhelmed by all this sudden attention. Not what I wanted."

"That's New York. You should know that it's impossible to keep anything out of the media for very long."

"You're right. On the other hand, I couldn't let the man die, could I?"

"Oh, no, of course not. Ben, you're still my hero."

A tone sounded in Ben's ear, and he checked the number of the incoming call: Howard Hopper, Cupertino, California.

Ben told Chana that he had to take the call, that he would call her back later, then clicked over to answer.

"Hey, Howie!"

"Ben! You're a TV star out here!"

"What are you talking about?"

"You're on CNN right now saving some police detective's life."

Ben sighed. "It's a lot less than it looks. Get my text?"

Hopper said, "I just sent you the GPS coordinates of your computer. It's in a house in Eatontown, New Jersey."

CHAPTER FORTY-THREE

B EN WAS NO STRANGER TO THE GARDEN STATE PARK-way, but never before had he traversed it at 3:00 a.m. at a hundred miles an hour in a police cruiser.

Ben sat up, slowly, so as not to wake Miryam, and peered through the bug-spattered windshield. Strung out ahead of his cruiser, lights flashing red and blue, were three large SUVs carrying a S.W.A.T. team, and a command car, bristling with antennae and bearing the NYPD's chief of detectives.

Their destination was Eatontown, a Monmouth County bedroom community notable for little besides its proximity to the faded glories of Asbury Park.

Eatontown police had established a perimeter at a distance around the house with Ben's computer. Howard Hopper's automated tracking system sent Ben an update every ten minutes confirming the computer's location in a 40-year-old, two-story frame home on a large, well-kept, grassy lot halfway down a street of similar homes.

The NYPD unit stopped half a block away and around a corner. Marko left the front seat and opened a passenger door, squatting on his heels in the street to talk to Ben.

"Here's how it's going down," he said in a low voice. "Jersey state troopers are bringing a warrant. In the meantime,

S.W.A.T. will seal off the house. When the warrant gets here, they'll go in. I'll follow with a couple of guys from the Chief of D's office."

Miryam sat up, blinking away sleep. "What is it that I'm supposed to do?"

Miryam had come at Ben's request because the house was owned by a family named Abboud, a distinctly Syrian Jewish name. Two Sephardic synagogues, whose members were mostly descended from Syrian immigrants, were within a mile of the house. Ben had supposed that, if a hostage situation materialized, Miryam's familiarity with the community, and her family's reputation, would be an invaluable asset.

Marko said, "Rabbi Ben tells me that that your late uncle was widely known and respected in this community. We think the people in this house might be part of that, and if we need to talk to them, they might trust you more than the police."

Miryam nodded. "Do I have to wear this vest? It's heavy."

Marko nodded. "Put it on, and stay in the car with the doors closed. Officer Foster will be right outside in case you need anything."

Behind them, a car turned the corner, doused its lights and crept forward until it was opposite Marko. Two men got out. Ben shuddered: Silhouetted in the streetlamp's glow, their high-brimmed hats reminded him of World War II-era German Army officers.

Marko said, "You have the warrant?"

The shorter man answered. "Signed and delivered. You in charge here?"

"I'm Marko, Detective Second, NYPD. Chief Kleiser is senior NYPD. Our S.W.A.T. should now be in position. The Eatontown force will serve the warrant."

"Take me to Chief Kleiser, and we'll get the ground rules straight."

Marko turned to Ben. "Both of you, stay in the car. Foster, a sharp eye.

"Rabbi, are you certain that the computer is still in that house?"

"As of five minutes ago. And in another five, I'll have another update."

"Good enough. Stay in the car. If Foster tells you to do something, do it."

With that, Marko moved into the darkness, followed by one of the state troopers.

Five long minutes went by until Marko reappeared. "Rabbi, is it still there?"

Ben said, "It is. Just got another update."

Marko went back the way he came. Ben rolled his window down and, by craning his neck, could see the house's second story. Only one light showed, in an upper window, and as he watched, it and every other light on the street winked out.

Instantly, spotlights from three vehicles bathed the front of the house. Four brawny men in black uniforms emblazoned with white letters that said NYPD SWAT knocked the door off its hinges with a battering ram. Flash-bang grenades, essentially big firecrackers, were thrown inside, and the rest of the team assaulted the house.

In less than two minutes, a man, a woman, two teenage boys and an adolescent girl were taken from the house in handcuffs and placed in three different cars.

Marko came out of the house with a silver laptop, which he carried with gloved hands to the car. Ben opened the door and peered at it.

"Turn it over," he said, and when Marko had done so, he pointed to a sticker with his name, in Hebrew, inexpertly scratched out.

"That is my computer," he said. "But I'd be surprised if

anybody in that house had anything to do with killing the desk clerk or stabbing Wise."

—◦◦◦◦—

EATONTOWN POLICE HEADQUARTERS WAS A modern, two-story structure of red brick and glass. Its small interview room couldn't accommodate all five Abbouds, so with Marko and Eatontown's rotund, balding Captain Squyres, they used the conference room. Squyres seemed uncomfortable; before a question could be asked, he left the room to confer with Chief Kleiser. A few minutes later, Kleiser told Marko to release Mrs. Abboud and the 10-year-old girl, and they were sent home in a squad car. Squyres returned and took a corner chair, plainly unhappy with the proceedings.

Marko then asked Ben to come into the room, and he sat down opposite Mikel, the younger of the two Abboud boys. He noticed immediately that both boys, who seemed younger than their 14 and 17 years, respectively, were dressed in skinny jeans, T-shirts and expensive Adidas shoes, while the older Abboud, a slender, olive-skinned man, wore only boxer shorts and an unfortunate ladies pink dressing robe.

Ben said, "I'm Rabbi Ben Maimon, and I'm here unofficially, to help the police."

Abboud peered at Ben closely. "I saw you on TV last night," he said. "You stuck your fingers in that guy's neck and saved him."

Ben sighed. Was this to be his future? Was he now forever the rabbi who sticks his fingers in necks?

Marko said, "The man Rabbi Ben here saved was a New York City Police detective. That detective was stabbed in a hotel room, and the computer that I found your sons using was taken from that room."

Abboud exploded. "You think my sons stabbed that detective? Is that why you burst into my house in the middle of the night?"

Ben said, "Please calm down, Mr. Abboud. Nobody likes to be shouted at."

Marko said, "Mr. Abboud, nobody is accusing you or your sons of anything. We just need to know how that computer came to be in their possession."

Ben looked at the boys. "How is it that both of you were awake and dressed at this hour? Why weren't you sleeping?"

Menachem, the older boy, puffed out his chest. "It's summer. I don't have to work tomorrow. I can stay up as long as I like."

Mikel said, "Me, too."

Their father looked like he wanted to smack them both.

Ben said, "I'm not saying that you had no business being up. I'm asking why? What were you doing at four in the morning that you were completely dressed?"

Captain Squyres said, "They were breaking into the Mac Shack."

Menachem said, "I didn't steal anything. And Mikel had nothing to do with that."

Squyres said, "He left a note and cash on the register."

The boy said, "I used to work there. Greg doesn't care if I take something, as long as I pay for it."

Squyres looked more uncomfortable than ever. "My son might not care, but you triggered the alarm. Whenever the security patrol comes out, there's a charge for that."

Marko said, "Hold on, Captain. The B and E is your bailiwick. I just want to know how these kids got their hands on the computer."

Mr. Abboud said, "What did you take from the store, Menachem?"

Ben said, "He took a MacBook Power Cord."

Menachem said, "How did you know that?"

Ben said, "Because the computer was on for four hours, and then it went off for a little over an hour, then came back on. But the guy who stole that computer left the power cord behind in the hotel room."

Marko said, "So you kids must have gotten a charger from somewhere."

Mikel, the younger boy said, "All we ever did was play K-Dice online."

Menachem said, "That's because everything except the Internet browser and some crappy remote control program was passworded. So I hooked it up to my old Mac and was running my password cracking routine, and meantime I played K-Dice against Mikel on my old machine. That's all."

Marko said, "Where did you get the computer, son?"

Menachem looked at Ben. He looked at his father. He said, "I want a lawyer."

Abboud said, "I am a lawyer."

Menachem said, "I'm not declaring bankruptcy, Dad. I need a real lawyer."

Ben said, "Mr. Abboud, may I have a word with you outside?"

Marko said, "That's a good idea, Rabbi. Why don't you and Mr. Abboud here get some coffee?"

Captain Squyres said, "I don't think there's any left."

Ben said, "I'll make some."

Ben found Miryam in the break room, eying a coffee maker from which ushered a thin wisp of steam and the sounds of brewed coffee.

Abboud said, "Marita?"

Miryam turned, frowning. "Do I know you?"

Abboud said, "Your great-uncle was Shemuel Benkamal. I went to his funeral. It was the first time I'd seen you since you were a little girl."

Miryam smiled, dazzling Ben. "I think I remember you, but there were so many people that day."

"What are you doing here, Marita?"

"Rabbi Ben asked me to come."

Abboud looked confused. "How do you know this Polonia?"

Miryam smiled again. "This Polish rabbi is my fiancé."

Abboud scratched his head. "Forgive me, Rabbi. We used to live in Bensonhurst, and I've known this little girl since she was born, though she doesn't remember me. My grandfather, of blessed memory, was business partners with her great-uncle Shemuel."

Ben smiled. "Let's get some coffee."

IN THE CONFERENCE ROOM, MARKO leaned across the table toward Menachem. "Now that the rabbi and your father are gone, you got something you want to tell me?"

Mikel said, "He doesn't want that rabbi to know that he was eating sausage pizza at Giuseppe's when he found the computer."

Menachem said, "My father would have a heart attack."

Marko said, "Why is that, son?"

Mikel gave the detective a look of incredulity. "You're not Jewish, are you?"

Marko said, "You were doing something Jews ain't supposed to be doing?"

Menachem said, "Sausage pizza. Pork sausage. And using money on Shabbat."

"Where was the computer?"

"It was in the booth when I sat down. Under a newspaper. I waited for someone to come back and claim it, but they never did."

"Where is this place, Giuseppe's?"

Mikel said, "On Monmouth Road, across from the Walgreen's."

"And what did you do with the newspaper it was wrapped in?"

Menachem scratched his nose. "I think it's still in my wastebasket."

———

IN THE BREAK ROOM, BEN handed Abboud a paper cup with steaming black coffee and sat down next to Miryam at the tiny table.

Abboud sipped carefully, and on the other side of the table, Ben slid his arm around Miryam's waist. She slid hers around Ben and leaned her head on his shoulder.

Ben said, "Excuse me, Mr. Abboud, but you said your grandfather was her uncle's business partner?"

"Yeah, back in Brooklyn. He came over from Aleppo with my folks when I was in diapers. *Abuelo*—that's Ladino for grandpa—had a little drugstore, a *farmacia*, and Mr. Benkamal was a kind of silent partner. I think he might have put up the money for the store lease or bought the inventory when it first opened. Something like that."

Ben said, "I heard that Mr. Benkamal was partners in several businesses."

"I think that's right. People—the older generation—said that he had a kind of Midas touch. If he was your partner, your business always did well."

Screened from Abboud's view, Miryam stroked Ben's leg.

Miryam said, "Mr. Abboud, was your family superstitious?"

"My family? A little, I guess. My grandfather definitely was. He always wore this leather thing around his neck, an amulet. Took it off to shower, then put it right back on."

Ben said, "How very interesting. What was in it?"

Abboud shrugged. "Some Hebrew writing on parchment. It kind of fell apart one day, about the time he got sick. My mother had it buried it with him, in the coffin."

The break room door opened, and Marco appeared, with the two boys in tow.

"Mr. Abboud, you and your sons are free to go. Captain Squyres will get you home. He's also going to take something from Menachem's wastebasket."

Abboud said, "What about the break-in?"

Menachem looked at the floor.

Marko said, "Captain Squyres is gonna hold charges in abeyance until your boy can work something out to pay for the security patrol charge."

Abboud said, "You and I are going to have a little talk, Menachem."

Ben got to his feet. "Mr. Abboud, may I have a word with you in private?"

Abboud followed Ben into the corridor and let the door swing closed.

Ben said, "The computer was taken from my room. There's a reward."

Ben handed him five hundred-dollar bills.

Abboud looked at the money in his hand and shook his head. "That's too much, Rabbi. Anyway, I don't need your money."

Ben said, "Think of it as a new front door."

"I really can't, Rabbi."

Miryam appeared. "Please, Mr. Abboud, allow my Ben this mitzvah," she said.

Abboud smiled. "If you put it that way, what choice do I have?"

Ben had a sudden thought. "Excuse me, Mr. Abboud, and I

apologize for asking a question from what looks like left field, but are you active in your synagogue?"

"I chair the *tefila*, the religious ritual, committee."

"Has anyone ever stolen a sefer Torah from your synagogue? For ransom?"

Abboud looked frightened. "You'd need to ask Rabbi Dibbo about that."

CHAPTER FORTY-FOUR

MIRYAM SAID, "I REMEMBER NOW. WE USED TO EAT here when I was a little girl. My parents spent a couple of weeks every summer over at Sandy Hook Bay."

"Here" was Sam & Harry's, a deli that began dishing it out in Brooklyn, made the jump to Monmouth County in the early '60s and, through three generations of one family, continued to serve the favored foods of the area's growing Jewish population.

At least, that's what the sign in the window said.

No stranger to delis, Marko ordered a corned beef omelet with cheese. Foster, who'd grown up in a small town near Poughkeepsie, found the menu foreign and settled for bacon and eggs. Ben and Miryam ordered lox and onions with scrambled eggs, and crisp latkes, potato pancakes.

Marko said, "You should try the corned beef," and pushed his plate toward Ben.

Ben swallowed. "It isn't kosher. And it's got cheese on it. That's why we're sticking to eggs, fish and pancakes."

"I thought this was a kosher deli?"

"Kosher style. To be kosher, restaurant or packaged food must be prepared under rabbinical supervision. If it was, there'd be a sign in the window. But any deli that serves bacon, or mixes milk products with meat, can't be kosher."

Officer Foster swallowed the last of his bacon and eggs and washed them down with a long gulp of his milk. "So this is what Jewish people eat?"

Ben shook his head. "It's actually Ashkenazi Jewish style, the cuisine of Jews whose ancestors came from Northern Europe."

Miryam said, "Some of my ancestors lived in Syria since Biblical times. We call them Mizrahi, Jews of the East. And others, the Sephardi, lived in Spain and Portugal for hundreds of years before returning to Syria. Their cuisines are very different from each other and from what Ashkenazi Jews like."

Ben said, "But in America, Mizrahi and Sephardi restaurants are hard to find."

Miryam said, "That reminds me. I had to call Mrs. Hedaya Friday afternoon and beg off from Shabbat dinner. I think she felt like I blew them off, until they saw you on TV. They called last night; they want to take us out for an early dinner tonight."

Marko said, "Not too early. The rabbi has to look at mug shots."

Miryam pursed her lips. "How long will that take?"

"A couple of hours, probably."

Ben said, "We can leave as soon as I talk with Rabbi Dibbo."

Marko said, "Police business or rabbi business?"

Ben said, "A little of both. I'm wondering why a guy who stabbed a cop and killed a man in Brooklyn, then stole a computer, would schlep it all the way out here, and then leave it to be found in a pizza parlor on a Saturday, when, chances are, it wouldn't be found by a Jew. And a place, not incidentally, about halfway between two Sephardic synagogues. That might mean something."

Marko said, "So that's what you're going to ask that other rabbi?"

"I'm going to ask him something else that might provide a hint to the answer."

Marko stood up and pushed his chair back. "Try to make it quick."

———◦◦◦◦◦◦———

WHILE MARKO, WITH FOSTER AND Miryam in tow, went to Giuseppe's in the faint hope of finding some counter clerk who might recall seeing a man with a silver Mac laptop from the previous day, Ben paid a visit to Congregation B'nai Yakov, a low-sprawling complex of red brick and recent construction. He found the front door open; a sign pointed him in the direction of Rabbi Dibbo's office.

Dibbo was a gaunt 50-year-old with pockmarked skin and a short, well-trimmed beard. He looked up from behind his desk when Ben tapped on the door.

"I'm afraid I have no time right now," he said. "Can you make an appointment Monday, or wait until after our meeting?"

Ben stepped into the room. "This will only take a moment, Rabbi Dibbo."

Dibbo looked again, then smiled. "I saw you on CNN yesterday! Saved that man's life in Williamsburg. What can I do for you?"

"I'm Rabbi Moshe Benyamin Maimon," he said, extending his hand.

"I know that name. Your father was head of Talmudic Studies at JTS?"

"My grandfather, of blessed memory."

"Of course, of course. I met him several times. A great scholar. What can I do for you? Would you like to join our book club discussion?"

"Thanks, but I just need to ask a couple of questions, and then I must get back to New York."

"All right. Ask away."

"Tell me about what happened when your sefer Torah was held for ransom?"

Dibbo paled. Then he got up and shut the door to his office.

"Who told you about that, Rabbi?"

"You'll learn that in due course, but I can't tell you. It's privileged."

"Why are you interested in this?"

"I'm working for The Jewish Museum of New York, trying to recover a stolen Torah."

"A word of advice, Rabbi. Tell the museum to just pay the ransom."

"What did it cost you?"

"In money, $50,000."

"And otherwise?"

"Seven families left the synagogue because of this. Two of our members went to the hospital with serious injuries. And I spent the most terrifying three days of my life."

"They took you and the Torah?"

"First the Torah. They demanded $25,000. We offered $5,000. They beat the president of the congregation and our cantorial intern with baseball bats and broke their legs. Then they grabbed me and doubled the price."

"Did you ever get a look at them?"

"I was blindfolded and kept in a closet the whole time. I don't know where, exactly, except it was a long ride. I think that they were Russians or Ukrainians."

"Jews?"

"I'm ashamed to say, but I think so. They spoke to me in Yiddish, which I don't know, then in English. And they fed me kosher food. Cereal and milk."

"Where did the money come from?"

"We raised some of it from the board. The rest we took from our building fund."

"And what about the Torah they took? Anything special about it?"

"A museum piece about 600 years old from Portugal, donated by one of our leading families, who also paid to have it restored."

"And when was this?"

Dibbo hesitated, thinking. "Three years ago, right after Passover."

"Was the Torah marked? Was it in the Universal Torah Registry?"

Dibbo shook his head. "It had just been repaired. We planned to have it registered, but they snatched it before we could."

"One more thing, if you don't mind: Who was your sopher, your scribe? Who did the restoration work?"

Dibbo scratched his nose, thinking. "I have his card here in my desk, somewhere. Can you call me tomorrow? I'll leave the name and phone with my secretary."

"Thank you. You've been very helpful."

"You're welcome to sit in on our class, but I'm already late."

Ben shook his head. "I'm also late. Thanks so much for your time and candor."

"Rabbi, please. Leave this alone."

"It's been more than three years. Why are you still frightened?"

"They said that if we ever told the police, they'd burn our building down with everyone in it. After what we went through, I take them at their word."

"Don't worry. I'm not going to the police about this."

They shook hands, and Ben left through a side door.

He found Marko pacing the sidewalk, his face a raging

maelstrom of competing emotions: anger, sorrow and frustration.

Ben said, "What's wrong?"

Marko said, "The sons of bitches! Walked right into the hospital!"

"I don't understand."

"It's Wise—they killed him."

CHAPTER FORTY-FIVE

I F THE NIGHT RIDE SOUTH HAD BEEN EXHILARATING, the day trip back to Brooklyn was flat-out fearsome. Foster flipped on the siren, and they flew north almost as fast as they had come south, with the added challenge of the Parkway's Sunday morning traffic as an obstacle course. Buckled in and wide-eyed, Miryam clutched Ben's arm for the entire trip.

En route, in bits and pieces as phone updates came in, Marko filled them in on Wise's murder: Around 6:00 that morning, while one of two officers guarding the detective's hospital room was using the men's room, someone started a fire in a stairwell. An alarm sounded, and a man in scrubs and a surgical mask thrust a fire extinguisher into the other cop's hands and told him to fight the fire. By the time the first cop returned from the men's room, someone had rolled Wise's bed into an elevator, slit his throat with a scalpel and sent him bleeding to the top floor, where he was found, minutes later, dead. The assassin or assassins escaped unnoticed in the confusion of the fire alarm.

By the time they reached the 72nd Precinct, Marko's inner seething was masked behind an icy calm. He sent Miryam home in a squad car, escorted Ben to a brightly lit table in the detectives bullpen and placed a stack of books in front of him.

"Look through these, and see if you recognize anyone. I'll send the artist over as soon as he gets in; this is supposedly his day off."

"Who's in these mug shots?"

"Guys we've arrested for anything big in Brooklyn in the last few years."

"I'm happy to look at them, but I'd also like to see some pictures of Russians, guys with gang affiliation."

"You want the Brighton Beach, Little Odessa crowd?"

"Just a hunch."

"I'll see what I can find."

"And, if you have any of guys who steal Torahs from synagogues, I'd like those, too."

"Eight or ten years back, that was a regular deal here. Maybe once a month."

"And then someone invented a system to give each Torah a positive, unique I.D. that can't be removed without replacing every page."

"So that's why they stopped."

"Except some didn't. Now they go after antique Torahs, very valuable ones, that haven't been marked because they've just been restored, or else they're museum pieces. And sometimes they take a Torah for ransom."

"That's what you talked to that Jersey rabbi about?"

"He's sort of an expert."

"I'll see what we can dig up for you."

Marko was back in half an hour and set a stack files on the table next to Ben.

"I'm tired. I started thinking about this Torah-napping stuff. Your dots don't connect," Marko said. "What's that got to do with murdering a desk clerk and Wise?"

Ben said, "About a week ago, an ancient Torah was taken from Miryam's uncle's home. While she was at his funeral, somebody knocked the back door off its hinges, went inside and did the same to a locked office door. They made off with a quarter-ton safe in which was locked that Torah, some gold coins and not much else."

"And you think it was these same guys?"

Ben shook his head. "No, that's not their style at all. I think the two guys who were following me were hoping that I'd lead them to whoever took that Torah."

"You said 'rare.' How rare?"

"Maybe one of a kind and priceless. Maybe a thousand years old. Maybe."

"No shit? What was a girl like—no offense, Rabbi, I'm sure she's smart, and she sure is beautiful, but she doesn't seem like the sort of person to own something like that."

"First of all, I'm not sure, and neither is Miryam, just which Torah was taken. But it was a Torah, or at least part of one, and it was very old. And it belonged to her great-uncle, her father's uncle, who probably brought it from Syria when he immigrated 65 years ago. He had no other heirs, so she inherited everything."

"Okay."

"I think they went to my hotel to force me to help them find that Torah. Then Wise walks in with the desk clerk, and they stabbed them and took off.

"They grabbed my computer because they thought it might lead them to the Torah. But they can't crack my passwords, so they take it out to hell-and-gone Jersey and dump it. It's a distraction, so that we'll think maybe somebody from one of those two Syrian Sephardic synagogues, somebody who knew Miryam's uncle, took it."

Marko said, "And while we're chasing that lead, they kill Wise. Why?"

"Because he saw them stab the desk clerk. He knew what

they looked like or maybe even who they are. He could put them away."

"Now the dots connect. Any luck with the pictures?"

Ben shook his head. "Mostly the wrong kind of thugs."

"I'm gonna go see if the artist is in yet."

Ben stood up, stretched his whole body, ran slowly in place for a few seconds. He hadn't run his usual five miles for almost three days, and his body craved exercise.

He sat back down, took a handful of file folders from the new stack and opened the top one. A slight, bearded young man in T-shirt, jeans and a Mets cap appeared at Ben's side.

"Excuse me," he said. "Are you the rabbi?"

Ben said, "Well, I'm a rabbi."

"I meant, are you the rabbi that saw the murder suspect? Saw his face, I mean? I'm Bill Roentke, the sketch artist."

Ben said, "I really appreciate you coming in on your day off."

"No problem. Wise was a real good guy. We're all trying to catch his killers."

"Then let's get started."

"Can you give me a sort of general description of the guy's face? Was he black or white or brown-skinned? Did he have a beard or a mustache?"

Ben turned the file he'd been looking at around so that it faced the young man. He pointed to a color photo in it.

"He looked just like this guy, Yevgeny Steinberg, a.k.a. Rabbi Eugene Stein, a.k.a. Hermann Stein, a.k.a. Gene Berg, but about eight or ten years older."

CHAPTER FORTY-SIX

B EN KNEW THAT HE SHOULD FEEL GOOD ABOUT FIND-
ing Steinberg's photo, but he was on the one hand exhausted from lack of sleep and on the other very much
aware that, if he'd found the picture a day earlier instead of
chasing around New Jersey, Wise might still be alive. But
when he shared this notion with Marko, the detective shook
his head.

Marko said, "You did good, Rabbi. If we hadn't gone down
to Eatontown, then you wouldn't have met that other rabbi,
and you wouldn't know to ask for the Russian O.C. files. It's a
rotten shame about Wise, but don't take any of that on you."

Ben said, "If I'd really thought about it, if I hadn't been fix-
ated on my computer, I think I could have—should have—made
the Torah-napping connection to the Russians without talking
to Rabbi Dibbo."

"Coulda, shoulda, woulda. You just go find your girl, have
that dinner out, whatever. We'll take it from here."

Ben said, "I'd like to be there when you make the arrest."

Marko frowned. "I am now off the Running Rapist Task
Force. This case is a very hot potato. The mayor's office is
calling Chief Kleiser every couple hours for updates. The two
palookas who were supposed to protect Wise are probably

looking at early retirement. Maybe no retirement, depending how hard the union decides to fight for them. The media is looking high and low to interview you. So you should get lost for awhile, because from here on out, it's all by the book. And there's nothing in that about rabbis on arrest ride-alongs."

"Any chance you could find something in that book about me questioning this guy after you bring him in?"

"Doubtful, but if he gives himself up or flips on the other guy, there's maybe a shot for you there. Don't get your hopes up."

Ben nodded. "One favor: Can you leave security on Miryam's house until you've got both of those guys in hand?"

Marko frowned. "We're keeping a team across the street, but now that we got a name and a face, we need everybody else on the hunt. Just be a little careful, okay?"

"Okay. And thanks for everything."

"Not at all. We owe you. I owe you, and always will. By the way, this guy we're looking for, Steinberg? Wise busted him twice for extortion, way back, but the Russians have good lawyers. Couldn't make it stick."

"I wonder why Wise didn't write his name out or something?"

"His artery—the docs put in a kind of shunt and had to keep him really still until it healed up. So they kept him doped. Out of it. When I talked to him, he just blinked once for yes, twice for no."

Ben turned to leave, and then turned back. "When's his funeral?"

Marko bit his upper lip. "Wednesday morning. I know you'd like to be there, but you oughta stay away. There's gonna be ten thousand cameras at that funeral."

"Because it's a cop funeral?"

"That, and because Cardinal Dolan is gonna say funeral Mass."

"I thought Wise might be Jewish."

Marko shook his head. "Roman Catholic, and I mean big-time. Knights of Columbus and Opus Dei. His brother is a priest in Rome. His uncle was a priest, knew Dolan from way back. So let me tell you what came down from Chief Kleiser. He found a patrolman about your size and build, red hair like yours, only he's maybe 25. Born in Ireland, talks a little bit of that brogue. At the funeral, he's going to be standing next to Kleiser, in civvies, wearing a black fedora. The media will be kept at a distance. If they want to follow that kid when the funeral breaks up, it's a free country."

Ben experienced a sinking feeling in the pit of his stomach.

"I did something... odd. Possibly illegal. You should hear it from me first," he said.

Marko looked amused. "Now what?"

Fighting the urge to smile, Ben explained how he'd found Steinberg and his accomplice watching Miryam's house and why he needed to get inside without being seen, then described his foray into St. Hermione's wearing priestly garb.

Marko burst into laughter. "Did you baptize any children, Father Horace?"

Ben shook his head.

"Say Mass? Marry anybody? Molest any choirboys?"

"Of course not."

"And you're worried about what, exactly?"

"I'm worried that, if Sister Agatha watches the funeral on television and sees a young officer that's been put there to make the media think he's me, she'll go to the archdiocese, or to the chief of police, and accuse this cop of impersonating a priest. I can't let him get jammed up on my account. And if the media gets a whiff of that, they'll spin it every which way and hound him forever."

Marko thought for a long moment. "Tell you what. I'll go see Sister Agatha and tell her he was working undercover. And I'll have a word with him at the funeral."

"I have a better idea. I'll see Sister Agatha and explain myself. She'll be angry, but truth is always best. And it turns out, the guys I was trying to avoid are cop killers."

"Let me get both them jerk-offs in cuffs, and I'll come with you."

———

BY 6:00 THAT EVENING, BEN felt much better. He'd run his five miles, plus one more for good measure, showered, had a nap and sent Chana a brief email update. He attired himself in a navy blazer with copper buttons with a subtle lattice design that on close inspection revealed a Star of David; a light blue short-sleeved shirt; a dark blue silk necktie with a pattern of tiny white Hebrew characters that spelled chai, life; and cream slacks over loafers with custom undersides that offered almost as much support and traction as running shoes.

Miryam was a stunning vision of loveliness in a lace shawl over a knee-length white sheath that set off her flawless olive skin. Around her neck, she wore a miniature of the Hamsa that Ben had noticed in her grandmother's wedding photo. Miryam took Ben's arm as they strolled into El Cuchillo, "The Knife," a well-lit Flatbush restaurant that melded Kosher Argentine-style beef with traditional Mizrahi and Sephardic dishes.

Ben was in such a rare mood that, when the Hedayas' dinner invitation turned out to be a hastily arranged surprise engagement party, he allowed himself the privilege of living in the moment, of putting aside the jigsaw puzzle he'd been struggling to assemble in his mind, to simply enjoy the outpouring of warmth from fifty strangers who came to meet the man whom Miryam had chosen for her husband.

Ben and Miryam joined the Hedayas: father, two sons, and their wives. In family groups, the guests trickled over to meet Ben and congratulate Miryam: the Bassouls, the Azraks, the HaCohens, the Cherbas, the Lofeses, the Kishks, the Zacharias—so many strange-sounding names that Ben lost hope of remembering any of them.

Most of the guests were families: Miryam's friends and their parents, plus a few infants, toddlers, grandparents and one sullen teenager who barely looked up from texting while he was introduced. Almost every family had a story, an anecdote from Miryam's childhood or school years, to share. To his surprise Ben learned that she had been a high school track star and tennis champion, co-captain of the debating team, class secretary one year and class treasurer another. And that she played piano, sang in a choir, and was a volunteer math tutor. And, no surprise, that Miryam was much beloved by her friends, admired but not envied, a trustworthy confidante to many and, on occasion, a class clown and cutup.

For a moment Ben found himself alone while Miryam chatted nearby with an older couple. Then he spied Cindy MacPherson across the room, beaming bashfully, and beckoned her over.

"I'm so happy for Miryam," the girl gushed.

"Only for Miryam?" Ben said.

Cindy blushed. "Oh no! For both of you. But Miryam—she used to baby-sit me, before her parents...."

"I understand."

As she turned to go, something caught his eye, a flash of silver.

"Cindy, wait."

The girl turned back, and Ben saw a silver pin on her sweater, a near-twin of the Hamsa that Miryam wore, but larger.

"Your pin—it's beautiful. Miryam gave it to you?"

Cindy touched the pin, almost caressing it. "Scott—my big brother—brought it back from Iraq."

Ben looked blank.

"Remember, when we were talking about Panama hats, I told you that he was in the Army?'

Ben nodded. "He bought that for you?"

"Uh-uh. He said he found it in a cave. In the desert, somewhere."

"I'd like to talk to your brother some time," Ben said, his mind whirling.

"He's in Afghanistan," she replied. "But he'll be home for Christmas."

Miryam returned, squealing with delight when she caught sight of Cindy. After a few minutes Cindy returned to her own table, another couple approached, and Miryam made introductions.

It was the first time since Rachel's death that Ben had been able to let himself go, and as this fact dawned on him and he felt the first pangs of guilty regret, he found himself experiencing the dissonance of simultaneous, contradictory feelings, of two minds seemingly regarding each other with wary tolerance.

Examining that idea, something clicked into place, deep down, an insight that he told himself he must revisit, something that might be the key to finding the Codex.

"Earth calling Ben," Miryam said, and Ben looked up at her beautiful face and smiled.

"Where were you?" she asked.

"Watching myself enjoy life in a way that I haven't in much too long."

"Welcome to my little world," she whispered. "What would you like to eat?"

Ben looked around, consciously inserting himself back into the scene. "Be my guide tonight, dear Marita. Order what you think I'd like or what you think I should try."

Minutes later, a waiter brought a huge slab of roast beef

pierced end to end by a gleaming chrome skewer topped by a wooden handle. Holding the beef vertically on a big wooden tray, he gripped the handle in one hand and with the other wielded an enormous knife, cutting long, thin slices from the roast.

The slices went on plates that went around the table; when everybody had been served, the waiter left the remaining roast and the slicing setup for those who wanted more, fetched another roast from the kitchen and went on to the next table.

Along with the beef came a succession of Syrian and Argentine dishes, including a salad of romaine with roasted red peppers, corn, and sliced black olives topped with a mint dressing; little pastries made of bulgur dough stuffed with vegetables, a dish of rice, lentils, and bulgur with grape leaves; cold tomato puree with onions and scrambled eggs; and *ballorieh*, fine threads of shredded filo dough filled with pistachio paste.

With so many interesting dishes, Ben sampled everything, eating slowly, savoring each new and exotic taste and between bites conversing with the Hedayas. Then a tall, bulky, older man in soiled chef's whites stepped from the kitchen, and the diners applauded. He answered with a mock bow and moved among the tables with an easy familiarity, speaking to each family in turn.

Finally, he arrived at Ben's table, and the senior Hedaya rose to introduce Ben to the chef and owner, Eli Mamrout, who leaned in and with a salacious wink kissed Miryam on each cheek. Then he shook hands with Ben and, standing between the couple, bent and whispered conspiratorially in Miryam's ear.

Miryam said, "A great honor! We're invited to sample desserts in the kitchen."

Ben groaned. "I'm stuffed," he said, and Miryam kicked him under the table.

Mamrout led the couple into the kitchen but ignored the waiting pastry tray and beckoned them into a cramped office, then shut the door behind them.

"Little Marita, I am so happy for you," the chef said. "And Rabbi, you are such a lucky man!"

Ben said, "The more I learn of Miryam, the more I marvel at my good fortune."

Miryam said, "It's me that's lucky. There is no better man than my Ben."

Mamrout said, "I saw you on the television. Tell me, did that man live?"

Ben shook his head, his mind flooding with sorrow. "Only a short time. In the end, he had lost too much blood."

Mamrout also shook his head. "A pity. Life is short. I brought you in here to share a great secret, a secret, Miryam, of your family, the Benkamals."

He turned and moved to a roll top desk, perhaps half the size of the one in Shemuel's home office, selected a drawer and pulled it out, laid it aside, then reached deep within the desk and came out with a small slab of unfinished wood. This too, he laid aside. He reached deep inside the space, crooking his elbow, into a secret compartment in the depths of the antique desk, to bring out an old manila envelope.

Very gently, Miryam bumped her hip against Ben's. He bumped hers back.

Mamrout turned to face the couple. "Miryam, you know that my father, *alev hashalom*, may he rest in peace, came from Syria with your father's uncle."

Miryam shook her head. "No, Tío Eli, I didn't know that."

"What happened is that in '47 there was a massacre in Aleppo."

Miryam nodded. "The Farhud. The Arabs looted the Great Synagogue and set fire to many Jewish houses."

"They killed many Jews. Some just disappeared. An Arab neighbor of your grandfather saved his son, and hid him in his own house until the danger passed."

"Saved my father? That's who you mean?"

"Yes. Nobody is sure what happened to your grandparents. They just disappeared during the attacks. Some time later, your uncle brought your father—he was just a little boy then—to our house, and they stayed with us for a few months. Later, we all left Syria together: My family, and your uncle, and your father."

"When was that, Tío Eli?"

"About 1949. The Syrians allowed Jews to leave, but they could not go to Israel. My father paid Shemuel and your father's passage on a boat from the city of Latakia to Cyprus and from Cyprus on a boat to Athens, and another boat from Athens to New York."

Miryam said, "That was very good of him."

Mamrout smiled. "And the reason that he did that, my father, was that the government allowed Jews to leave, but they could take nothing but the clothes on their backs. But Shemuel was friends with a man who could make any sort of passport, any document at all, and it would always pass for the real thing. So Shemuel got everyone a passport—my father, my mother, my two sisters and me—and U.S. visas, that said we were Lebanese Maronites. Nobody stopped us when we sailed to Cyprus."

Ben said, "That's an amazing story, Mr. Mamrout."

Mamrout smiled again. "In Aleppo, my father owned several businesses and a restaurant. He was quite well-to-do. And because of Shemuel and his friend's documents, because they said we were Maronites, not Jews, my father was able to take most of his money. He wanted to go to Buenos Aires, where we have family. Shemuel had relatives there also, but he insisted on New York. And so my father started this place and two others, and they all did very well."

From the envelope, he took a silver cylinder covered with ornate filigree. It was three inches long and about a half-inch in diameter, suspended from a simple silver chain.

Miryam said, "A mezuzah?"

"An amulet. Your uncle, my father, that whole generation—very superstitious. Shemuel took this off his own neck and gave it to my father many years ago, and told him that it would keep him safe from evil. Bring him luck. And so it did. My father was so grateful for Shemuel's help in leaving Syria, and for insisting that he come to New York, and I think for this amulet, that he made him a silent partner in this place. Every week, he gave Shemuel a share of profits. When my father died, I offered to continue that, but Shemuel said that it was too much, that the debt had been paid."

Miryam said, "Thank you so much for sharing your father's story, Tío Eli."

Mamrout held out the amulet for Miryam. "This came off your uncle's neck. It belongs on yours. Please, take it."

Miryam took it, hugged Mamrout and kissed him on both cheeks.

Mamrout said, "You shouldn't say about this. It's private, family."

"Of course," Miryam said.

"Come, let's look at those desserts," said Mamrout and led them into the kitchen.

CHAPTER FORTY-SEVEN

IRYAM HELD THE DOOR SO THAT BEN AND MAM-rout could carry a massive tray of pastries out of the kitchen. Walking backward at one end with Mamrout on the other end as his guide, Ben became aware that the room was silent, and he wondered why.

The two men laid the tray on an empty table and turned to find all eyes directed to Ben's former seat at the Hedayas' table. In that chair, his back to Ben, sat a tall, muscular man in his mid-20s. He had long hair and wore skinny jeans below a short-sleeved shirt that showcased the wide chest, bulging biceps and forearms of a bodybuilder.

Miryam moved to Ben's side. "That's Jake Cassin," she said, in a low voice.

Ben tensed.

Miryam whispered, "He usually carries a gun."

Cassin turned in his chair, a smile on his face, and got to his feet.

"Welcome, everyone!" he shouted. "We're here to celebrate Marita's engagement, and I thank you all for coming!"

A low murmur of disbelief swept the room. Near the front, a family of six stood up and headed for the door.

The door opened, and two tough-looking Latinos barred

their way. Cassin looked directly at Ben. "But you seem to have forgotten to invite Marita's fiancé!

"Me.

"We must honor the customs of our people, the laws of our ancestors. It's for a father to find his son a bride, as Abraham found Rebecca for his son Isaac. As Shechem asked his father, King Hamor to arrange a marriage with Dina—"

"—except that was after Shechem had raped Dina," Ben said.

A look of annoyance flitted across Cassin's features but was quickly replaced with a smile. "I see we have a rabbi with us tonight."

Ben took a step forward. "I am a rabbi. But I must also point out that I'm also Miryam's fiancé. And you are intruding on a private party."

"How can you be Miryam's anything? Did your father discuss marriage with the head of her family, with Tío Shemuel Benkamal?"

"Of course not. This isn't Syria, and we're long past Biblical times. A woman marries as she chooses. I'm sure you're an observant man, Mr. Cassin, well-schooled in the Laws of Moses, but Miryam doesn't choose to be your bride. So, please, spare yourself further embarrassment. Take your little gang of goons and leave us in peace."

Cassin's smile was that of a wolf considering how best to dine on lamb.

"You, mean, spare you embarrassment. My father and Shemuel Benkamal had an understanding. Solemn promises were exchanged between our families. Money changed hands. You're an interloper, a stranger, and you're trying to steal that which is mine."

"If you have a claim against Mr. Benkamal's estate, then talk to Miryam's lawyers. It has nothing to do with her engagement or our plans to marry."

"It has everything to do with it. Miryam has been my fiancée for almost six years. It's long past time that we married. And suddenly you show up."

"Listen to yourself! You're playing the villain in a scene out of a bad production of Romeo and Juliet."

Tittering and muted laughter swept the room, and Cassin's face darkened.

Ben said, "This isn't Shakespeare. Give it up. Go home."

Cassin took a few steps toward Ben, raised his voice a notch. "This is no performance, little man. I'm here to expose you."

"Expose me? What are you talking about?"

He was glaring now, furious, partly because Ben seemed calm and assertive when he should have cowered in fear. "You're a fortune hunter! A fraud, not even a real rabbi! You have no congregation! You don't work in a yeshiva. Maybe you have a rabbinical degree, maybe you don't, but you're really just a con man, a swindler."

Ben laughed. "What nonsense."

"You live in Massachusetts and came here as soon as you heard Miryam's uncle died. You use your Hebrew name instead of your legal name, Mark Thompson Glass, because, like your father, you're known to prey on synagogues and rich Jews. And now you're after Mr. Benkamal's money, Miryam's inheritance."

Miryam moved to Ben's side. "Jake, I don't know whether to laugh or cry. In high school, I never heard you put more than three sentences together. This is what you learned in college? How to make an ass of yourself?"

"This isn't about me. Did you know that this shrimp's father was on the FBI's most-wanted list for 30 years?"

Miryam turned crimson. "Did you know that it is forbidden to attack a child for his father's crimes?"

"He isn't a child."

"And did you know that Ben's parents divorced when he was in diapers, that he never knew his father, has never heard from him even till today?"

Cassin sneered. "How would you know this? You met him only last week!"

Ben was wondering the same thing.

"Rabbi Zeev has known Ben since he was a little boy. He told me all about him."

Ben found his voice.

"Mr. Cassin, you're not making any friends here. I suggest that you go home."

"Are you gonna make me go home?"

Miryam laughed, the sound of tiny silver bells. "That's the Jake I remember."

Ben said, "I can't make you go home. But I can certainly make you wish to God Almighty that you had."

More laughter came from around the room.

The elder Hedaya got to his feet, followed instantly by his two sons. "We can make you go home," he said.

Old Eli Mamrout took a carving knife from a table and stepped forward. "And I will make you go. Get out, or I'll carve you into little pieces and feed them to my dogs."

Cassin knew that he was beaten, but he couldn't back down in front of underlings. He turned to the pair near the door. "Ordoñez, the car. Rivera, my piece."

The smaller of the two men reached under his shirt and produced an evil-looking automatic. He stepped forward, arm extended, and Cassin turned to take it.

The instant that Cassin's head turned, Ben launched himself. In four long strides, he closed the gap; as Jake turned back, gun in hand, Ben arrived, feet first, knees locked, a human missile that struck Cassin's lower torso with force enough to knock him down.

Ben landed on his own back and shoulders, then arched his back, planted his legs and pushed off with both hands to pop up into a standing position as Cassin, gasping for air but still gripping the gun, brought his hand up. Ben dropped, landing on Cassin's chest with his right knee and smashing his nose with the heel of his right palm, then snatching the pistol away.

Ben stood up, gun in hand, looked at the crouching Rivera, and then at Ordoñez, near the door. Both held up their hands, palms out, and slowly backed out the door.

Ben removed the magazine, cleared the chamber, and then jammed the gun into a back pocket. Reaching down, he grasped Cassin's upper arm and pulled him to his feet. Miryam handed Cassin a clean table napkin, which he applied to his bleeding nose.

Ben said, "Mr. Cassin, I apologize for striking you without warning. But I couldn't permit you to have a loaded gun in a room full of people."

Cassin mumbled something that sounded like "Shishisntfkngoba."

Mamrout said, "Get out, Jake. Don't come back."

Ben watched Cassin head for the door. "You can pick up your gun at the 72nd Precinct. They'll probably ask to see your permit."

Head down, Cassin went out the door.

Less than a minute had passed since he'd turned to reach for the pistol.

Miryam wrapped both arms around Ben. He hugged her, feeling her heart beating frantically against his own chest. After a long moment, they moved apart and turned to find the other guests, mostly standing, eyes wide and mouths agape.

Ben said, "That's the floor show, folks. Now, how about some dessert?"

CHAPTER FORTY-EIGHT

B EN SAID, "SO YOU WENT AND CHECKED ME OUT WITH Rabbi Zeev."

Miryam said, "Of course. A wild-eyed, killer-dog-taming, fence-jumping, Catholic priest claiming to be a-rabbi searching for a thousand-year-old Torah pops into my back yard, and I'm supposed to just believe whatever he tells me?"

"Wild-eyed?"

"A figure of speech. You were staring at me."

"You were almost naked."

"True, and you averted your eyes and asked me to get dressed, which immediately told me that you weren't a creep, but I will always remember that, at the moment we met, your eyes were as big as saucers."

"Child's tea-set saucers?"

"Grandma Jolly Green Giant's best."

Ben laughed. It had been a long time since he could laugh so easily.

Miryam rolled over. Her bed was small for an adult, but she was tiny and had slept in it since junior high. Sharing it with Ben while fully clothed and lying atop the covers was a challenge. She pushed one arm under him and snuggled against his side, replaying in her mind the events of an hour earlier.

"Black Belt Ben," she said. "Where did you learn those moves?"

"Mostly at the 92nd Street Y. And then in Israel. The IDF offered a course in self-defense that included some basic Krav Maga, their hand-to-hand combat system."

"Did you know you were going to become Rabbi Jason Bourne?"

"I knew that I was a runt. I knew that almost every boy in every one of my classes was bigger and stronger than me. I knew I didn't like getting pushed around, punched, kicked, or tripped. And I knew that I was never going to be very big."

"I have another confession, Father Ben."

"I'm almost out of Hail Marys, the Our Fathers have been recalled, and Acts of Contrition are on back order from Rome. Still want to confess?"

"Watching you kick Jake's ass made me wet."

Ben was on his back. He rolled his body so he could see part of Miryam's face. "I get the impression that you're very frequently wet."

"That's a kind of intellectual or emotional wet. This was physical, visceral."

"If I'd known that it was going to have that kind of effect, I could have made it last a little longer."

"I don't think so."

"You don't? Why?"

"Because you're a runt. By the way, I love that you're a runt. I love the way our bodies kind of fit together. David is so tall. We never quite meshed that way."

"I think you just changed the subject."

"I meant, because Jake is so much bigger and stronger, the only chance a smaller man has is to knock him down and finish him right away. You know that."

"Wow. Do you know how many times I've tried to explain that concept to other guys, and they just don't get it?"

"I'm a runt, too, Professor Ben. I think about what to do if someone attacks me."

"You're actually Wonder Woman, aren't you?"

"Maybe, and maybe not. I don't reveal my secret identity to just anyone, you know."

Ben giggled. "Sometimes, you make me feel like a teenager."

Miryam pulled her arm out from under Ben and sat up. "What do you think we'll find in the secret compartment?"

"In the desk?"

"Yeah. And there's a secret room downstairs in the basement. I think."

"One thing at a time. I have no idea what we'll find in the desk. A will, I hope. But Miryam, we might find something that changes what you know about your uncle."

"He was a mystery when he was alive. Maybe I'll find some answers."

"What are your questions?"

"Well, we were just talking about size. I'm tiny. My parents were tiny. In the few family pictures I've seen from Aleppo, my relatives were all small people. Tío Shemuel was a giant; until he got old and started to hunch over. How come he's so tall?"

"It's unusual, but I've known families with four or five kids and one kid grows up to be a head taller or a head shorter than the others. It happens."

"Yeah, but judging from those family snaps, he didn't even look like the others. His eyes were wider apart and thinner. His nose was kind of hooked. My father and his parents had straight noses. Little stuff like that. Plus, tonight Mr. Mamrout said that I had relatives in Argentina. Tío Shemuel never mentioned them, not once. Why?"

"You're worried that you'll find out that he wasn't really your uncle?"

"I know, it sounds stupid."

"We'll look tomorrow, after breakfast."

Across the room, on the dresser, Ben's iPhone rang. A moment later, Miryam's cell phone rang, followed almost instantly by the house phone, a landline.

Ben said, "Don't answer. Call them back."

Miryam said, "What if it's important?"

Ben hopped out of bed and went to his phone to see who was calling.

"It's Detective Marko," Ben said.

Marko said, "I thought you agreed to lie low until after Wise's funeral."

Miryam called out, "Ben! You're on television again! And on YouTube!"

Ben said, "I thought you said to get Miryam and take her to dinner."

Marko said, "Goddamn cell phone video cams are everywhere now. The whole damn thing is on WNYW, starting with 'I can't make you leave, but I can make you wish to God Almighty that you did,' and ending with Dirty Harry, Jr., telling him where to pick up his gun."

Ben sighed. Publicity was the last thing he needed.

"I only did what I had to do."

"You're just one surprise after another. Should have given you a vest and put you through the door down in Eatontown. You ever think about joining up?"

"The pay sucks."

"It does. Listen, Rabbi: All kidding aside, you kinda dodged a bullet on this, publicity-wise."

"How's that?"

"The kid that shot the footage gave your name as Rabbi

Ben Camel. And he never got a clear shot of your face until you turned away, and that's just a few frames."

"So that's why there's no circus outside Miryam's front door. Tell me, Detective, why did that guy—his name is Jake Cassin—have to ask one of his gangbangers for a gun. Why wasn't he carrying it himself?"

"I'll check, but I'd make book that he's on parole. He gets stopped, he's carrying, he's back in custody. On a related subject, what did you do with that gun?"

"In the restaurant safe. It's in Flatbush. 'El Cuchillo.'"

"There are a couple of murders that we're hoping that gun might tie up to."

"I don't know about that, Detective. From what I've heard, Cassin is more the type to break your windows, torch your car or, if he's really pissed, shoot your knee cap."

"We'll see. When's that place open?"

"I imagine he does a nice lunch. Maybe late morning."

"We'll send someone. You should think about taking a little trip, stay out of the limelight in, say, a Jersey hotel, for a few nights. Maybe take a trip to Philly."

"I think we're good right here. Anything new on Steinberg?"

"You'll be the first to know."

"First after your boss, and the chief of detectives, and the mayor, you mean."

"Yeah, that's what I mean."

"Good hunting, Detective."

CHAPTER FORTY-NINE

———

MIRYAM SAID, "WAKE UP! YOU HAVE TO HELP ME find the secret compartment!"

Ben groaned and opened one eye. "Okay, okay. But first I have to do my stretches, and then I have to take my pills, and then I'm going to run and come back and take a shower and have breakfast."

"Android Ben! How do I reprogram you?"

"You. Cannot. I. Am. Obsolete. No. One. Remembers. How. To. Modify. My. Ancient. Source. Code."

Miryam giggled. "I'm making oatmeal. The real thing."

"My go switch is under my lips. Push that to get me started."

Miryam leaned in, and slowly, passionately, they kissed.

"Why don't you just skip the stretching and get naked with me," Miryam said. "That's gotta be a better workout than anything else you could do in half an hour."

"I've been thinking about that."

"Think harder."

Ben opened his other eye.

Miryam said, "Isn't it time to stop thinking and start acting?"

"Before we have sex, we have to go see Bert Epstein, my doctor. Both of us—but he's up at Harvard. We'll find out what we can do safely and what we shouldn't."

———

"I think that you think too much, Doctor Ben."

Ben sat up, put his legs on the floor of what had been the housekeeper's room, and put his arms around Miryam, nestled his head against the thin fabric over her breasts. "You are very precious to me, Marita. I just can't endanger your health. The virus is a killer, so be a little more patient with me, please."

Miryam said, "I love you, Doctor Ben."

"And I love you, Wonder Woman," Ben said.

"Finally!" she sobbed, and began to weep. Ben held her tight.

When she was calm, Ben said, "What was that about?"

"You're such an idiot. What took you so long to say that you loved me?"

"Fear."

"But you're the most fearless man I've ever met."

"I was afraid of myself, of giving in to my emotions."

"It feels good, doesn't it?"

"Yeah. Now let me get changed and out the door before I forget and do something that we'll both regret."

FEELING GOOD, FEELING WARM, FEELING strong, Ben ran down Bath Avenue as far as Stillwell, a little more than three miles. He had just started back when his phone rang: Chana.

He didn't really want to talk to her, but he took the call, explained what had happened in the restaurant before Cassin intervened, then quickly changed the subject to the amulet that Miryam had received from the Mamrout.

Chana said, "Do you think she'd let us open it and examine whatever's inside?"

Ben said, "I'm pretty sure she will. Look, I'm on my morning run, and when I get back, we're going to look for a secret compartment in her uncle's desk. No telling what we'll find in there. And in the next few days, I'm sure that I'll be able to speak with some of the people that might have pages from the Codex in amulets."

"All good, Ben. But you need to get to the bottom of this quickly. Mrs. Shapiro—Aviva— called early this morning. Yossi has reason to suspect that Mossad has taken a more active interest in you, thanks to all the publicity you've had lately."

"I'm really sorry about that, Chana, but there wasn't much I could have done to prevent it."

"I know, Ben. Trouble seems to find you. When am I going to see you?"

"Maybe tomorrow or Wednesday, if I find anything new to bring you."

"Or we could just have lunch. Or dinner."

"We could, but Chana, if I'm fighting the clock now, I'm going to need as much time as possible here in Brooklyn."

"You're right. But I do miss you, Ben."

"Chana, there's something you could do to help. Can you make a call for me?"

"Sure."

"Call Rabbi Dibbo at Congregation B'nai Yakov in Eatontown, New Jersey. His secretary has the name of a sopher stam, a scribe who works on Torahs, tephillin and mezuzahs, that I want to talk to as soon as possible."

"*Dibbo at B'nai Yakov.* I'll call him."

"Thanks, Chana. And if you get a phone number, text it to me?"

"You got it, Ben. See you soon, I hope?"

Ben broke the connection, feeling rotten. He'd exchanged no promises with Chana, made no vows or declarations, but nevertheless felt as if he had betrayed her.

BEN ENTERED THROUGH THE KITCHEN and found the table set for two. Boiled eggs cooled in the sink and a bubbling pot of oatmeal simmered on the stove.

"In here!" called Miryam, and Ben followed the sound of her voice down the hall into her uncle's office, where she sat behind the desk, all smiles, beaming like she'd just won the Mega Millions Lottery.

"Are those canary feathers sticking out of your mouth?" Ben asked.

"I just couldn't wait," she said.

"What did you find?"

"Loads of stuff. My father's will. Bank books. Financial records. The deed to this house. An insurance policy."

"That's wonderful! Wait, did you say your father's will? Not your uncle's?"

"I have his old will, remember. That will have to do, I guess. Anyway, this will says that my dad left everything to my mom, and if she didn't survive him it all went to me. Tío Shemuel had power of attorney until I turned 21."

"And you didn't know about this?"

"It never crossed my mind to wonder about it. I was a little girl, my parents were gone, I was well taken care of. Now I know that this house has belonged to me for years."

"I wonder why your uncle never said anything?"

"Me, too. Is something burning?"

"The oatmeal!"

Ben dashed back to the kitchen, and the next several minutes were filled with salvaging the oatmeal, peeling eggs and pouring juice and coffee.

Ben watched in amazement as Miryam mixed olive oil into her oatmeal, and then sprinkled it with salt and pepper. She was equally amused to watch him pour milk on his, and then sprinkle in raisins.

As he was about to take his first bite, Ben stopped and put his spoon down.

"Chef Ben, do you have a problem with the food?"

"No, no. I just had a thought. Let me think about it some more while we eat."

As they ate, Miryam busied herself examining each of the new documents.

"This is strange," she said. "It's my father's life insurance policy. My mother is primary beneficiary, I'm secondary."

"You ever get that money?"

"Never."

"Then they still owe it to you. With interest. I hope it's a lot."

"One million dollars. Double for accidental death."

Ben looked surprised.

"He was an oncologist. If he'd lived a few more years, he would have made a lot of money."

Miryam took a spoonful of oatmeal, put it in her mouth, chewed, swallowed, then picked up a bank book. Her eyes widened in amazement, and she passed it to Ben.

It was a savings account with the Flushing Savings Bank, and the last deposit, for $2,404, was about four months earlier. The balance was just over $250,000.

Ben said, "That's a lot to keep in a savings account."

Miryam handed him another bank book. "Northfield Bank, last deposit about two and a half years ago, balance $248,471."

The names on both books were the same: Isaac and Aida Benkamal.

"Your parents?" Ben asked.

"Yes," she replied, tight-lipped, fighting for control. "Detective Ben, tell me how there could be a deposit four months ago when my parents have been dead for years?"

"Perhaps your uncle didn't close the accounts when your

parents died. Anyone can make a deposit into an account. All you need is the number. And he seems to have made deposits every couple of weeks or so."

"Ben, there are nine more bank books. And all the balances are for around $250,000. There must be three million dollars in these accounts."

"That explains the bags of cash you found around the house. For some reason, he stopped making deposits a few months ago."

"After Beneficia died. And after he fired the woman who replaced her."

Ben thought for a moment. "Miryam, is each of those accounts in a different bank?"

Miryam flipped through the stack. "Yes, eleven different banks. I never knew there were so many banks in Brooklyn."

"That's the answer. He ran out of banks to open accounts in. And he stopped at $250,000 because that's the F.D.I.C. insurance limit."

"My uncle was going around opening bank accounts in my parents' names, years after they died?"

"Maybe. Or maybe he opened the accounts while they were still alive. He must have been getting that cash for years and years, and he needed a place to keep it."

"My God."

"Miryam, do you recall how you found out about your uncle being in the hospital?"

"Rabbi Zeev called me."

"And when he was taken to the hospital, did he have anything with him? A wallet, driver's license, anything like that?"

Miryam nodded. "A wallet."

"Do you remember what was in that wallet?"

"It's upstairs, in his room."

"Let's finish eating, and then while you go get the wallet,

I'm going to try to find the second secret compartment in that desk."

"Another one? How do you know?"

"I don't know for sure. But, if we reason it through, then there's a good chance there is a second one."

"This is one of those rabbi things, isn't it?"

"It's called pilpul, roughly translated as 'sharp analysis.' It's a way of finding the hidden meaning in texts."

"Take me through this, Rabbi Ben."

"Iffffffff ..." he began in a sing-song, "iffffffff we saw the only two antique roll-top desks that had secret compartments that would be very unlikely.

"So, it is more likely that most antique roll-tops have secret compartments. Iffffff that is the case, then most people who own or use or are often around one will know about that compartment.

"In that case, the compartment is hidden but not secret.

"In that case, anyone who owned such a desk and wanted to hide something from anyone who might know about the hidden compartment would either hide it someplace else or create a second, more-hidden compartment that only he knew about."

Miryam shook her head in wonder. "And that would be just like my uncle. Rabbi Ben, you are amazing."

"Tell me that if I find the second hidden compartment."

CHAPTER FIFTY

MIRYAM ENTERED THE OFFICE TO FIND BEN ON HIS hands and knees under the desk.

"Find it yet?" she asked.

"Not yet," he replied. "May I see the wallet?"

Ben sat down at the desk, and Miryam put the wallet in front of him, and then stood behind him, her right arm resting on his left shoulder. He opened the wallet and emptied it, stacking its contents in front of him. Then he went through it:

Forty-two dollars.

A library card in the name of Shemuel Benkamal.

A New York State Non-Driver I.D. Card issued to Isaac Benkamal but with a photo of Shemuel taken some years earlier.

A photo of Miryam as a young girl.

A photo of Isaac and Aida, Miryam's parents, in wedding finery.

A coupon for a local kosher pizzeria.

Cash register receipts for groceries from three stores.

A business card from a taxi company.

A business card from a plumber.

A folded subway map.

A list of names and telephone numbers.

A deposit receipt from Emigrant Savings Bank for $2,800.

Ben said, "Anything else in his pockets?"

Miryam shook her head. "A handkerchief and house keys."

"Let's look at those keys.

Miriam went upstairs and returned to lay a ring of keys on the table.

Ben said, "We should try to match each one to a lock."

Miryam nodded, yes.

"Miryam, did the hospital send a bill for your uncle's care?"

"Not yet."

"What about his death certificate?"

"The funeral home called last week and said they'd need his Social Security number before they could apply for one on my behalf, but I haven't been able to find it."

Ben said, "Do you have utility bills? Phone bills, gas, water, electricity?"

"In the kitchen. Should I get them?"

Ben nodded, and when Miryam returned, he spread them out on the desk. They were all in the name of Isaac Benkamal.

Ben shook his head. "Miryam, do you see what's missing from this?" he said, indicating the contents of Shemuel's wallet.

Miryam shook her head. "He hated credit cards. Never had one."

"Every American citizen, every legal resident, gets a Medicare card at age 65. They carry it with them in case they have a heart attack, a stroke, the emergency room."

"But I don't see one," Miryam said.

"It's not there. Here's what I think, Miryam. I think he never got a Social Security number, so he never got Medicare. I think he put his own picture on your father's I.D. and used that if he needed to show an I.D. He paid cash for everything. The house was in your name. Bank accounts in your parents' names. The phone, the utilities—all in Isaac's name. And if

Shemuel didn't have a Social Security number, he didn't file tax returns."

"What does that mean, Ben?"

"Shemuel made himself invisible to authorities. Off the grid."

"What about the census? Beneficia said that, last year, someone came to interview them."

Ben thought for a moment. With a shock, he saw how the pieces fit together. A chill ran up and down his spine as he realized that he would now have to broach the delicate subject of murder.

"Miryam, the housekeeper—Beneficia—would she do anything your uncle asked?"

"Anything except sleep with him."

"She died, you told me, last February. That's years after the last census was finished. Then Shemuel hires a replacement, finds her poking around in this room full of secrets, and fires her. Not long after that, he dies in a freakish skateboard hit-and-run."

"Where are you going with this, Ben?"

"I think they were both murdered."

"What! Why?"

"Your uncle for his money, for this house. Beneficia because she was in the way."

"Did you just come up with this? More rabbi reasoning?"

"I thought their deaths were suspicious as soon as you described them. But just now, you gave me the missing piece: the how. It was the census that made it possible."

"Go on."

"We see that your uncle was trying to remain invisible to authorities, so he probably had Beneficia tell the census enumerator, who was probably a fake, that she lived here alone, that he was a visitor. Then his name wouldn't be recorded."

"That makes sense."

"The Census Bureau hires tens of thousands of temporary workers. They don't do thorough background checks. Miryam, I really hate to mention this, but there are people in every city, in every country, who prey on the sick, and the weak and the elderly. It is their life's work. What if the census worker was one of those? Put it another way, if you were one of those people, if your profession was exploiting old people, what better way to look for victims than to become a census enumerator? Someone who can visit any house without arousing suspicion? And maybe keep visiting houses years after the decade census."

"Ben, you're scaring me."

"I'm truly sorry. But you need to hear this."

"Okay," she whispered.

"Those who prey on the elderly typically befriend them, insinuate themselves into their lives. Sometimes, they find a way to injure them, make them sick, or even poison them, anything to make them totally dependent on a caregiver. The caregiver manipulates them into signing papers they don't understand, loots their bank accounts, steals their property, sells their house or takes out a mortgage and steals the proceeds. The police call these kinds of scams 'Gypsy cons.'

"What if this census worker decided to get rid of Beneficia so that he or she could work that kind of a scam?"

"You think somebody threw a Coke on our steps just to hurt Beneficia?"

"Threw a Coke over a fence six blocks from the nearest fast-food joint, threw it to land right on the top step on a freezing night? Simple carelessness? I doubt it."

"But why?"

"Two possibilities suggest themselves. Either they believed that she lived here alone, and she became their initial target, or they suspected that she was lying and was Shemuel's caregiver. If the former, they wanted to incapacitate her, then move in, literally move in to the house, in the guise of caring for her. Then they loot the house, steal her money, and maybe even sell the house right from under her.

"But if they thought that Shemuel lived here, then he was the target. Beneficia was just in the way. If they watched the house for a few days, they'd see that she went out every morning for the paper; they wanted her to slip, break a leg, fracture her hip. Instead, she fractured her skull. Dead, she's still out of the way."

"There are really such horrible people?"

"More than you might imagine."

"And they're all Gypsies?"

"Not at all. That's just the name of this type of confidence game. Typically, it's a small group of people who are related to each other. One throws a Coke over a fence. Another skateboards down a street and bumps an old man. One befriends a crippled victim, takes care of him, moves into his house. It's a long-term con, and often these groups have three or four cons going at one time."

"How do you know all this?"

"Because, dearest Marita, I am not your ordinary, garden-variety rabbi."

"No, you're a fence-jumping, beast-taming, heart-stealing, kung fu-master rabbi."

"Whose business it is to know things like this, just as much as it is my business to know who to ask when I don't know something like this. I called a police detective I knew, and he filled me in. Not Marko, another one."

"This is horrible news. But I love you for telling me."

"And I just love you. And it feels so good to say that."

"Oh, Ben. This is hard on you, too, isn't it?"

"It is. It's hard seeing you suffer mental anguish. Shall I continue?"

Miryam bobbed her head up and down.

"Okay, so Beneficia is gone, and suddenly, I'm supposing, before he even gets around to looking for a new housekeeper, here is this attractive woman, younger than Beneficia, maybe in her 40s, who says she's looking for a job, even a temporary one."

Miryam's mouth flew open. "That's just what happened. She approached him in a supermarket, said she was looking for a job, did he know anyone who needed a housekeeper, a cleaning lady. But how did you know?"

Ben shook his head. "A logical surmise. It's how the con might work."

"But why did they kill him?"

"Shemuel threw her out, but they had invested time in this, and by then they might know that people came over bringing bags of money. Unless she only worked days and the bags came at night.

"Anyway, they went to Plan B: Get the skateboarder to knock him down, maybe fracture his hip, get somebody else into the house twenty-four and seven."

"So they didn't mean to kill him?"

"Probably not."

"Then they came to take the safe?"

Ben stared at Miryam for a long moment.

"Maybe! I never thought about that. They must have known that it was here. You told me he never locked it, and you told me that he caught her in this locked room. So—"

"It might have had nothing to do with the Torah I put in it," Miryam finished.

Ben thought for a long moment. "Supposing all that we've talked about is what happened. Now you're a bunch of con artists, and you crack your stolen safe, and inside you find some gold coins, a gun, and some papers. Miryam, how many gold coins?"

"Maybe a dozen or so. They were pretty heavy."

"Maybe one-ounce Krugerrands?"

"I've heard of them."

"South African gold coins worth, maybe, $1,250 each. So their big score is fifteen thousand dollars, give or take. And an old Torah. What does a grifter do with an old Torah?"

Miryam thought for a moment. "Find someone who buys stolen Torahs?"

"Or maybe someone who steals them."

"So the Gypsies, or whoever they were, show some Torah thieves what they found in the safe, and the Torah thieves... what?"

"If they steal Torahs, they know what it is. They buy it from the Gypsies. The Torah thieves are Jews. They ask around. They find out who Shemuel was. And they think, if there was one Torah, then maybe there are more. Or other valuable old scrolls."

"And then you show up."

"They watch Rabbi Zeev's house, because if someone steals Benkamal's Torah, he's the guy who'd want to find it. So they follow me, and they stake out this house. And they try to break in. And they go to my hotel room."

"To kill you?"

Ben shook his head. "Probably to use me to get into this house. And for any cash they might get from a ransom, of course."

"Then why kill the desk clerk?"

"They were in my room when Wise and the clerk walked in on them. The bad guys stabbed them, grabbed my computer and ran."

"And they went back to kill Detective Wise because he could identify them?"

Ben nodded, yes.

Miryam pulled Ben's chair back to sit in his lap, and in silence they held each other tight for a long moment.

Miryam said, "But why? Why did my uncle want to be officially invisible?"

Ben said, "That's the question, isn't it?"

Abruptly, Miryam got to her feet and took the keys from the desk. "I'm going to try to match these up," she said.

"And I'll try to puzzle out this desk."

BEN WAS FRUSTRATED. HE HAD removed all the drawers, then felt for movable panels but found nothing. He returned to the empty space left by the desk's center drawer, reached deep inside, and felt the back panel. It was smooth and seamless. He dragged his fingernails across the back, found nothing but smooth, finished wood. The sides were finished, and the top as well.

That made him think: Why would anyone finish the inside of a desk drawer?

On his knees in front of the desk, he inserted his right arm in the hole again, palm upward, and dragged his fingernails across the finished smoothness until his index fingernail caught on something. Gently, he scratched around, found the seam, which seemed very short. He pushed upward, and he felt it give, just a little. He pushed upward while pushing the panel to his left, but it remained blocked. He tried to push it the other way, but his wrist wasn't built to go that way.

"Find anything?" asked Miryam, and Ben turned to see her in the doorway, her hair a riot of unruly curls, as fetching a pose as he'd yet seen her strike.

"I think I'm getting warmer. Let me try one more time."

This time, Ben put his left arm inside, palm up, found the panel with his fingernail, pressed up and rotated his wrist to the right.

He felt it move.

Still pressing upward, he rotated his wrist still further. The panel swung out of the way. He put his finger through it, probing, and felt something long, narrow and metallic. A key hole. He removed his arm, then smiling, turned to look at Miryam.

Miryam said, "What is it?"

Ben said, "This is really well-thought-out. Most people are right-handed. When your palm is facing upward, you can't rotate your wrist away from your body, only toward it. It won't open with the right hand. Opening it requires that the left hand be rotated to the right, which it does easily.

"Let me see those keys."

Miryam handed him the ring, and he selected a tiny, old-fashioned key and held it up between thumb and forefinger.

"You find where this goes?"

Miryam shook her head. "Not that one. And not two others."

Ben removed the key from the ring, transferred it to his left hand, and poked it deep inside the hole. He probed upward through the open panel, felt the key go into the lock, and turned it clockwise, the way most locks closed.

With a loud click! the center portion of the desk, the writing surface, sprang up, revealing a locked drawer.

"My God," Miryam said. "Safecracker Ben, you found it!"

"You mean, Talmudist Ben. There's no way anybody finds that by accident. You have to know it's there, somewhere."

"But why couldn't we see it?" Miryam asked.

Ben peered at it. "It has little overhangs on all four sides that fit into tiny grooves on the desk. When it's locked down, it blends in with the parquet design of the desktop."

Ben tried the little key from Shemuel's ring. It fit the lock of this drawer.

Ben got to his feet. He handed the key to Miryam.

She hesitated.

"I'm almost afraid to open this," she said.

The kitchen phone rang.

A moment later, Ben's iPhone sounded a familiar ringtone.

"It's Chana," Ben said.

CHAPTER FIFTY-ONE

CHANA SAID, "THE NAME OF THE SCRIBE YOU ASKED about, the sopher stam, is Rabbi Jason Silber. I emailed his contact information."

Ben said, "Thanks for doing that. Do you find it strange that a sopher stam with an Ashkenazi name would be asked to repair a 600-year-old Torah made in Portugal? A Sephardic scroll?"

"Odd, yes. Unheard of, no."

"Have you ever heard of this guy Silber?"

"No. And I have to get back into a meeting with my lawyers. Talk to you later."

Ben hung up and turned to find Miryam, smiling. "That call was a lawyer. Chana had him call me about my grandfather's estate."

"Great. But it looks more like he'll be settling your parents' estate, doesn't it?"

"What can I tell him about all this?"

"He's your attorney, and whatever you tell him is privileged. He needs to know everything, so he'll know how to deal with it intelligently. And he can't, by law, divulge it to anyone without your permission."

"It was really nice of Chana to refer him."

"She's a good woman. I told you that."

"You always know who to trust."

"It just seems that way now. I've been wrong often enough."

"Shall we see what's in the secret drawer?"

Before Ben could reply, the kitchen phone rang again, and Miryam answered it, speaking in a low voice for a few minutes, and then hanging up.

"That was Deb HaCohen, one of my closest friends in high school."

"We met her last night, didn't we? The redhead?"

"Yes. Her parents would like us to come for dinner tonight. She says she has a surprise for us, but the surprise is only tonight. If we can't make it ..."

"It's fine. But when you call her back, tell her we've been eating a lot lately, and a simple meal, something light, maybe just dairy, would be best."

"I'll tell her, but her mother is a really good cook."

"Call her back later. Let's go see what's in that drawer."

Ben followed Miryam back to the office and stood behind her while she opened the drawer. She took out a small, leather-covered notebook, a worn leather wallet, a small automatic pistol, a thick accordion folder and a stack of passports.

Ben said, "The light in here sucks. And now I think that's not an accident."

Miryam said. "Let's go back to the kitchen."

Minutes later, when they were seated side by side at the table, Miryam opened a passport, issued by Syria in 1948, and they found themselves looking at a cropped miniature of a photo they now knew to be a fake: Shemuel with Isaac in his lap.

"The plot thickens," Miryam sighed.

The passport was in English and Arabic: The holder's

name was given as Sam'wa'eel bin Kamal; the child was Ishaq bin Kamal.

Miryam said, "Just like what Mr. Mamrout told us."

Ben said, "And now, maybe, we know why he doctored the picture."

Miryam opened the second passport and stared: It had been issued by the Soviet Union. The holder was Daudov Khanov, and the picture was of a very young Shemuel.

Ben said, "'Daudov Khanov' is a russification, a Russian adaptation from another language, maybe Chechen or Arabic. Drop the last syllable, and he becomes Daud Khan, which is the Arabic equivalent of David Cohen."

"So his real name was David Cohen?"

Ben shrugged. "This says he was born in Grozny in 1919. That's in what's now called The Chechen Republic, a tiny Islamic country in the Caucasus Mountains. According to legend, pagans of that region were converted to Judaism by Syrian refugees. In the Middle Ages, many Chechens became Jews. Part of the area that includes present-day Dagestan and Chechnya was a Jewish state called Khazaria. Later, most of them converted to Islam."

"What would he be doing with a Russian passport?"

Ben shook his head. "Soviet, not Russian. Issued in 1941, during the Second World War. The Soviets had a strategic interest in the Middle East because of its oil and because of the Suez Canal, which was then controlled by England. Don't forget that they were allied with England in World War II. But before that, between 1939 and 1941, Stalin and Hitler were joined at the hip against England. Until Hitler invaded Russia."

"That was the Molotov–Ribbentrop Pact?"

"Exactly right."

Miryam frowned. "Could he have been a spy, sent to Syria to report on what the British were doing?"

"You might have something there. The Soviets had spies in Britain going back to the '30s, at least. If he wasn't a spy, then maybe an agent provocateur, someone whose mission was to stir up trouble for the British. After the First World War, France controlled Syria. Germany defeated France in 1939, and the Vichy government, a Nazi puppet, tried to hold Syria, but the British and Free French drove them out."

"But Professor Ben, my great uncle would have been very young in 1939. Would they really send a kid to be a spy or to stir up trouble?"

"Maybe he wasn't alone. Perhaps he was part of a team."

She picked up the third passport.

The kitchen phone rang again.

"Were you always this popular?" Ben asked.

"Always. I was very cute as a kid."

"You're still kind of cute."

The phone rang again, and Miryam jumped up and answered it.

"Hello," she said. "Yes, Officer Novello, I remember you. You came over when Rabbi Ben found some bugs in the house."

This was all for Ben's benefit, so he smiled. Miryam listened for a few minutes, periodically making small sounds to show that she was still on the line.

"Oh, thanks for asking, Officer Don Novello, but I'm kind of engaged right now," she said. "Yes, to be married. With a ring and everything."

"Yes. By the way, Officer Don, did you ever find that guy who likes to dress up like a priest?"

"You found his hat, and it was all chewed to pieces?"

"Oh, sure. If I ever get disengaged, I'll give you a call, and we can go get that pizza or something."

She hung up the phone, giggling. "Officer Novello wants to jump my bones."

Ben started. "He said that?"

"No, he said he thinks I'm cute and wants to take me for kosher pizza."

"Any word on the origins of those listening devices?"

"He said he'd send me a report, but the crime lab thinks they're at least 20 years old and haven't been in working condition for a long time."

"Curiouser and curiouser."

"Father Ben, are you really, actually going to marry me?"

"If I can find the right rabbi to perform the ceremony."

"That's right. I'm a millionairess now. We can't have just any rabbi."

"So you're feeling a little better now, dearest Marita?"

"Whenever a cop asks me out, I get all tingly inside."

"One of these days, I guess, I'll have to ask you out."

"That's how the Ashkenazi do it? First they get engaged, and then they date?"

"Pretty much, yeah."

"Father Ben, do you want to jump my bones?"

"Oh, very much. But first I want to look at the rest of Shemuel's mystery box."

"You are a very strange priest, you know that?"

And they both giggled.

CHAPTER FIFTY-TWO

MIRYAM HANDED BEN ANOTHER PASSPORT. HE opened it to stare at the picture of a vigorous, mustachioed man in mid-life. According to La Republica Argentina, the passport was issued in 1968 to Señor Samuel Beneficio Camello. Visa stamps marked a dozen stops in Buenos Aires and Miami, with visits to Panama, Rio de Janeiro, Geneva and Beirut. The last entry was 1978.

"Very interesting," Ben murmured.

"This was all before I was born," Miryam said. "He never mentioned that he went to South America."

"What does Camello mean?"

"A camel."

"The Beneficent Camel. Sounds like a saloon."

"Here's the last one," Miryam said, and opened it.

"Wow," Ben said. "A French diplomatic passport! Still valid! According to this, Shemuel is Abderahim Bouteflika, born in Fez, Morocco. Two years ago, he visited Beirut, Geneva, Bahrain and Monaco. The year before, Geneva, London and Majorca."

Miryam said, "That's impossible!"

Ben said, "Miryam, when you were a child, did Shemuel ever go away?"

Miryam pursed her lips, deep in thought. "In the winter.

After Hanukah, he always left on business. He was back before Purim. My nanny, and Beneficia, took care of me. He always brought us the most amazing gifts."

Ben said, "A little while ago, when I asked about Beneficia, you said that she'd do anything for Shemuel except sleep with him. Did he have a girlfriend?"

"Tía Hadassah, his wife, died the year I was born, and I came to live here after my parents died. I think my uncle did have girlfriends, but he didn't bring them here. He often went out in the evening, and once, when I was a teenager, I asked where he was going, and he just smiled. Another time, he said that he was going to see his girlfriend, but I thought he was joking. When I asked Beneficia where he'd gone; she'd shake her head and roll her eyes."

"All that sounds perfectly normal. A man in good health, even into his 80s and 90s, might very well enjoy being with a woman now and then."

"Sex, you mean."

"Yes, sex. Like you never, ever, think about it."

Miryam giggled. "Why did you ask about this?"

Ben held out the passport. "He's got money, he's got time, he's single, why not travel? Take your girlfriend to Europe or the Middle East. Or go alone and find a new girlfriend for a few days."

"A prostitute, you mean?"

"Not necessarily. But at his age, with money to throw around, probably."

"But where would he get a passport like that? A French diplomat? My uncle?"

"He was off the grid. Officially invisible in this country. He couldn't very well apply for a U.S. passport."

"Mr. Mamrout told us that in Aleppo, Tío Shemuel knew someone who could make phony documents."

"I think Shemuel made these. I think he was the forger."

"What?"

"Remember the doctored photo of him with your father? A forger's work. He knew a forger in Aleppo, and he found another forger here? Where would he get real passports? From France, Argentina, the Soviet Union?"

Ben went on with the inventory, extracting from the accordion folder a handful of yellowing documents written in Arabic or Hebrew and a current International Driver's License in a name matching the French passport, Abderahim Bouteflika, as well as another, expired, for Samuel Beneficio Camello, and various other papers in either name. He inspected the gun, which was loaded, a German-made Walther PP, .380 caliber, manufactured in 1936. Finally, he looked at the notebook, counted thirty-seven names on several pages, followed by sequences of numbers and letters in at least three alphabets.

Ben remarked on each item; Miryam heard but no longer listened. She was years away, burrowing into her early life like some cosmic mole, viewing a phantasmagoric newsreel of her years in this house, her uncle's mysteries swimming into focus, one by one: a strange look passing between Shemuel and a visitor, an overheard fragment of a telephone conversation, nocturnal arrivals and departures heard but never seen, hushed voices at the foot of the stairs. Awakening, nude, on a stifling summer night to find an empty chair next to her bed. Shemuel on tiptoe on a chair, a tiny metal gizmo clenched between his lips as he unscrewed a light bulb, a child's stream of innocent questions answered with a single lie: business.

But now she knew that the man she'd loved and trusted and obeyed as her father's uncle, as Shemuel Benkamal, Syrian refugee, community leader, businessman, was someone else. Several someones. She ached to know whether he was indeed her father's uncle. Was her father, Isaac, even really her father?

And if Isaac, who departed from her life at such a tender age, was not her father, if his blood didn't pulse through her veins, then who was she? To whom did she belong? To what family, what clan, what race?

Miryam began to weep. "His whole life was a lie," she muttered. "Was he even really my uncle? If not, then who the hell am I?"

Ben wrapped his arms around her. "He got your father out of Syria," he said. "He gave him a good life: protected him, fed him, clothed him, sent him to college and then to medical school. And he took very good care of you: kept you safe, made sure you were healthy and educated. Does it really matter what name he was born with?"

"It does," she wailed. "It's probably stupid, but it does."

"Tell me why. How does it make you feel?"

Miryam untangled herself and stared at Ben. "It's Head-shrinker Ben now?"

"Best Friend Ben."

"I feel ... confused, lost, the opposite of grounded. If I can't believe in Tío Shemuel, or Abe Buottofuco or whatever he called himself, what can I believe in?"

"Believe in yourself. Believe in your strength, your wisdom, your patience, your capacity to grow and learn."

"That's it? I'm on my own?"

"We're all on our own. In the end, we completely depend only on our self. It's just that you discovered this so suddenly and in such a terrible way."

"What about you, Best Friend Ben?"

"I have depended on myself, and only myself, for many years. In fact, I was just about the same age as you are now when my grandparents died ..."

In his mind's eye, Ben relived the funeral. Every seat in the vast synagogue on Manhattan's Fifth Avenue, the largest in the world, was filled with a mourner. Eighteen rabbis delivered eulogies. Afterward, Ben had returned to an empty Brooklyn apartment, walked through its empty rooms in a daze, not knowing what to do, then left and never went back, paid someone to pack everything up and dispose of it. All that remained of his grandparents was a pair of graves in Jerusalem and a sealed box of pictures and papers that he had been unable to confront for almost fifteen years.

"Ben, where did you just go?"

Ben blinked and returned to Miryam's kitchen.

"Sorry. I was recalling my grandfather's death and how empty it made me feel, how powerless and alone and afraid."

"That's me, right now," Miryam said.

"You knew—Rabbi Zeev told you—that my father left when I was an infant. But did you know that my mother took her own life nine years later?"

Miryam's eyes filled, and she shook her head. "I'm so sorry," she murmured.

"I knew nothing about my father. I was told that he died in a plane crash, that he wasn't even Jewish, and nothing more except that I looked like him. My mother destroyed her wedding pictures. My grandparents ducked my questions ..."

"Miryam, forgive me. I'm being selfish. You don't need to hear this now, when you're trying to wrap your head around your own family's betrayals."

"Of course I need to hear it. Talk to me, Ben."

"You're sure?"

"Yes, yes, yes. Please. Tell me how you got yourself back together."

"It's a process. My grandparents were old. I'd kind of expected that they'd die. Still, when my grandfather, especially, went, it was a shock. But I had Rachel, my wife, to help me through it. Then, bang! She's gone. It was a long time, several years, before I could come to terms with that. I had friends that I could turn to for advice, but when it came to the big issues—where would I live, what would I do with my life, what kind of person did I want to be, who was I in context with the rest of my world—I was alone, a solo act. For every issue, important or trivial, I was on my own. Then I learned that I had the virus, H.I.V., and I had to learn to take care of myself in other ways. There was no one else. So I did. I do. I don't look for others to solve my problems. It's up to me. And it wasn't until I could dispassionately recognize myself in that context, accept that it was counterproductive to surrender to anger or self pity, that I gradually found it easier to cope."

Rachel said, "Is it still hard for you?"

"Sometimes. Yes. But one night about a month ago, out in California, I was running through a Jewish cemetery—"

"Wait! Running through a cemetery at night?"

"A very long story. I was helping a synagogue that—never mind, I'll tell you all about it another time. The point is, I came across my father's grave."

Miryam gasped. "What?"

"We have the same name. Same legal name. I don't know about the Hebrew. So when I saw my name on a tombstone in a Jewish cemetery, it stopped me. I thought for a moment that in some freakish way I'd found my own grave.

"I'd gotten to know some police out there. They showed me my father's criminal record. He was a terrible man, a thief who preyed on Jews."

"That's what Jake Cassin was going on about? That was all true?"

"My father didn't die in a plane crash. That was a lie that my grandfather told me. Told everyone, I guess. My father was a lifelong swindler and con man. Specialized in synagogues. And he was Jewish. Another lie."

"How terrible for you!"

Ben said, "You're the first person I've ever told about this."

Miryam took Ben's hand. "Who could imagine that a rabbi dressed as a priest leaps into my back yard, steals my heart, and it turns out that he lost both parents in childhood, was raised by old people and then discovered that his family had hidden a shameful secret from him," she said. "You're just like me. We must belong together."

"There's more," Ben said. "After I found my father's grave, I learned that he'd died only the year before. He had a nice tombstone. There were pebbles on it. I realized that somebody must have put that up for him; someone must have arranged his funeral, left the stones to mark their visit. So I went looking. A couple of weeks ago, just before I came to New York this time, I discovered that I have a sister and a brother."

"Amazing!" Miryam said.

"Half-sister, half-brother. Three different mothers. And they resemble me. In fact, my sister freaked out when I turned up because I look so much like our father.

"But Miryam, this is very strange. When I went to see Rabbi Zeev—he knew my grandparents and me as a child—he at first mistook me for my grandfather."

Miryam sighed. "He's so old. Sometimes, he doesn't recognize people right away."

Ben shook his head. "That's not it. He quickly corrected himself. But he insists that I strongly resemble my grandfather of fifty years ago, when he was about my age now. But how can that be? I'm certain that my grandfather was my mother's father."

"I don't understand."

"How can I be a dead ringer for both my father and my mother's father? How could my mother have a child with someone who looked just like her own father?"

Miryam said, "Unless—is it possible that your mother and father were ..."

"Siblings," Ben whispered, "which would make me a *mamzer*, a child of incest, forever impure, forever barred from marriage to a Jewish woman."

CHAPTER FIFTY-THREE

———

MIRYAM SHOOK HER HEAD, SPEECHLESS. A TEAR trickled down her cheek.

Ben said, "That last part, the possibility that I might be a *mamzer*? I've only began to suspect it for a few days."

Miryam found her voice. "There must be another explanation, has to be. And I know you well enough now to believe that you'll find it."

"You think so?"

"You can't be a *mamzer*. But even if you are, even if we can never have a Jewish wedding, I want to be with you."

"Miryam, do you understand that the children of a *mamzer* are also *mamzers*, and their children as well, and so forth, for ten generations or more?"

"Yes. I want to have your children. I want to grow old sleeping next to you."

Ben reached over and took her face gently between both hands. "I can't tell you—I don't have the words—it amazes me and overwhelms me that you feel that. Especially for somebody that's never even been past first base."

"We could go upstairs and have all the home runs you want," Miryam said, "right now."

"We've been over this. H.I.V. League rules: We must go see

the team doctor, do the tests, before we can pick up our balls and bats. But what I wanted to say, what I need to tell you, is that even if it's okay to play ball in a way that won't infect you—besides Jewish law and ancient incest taboos, if I'm actually a *mamzer*, there are very good reasons to avoid having children."

"Like what?"

"Incest greatly increases the chances that a child will have one of a bunch of really terrible genetic diseases that pop up among the Ashkenazi much more often than in other populations."

"For example, Doctor Ben?"

"Tay-Sachs, cystic fibrosis, Gaucher's, Niemann-Pick— there are about a dozen, I think, each more terrible than the last. The genetics are well-known. If my parents—"

"—Ben, that's it!"

"What?"

"That's the answer. Have your DNA tested. Maybe they can tell if you have any of those genetic markers."

Ben smiled. "And if my parents were closely related. What time is it?"

Miryam craned her head to look at a wall clock. "A little after noon."

"It's Monday. I might be able to catch my doctor before he meets with the head of hematology."

"You know your doctor's daily schedule?" Miryam asked.

"He's a close friend and my classmate at M.I.T. The head of hematology, Brad Cho, was his classmate in med school. They have lunch every Monday."

"You went to M.I.T. before you became a rabbi?"

"The calculus is excellent preparation for the Talmud."

"Doctor Ben, Father Ben, Professor Ben, Jason Bourne Ben—and before that, Nerd Ben?"

"That's me."

Ben pulled out his iPhone and thumbed his speed dial. To his surprise, Bert Epstein picked up on the second ring.

"Hey Ben," he said. "I've just got a minute before Brad gets here. How's it going?"

"Still a puzzle," Ben said.

"I know, you can't talk about it. What can you talk about?"

"DNA. Is it possible to look at human DNA and determine whether an individual's parents were closely related: siblings, cousins, mother-son?"

"You're asking about consanguinity? Incest? Whether it's possible to determine from DNA whether a particular individual was born of an incestuous relationship?"

"Exactly."

"Well, it would be simple if you also had the DNA of that individual's parents."

"Let's say, for the purpose of this hypothetical, that I don't and can't get it."

"Ben, you've stumped me. I'll ask around for you and, when I get a half-hour or so, do a quick search of the literature."

"At your early convenience, and thanks."

"My pleasure. Here's Brad. Gotta go. See you soon?"

"A few weeks, maybe sooner."

Ben hung up and shook his head. "He'll check for me."

"In the meantime, Rabbi Ben, maybe you could apply your Talmudic training to the subject."

Ben looked mystified. "The Talmud says nothing about DNA."

"How tall was your mother? What color was her hair? Did she look like your grandmother?"

Ben smiled. "Of course. My mother was … I don't know how tall she was. I was a kid when she died. She was a grownup. My grandparents were grownups. They were big, I was small."

"What about her hair?"

"Bubbe, my grandmother, had gray hair. Mom's was kind of a reddish blonde."

Ben and Miryam looked at each other for a long moment.

"This isn't helping," Ben said. "But you're right. Let me look at the problem like a rabbi would. Could my grandfather have had two children, a boy and a girl, and not tell me that I had an uncle? Or my mother—could she have failed to tell me that she had a brother?"

"If there was some reason why you shouldn't know about him."

"That reason could only be something shameful. But, if he had a son who did something so shameful that he couldn't talk about it, that would probably be …"

"Incest," Miryam finished.

"But if I was the child of incest, wouldn't an ethical man, a highly respected scholar admired for his saintliness, wouldn't a man like that tell his grandson that he was a child of incest?"

"He would, except—"

"—if he feared that it would ruin his own reputation," Ben finished.

They looked at each other again. "We're right back where we started. Incest is such a terrible taboo that some people would do anything to avoid it."

"Wait," Miryam said. "What about your birth certificate? Wouldn't it list your mother's maiden name?"

"That's another clue. It's illegible."

"How could it be illegible?"

"The original form was badly erased and something written over it. What I have, at home, is a photocopy, and her maiden name is impossible to read."

For the third time in ten minutes, they stared at each other.

Finally, Ben said, "This is a waste of time. The answer is in my DNA and in a box of pictures and papers that I've been waiting to open for fifteen years."

"Waiting for what?"

"For a good reason to delve into my family history. And now I have one."

CHAPTER FIFTY-FOUR

B EN SAID, "THE SOONER I CAN FINISH WHAT I CAME here for, the sooner I can go home and look through that box of pictures and stuff. You up for more of Shemuel's stash?"

"Let's do it," Miryam agreed.

The kitchen phone rang again, and she jumped up to answer it. After a few minutes, she laughed and hung up.

"That was Deb again. Are we going for dinner tonight?"

"Sure."

"She said that I should wear my Hamsa. And that's weird, because nobody's ever mentioned it before."

"Anything special about it?"

"Only that my uncle had it made in Tel Aviv and gave it to me after my parents died. It's a miniature of the one my grandmother wore."

"The one in the picture you showed me?"

"Exactly."

Ben scratched his head. "Anything else?"

"I could go get it?"

"While you're at it, could I look at the amulet? The one Mr. Mamrout gave you?

Miryam went upstairs, and Ben returned to the stack of papers he'd taken from the accordion file. The first brought a smile to his lips.

"What's so funny?" Miryam asked as she returned.

Ben unfolded a parchment and set it in front of Miryam. "Know what this is?"

Miryam started to read, then squealed with joy.

"It's a ketubah! My grandparents' wedding contract!"

"On the 15th of Shevat, in the year 5702 according to the Hebrew Calendar, a marriage contract between Yitzchak Benkamal of Aleppo and Naomi Moshon of Damascus is made. The groom will provide the bride's family with a she-camel no more than two years old ... The bride is to supply her own bedding and clothing for every season for one year ..."

Miryam smiled. "So my grandfather's name was Yitzchak, or Isaac, the same as my father. I never knew that, because my father could recall only his mother's name."

"No Ashkenazi family would ever name a child after a living person. It's considered bad luck for the one whom the baby is named after."

"And you say that the Sephardi are superstitious?"

"Point taken. It's human nature, I guess. That's probably why the Torah warns us against it in Dvarim—Deuteronomy. And, ironically, that's the only one of the Five Books of Moses that isn't missing from the Codex."

"Just to prove that I have no superstitious beliefs, I'm going to name our first child after you."

"Don't I have something to say about that?"

"Of course. We'll have several children and name them Father Ben, Sister Agatha, His Eminence Dolan—like that."

Ben couldn't help laughing. It was good to see that Miryam's spirits had lifted.

"What do you make of the reference to a she-camel in the ketubah? Is there any significance to that and the fact that Benkamal might be translated as "son of a camel'?"

"My uncle told me that, before the Expulsion of 1492, when my ancestors lived in Spain, the family raised camels for the Sultan of Granada."

Miryam shrugged. She handed him her Hamsa, which was on a silver chain.

Ben peered at it closely, and then smiled. "Did you know that there's a camel in this design?"

"No! Where?"

Ben turned the pendant around until it faced Miryam and, with the tip of a pen, traced a gold thread woven into the design. "That's the profile of a dromedary," he said. "Elongated, stylized."

Miryam smiled. "Now I see it!"

Ben said, "I just thought of something," and pulled out his iPhone. "My Jewish calendar app."

"Well, sure. Today, you're pretending to be some kind of rabbi, right?"

"The kind who must buy every app," Ben said, and thumbed in Shevat 15, 5702.

"Ah ha," he mumbled. "Miryam, my love, what if I could tell you the menu for your grandparent's wedding feast?"

"That's some app."

"Class, who can name the Shivat Haminim, the seven types of agricultural products for which the ancient land of Israel was famous?"

Miryam raised her hand and waved it. "Professor! Rabbi! Me! I know them! Wheat and barley, grapes, figs and dates, olives and ... pomegranates?"

"A gold star for little Miryam. Next, February 2, 1942, corresponds to Shevat 15, 5702, which was—"

"My grandparents got married on Tu b'shevat? The New Year of Trees?"

"It's considered a very auspicious day for marriage. In Deuteronomy—I'd have to look up the verse—we are told that 'a man is akin to the tree of the field.' So their wedding feast would also have been a Tu b'shevat seder, a formal dinner with storytelling and prayer, at which the seven species of ancient Israel were served."

"You see how this must be *beshert?* If you hadn't leaped into my back yard, I might never have found this, and I certainly wouldn't have known to look up the date."

Ben said, "One thing bothers me. Shemuel had your Hamsa made in Israel?"

"So he said."

"There's no Israeli entry visa stamp in any of those passports. He must have done it over the Internet or through a local jewelry store."

"My uncle never used a computer. But his friend Mr. Kelsi was a jeweler."

"Still in business?"

"He died a few years ago. I was in high school. His children run the business."

"It might be interesting to look at your grandmother's wedding photo under a magnifying glass and see whether there's a camel in her Hamsa."

"We don't have a magnifying glass."

Ben held up his iPhone. "Get the photo."

When she left, Ben took a letter from the accordion file. Postmarked Haifa and dated June 1997, it was written in a shaky, old-fashioned German hand that Ben found difficult to follow. But German is somewhat like Yiddish, which Ben could sometimes follow. German also has many words similar to English; Ben understood enough to realize that Miryam should not see it until he could get an accurate translation.

Miryam returned with the photo. "Take it out of the frame?" she asked.

"Not necessary," Ben replied. He laid it on the kitchen counter, and then used his iPhone camera, zooming in on the Hamsa. He showed the picture to Miryam.

"Can you zoom in more?"

"Oddly, there's an app for that," he said, and touched the screen to bring it up. The image was pixilated but clear enough to see the delicate filigree outline of a camel.

"Wow," Miryam said, "Whoever made mine did a very good job. Do you want to look at the amulet now?"

Ben took the silver cylinder, turned it over in his fingers, looking for way to open it. "There," he said, "If you look closely, it's been soldered, and then brushed smooth. So there might be something inside. It might be better to let Chana's people open this."

"Okay. When are you going over there?"

"Maybe tomorrow morning, if that works for her. I'll text her."

"Anything else to look at in the file?"

"I think so, but I'm getting a little antsy. Can I take you to lunch?"

"I thought you said you were antsy, not hungry?"

"We'll go for a walk along 13th Avenue, and that will cure my antsy, and then I'll be really hungry."

"Too bad we can't play a few innings of baseball. That's always good for antsy."

"As soon as I'm off the Disabled List, you can get season tickets."

"I'll go change clothes. Would you put all that stuff away in the office?"

"Go," said Ben. As soon as he heard Miryam on the stairs,

he laid the German letter flat on the kitchen counter and took out his phone. Steadying himself, he took a picture, and then returned it to the accordion file with the rest of Shemuel's mysteries.

CHAPTER FIFTY-FIVE

D ETECTIVE MARKO CALLED JUST AS BEN AND Miryam were sitting down to salads in a sparkling new Italian deli on 13th Avenue. Ben excused himself and went back outside to take the call in the shade of the sidewalk awning. He leaned against the cool brick and listened to Marko talk about several leads the NYPD was pursuing.

"Then you actually have no idea where to find Steinberg?" Ben asked.

"Not yet. But Hizzoner the Mayor dug around in his other pants and came up with some spare change for a reward."

Across the street, a city bus pulled away from the curb, revealing a short, burly, bearded man in a Sikh turban sitting on a bus bench with a backpack in his lap. There was something familiar about him, Ben realized, very familiar.

"How much is the reward?" Ben asked.

"A million," Marko replied. "It was on TV about an hour ago."

"And this is for what?"

"Information leading to the arrest and conviction of the person or persons responsible for the murder of Detective Leonard Wise, the usual boilerplate."

"God bless billionaires who love being mayor."

"You said it, Rabbi."

"Listen, Detective: I'm outside an Italian Deli called Furillo's on 13th Avenue, and I'm pretty sure that Yevgeny Steinberg is across the street sitting on a bus bench."

"This is no time to kid around."

"He's wearing a turban, like Sikhs do, and he's got a beard, but I'd bet my life that it's Steinberg. I'd also bet that he wants me to see him, that he wants me to go back inside and grab Miryam and go out through the kitchen and into the alley, where I'll also bet his pal is waiting. Which is about how it went down the last time we played this game."

Marko said, "If this is a joke—"

Ben said, "No joke. I'm going back inside and let him watch me eat my salad."

"We'll have someone there in five."

"Right behind the bus stop is a hair salon called Helene's. You might want to send a couple of guys in through the back door. The southbound bus just left, so I'd put a couple of plain-clothes guys on the next one, which is maybe ten or twelve minutes out, and when they get off the bus, have the officers in the salon come out and join the party."

"You should have been a cop. Anything else I oughta know?"

"Don't forget the guy in the alley. He might have done the wet work in the hotel."

Marko said, "I sure hope this isn't a wild goose chase."

"Me, too," Ben said. He went back inside; before sitting down with Miryam in the half-empty deli, he asked the waitress to move them to a window table.

As they dug into their salads, Ben consulted his wristwatch. When five minutes had gone by, he took out his iPhone and showed Miryam how to shoot video with it. A few minutes later, as a southbound bus came into view, Ben handed her the phone.

"The show is about to start," he said.

"What are you talking about?"

"Look across the street. When that bus pulls away, start shooting video. Just let it roll until you're sure it's all over."

"Director Ben, have you lost your mind?"

"Start shooting now," Ben said, getting to his feet.

"Where are you going?"

"Not far," Ben said.

He picked up a chair and positioned himself near the kitchen door. A moment later, a man with a gun ran through the door and shoved a waitress aside.

Both feet planted, Ben twisted his hips and swung the chair at shoulder level. The wooden chair flew into pieces. The man tumbled backwards. The gun skidded across the floor. Ben stepped on the gun and put his other foot on the man's crotch.

Ben said, "Don't even try to get up."

The man tried to sit up, and Ben stood on his crotch, evoking a scream.

Officer Novello, in the same cheap suit he'd worn to the Benkamal home, came through the kitchen door, his badge clipped to his collar, gripping a gun in both hands. Right behind him came three more officers similarly equipped.

Novello said, "What are you doing here?"

Ben said, "You should try the salads. Everything's fresh. They're really excellent."

"Is that your gun?" Novello snarled.

"No. I accidentally stepped on it while I was trying to help this man up."

"Why is he lying on the floor?"

"I might have hit him with a chair."

"Looks like assault and battery, possession of an unregistered firearm, and criminal vandalism," Novello said. "You're under arrest."

A bulky man with a receding hairline and clad in immaculate cook's whites stepped out from behind the counter and shouted something in Italian to Novello that evoked titters from the two middle-aged waitresses. Novello's face flushed deep red.

Marko pushed open the front door. "We got him!" he announced. "What's all this?"

Ben said, "Officer Novello here is just about to arrest Steinberg's accomplice."

"Good work, Novello," Marko said.

Ben put a pair of hundred-dollar bills on a table and turned to the man in whites. "I'm very sorry that I broke your chair."

"It's okay, it's okay. And that was the sweetest swing I've seen in Brooklyn since the Duke of Flatbush went west," the counterman said. "You and your lady come back and try one of my hero sandwiches, on me."

Ben smiled. "I'm sure we'll be back."

"Hey, what's your name?"

"Ben."

"Just Ben? That's it?"

"Rabbi Ben."

"Hey, you're the guy kicked that punk's ass over on Flatbush Avenue, right?"

Marko put a hand on Ben's shoulder. "I need you to come down to the station and I.D. these two—for the record."

Ben turned to leave, and the deli owner called out, "Hey, I'm gonna name one of my hero sandwiches after you."

"I hope it's kosher," Ben said.

CHAPTER FIFTY-SIX

BEN SAID, "MIRYAM'S COMING WITH US."
Marko shrugged, and held the door as they climbed into
the back seat.

As they pulled away from the curb, Foster at the wheel,
Ben leaned forward and tapped Marko's shoulder. "It'll be
tough to convict those guys of killing Wise," he said.

"You're right, Rabbi," Marko replied. "And the guy we just
nabbed says his name is Raghubir Sikh."

"Oh, sure. A few days ago when he left the hotel, he was
clean shaven."

"Oh, no worries on that score. We'll print him and pull his
beard off."

"Do you have enough to put him away?"

Marko shook his head, no. "You saw Steinberg leave the
hotel, but not his accomplice, and the guys who killed Wise in
the hospital wore surgical masks. We've got Steinberg's palm
print on a newspaper that a kid says your computer was
wrapped in, but any halfway smart lawyer can turn that into
coincidence. Everything else is circumstantial: no murder
weapon, no witnesses and no provable motive."

"I might have a few things that could help you build a
lesser charge against them. Maybe a way towards getting them

310

to talk, maybe lead you to evidence that could make murder charges stick."

"Shoot."

"Miryam told me that, one night last winter, somebody threw a McDonald's cup over the fence of her uncle's house to land on the stoop. The closest McDonald's is six blocks, so this was no accident. The liquid in the cup freezes; next morning, Beneficia, her uncle's housekeeper, goes to get the newspaper, slips on the ice, fractures her skull.

"She dies; a few days later, the uncle is in a supermarket, and this pretty, 40ish woman stops him and says she's looking for a job, does he know anybody who needs a housekeeper. He hires her, but a couple of weeks later, he catches her in his locked office, trying to get into the locked desk."

"Sounds like a Gypsy scam," Marko said. "A long con to siphon off his assets."

"Exactly. So Miryam's uncle, Shemuel, kicks this woman out. A few months later, he's walking to the library when a skateboarder, a big teenager, knocks him down and keeps going. Shemuel falls, hits his head, fractures his skull. Four days later, he's dead, too."

"More and more like a Gypsy con," Marko said. "They didn't want to kill him; they wanted to break a leg or fracture a hip so they could get someone into the house."

"That's pretty much the way I saw it," Ben said.

"So then what?"

"They've got months invested in Shemuel, so they won't want to walk away. Miryam flies in from California, finds an old Torah, which might be priceless. She locks it in the safe. While she and the neighbors are at her uncle's funeral, somebody takes the back door off its hinges, does the same number on the office, and takes the safe. I'm guessing, but I'd say it was the same gang that killed Beneficia and Shemuel."

"Where do you fit into this?" Marko asked. "For real?"

"The Jewish Museum in Manhattan asked me to try to find this Torah, which, if it's what they think it is, belongs in a museum," Ben said.

"You came looking for that, and you two hooked up? That's what happened?"

Miryam blushed. "We haven't actually hooked up," she said. "Though it's not for my lack of trying. Ben is kind of old-fashioned that way."

"You're a better man than I," Marko said, with a smirk.

"No comment," Ben said, and Foster, behind the wheel, burst into laughter.

"Anyway," Ben continued, "in that safe were some gold coins, some papers, and that Torah. But probably they don't know what to with a Torah, so—"

"So they sell it to Steinberg and his crew. Torah 'nappers from way back."

"Exactly. But Steinberg is also a kidnapper and an extortionist. And he's been in Brooklyn long enough to have some idea who old Shemuel was: one of the wealthiest and most respected members of the Syrian Jewish community. If there's one priceless Torah, then there might be another. Or some other valuables. So he tries to break into the house again. They follow Miryam to Rabbi Zeev's and find out he's the most important rabbi in the community. Then I show up. They don't know who I am or what I'm about, so they follow me. I stupidly act like I'm trying to hide something and run, which makes them want to watch me even more. When I'm away for the night, they try to break into her house again."

"That was the night I arrested you," Marko said.

"One more thing," Ben said. "It's got to do with how this con might have been set up in the first place. But I think Miryam should talk about this. Are you okay with that, sweetie?"

"That's the first time you ever called me 'sweetie,'" she said. "Got to make a mental note that it happened in the back of a cop car on the way down to the station house. Just in case someday our kids ask."

Everyone laughed.

"My uncle, Shemuel Benkamal, was a very private guy," Miryam began. "No, let me start over. My Ben isn't such a funny man. He's got a sense of humor, but he doesn't tell a lot of jokes. But he has other... qualities. I guess you could say he gets his Sherlock Holmes freak on. A lot. So when we were talking about how my uncle and his housekeeper died, and he explained what a Gypsy con was, we sort of wondered out loud about how someone would go about finding an old, rich guy to scam. Because my uncle, he wasn't one to flaunt his money. He kept a low profile. Just one of the neighborhood geezers.

"So we tried to game it out backward, and we decided that, if you were the kind of person who went around looking to prey on old folks, then you might get a job with the census department..."

Marko said, "That's brilliant, Ms. Benkamal. And that gives us something to run down. I'm sure the Feds have records on who they hired to do interviews in your uncle's neighborhood, and their supervisors, anyone who might have had access to the raw data."

"One more thing," Ben said. "Neither of the guys you just nabbed should hear the word 'cop killer' from anyone. Let them think you're working the Gypsy con, looking to recover the safe and the Torah. You can threaten to charge them for the murders of Shemuel and Beneficia. Get a search warrant and find that Torah, which might have some fingerprints that would tie them to the Gypsy scam or help I.D. the guys who killed Miryam's uncle."

"Like I said on the phone, you shoulda been a cop," Marko

said. "Maybe they'll give us the Gypsy con guys for a pass on receiving stolen property. Then we come back at them with murder charges."

"Which puts them deeper into the original con and gives you a shot at playing Steinberg against the guy who came into the deli waving a gun," Ben added.

"Gave his name as Soper. George Soper. Did Novello really deck him?"

"I'll show you the video," Miryam said. "Ben hit him with a chair, and he went down like the Titanic."

"You were supposed to be shooting the action across the street," Ben said.

"By the time the bus got out of the way, that Steinberg guy was face down on the sidewalk," Miryam explained. "There was nothing to see. All the action was in the deli."

"At first, I thought he was Steinberg's boss," Ben said. "Now I think it's the other way around: It's Steinberg who goes around wearing all different disguises."

Miryam said, "How did Ben know he would come in through the kitchen?"

Marko said, "Your boyfriend here was two steps ahead of those guys. On the phone, he told me that he thought maybe Steinberg had a guy in the alley to intercept you kids if you tried to escape through the back door."

Ben said, "The precinct house is two blocks away. The police have no time to formulate a fancy plan, so they put a car at either end to seal off the alley. Where does that leave somebody waiting for us? He's going to try to escape through the deli."

Marko said, "You're handy with your fists and feet. Why'd you hit him with a chair?"

"Same reason that you arrest a rape suspect with a dozen guys. I wanted it over before someone got hurt or killed. And I forgot to bring a baseball bat."

Miryam said, "And besides that, he only gets to play baseball with me."

CHAPTER FIFTY-SEVEN

———————

MIRYAM BRUSHED IMAGINARY LINT FROM BEN'S sports jacket, and then rang the bell. The door flew open, and they were welcomed into a bright, air-conditioned room where Deb's parents, Perlita and Eduardo HaCohen, greeted Ben effusively and kissed him on both cheeks as if he was some long-lost friend instead of a man they'd met for the first time the previous evening. Miryam got the same welcome, plus a hug from Perlita.

Tall, elegantly blonde and just beginning to show the wear and tear of living almost five decades and raising two children, Perlita beckoned toward the sofa. A shorter, plumper and somewhat older version of herself got up and hurried over.

"This is my cousin Malka," Perlita said. "She's visiting from Buenos Aries."

"I am so pleased to meet you both," Malka said, smiling, in heavily accented English. "But I am not the surprise. This way, please."

She led them down a hallway to a dimly lit bedroom where a tiny, wizened woman in a wheelchair sat watching a Spanish-language television program. "This is Tía Fruma, my mother's younger sister," Malka said.

"Her ophthalmologist came to New York to teach for one

year—a new procedure that he developed—and Tía Fruma is now recovering from that procedure, to repair her retina," Malka continued. "She must be away from bright light for two more days. We will fly home very early tomorrow morning, in order to land in darkness."

Fruma looked up and said something in what Ben took to be Argentine Spanish.

Malka said, "She speaks only Spanish, Ladino and Arabic. She asks that we all come closer, but especially Miryam."

Miryam knelt on the carpet next to the wheelchair, and Fruma raised a remote and fumbled with it until the television set went off. She peered at Miryam closely, as though trying to examine her face in minute detail. Then she looked at Miryam's Hamsa, fingered it, touched her own brooch; it seemed identical to Miryam's, except larger. It was, Ben realized, about the same size as the one Cindy had worn to the party.

"My eyes are not so good, but there is nothing wrong with my memory," Fruma said, with Malka translating for Ben. "You, child—you look so much like my baby sister, Naomi. And your Hamsa is like the one I gave her, but smaller. Tell me your name?"

"Miryam," she replied, in a tremulous voice.

"And your father's name?" Fruma asked.

"My father, of blessed memory, died when I was little. His name was Yitzchak, Isaac."

"What was his father's name, child?" Malka translated.

"The same as his own, Yitzchak."

"I am from Damascus," Fruma said. "I am a Moshon; my sister Naomi married Yitzchak Benkamal of Aleppo in 1942. Their chuppah, or wedding canopy, was on the 15th day of Shevat, and the wedding feast was a Tu b'shevat seder attended by more than 500 guests."

Miryam burst into tears and stood to embrace Fruma. "You are my grandmother's sister," she sobbed. "I thought that I had no family left at all."

Ben put an arm around Miryam's shoulders.

After several minutes, she stood up and kissed Fruma.

With Malka translating, Fruma asked, "How did you come to be here, in New York? Are your grandparents still alive?"

Miryam said, "I don't know what became of my grandparents. My father came here as a young boy, with his uncle Shemuel. Tío Shemuel died last week. I always believed that my father's parents disappeared in the Farhud."

"No. That is not right," Fruma said.

Miryam said, "When was the last time you saw your sister, Auntie?"

"A few days after the Farhud, Naomi and Yitzchak came to Damascus with their little boy. Their house had been burned and looted, but they were not injured. They wanted to leave Syria, but they had no passports, no documents. The Arabs didn't want Jews to go to Palestine. Everyone thought it would soon become Israel. But Yitzchak thought that, if he could get to Amman, in Transjordan, it would be easy to find a way to Jerusalem. So my husband found someone who made false documents."

Ben said, "A forger?"

Malka said, "Yes, what we call un fraguador," and Fruma nodded her head vigorously. "Yes, a forger. From this man, they got Syrian passports, under Arab names. And he also found someone to take them to the Golan, above the Galilee. Transjordan was just to the south. My husband and I wanted to leave, too; even before the Farhud, there was no future for Jews in Syria, but there was no place to go. If Palestine would again be Jewish... now there was some hope, you see?"

Miryam said, "Why didn't you go with them?"

"I was six months' pregnant, a difficult time for me, so my husband decided to go with Naomi and Yitzchak as far as the border. Later, after the baby came, we would join them in Jerusalem. Or so we thought."

Suddenly, Fruma began to weep. "I have outlived three husbands," she said through Malka. "My first was also a Benkamal, a cousin of my sister's husband. His name was Shemuel."

A chill ran down Ben's spine.

Miryam reached out to embrace Fruma again. "Why are you crying, Tía?"

"Because Shemuel never came back," she cried. "The police said they found his body in the river, the Euphrates River, near a little town, Abu Kamal. They said that he drowned trying to get into Syria from Iraq, that he carried a false passport, that he was a Zionist spy. But how can I believe that? He left from Damascus with my sister and her husband to go south, to Amman. Abu Kamal is hundreds of miles east, in the desert. And why would he have a British passport? It doesn't make sense, even now."

Ben said, "Please, was your husband a very tall man?"

Fruma listened to Malka translate, and then shook her head. "No, no, he was a chato, a shrimp. Like you! All the Benkamal men are short."

Ben said, "Fruma, did you ever meet this forger?"

"No, no," she replied. "Yitzchak and Shemuel did all that."

Miryam turned to Ben, "What do you make of all this?"

"I'm not sure," Ben said. "It sounds... It's a lot to consider. Let me think it through a few times."

"My dear child, we must leave tonight," Fruma said. "You must come to Buenos Aries. You have many, many cousins there. Everyone will be so glad to see you."

"I will come, Tía Fruma," Miryam said, her eyes glistening. "Very soon."

CHAPTER FIFTY-EIGHT

M IRYAM SAID, "BEN. I LIED TO YOU, AND I'M VERY sorry."

Ben stopped and turned to face her. They were only steps from the HaCohen home, and the sodium vapor glare of nearby streetlights bathed them in a strange, other-worldly scrim of orange shadow and light.

"What are you talking about?"

"The day we met. When you jumped into the yard dressed as a priest and I told you that I was engaged to David."

"That wasn't true?"

"Do you hate me? For lying to you?"

"Of course not."

"I was engaged to David. I broke it off last winter, when Beneficia died. I wanted to come for her funeral, and I wanted him with me to meet Shemuel. David had something planned for that weekend, something that didn't include me, and he wouldn't come, and he wouldn't tell me what it was. We argued about it, and in the end I didn't go to the funeral, either. It turned out that his big, important event was a poker game. He was a selfish schmuck, and I dumped him.

"When you showed up, a strange man dressed as a priest but claiming he was a rabbi, I didn't think too clearly. I was a little afraid of you. I wanted you to think that I wasn't alone, that I had a man. So I lied."

Ben looked disconsolate. "This is quite a blow to my masculinity, Miryam," he said. "I've been telling myself that I'm a smoking hot, macho superstar hero who got this supermodel to break up with her fiancé less than twenty-four hours after meeting me."

"You're teasing me, right?"

"Only a little. Miryam, none of this matters now. Neither of us is the same person we were even a week ago. I really fought against this, but your womanly wiles were just too much for me. I have come to love you fiercely. I believe that you love me."

"I'm crazy about you, Father Ben. But everything I thought I knew about my Uncle Shemuel—it's all lies. He was evil! I don't want us to start what I hope is the rest of our lives together with a lie. I don't want lies between us, not ever."

"You had me at 'Father Ben.' But I'm not sure what you mean about Shemuel."

"You heard her. Tía Fruma. My grandparents didn't disappear in the Farhud the way Shemuel said. Their house was burned, and they went to Damascus with their baby. With my father. Fruma's husband, Shemuel, got a forger to get them passports and someone to guide them across the border. Instead, he takes them in the wrong direction, hundreds of miles away, into the desert, into Iraq. Fruma's husband 'drowns' in the Euphrates River with a phony British passport in his pocket.

"Then we find that my Shemuel has a stack of phony passports, a doctored picture of himself and my father. Don't you get it, Ben? Can't you connect the dots?"

"I've been thinking about it nonstop through dinner. And I think you're probably right. I think your grandparents couldn't wait to get out of Syria. Maybe they were carrying important scrolls, perhaps part of the Codex, from the Aleppo synagogue. So instead of waiting, instead of trying to get to South America or the U.S., they tried to get their sacred treasure to Jerusalem, where they thought it would be safe.

"I think Fruma's husband found a forger, and he offered to take your grandparents to Amman. Instead, he took them and your uncle into the desert. Maybe he drugged them. Then he either killed them or abandoned them. Before that happened, he elicited enough information from them to pass himself off in Aleppo as Shemuel Benkamal from Damascus. He took their baby to give himself credence and as a means to convince Aleppo Jews to give him money, to enable him to leave Syria. Or something like that. Is that what you think?"

"What else could it be?"

"I'm not sure of anything. It sounds possible, a logical extension of the facts. But then let's not forget, he wasn't all bad: He raised your father, he took care of you."

"But it was all an act, part of his cover story."

"I wouldn't be so hard on him. We don't know everything yet. There are more papers in that mystery folder that we should look at."

Miryam moved next to Ben and surrounded him with her arms. "You have such a good heart, Rabbi Ben. On the days when I actually believe in God, I'm sure He sent you to help me get over being raised by Shemuel or Daud Khan whatever the hell his real name was."

"On the days when I actually believe in God, I believe that you are my earthly reward for all that She expects of me in the world to come," Ben said. He showered kisses on her face, hugged her and held her for a long time.

Miryam said, "What are we going to do now?"

"It's still early. Let's go back to the house and see what else is in that folder."

BEN HAD BARELY OPENED THE folder when he heard Miryam calling. He laid it carefully on the kitchen table and ran upstairs in time to see himself in an Italian deli standing on a man's chest. The shaky video cut to another scene, Ben leveling Jake Cassin in another restaurant, and then a final cut, him cradling Detective Wise's head in his lap, his finger still poked inside his neck. A breathless announcer invited anyone who knew the identity of the "YouTube Rabbi" to contact the station for a cash reward.

With all three clips looping the background, viewers were treated to a round-table discussion by a trio of talking heads speculating on whether the NYPD had a secret undercover weapon or whether the "YouTube Rabbi" was an out-of-control vigilante.

Ben's phone rang, and he turned it off.

"Obviously, there was another cell phone with video in the deli," he said.

Miryam's phone rang, and then the downstairs phone rang. She made no move to answer either. "I don't know whether to laugh or cry," she said.

"There's nothing we can do about this, so let's just ignore it," Ben said.

THE NEXT MORNING, AFTER HIS run and shower, Ben sat down to bagels and soft-boiled eggs. He was on his second cup of coffee when the kitchen phone rang. Ignoring Ben's look, Miryam took the call. She spoke softly into the phone, and then hung up.

"That was Esperanza."

"Rabbi Zeev's housekeeper?"

Miryam nodded, yes. "Did you know that she's Beneficia's daughter?"

Ben shook his head. "I don't know much about her at all, except that she's very protective of Rabbi Zeev."

"That's how Beneficia was with... Shemuel, or whoever he was. Anyway, Rabbi Zeev would like to see you."

"I was going to go into Manhattan, but I can go later. Will you come with me?"

"Sorry, Rabbi Ben, but I have errands of my own to run."

"Did Esperanza say what time?"

"I think she means now."

Ben got up. "I'll brush my teeth and be off."

"Did you take your pills? Your anti-retrovirals?"

Ben smiled. It felt good to have someone concerned about his health.

"I swallowed them all before I went out on my run," he said.

Miryam frowned. "Ben, before you leave—do you speak German?"

Ben shook his head, no. "You found that letter from Haifa?"

"Yes. I want to know what it says."

"Try Brooklyn College—their modern languages department."

"It's summer."

"There's bound to be a few teachers around."

"I've got a better idea, Professor Ben."

"What's that?"

"I'll let you know if it works out."

"Maybe I'll walk part way with you? Which way you headed?"

"South, I think. And you're going east."

Ben took a final bite of his bagel. By the time he'd rinsed his dish in the sink, he heard the door lock behind Miryam.

CHAPTER FIFTY-NINE

E SPERANZA OPENED THE DOOR, FAVORED BEN WITH A hard stare, and then, still silent, led him down the hall to Rabbi Zeev's study.

"Benny!" Zeev said, and slowly, unsteadily, stood up. "Thank you for coming."

"Please, Rabbi, sit down," Ben said, taking Zeev's hand and shaking it gently.

Zeev lowered himself into an overstuffed armchair and gestured for Ben to sit beside him in a straight-backed model.

Esperanza brought iced mint tea, and Ben sipped it, waiting for Zeev to begin.

"Benny, the wonderful thing about a long life is that there are so many surprises. And the wonderful thing about a life serving our people is that sometimes those surprises also serve the Lord. But you have no idea what I'm talking about, do you?"

"My grandfather, of blessed memory, taught me to listen before asking questions."

"Ah. When you told me that you were looking for the Keter, the Codex of Aleppo, I mentioned that many years ago there had been some talk about Shemuel selling amulets, maybe some of the missing pages from the Keter. And that when Yosaif Aharoni died, his family found an amulet with a page of text that probably came from a very old sefer Torah, maybe even from the Codex."

"I recall the conversation, Rabbi. Aharoni sold men's clothing, you said."

"Yes, excellent. So I won't have to go into that again. Well, one of the advantages to being an old rabbi is that you know many younger rabbis, and on the rare occasions when you tell them something, they're inclined to listen. You understand?"

"I do, Rabbi. What did you say, and to whom did you say it?"

"Ah, right to the point and saving my time. Good. Benny, you know that I'm so old now that I won't let Esperanza buy green bananas?"

The twinkle in Zeev's eye said that he was joking. Ben laughed.

"It occurred to me, after the last time we spoke, that perhaps one or another of the rabbis in our community might have heard something about an amulet or a page from the Keter. After all, my generation, we who came from Syria, is almost gone now. Their families may have found such things without appreciating their true nature. Then I thought, why not make this a teaching opportunity, a chance for our community to look at its recent history with fresh eyes, to teach our young about the dangers of magic, why superstitious beliefs are not harmless, that they defy and diminish the word of God."

"I wish that I had had the wisdom to suggest that, Rabbi," Ben said.

"All in good time, Rabbi. You serve in other ways, and may I say, although I don't have a television set, and I have no idea what the you tube could be, I have heard that you are now a video star."

Ben laughed again. "It's just that everybody, even children, now carries a cell phone with a video camera. There's no place to hide."

"You, as well, Rabbi? You have such a device?"

Ben took out his iPhone and clicked on the video camera, then pointed it at Zeev.

"You should say something," Ben said.

"Allow me to share the good news, then. Last Shabbat, seven rabbis used their sermons to tell their congregations about magic, amulets, superstition, about the missing Keter pages. And I am pleased to tell you that many people have came forward. More than I could have imagined."

Ben turned the camera off, then hit playback and let Zeev watch himself speaking.

"It's very small," Zeev said. "And the sound isn't clear."

Ben nodded. "But good enough for television. And, there is a place on the Internet where people can post these short videos. That is called YouTube."

"Someone once tried to explain to me about the Internet. All I can visualize is an enormous Russian doll filled with some kind of information, words, pictures, movies, with a slightly smaller doll inside it and smaller one inside that. Except that it goes in both directions, infinitely smaller and infinitely larger, at the same time. And all these dolls are somehow connected to each other."

Ben suppressed a chuckle. "The internet is just a system for connecting computers, all kinds, very small ones, very big ones, in-between ones. Some are connected by phone lines, some by a much faster method called optical cable—the same thing used for cable television—some by radio waves. And every one of them can exchange information with any other one. This information, as you said, can be words, pictures, video, even music or sound. It's a wonderful tool. It's also a terrific way to waste time looking at silly things. Like fuzzy videos of me."

"Thank you, Benny, although I'm not sure I fully grasp all that."

Zeev turned and took a thick manila envelope from his desk. "There are seventeen pieces of parchment in here. From what my old eyes tell me, some might have been inscribed by the same sopher stam. But whether they are from the Keter, I can't tell."

He handed the envelope to Ben. "Each one has a tag, with the family name. They all agreed that, if their page is from an important Torah—not necessarily the Keter—then they will allow me to decide what to do with it. If not, then each will be returned."

Ben felt an immense load lift from his shoulders. "Rabbi, you have done my job for me!"

"Then I have served God," he said. "And now, before I get too tired, I want to ask you a personal question, Benny."

"Anything, Rabbi."

"What is the nature of your involvement with the Benkamal girl, Miryam? I have heard that you are to be married."

"Yes. We have chosen each other. I should tell you, one rabbi to another, that until we stand under the chuppah together, we will not be intimate. She is very young, and she has gone through several shocks, starting with her uncle's death. I cannot, will not, ever take advantage of her. So we are engaged, and I will make sure that we delay our marriage until Miryam has ample opportunity to change her mind. But I hope that she doesn't change it, because she's a wonderful woman and I love her."

Zeev beamed. "I am happy for you," he said. "Esperanza has known Miryam since she was a baby. When she heard that you stay in her house, she was concerned."

"I'll ask Miryam to call her."

As if on cue, Esperanza appeared. "Rabbi Zeev must rest

now," she said, and ushered Ben, clutching the big envelope, out the front door. It was only when the door had closed behind him that he realized that he still had unfinished business with Rabbi Zeev.

———oooOooo———

WALKING BACK TO MIRYAM'S HOME, Ben pulled out his phone and glanced at the missed calls list: three calls from Chana, two each from Detective Marko and Bert Epstein, one from Rabbi Dibbo in Eatontown. Next, he checked his email and was chagrined to find one or more messages forwarded from his Gmail account from each of nine different television news departments and the New York Post. Each asked him to contact them immediately. He realized that Cindy MacPherson must have been the source. He tried to be angry with her, but failed. She had no idea that he wanted to stay out of the limelight—and had failed miserably—and she was of an age and lived in a time when celebrity, however brief, seemed like a good thing.

Chana answered on the second ring; she had news to share, she said, she had seen him on YouTube again and on television, and did he have any news of the Codex?

"I have lots of news. Much good stuff. Can I take you to lunch today?" Ben said.

"Meet me at the museum about 1:30," Chana replied. "I can't wait to see you!"

Ben clicked off, looked at his watch: a little past ten. There should be time to pick up some things from the Benkamal house and then stop at St. Hermione's.

CHAPTER SIXTY

B EN SLIPPED INTO THE CONFESSION BOOTH AT ST. Hermione's Church and waited for the priest to acknowledge him.

Several seconds ticked by until Ben said, "Hello? Anyone there?"

Father Monaghan said, "How long since your last confession?"

Ben said, "This is my first. I'm not a Catholic, nor do I intend to become one."

The window between the two halves of the booth slid open, and Monaghan peered at Ben. He saw a compact man in a dark blue sports jacket, a blue shirt and khaki slacks. On his head was a navy yarmulke with a subtle Star of David pattern in lighter blue. "If this is your idea of joke, son, it ends right now," Monaghan growled.

"I'm Rabbi Ben Maimon. I need to talk to a priest, but I had no idea where to find you until I walked in and saw the line. And I thought, Why not? He's meeting with people, hearing about their problems, and so he'll probably be okay with hearing about mine. I waited until everyone else finished."

"You're really a rabbi?"

Ben passed his old Jewish Theological Seminary I.D. card through the window. "The picture was taken ten years ago," he said.

Monaghan looked at the card, looked at Ben, handed the card back.

"You could have come to my office, Rabbi."

"There was no one in it and no one to ask where you were."

The priest sighed. "I usually hear confessions on Saturday afternoon, but last week was my niece's wedding.... Our budget's a little thin these days; my assistant works only afternoons and I rely on a volunteer before lunch. She didn't show up today."

"Well, do you have a minute?"

A bulky, towering man with thick, curly hair the color of brushed pewter stepped out of the booth. "We'll be more comfortable in my office," he said.

When they were seated and Ben had declined coffee, Monaghan said, "So?"

"A few days ago, I paid a visit next door to Sister Agatha, dressed as a priest—"

Monaghan jumped up. "You! Of course—short, red hair—I should call the cops."

"You may well do that, but please, hear me out first, one clergyman to another."

A wary expression on his face, Monaghan sat down slowly.

Ben said, "About two weeks ago, a house on the next street east was burgled. Someone took the kitchen door off its hinges, went inside, removed the door from a home office, and then made off with a small safe."

Monaghan said, "It was two men in coveralls and a pretty, dark-haired woman."

Ben's jaw dropped. "You saw them?" he gasped.

"Every morning after breakfast, I walk around the block, twice. Used to run, but these old knees of mine have other ideas now. First time I went around that morning, their truck was double-parked, blocking the street, and a UPS guy in a delivery van was honking. Second time around, the safe's on a dolly, and they're pushing it to where they'd parked. The sidewalk is all broken over there, and the woman was telling them to be careful with the safe, and they were looking annoyed and taking it very slow."

Ben said, "Could you identify these people?"

"The woman greeted me by name. Hers is Kizzu or Kizzya, something like that. I've seen her in church. Maybe she's taken Communion here. I can I.D. one of the men, I think. Short, barrel chest, a handlebar mustache, but if I was a betting man, I'd put a year's salary that the mustache was a fake. The other one was a little taller, slender, kept his head down. What's all that to do with impersonating a priest?"

"Everything," Ben said. "The house belonged to Mr. Shemuel Benkamal—"

"Of course. Tall, very Semitic looking, almost like an Arab. Lived here for at least the thirty-two years that I've been at St. Hermione's. Used to pass him on the street, me going one way around the block, him the other."

"He died two days before the burglary, and his grand-niece and the neighbors were at the cemetery for his funeral when those guys broke in and took the safe."

"And you were going to explain how this relates to your masquerade?"

"In that safe was a Torah, a very old and historically valuable one, or so the grand-niece believes. Her name is Miryam, and she told Rabbi Zeev—"

"I know who that is," the priest said, interrupting. "If you fellows had bishops, that would be him."

"Rabbi Zeev made inquiries in Jewish circles, and the Jewish Museum of New York asked me to speak with him, then find that Torah, which belongs in a museum."

"And presently," Monaghan said, "you'll explain why you

put on a Roman collar and a phony brogue and pretended to be a priest and convinced Sister Agatha that His Eminence, Cardinal Dolan, was coming to visit."

"I will," Ben said. "Two men followed me from Rabbi Zeev's home. When I drove by the Benkamal residence later, I saw both of them parked, watching the house."

"Go on."

"About three days after I first saw them, those two stabbed a police officer and a hotel desk clerk. The clerk died. The police officer was taken to the hospital—"

"Wait! I saw you on TV carrying that man's head. Your finger was inside his neck pinching his carotid artery to keep him from bleeding to death. That was you, wasn't it?"

Ben nodded. "Two days later, those same two went to the hospital and murdered the officer, Leonard Wise. His brother's at the Holy See, his late uncle was a priest, and he, Detective Wise, was personally acquainted with Cardinal Dolan."

"And his funeral is tomorrow," Monaghan murmured.

"I'll get to that. To back up, before they stabbed Wise, those guys were watching the house. I didn't know who they were or what they were up to, but I didn't want them to see me at the Benkamals' front door. There's no alley. The only other way I could think of was to use the overhanging tree limb and swing myself over the playground fence at St. Hermione's School and into the back yard of the house next door."

"The one with the big mastiff?"

"Samson. I didn't know there'd be a dog, but just in case, most dogs like bacon."

"A rabbi carrying bacon? You can't be serious."

"You take kosher turkey pastrami and pan fry it. I doubt that the dog cared. Anyway, then I crossed through three more yards until I got to the Benkamal yard."

Comprehension crept into Monaghan's eyes. "But you

couldn't just climb over a twelve-foot fence into the schoolyard. Someone would have called the police. You had to find a way to get invited into the schoolyard. And then you just vanished."

Ben nodded. "Exactly. So I tricked Sister Agatha. Now, you mentioned the funeral tomorrow. That video you mentioned was on local TV, on YouTube and then CNN, me helping Detective Wise, and because I wasn't identified, the NYPD would like to leave me out of this. That suits me as well. The police found a young patrolman. From a distance, he resembles me, and he'll wear civilian clothes and stand near the chief of detectives at the funeral. The media will be kept at a distance, and some of them may believe that he is me."

"Then you must have friends in the police."

"A few. Detective Wise was one. The police want to find the men who killed him. I want to recover that Torah. I think it's also possible that the same men who burgled the Benkamal house might be responsible for Shemuel's death."

"You think that they hired some skateboarder to roll by and knock him down?"

Ben looked surprised. "You know about that?"

"It was two blocks up the street, in front of the library. Everybody in the neighborhood knows. I just assumed it was an accident."

"The police, Miryam Benkamal, and I think that it was murder. And we think that the woman you saw, the one with the safe movers, might be involved in that."

"And now that I know why you impersonated a priest and annoyed Sister Agatha, why are you here? What do you need from me?"

"If Sister Agatha watches that funeral tomorrow, and she sees that young patrolman, she might accuse him of impersonating a priest. That kind of accusation, though false, could follow him for life. I want to spare him all that."

The priest scowled. "What the hell kind of rabbi are you? Who do you work for?"

"I work for people who need my help. And I'm the kind of rabbi that solves problems and tries to do the right thing."

"A sort of Jewish paladin?"

"Exactly. You speak French?"

"Minored in medieval literature at Yale. Fat lot of good that's done me."

"I feel badly about deceiving Sister Agatha. I hope you'll come with me when I apologize to her. That's why I'm here."

"That's it?"

"I don't want that patrolman jammed up, and I want to offer Sister Agatha the opportunity to forgive me. If you're with me, she might at least give me a chance to explain, and then to apologize."

"She might still call the police, you know."

"If she does, will you try to get her to call Detective Marko at the 72nd Precinct to make a report? He was Detective Wise's partner."

"You really want to talk to her? Because now that I know what happened, I think I could persuade Agatha to just forget about all this."

"I owe it to her, I owe it to God, and I owe it to myself, Father."

"You can call me Walt."

"I'm Ben."

"Well, Ben, now that you've shown me that you're actually a rabbi, I'll call Agatha and tell her we're coming."

"One more thing, Walt. I need you to tell Detective Marko what you told me about the two men and the woman with the safe. I'm pretty sure he arrested those two men yesterday afternoon."

"But not the woman?"

Ben shook his head. "Still at large."

CHAPTER SIXTY-ONE

IRYAM GLANCED AT HER WRISTWATCH: TWENTY minutes before noon, and already a line was forming in front the Jewish Community House of Bensonhurst, seniors queuing for the daily one dollar kosher lunch.

She had been raised by elderly people, and they intimidated her. She knew this, had long ago accepted it. Now, she told herself that she needed to get past her feelings of inferiority. She was a graduate student at one of the world's elite universities and had taught classes to freshmen and sophomores. She had presided over classrooms of three-year-olds. And she had watched Ben for a week, noticed his poise, his confidence, his strength. Who knew what he felt inside? Probably he's just as fearful as everyone else, she told herself, except that he had learned to wear an imaginary cloak of strength. She would borrow that cloak, slip into a garment of poise and confidence.

Miryam had spent the preceding two hours in the library, searching first English language and then foreign language newspapers and wire services on Lexis-Nexis, an Internet-linked newspaper and wire service database. She found no mention of a ferry disaster in Turkey in the year her parents died or in the five years before and after. No ferry had foundered in the Bosporus Strait, in the Black Sea, the Sea of Marmara, or the Aegean.

So Shemuel had lied about that, too.

Miryam knew no German, but she had nevertheless been

able to pick out the names of her parents, Isaac and Aida, as well as her own, in the letter. So it had something to do with her family, and she meant to know what.

Miryam positioned herself near the center of the line, took several steps backward, and yelled at the top of her lungs, "Excuse me! May I have your attention!"

A few heads turned, but most of the people in line remained fixed on the door to the cafeteria. Miryam reached into her jeans pocket, took out a handful of twenty-dollar bills, and waved them over her head.

"I've got a hundred dollars for the person who can translate a letter in German into plain English!" she yelled.

A murmur swept the line. Heads turned. A rotund woman pushing a walker broke away from the line and began making her way toward Miryam. A thin, stooped man in threadbare clothes, limping painfully, beat her by a step.

The woman said, "I had farther to come and I'm handicapped, so actually I was first."

The man said, "You're full of shit, Clara. I've got no cartilage in my knees—that's not a handicap? And you're always cutting the line with that walker! Today it ends, or we're going to go round and round."

The woman said, "Stuff it, Mintz, or I'll call the Social Security and tell about—"

"Sheket!" Miryam yelled, surprising herself. "Quiet! Stop it, both of you. You're behaving worse than my three-year-olds! I will give you each a hundred. What I want from you, one at a time, in private, is an English summary of this letter."

"You first, Mr. Mintz," she finished, and led him to a bench, where they sat side by side. Miryam handed Mintz the letter, and he skimmed it, quickly, and then read it again.

"It says that they were disappointed when their beloved daughter Aida, her husband Isaac and their granddaughter

Miryam didn't arrive the previous month, and they are both shocked and still mourning their untimely deaths. They appreciate that he, the person they're writing to, generously sent them money orders with the $20,000 payout from their son-in-law's life insurance, and they intend to use some of it to establish a scholarship fund at Tzvia High School in their daughter's name. They say that their son-in-law Isaac has cousins, and they were all looking forward to meeting him for the first time, so they also offer condolences. And they ask whether the authorities have found Aida or Isaac's remains in Long Island Sound and whether the Coast Guard was still looking for their boat.

"And then there are a few lines about their hope that he might come to Israel and meet them sometime."

Her head spinning, Miryam handed the man five twenties, then beckoned to the woman, Clara.

Clara took longer to read the letter, but her translation was almost identical.

Miryam counted out the money, thanked her, and sat, thinking, while Clara hobbled away, triumphantly clutching her earnings.

Miryam decided that the letter meant that her parents had planned to visit her maternal grandparents in Israel. Instead, Shemuel told them that she and her parents had drowned in a boating accident in Long Island. And he had sent them some money.

Untraceable money orders, of course.

But why? And what had actually become of her parents? If they had drowned in Long Island Sound, why had he always said that they had died in Turkey? Why tell her mother's family that she, Miryam, was also dead?

What kind of monster was the man who had raised her?

Miryam got up and headed back to the library.

CHAPTER SIXTY-TWO

―――――――

MUCH TO BEN'S SURPRISE, WITH FATHER MONAGHAN at his side, Sister Agatha listened quietly to his explanation and accepted his apology with only token sarcasm.

"Now that I have the full story, I'm inclined to forgive you, Fath— I mean, Rabbi. What is it now that those stiff-necked members of our family-in-faith, those who refuse to see the error of their ways—the Jews. What do Jews do for penance?" Sister Agatha asked.

Ben smiled, recognizing his own words thrown back at him. "First, we apologize to anyone whom we have offended. Second, we try to make things right."

Ben took a thousand dollars in hundreds out of his pocket. "I'd be honored if St. Hermione's School would accept a small donation that would atone for some of the inconvenience I caused its director, Sister Agatha."

Agatha nodded. "I know exactly what that will be used for, Rabbi. There are always children whose families cannot afford to send them here, and this will enable almost one child to attend the second session of summer school this year."

Ben reached into his pocket and counted out another thousand dollars.

―――

"Thank you," Sister Agatha said, in her normal voice.

"After making things right with the wronged person," Ben continued, "we publicly and formally repent our sins on Yom Kippur, the Day of Atonement. We seek God's forgiveness."

"Not God's grace, Rabbi?" asked Monaghan.

"That's not a Jewish concept," he replied. "Christians understand grace as God's unconditional and undeserved love. If an individual firmly believes in Jesus Christ as his savior, that grace will be bestowed upon them. Jews believe that everyone has the power and the choice to obey God's laws and that it's up to each of us to exercise that choice. When we fail to obey those laws, and most of us will, we beg forgiveness by making amends here on Earth, by demonstrating our contrition with deeds. We believe that our actions, not our intentions or beliefs, are the basis for obtaining God's mercy."

Father Monaghan said, "You don't believe that God speaks to individuals?"

"Not in those terms, no. We believe that there were prophets to whom God communicated directly, but the era of prophetic revelation is now long past. I believe that God gave each of us the power to discern right and wrong, the sense to educate ourselves about what God expects from us—which is pretty much a lifelong occupation—and God therefore expects us to make choices. We are human; therefore, we sometimes make bad choices, we forget why we were put here on earth, we behave badly, we indulge our greedy tendencies, what in ancient times was called the evil inclination. For all that, there is tshuvah, repentance, or turning back to Godly ways, and there is atonement."

"All very instructive. We should have the Rabbi in to talk to our lay leaders some time," Monaghan said.

"I'd be pleased. And now, I'm sorry, but I have an appointment in Manhattan."

BEN DROPPED A TOKEN IN the turnstile and stepped onto the platform. Looking around, he was surprised to see people talking on cell phones; apparently, this station was among the first in New York to get the new WiFi and cell service.

He pulled out his iPhone and called Marko, who told him in rapid-fire fashion that fingerprints confirmed Steinberg's identity and that the man arrested with him, "George Soper," had no criminal record. Both demanded lawyers and refused to answer questions.

Ben said, "I just spoke with Father Monaghan at St. Hermione's, and he can I.D. at least one of the two men who took the safe out of Benkamal's house. His description sounds like Steinberg. He also said there was a woman with them, and he thinks he's seen her at his church before."

"Where are you now?" Marko asked. "Can you meet me at St. Hermione's?"

"I'm in the subway on my way to Manhattan; I'll be back in Brooklyn tonight."

A train pulled in and stopped. "I'll call back," Ben said, and ran for the train.

CHAPTER SIXTY-THREE

———————

Ben slipped into Chana's office at the museum and smiled when she looked up.

"I'll go first," Chana said, grinning from one tiny, perfect ear to the other, hardly able to contain her excitement. "I found out why Mo has been such a bastard about a divorce."

"Anything to do with a criminal investigation?" Ben asked, joking.

"Whoa! How did you know that?"

"A wild guess. But this seems to be the season for going after hedge funds and pirate financiers. The FBI, SEC, or somebody else?"

"The SEC and the state of New York, so far. Allegations of insider trading."

"And since a wife can't be compelled to testify against her husband, but an ex-wife is fair game ..."

"Exactly," Chana said. "I was interviewed by the SEC, twice, and by the FBI, who are staying out of it for now, and the New York attorney general's office. And they all agree that I really know next to nothing about how Mo runs his business."

"Then why are you so happy?"

"Because, dear Ben, both agencies gave formal notice to my husband's lawyers that they won't call me as a witness even if I'm no longer his wife, if his lawyers will also agree not to call me. And he signed off on that."

———

"So at this point he's got no reason to further delay the settlement?"

"Exactly. Morris's lawyer named a number, which was about a tenth of what he should pay, and my lawyer demanded triple that, and he agreed."

"That's wonderful news, Chana."

"My head is swimming with the possibilities. Eighty million dollars!"

"I'm so glad for you. Truly, you deserve every cent."

"Thank you. New subject: Ben, do you know that they're calling you 'The YouTube Rabbi'?"

"Yeah. A pain in the neck! I've got emails from every TV station in the city, begging for an interview."

"What are you going to do?"

"Nothing. In two weeks, they'll be on to the next big thing, and I'll be forgotten."

"I don't think so. You live the kind of life where trouble constantly finds you. You won't be old news in two weeks or two months or two years."

"Well, as far as this job is concerned, in a week I could be done, finished, mission accomplished and back to Cambridge."

"What? How?"

"Or not. The police arrested the two men who burgled Benkamal's house. They aren't talking yet, but there's a very credible eyewitness who can put them with the safe on the street in front of Benkamal's house. In the meantime, thanks to Rabbi Zeev, I bring you eighteen Torah fragments, possibly from the Codex, for scientific and scribal analysis."

He held up the envelope and repeated what Zeev had said about enlightening the Jewish community in his part of Brooklyn, and how people had come forward with amulets and scraps of Torah pages.

Then he produced the passports from Shemuel's mystery

drawer, described other finds, and detailed what he and Miryam had learned about Shemuel Benkamal.

Chana pursed her lips. "So you believe that Shemuel might not have been his real name and that he probably wasn't Miryam's great-uncle at all?"

"More to the point, he might have murdered the real Shemuel Benkamal to steal his identity and killed Miryam's grandparents, Isaac and Naomi."

"Do think he was even Jewish?"

Ben thought for a long moment. "If... we suppose that he was a Chechen, and that he was sent by the Soviets into Syria during World War II, then I think he might well have been a Jew who could pass for a Muslim when he wanted to."

"Why?"

"This is all supposition, but it would be easier for a Jew to find ideological motivation to undermine or influence an Arab state adjacent to Palestine than it would for a Muslim. The Soviets had troubles with Muslim republics because Communism was the state religion. That wouldn't bother a Jew who was committed to the illusion of equality and social justice that Communism claims to offer. Also, if they were anticipating the emergence of a Jewish state, there were millions of Jews in the Soviet Union, many of them committed Communists. Send enough of them to Israel, and maybe they could take over that country."

Chana said, "And in Syria, a Jew would be able to get support from other Jews, an oppressed minority that had no sympathy for Arab nationalism."

"Exactly. A more practical matter: One of the items we found was a notebook with coded entries. Is there someone at the museum with a background in cryptography?"

"Aliza Weiner, a consultant. You'll like her—she's petite, very cute, and single."

"Good. We should also give her a list of the amulet owners."

"You have a theory about how Benkamal ties in with the amulets?"

"I do. But only some of those eighteen parchments are in amulets. Four were simply folded small enough to fit in a wallet or a change purse. My theory is that Benkamal, or Daudov Khanov, whom I now suspect was a document and photo forger, exchanged amulets for minority shares in small businesses.

"Isaac and Naomi came from a wealthy merchant family. They were trying to get out of Syria and presumably would have taken as much money as they could with them. If Shemuel—Khanov—killed them, wouldn't he rob them, as well?

"So when he arrived in Bensonhurst and started peddling amulets, perhaps he also put up a little cash, along with the amulet. It's a sweet deal: You get some money, maybe enough to buy materials or a start-up inventory, and a holy amulet that would ensure your success. In return, Khanov, or whoever he was, took, say, fifteen or twenty percent of the net. For the next fifty years, he has a stream of cash from multiple small businesses.

"That's my theory."

"That's great work, Ben. And, if he was actually a Soviet spy, he's got two good reasons to keep a low profile: the KGB and the FBI."

"You're right! I didn't think of that. Shall we go eat?"

Chana frowned. "Sorry," she said. "Can't do lunch today. I have to go downtown and sign some papers now, and then I have a late class. I'll call Aliza on my way downtown and see whether she can come over this afternoon. You should take her through all the stuff that you told me: the forgeries, the murders. If she can't come now, I'll meet with her later or set up a meeting for the three of us.

"Is there anything else we need to talk about now?"

Chana's sudden all-business attitude left Ben wondering whether something had changed between them. It made him feel uneasy, as though she was withdrawing from him, and he didn't know why.

Ben said, "Three things."

"Quickly?"

"Shemuel is dead, and the police won't be interested in who he was. I'd also like to spare Miryam any public embarrassment. Can your people work up these passports and tell me which, if any, are authentic?"

Chana pulled a face. "I'll ask. Budgets are always tight."

"If it becomes an issue, I'll find the money."

"Okay. What's next?"

He handed her a faded parchment written in faint, oxidized Arabic and stored between two sheets of what Ben hoped were acid-free paper.

Chana glanced at the parchment, and then stared, her face registering surprise. She read carefully, her excitement growing with every line.

"Where did you find this, Ben?"

"In a secret compartment in an old roll-top desk in Benkamal's office."

"I'll need to have the ink and paper analyzed, but this appears to be a letter sent from Egypt about the year 1199 or 1200 to the chief rabbi of the Great Synagogue of Aleppo. The sender signs his name Mūsā ibn Maymūn."

"No! A letter from Maimonides?"

"It's a detailed response to a rabbi's inquiry on an issue of *halakhah*, Jewish law."

"Do you think it's genuine?"

"It might be a copy, but if it is, it's either hundreds of years old or …"

"It was found among the possessions of a skilled forger."

"For that reason alone, it's suspect. If it's genuine, it's a priceless find. We'll see what the lab says. What else?"

"After I found the letter, I looked for something to carry it here in. Eventually, I found some paper. But before I did, I poked through a book shelf and found this," Ben said, and handed her a small book, its cover, in Arabic script, faded and torn.

"Oh. My. God," she breathed. "An early copy of The Kitab al Khazari, by Yehuda Halevi. The original was hand-made about half a century before Gutenberg."

"It was in a bookcase, among many other books. Hidden in plain sight. And now that you've translated the title, I think it might be genuine."

"Ben, I have to leave. Can you make this fast?"

"The book is a defense of Judaism in the form of a mythical conversation with the king of the Khazars, after which the king and his subjects convert to Judaism. Chechens are descendants of the Khazars. And that's where we think Shemuel actually came from."

"You're probably right," she said, then hurriedly packed her briefcase and left without even a hug.

Something was going on, Ben realized. Maybe it was the eighty million dollars, but Chana was no longer interested in him romantically.

He was glad about that, because he had dreaded the discussion that would follow when he told Chana about Miryam. Even so, her sudden coolness toward him was more than merely puzzling. He felt a little hurt. She'd rejected him and he didn't know why.

CHAPTER SIXTY-FOUR

B EN BROUGHT THE AMULETS, THE NOTEBOOK, THE Kitab al Khazari and the other documents from Shemuel's secret drawer down to Dr. Wilson's basement lab and left them with his technician. Then, hungry, he went upstairs to the cafeteria, ordered an egg salad sandwich, and after eating it went out to the veranda to return calls.

First was Marko, who said that he'd spoken with Father Monaghan: The priest was on his way over to be interviewed, to confirm that Steinberg and Soper were the men he saw with the safe, and to help find the woman he'd seen with them.

Ben then called Bert Epstein. "What's up?" he said when Bert answered.

"I have an answer to your inquiry about consanguinity and DNA."

"Do you need samples from all concerned?"

"I thought that would be the case, but I found a recent article in The Lancet. A study at Baylor University unexpectedly discovered several cases of presumed incest through what's called an 'absence of heterozygosity.'"

"You're going to have to explain that one, Bert."

"Most people get roughly half of their genes from each parent; that's heterozygosity. But when closely related people, whose DNA is already similar to each other, create offspring, their DNA has large blocks in which genes inherited from the mother and father are identical. Many children of incest also show a high number of DNA markers for certain heritable diseases."

Ben swallowed. He was about to withhold information from his doctor and didn't feel good about it. "Thanks, Bert. I've got a blood sample. Who can I send it to that would discretely examine it for evidence of incest?"

"Send it to me. I'll have the DNA extracted and let my postdocs work it up as a teaching experience."

"In other words, you're not going to tell them what they're looking for?"

"Exactly. And if they report nothing unusual, I'll have a look at it myself."

"I'll overnight the sample. Thanks, Bert."

"You're welcome. When are you coming home? You're about due for your semiannual workup."

"A couple of weeks, maybe less. See you soon."

Ben clicked off and dialed Rabbi Dibbo in Eatontown.

"I saw you on YouTube yesterday," Dibbo said.

"So you were the guy who clicked in," Ben replied.

"Very funny. The reason I called, the guy you clocked with the chair—in the deli—he used to be a member of my congregation."

"You mean, there in Eatontown? Or someplace else?"

"Here. Joined four or five years ago. He was one of the people who canceled their membership after the, uh, ransom was paid."

"You recall his name, Rabbi?"

"George Soper. It was kind of odd for an Ashkenazi to join a Sephardic congregation. I asked him about it, and he said his grandmother was Sephardic."

"And he was the guy with the gun that I hit with the chair? For sure?"

"I'm absolutely certain."

"What can I do with this, Rabbi Dibbo? If I tell the police, they'll want to know who identified him. If I send them to you, will you tell them about the ransom?"

"I spoke with the key players on my board about this yesterday, and the consensus is that Soper must have been involved in that business. If he's in custody, he can't hurt us. I release you from your promise. You can tell the police what I told you."

"Thanks, Rabbi. You've done something good."

"I hope so."

Ben clicked off and stood, lost in thought, for several seconds. Something was familiar about the name George Soper, but he couldn't quite recall it.

Ben's phone rang, but when he answered there was only silence. He clicked off; a moment later, the phone rang again, and Miryam, crying, almost incoherent, begged him to meet her in front of Sloan-Kettering Memorial as fast as he could get there.

"Fifteen minutes. I'm on my way," he said.

CHAPTER SIXTY-FIVE

B EN GOT OUT OF A CAB ON YORK AVENUE AND SAW Miryam sitting on a low curb in front of a tree. Behind her a high fence of steel pickets protected a complex of blocky, low-rise buildings of pale red brick.

Miryam ran to him, and they held each other for a long moment. When he finally broke their clinch and looked at her, he saw bloodshot eyes and a puffy face streaked with mascara.

Ben said, "Tell me."

Her story came tumbling out in random fashion, getting the letter translated, the library, the results of her Lexis-Nexis search, a second visit to the library.

"Ben, I'm no expert at this, but my father was a doctor, and if he died, you'd expect to find something in the newspaper, an obituary, and a death notice. And I didn't," she wailed. "Could he still be alive?"

Ben held her again for a long moment.

"I don't see how that could be," he said.

"Do you think Shemuel murder—"

"Yes."

"And my mom?"

"The same."

Miryam began to cry, long, agonizing sobs, a river of tears that went on and on.

When she had cried herself out, Ben led her back to the curb, and they both sat down. "Why are we here, at Sloan-Kettering?" Ben asked.

"My father worked here. He was a Fellow in oncology. I thought that somebody might know something about what happened to him ..."

———⚬⚬⚬⚬⚬———

THE ASSOCIATE MANAGER OF HUMAN Relations was a trim, businesslike woman in her late 40s who listened carefully as Miryam explained that her father had been employed there until the summer of 1997. Was there a record of why he left his job?

"I'm not sure that there is, and I'm not sure that I could share that with you if there was," she said. "What is this in regard to?"

Ben said, "Miryam was eight years old in 1997. She has always believed that her parents drowned in Turkey while on vacation. Now she has reason to believe that this was not the case. It would be helpful if there were some record of the manner of Dr. Benkamal's departure. Did he resign? Did he simply stop coming? Was he fired?"

The woman thought for a long moment. "I'll see if we have anything. But if he didn't leave of his own volition, I may not be able to tell you much more than that."

"Whatever you can do, I will thank you," Miryam said.

They waited in silence for twenty minutes until the woman reappeared. She carried a single sheet of paper.

"Dr. Benkamal resigned his post in June 1997 to accept a position with Hospital de Niños in Buenos Aires. This is a copy of his letter of resignation," she said.

The letter was short and succinct: He had accepted a job in Argentina and requested that his final paycheck be sent to his home in Brooklyn.

"May we take this?" Ben asked.

"Certainly," the woman replied.

They rode the elevator five floors down to the ground floor in silence.

Ben broke the silence. "Obviously, we'll have to check with that hospital in Buenos Aires. But, based on the letter from your mother's parents and your own experience with Shemuel, I think we should get the police involved. They'll be able to check with their opposite numbers in Argentina to find out whether your father ever worked at that hospital. My guess is that he killed them both."

Miryam began to weep again. "Why?" she wailed.

"We may never know. But there might be a clue in the letter from Haifa. Your parents were planning a trip to Israel to see your mother's family. But if your father had cousins in Israel, they probably knew that the only Shemuel Benkamal of his generation drowned in the Euphrates many years ago. And that he was much shorter than the man now using that name and pretending to be Isaac's uncle. Maybe Shemuel feared that his masquerade would be exposed, and he dealt with that threat the way he usually did."

"God. Oh God. How could he do that? What kind of a monster was he!"

They went out through the parking lot and then a gated entrance and stood on the curb, leaning against each other, holding hands.

CHAPTER SIXTY-SIX

THE TAXI WAS CROSSING THE 59TH STREET BRIDGE when Ben's phone rang.

"Can you come by the precinct right away?" Marko asked.

"On our way. Hey, remember that rabbi I went to see in New Jersey?"

"What about him?"

"A couple of hours ago, he told me that Soper, the guy from the deli, joined his congregation about four years ago. The following year, somebody snatched their very valuable Torah and held it for ransom. When they tried to negotiate a price, they grabbed Rabbi Dibbo, held him for ransom and doubled the price. The synagogue paid up, and then this guy Soper left the congregation."

Marko said, "So you think it was an inside job? Soper was in on it?"

"You should call Rabbi Dibbo. And we've got more to tell you about Miryam's uncle Shemuel. We think he killed her parents."

"He was never my uncle," Miryam whispered, her face a mask, far beyond tears.

MARKO SAID, "LET ME GET this straight. You think the old guy, Shemuel Benkamal, killed his nephew and the nephew's wife—your parents, Ms. Benkamal?"

Miryam nodded. "But he wasn't actually my father's uncle. He was an imposter."

"He told everyone that they'd drowned in a ferry boat accident in Turkey?"

Miryam said, "He told me that. He also told me that my mother's parents were dead, but they weren't, and he told them that my parents died in some kind of boating accident in Long Island Sound. Yesterday, I met my great aunt, my grandmother's sister, for the first time—she was visiting from Argentina—and she said that her husband was named Shemuel Benkamal and he was murdered in 1947. And we found a bunch of old passports with Shemuel's picture but all different names. So we think the man who killed my parents, Shemuel, also killed the real Shemuel and took his identity."

Ben said, "It can't be hard to verify whether Isaac Benkamal ever went to Argentina and whether he ever worked for that children's hospital in Buenos Aires, which is what his resignation letter to Sloan-Kettering said."

"We'll pursue that," Marko said. "I'll get the feds to ask Argentina whether your father and mother ever arrived in Buenos Aires. There should be records of that. But it's gonna take awhile," Marko said. "Ms. Benkamal, you need to understand that while the murder of your parents is a very serious matter—every murder is—the suspected killer is now dead. So to be brutally honest, this is not going to get the priority, the attention that the suspected murder of your uncle—"

"He was never my uncle," Miryam interrupted. "He killed my uncle."

"I understand. Anyway, we're about to pick up the woman that was with Steinberg and Soper during the safe heist."

Ben said, "Heist?"

Marko smiled. "The power of words. We get a little more support from the higher-ups when they think it's a major crime. And guess what? It was major, because two people probably got murdered in the deal."

Ben said, "Back up. You're 'about' to pick up that woman?"

"Qetsiyah Sarkissian, a.k.a. Kizzy Sark, a.k.a. Ketsiyah Tabbash. Three arrests, no convictions, all for the sweetheart con."

Miryam said, "What's that?"

"Pretty woman finds a loser—old, or fat, or ugly, whatever—and convinces him she's in love with him. Then she cleans out his bank accounts and disappears."

"People really do things like that?" Miryam asked, wide-eyed.

"Every day, Ms. Benkamal, every freaking day. By the way, you were right about Kizzy and the census. She was a temporary hire, an enumerator, in 2000 and again in 2010.

"Anyway," he continued, "Kizzy applied to St. Hermione's for a scholarship to summer school for her kid. A few months ago, that was. Left a cell number, but no address. Your new pal, Sister Agatha called her today and said they got more scholarship funding and, if she'd come in and fill out an application, they'd consider the kid for the second summer term."

Miryam said, "You're not really going to arrest her at school?"

Marko shook his head. "Out front. The priest will make the I.D. from inside a Con Edison shop van with a one-way window."

"Why did you want us to come down?" Ben asked.

"I'm gonna need a formal statement from Ms. Benkamal about the events leading up to your... to the guy you used to think was your uncle, his death. And now, the rest of that, how he might have killed your real uncle, all that."

Miryam said, "Okay, let's get started."

While Miryam sat with Foster to write out what she knew about the deaths of Beneficia and Shemuel, Ben took Marco aside.

"I've got another theory about how the safe... heist happened," he said.

"Shoot," Marko said.

"I think the woman—Kizzy, you said her name is?"

Marco nodded, yes.

"Kizzy worked in the house long enough to find some things that she thought might be valuable. For example, in his office I found a rare, handwritten book that might be 500 years old. It's worth a fortune to a collector. Millions. It was on a bookshelf; I think she found it hidden away someplace and moved it there so that it would be easy to grab later. It looked very old, but otherwise Kizzy probably couldn't tell what was what. Maybe she managed to take a couple of items, maybe not, but then the old man fired her.

"After killing the housekeeper and then the old man, she brought Steinberg and Soper in because they could tell her what was worth stealing. Maybe they planned to put everything they stole in the unlocked safe, and then take the safe out. You can do that in broad daylight if you act like you're just going about your business.

"But then things went wrong. Miryam put an old Torah in the safe and locked it. So they take the safe and anything they can stick in their pockets, but then the UPS guy starts honking because they left their truck double-parked. So they have to move the truck. Then they meet the priest on the street, he recognizes Kizzy, and she decides to keep going because they don't know if Father Monaghan called the police.

"They get away with the safe, but they know there's more to steal in the house. They want to go back, but then Miryam moves in. Maybe they follow her to Rabbi Zeev, and they find out who he is. Then they keep an eye on his house. When there's no hue and cry, nobody coming around to arrest Kizzy, they think they're in the clear.

"Then I show up at Rabbi Zeev's. If they've been watching the house, they know I'm new, not one of his usual visitors, who are mostly old rabbis. Maybe they even paid somebody on the block to tell them who the regular visitors are.

"Then I caught Steinberg following me and over-reacted. So they got interested in what I do and where I go. They found out where I'm staying. That led to Wise getting killed. But before that, when there were a few hours when nobody was at the Benkamal house, they tried to break in again to take more stuff."

Marko nodded. "Yeah, I like that. That could be just how it went down."

His phone rang, and Marko picked up, identified himself, and listened.

"Well, what are you doing about it?" he growled, listened more, and then hung up.

"Good news is that Father Monaghan I.D.'d Kizzy. The bad news is that, when she noticed the Con-Ed van, she took off running."

Ben said, "She got away?"

Marko scowled. "For now."

"I've got one more lead for you to check out," Ben said. "I've been meaning to call this guy but haven't got around to it. Three years ago, just before that Torah got stolen from Rabbi Dibbo's synagogue, they had it repaired."

Marko said, "You think that maybe the guy who did that work tipped Steinberg?"

Ben shrugged. "His name is Rabbi Jason Silber. He lives in Williamsburg."

"Maybe we should go talk to him," Marko said.

"We?" Ben said.

"Ever do any consulting work?"

CHAPTER SIXTY-SEVEN

R ABBI SILBER WAS A COMPACT, BEARDED, FASTIDI-
ously neat man in his late 30s. He showed Marko, Foster
and Ben to a small, well-lit workspace in a corner of the
dining room of his modest third-story apartment across from
Sternberg Park.

"Everything to do with my sopher work, I keep here," Silber said. "You're welcome to look around."

Marko said, "What if what we're looking for is in another room?"

Silber shrugged. "I have nothing to hide. My wife is at work; my kids are in camp. Look at anything you like. Just, please, be very careful touching any of the Torahs. Some of them are very old, and the parchment is brittle."

Marko said, "Do you know Yevgeny Steinberg?"

Silber shook his head. "Not a name I'm familiar with."

Marko consulted his notebook. "What about Rabbi Eugene Stein, or Hermann Stein, or Gene Berg?"

Silber shook his head. "Please, officer, what is this about?"

Marko handed him two booking photos taken of Steinberg, one with the Sikh turban and beard, the other bareheaded and clean-shaven. "Recognize this man?"

Silber's eyebrows shot up. "Rabbi Altarstone! Is he in some kind of trouble?"

Marko said, "How do you know him?"

"He's a collector. Sometimes, he brings Torahs to be repaired."

"Have you seen him recently?"

"About two weeks ago. What's going on? Was that a mug shot you showed me?"

"The last time he came here, what was his reason?"

"He brought me a pile of old parchments to look at. He wanted an estimate of repair costs, and an informal appraisal."

"Do you still have them?"

"Of course," Silber said, moving to a tall steel filing cabinet and opening the bottom drawer. He removed a battered red makeup case and placed it on his worktable.

Ben's heart began to pound.

"Excuse me, Rabbi Silber," Ben said. "Have you looked at that yet?"

"Just for a few minutes. Please understand: I can't make a living as a sopher, so I also have a couple of part-time jobs. I really only get to work as a sopher stam about three afternoons a week. Sometimes in the evenings. In fact, Rabbi Altarstone called a couple of days ago. I called back, but I haven't been able to reach him yet."

"Would you mind opening that and telling us what kind of Torah it is? Now?"

"Oh, I know what it is. I just haven't been able to go through it, page by page, to see enough to make an estimate of what it would take to repair it."

Ben said, "What is it?"

Silber unzipped the case, revealing a stack of yellowing parchments. "This is not a Torah, but a *Tanakh*. Handmade. Mizrahi, probably Mesopotamian, likely Kurdish, 17th century or thereabouts."

Ben let his breath out. It was not the Aleppo Codex. His quest was over.

Marko said, "What would a thing like that be worth, Rabbi?"

Silber shrugged. "There aren't many like this. To the right collector, maybe in the low six figures. But it's in poor condition; it would take months of work to restore it. It really belongs in a museum."

Ben said, "May I look more closely?"

Silber stepped back. "Please try not to touch it," he said.

Ben put his face as close to the page as possible. "That's a remarkably delicate hand," he said. "And the pages are smaller than most I've seen."

"Almost feminine," Silber agreed. "Although four hundred years ago in Mesopotamia or elsewhere, no woman would have been allowed to write a sefer Torah."

Ben said, "What about a woman sopher, a sopheret, making a Torah for other women to study? Such as Miriam bat Benaya, the 15th-century Yemenite scribe?"

Silber frowned. "Unlikely. Bat Benaya wrote prayer books and other Hebrew items, but never a Torah. Remember, in that time, women didn't study Torah ..."

Marko said, "I hate to break up your little rabbinical confab, but I have more questions for you, Rabbi Silber."

"Of course."

"Did Rabbi Altarstone ever come for anything other than repairs or appraisals?"

"He calls once in a while to ask if I'm working on anything interesting, and if I am, he might come over to see it. A few times, he's offered to buy a scroll, but I always refer him to the owner, which in every case was a synagogue."

Ben and Marko exchanged looks.

Marko showed George Soper's booking photo to Silber. "You know this man?"

"I haven't seen him in years, but he looks like the son of the man I studied under to become a sopher."

Ben said, "Is he a sopher, as well?"

Silber shook his head. "He had the hand-to-eye coordination, and he was pretty knowledgeable, but it takes more than a steady hand, an appreciation of Jewish law, an understanding of parchment, ink and writing styles. To make or repair a holy Torah, or a scroll to put inside tefillin for morning prayers, even a scroll for a mezuzah to hang on a doorpost, a scribe must live an observant life. He must be of good moral character..."

"And Soper wasn't?" Marko finished.

"Soper? Who is that?"

"The man in the photo. That's the name he uses."

Silber shook his head. "He's got two or three older brothers. I'm not sure if I ever got all their names straight, but the family name is Tobias. I think his name was Jeremiah or Gershom."

Ben said, "You suggested that he wasn't of good moral character?"

Silber frowned. "Gossip and tale-telling—*lashon hara*—is forbidden. I try to avoid it."

Marko said, "This is a murder investigation. We believe that this man murdered a police officer. If you know something material to this investigation, tell me now, or I'll have you charged with obstruction of justice."

Silber seemed stunned. "I really don't know much about him. Just that he supposedly drank, that he used cocaine, that he gambled, that he broke into stores and houses sometimes. Stuff like that. But that was years ago."

Ben said, "Was he also his father's student?"

"He came and went. None of his brothers seemed interested. His father was disappointed because he came from a line of sopherim, several generations."

"Can you think of why he'd use the name George Soper?"

Silber laughed. "That's a good one."

"What are you saying?" Ben asked.

"That's the name of the man who put Typhoid Mary away," Silber replied.

Marko looked blank.

Ben said, "Of course. A hundred years ago. Typhoid Mary, Mary Mallon, was a cook who spread the typhoid bacillus but was herself immune to the disease. She was a carrier. Soper was the New York Public Health guy who tracked her down."

Marko said, "Why would that be funny to you, Rabbi Silber?"

"Because Mr. Tobias, my teacher, used to say that his father, who committed suicide, had ruined the family name, had turned them all into Typhoid Marys."

Ben said, "What did he mean by that?"

"Mr. Tobias's father died almost ten months before he was born. The community regarded his mother as an adulteress and him as a *mamzer*."

Ben's blood ran cold. "According to halakhah, Jewish law, a child born within a year of the father's death is nevertheless regarded as his legitimate offspring," he said.

"Exactly. But down in Bensonhurst, among the Syrians, they have their own ideas. When Mr. Tobias grew up, he went to Israel and learned to be a sopher, following his family's tradition. The Brooklyn Sephardim wouldn't let him near their Torahs, their mezzuzim, their tephillin. He couldn't even get ketubah work. He had to change his name and move to Queens. The Hasidic rabbis didn't want any part of him, either. He worked menial jobs and made a little extra money teaching young men a sopher's skills."

Ben said, "He's retired? Do you know where he lives?"

Silber shook his head. "Died a few years ago. He wasn't even 60."

Marko said, "Sorry, but we're going to have to take the

Torah. It's evidence in a murder investigation. Foster, would you bag that, tag it, give the rabbi a receipt?"

As Foster broke out an evidence bag, Ben turned to Silber. "One more question, Rabbi: Have you ever seen George Soper, or Gershom Tobias, whatever his name is—have you ever seen him on a skateboard?"

Silber said, "All the time. Him and his brothers. They zoomed all over Queens on them, snatching bottles out of liquor stores, grabbing stuff from sidewalk stands and skating off. He was an expert."

CHAPTER SIXTY-EIGHT

THEY WERE HEADED SOUTH ON THE BROOKLYN QUEENS Expressway, across the river from a glowing Manhattan skyline haloed by the dying sunset. At the wheel, Foster volunteered that it was a long way around Brooklyn but the fastest route back to Bensonhurst.

Marko bobbed his head in agreement, then swiveled in his seat to look at Ben. "Do you figure Soper was the skateboarder who knocked Benkamal down?" he said.

Ben said, "Probably."

"What do you think he was doing by calling himself George Soper?"

"Soper is a variant spelling of sopher. Gershom, if that's his real name, sounds something like George. It's from the Hebrew, meaning 'a stranger there' or maybe 'stranger is his name.' So maybe George Soper means to say, 'The stranger scribe.' That's his private joke, a play on words: He was trained as a sopher, a scribe, and his family was exiled, treated like strangers in their own community and then as strangers when they moved on.

"But the reference to Typhoid Mary also could mean that he sees himself as tracking down a person who caused death and grief to innocent people. From what we now know of Benkamal, that's accurate. Or maybe he thinks Benkamal seduced his grandmother and that led to his grandfather's suicide. Hard to say what he's thinking."

"What if his name is Jeremiah?"

"That means 'God will raise up.' Jeremiah was a prophet whose warnings of impending doom were ignored until it was too late."

"So that might work, too. Maybe he tried to intimidate Benkamal or to extort him, and he was ignored. Or maybe by acting against Benkamal, he raised himself up."

Foster said, "Excuse me, Detective, Rabbi. Maybe he isn't as smart as you think. Maybe he just needed an alias and didn't think about it too much."

Ben smiled. "Or maybe he didn't even make it up. Maybe Steinberg did. Either way, Detective, do you have enough to charge him with murder?"

"Enough to charge him with breaking and entering and with grand theft. Enough to get a search warrant for his house and car. Maybe we get Steinberg to flip on Soper, Tobias, whatever his name is, in the murders."

"Don't forget Kizzy. She could have thrown the Coke over the fence herself."

"We've got her place staked out. If she comes back for her kid, we'll nail her."

Ben sighed. "I feel badly for that kid."

"Collateral damage. Can't be helped."

Thinking aloud, Ben said, "Maybe Kizzy was a solo when she got Benkamal to hire her. She saw what he had in his house and got Steinberg, and maybe Steinberg brought in Tobias because he has scribal training and could tell what might be valuable."

Marko said, "And he used Tobias on the Eatontown job. Maybe Steinberg learned that Silber was repairing this Torah, offered to buy it, and Silber innocently gave him the owner.

Steinberg needs an insider to maybe leave a synagogue door open, or tell him when it would be easy to snatch the Torah. So he gets Tobias, a.k.a. Soper, to join that congregation."

"That makes sense," Ben said. "Tobias was raised in a Sephardic home."

Marko said, "If he killed Benkamal, was that personal or not?"

"It was better for Kizzy to put Benkamal in a hospital, get someone into his house to gain his confidence, make him dependant on them, so they could loot it and empty his bank accounts. She needed help for that, and Tobias was comfortable on a skateboard. He's skinny, not that tall. In the right clothes, maybe a hat, zipping by on a skateboard, he could pass for a teenager."

"I wish we knew what that Typhoid Mary business really meant."

"Maybe I'll go see Rabbi Zeev tomorrow, if he's up to it, and see if he remembers anything about Tobias's grandfather."

"Rabbi, was that the Torah you came here looking for? The one we took from Silber?"

"It was the one stolen from Miryam's house. The case is a perfect match for her description. But it wasn't the one that I hoped to find. That's still missing."

"Missing how long?"

"Since 1947."

"So your job is pretty much finished?"

"It is. I'll call my boss in the morning and give her the news."

"She's gonna be pissed that it wasn't the one you thought it was?"

"It was always a long shot. Anyway, the one we have, if I can get Miryam to donate it to the museum, will make a nice consolation prize."

BEN LET HIMSELF INTO THE darkened house, and then switched on the light. He'd tried to call Miryam from the car, but his calls went to voice mail. Where could she be?

"Hello!" he yelled. "Miryam?"

"Down here!" came her voice, muffled as though she spoke through a wall.

Ben found the basement door open and descended to the concrete floor. To his right was a wall now pierced by a jagged hole about three feet wide. A pile of plaster and drywall lay in front of it. Dim light came through the hole. Ben stuck his head inside and saw a short, steep, narrow flight of stairs. At their foot was Miryam, her jeans and T-shirt covered with plaster dust. A flashlight, propped on a step, illuminated a wall with a second, smaller hole that she was making with a hammer and a crowbar.

"What are you doing?" Ben said.

"I thought there was a secret basement room, and here it is," she said.

"You must be exhausted," Ben said.

"I guess."

"Why don't you come upstairs and get a shower, while I make something to eat?

"Ben, I really have to know what's in this room!"

"It's waited for years. It will wait one more night."

Miryam sighed, then laid the tools on a step, grabbed the flashlight and came back through the hole.

Ben said, "I'd hug you, but you're covered with schmutz."

"Why don't you take a shower with me?"

Ben grinned. "I'm very tempted. Instead, I'm going to make an omelet."

CHAPTER SIXTY-NINE

THEY ATE SLOWLY, EYING EACH OTHER, EXCHANGING invisible love messages, as Ben described his visit with Silber, finding the lost Torah and sharing some of the revelations about Steinberg and Tobias, a.k.a. Soper.

Miryam said, "So the Torah that I found in the red case wasn't the Codex? This whole thing was just a wild goose chase?"

His mouth full, Ben shook his head, swallowed. "Nothing wrong with a wild goose chase when you wind up catching the wild goose!"

"And take a gander at what I caught."

They giggled, and then looked at each other some more.

Finally, Ben said, "About your Torah. It's actually a *Tanakh*. It might be unique, and almost as valuable, in its own way, as the Codex."

"Explain, Great Goose Hunter Ben."

"Based on what Rabbi Silber told us, if you were to spend a thousand dollars or so and have the paper, ink and calligraphy analyzed, I'm of the opinion that it might prove to be an incredible find, something that no one in our time suspects had ever existed."

"You have my complete attention."

"Silber's quick look of the pages led him to believe that the Torah was made in Mesopotamia, meaning present-day Iraq and eastern Syria. But he also suspects that it might be of Kurdish origin."

"What does that mean, exactly?"

"The Kurdish people have their own culture and language, and from the 16th century, their territory, Kurdistan, was a self-ruled part of the Ottoman Empire. After World War II, Iraq, Turkey and Iran divided the Kurdish territory.

"Jews were exiled to ancient Babylonia after the destruction of Jerusalem in 587 BCE. Some migrated northward to live among the Kurds. The heart of Jewish Kurdistan was the present city of Mosul, near the ruins of ancient Nineveh.

"Silber said he thought your parchments were 17th century. I had a quick look at it; I'm no expert, but I've read from many Torah scrolls, and the calligraphy was unlike any that I'd ever seen. Very delicate. As if it was written by a woman."

Ben paused to let that sink in.

"Hold it," Miryam said. "A woman can't make a sefer Torah. I remember that from a lecture at The Technion, in Israel."

"That is the prevailing interpretation of halakhah, although there are more recent interpretations, as well. But let's put that aside for now. Anyway, it was a *Tanakh*, a codex or book, written on both sides of the parchment. Not a scroll. Not a sefer Torah."

"But women weren't allowed to be scribes, either."

"Have you heard of Asenath Barzani?"

Miryam shook her head. "Who is that?"

"She was born about 1590 and lived to be 80. Her father was a famous rabbi, a mystic and Kabbalah master who started yeshivas in many cities throughout Kurdistan. He had no son, so he taught Asenath to read and write Hebrew—something that was almost unheard of for women in that era—and to pray, to understand and interpret Torah and Talmud, to embrace the kind of piety followed by observant Jewish men of her day.

"Asenath married her cousin, also a noted rabbi, and they had a couple of children. Her husband ran a yeshiva that her father had founded in Mosul. But Asenath's husband died very young. To support her family, she took his place."

"Wait," Miryam protested. "A 17th-century woman running a yeshiva for men?"

"She was quite extraordinary: The first Rosh Yeshiva, the first woman dean and head teacher of a men's Talmudic academy, in all Jewish history. And in the context of her times, she met the definition and in all ways fulfilled the duties of a rabbi, a teacher."

Miryam's face registered surprise. "She was the first female rabbi?"

"Many think so. I think so. There's much, much more. Miracles are attributed to her. More to the point, she wrote poetry, in Hebrew, and some of it has survived."

"And you think she wrote my *Tanakh?*"

"It's a good possibility. There is a commandment that every man is obliged to write a Torah. She was a woman living, in many ways, a man's life; I think that, if she wrote it, it was not for worship services, because this wasn't permitted, but for other women to study."

"I am amazed, Professor Ben, at the width and depth of your knowledge."

"Thank you, Grasshopper. And my mind is constantly boggled that anyone as smart and beautiful as you would ever favor me."

"Don't forget rich, Father Ben. I'm also rich."

"It crossed my mind, but that leads us to a whole different discussion."

"So how do I find out about my *Tanakh?*"

"You ask the police to release it, and eventually they will, because, after all, it's a valuable religious object. Then we could take it to the Jewish Museum for analysis. They may be able to find samples of Asenath Barzani's calligraphy, perhaps from her poetry, and that could serve as a basis for comparison to determine authorship."

"Or we could take it to Israel," Miryam said.

"Of course. But Israel now is in the grip of powerful Orthodox rabbis, both the Ashkenazi and the Sephardic. Anything that might conflict with their views of proper behavior is immediately suspect. Depending on how offended they decide they want to be over a *Tanakh* allegedly written by a mere woman, it might take decades to fully evaluate it. It might even get lost or misplaced. Or burn up in a mysterious fire."

"Are you serious?"

"Completely. It would be wise to get a preliminary opinion here in the States before you take it overseas. Let the scholarly community take note of the find. Then the haredim could try to discredit their findings, but they won't be able to sweep it under the table."

"Okay. Detective Ben, I want to ask you something else."

"You've already had your shower."

"I'm serious."

"Tell me."

"What do you think we'll find in the basement?"

"A forger's studio. A place to make high-quality counterfeit documents."

"What makes you say that?"

"There's no other place in this house where he could have worked on documents. Unless he had the equipment removed long ago. He had to work in secret, so he couldn't chance letting anyone know. Not you, not Beneficia, not a casual visitor.

I've been thinking about that for days, since you first mentioned the possibility."

"I'm very tired," Miryam said.

"Me, too. And tomorrow I have a full day. I've got to see Rabbi Zeev, and I have to go tell Chana that the Aleppo Codex was never in this house."

"Will you sleep with me tonight?"

"I will sleep with you. But we will sleep, nothing more."

"No kissing?"

"We'd have to set some parameters. But we could have some kissing."

CHAPTER SEVENTY

AS IT TURNED OUT, THERE WAS QUITE A LOT OF kissing.

Ben awoke feeling good. He'd slept well, Miryam had almost recovered her former good cheer, and his once-daunting hunt was all but completed: He'd found the stolen Benkamal codex; Steinberg and Tobias were locked up; Kizzy was on the run. Catching her, prosecuting and convicting them—that was for the police and the courts.

By 7:00, he was pounding the warming asphalt, pushing hard, going full tilt the last mile, reassured by the knowledge that he still had plenty left afterward. By 8:00, he was under the shower, and by 9:00, after a bagel and coffee, he walked Miryam to the subway so she could meet her new estate attorney in Manhattan.

Ten minutes later, Ben knocked on Rabbi Zeev's door.

"Next time, you must make the appointment," Esperanza hissed. "He is not well."

"I'm very sorry," Ben replied. "I shouldn't be long."

Ben found Rabbi Zeev at his desk, staring out the window. He turned to greet Ben, and after a moment of confusion, his face composed itself into a smile.

"Shalom, Rabbi!" he said, wheezing a little.

"Shalom, Rabbi," Ben replied. "Sick today?"

Zeev spread his palms and pursed his lips as if to say, What's new?

"Benny, every day is a gift from God. Even the days when I don't feel so well."

"Then I'll be quick," Ben said. "Were you here, in Bensonhurst, around 1950?"

"We came the following year, just before Pesach, Passover. My wife was very upset because we had sold most of our possessions and had no money for Pesach china. So we used paper plates. It seemed odd at first, but it was fine."

"Do you remember anything around that time about a sopher stam who took his own life, and later his wife had a baby that people suspected wasn't his?"

"Do you know the name, Benny?"

"Tobias."

Zeev sank deeper into his chair, closed his eyes for so long that Ben feared he had gone to sleep.

Abruptly, the old man opened his eyes and smiled.

"The name wasn't Tobias. It was Tabush, Tabbash, Tebele—something like that. He jumped from the Brooklyn Bridge, I think. Maybe the Williamsburg. One or the other. There was no funeral. They never found his body, just clothes. His shoes. A note.

"I was a young nobody. The reason I remember this is because the halakhah, the law, on the child is very clear, but the old men, the graybeards—"

He stopped himself. "And now, I am the graybeard. It's ancient history, Benny. What is this to you, now, after so many years?"

"What was the trouble about the halakhah? What do you mean by that?"

"The boy was born less than a year after his father died.

More than nine months but less than ten. There's no doubt about the law: He is the dead man's son. I told them, the other rabbis, but they had opinions about the wife. About why the man killed himself.

"They could have made things right, but they said nothing at all. That poor woman. She was very beautiful. She had good jewelry and nice clothes, and for that the neighborhood busy-bodies all but stoned her. She had to leave. I heard she went to Israel."

"I'm sorry that I upset you, Rabbi."

Zeev waved his arm, as if to say, it doesn't matter.

"Rabbi Zeev, I met that sopher's grandson. When his grandmother was accused of adultery and then his father was treated as a *mamzer*, it ruined their family."

Zeev nodded and was silent a long time. "That was a terrible thing. This has to do with the Keter?"

"In a way. I found the Benkamal parchments, the stolen one, yesterday. The grandson seems to have had something to do with stealing it, but it wasn't the Keter. It was a codex, a *Tanakh*, but it was made in Iraq or Kurdistan, about 350 years old."

"So. Then you'll be leaving. Going home?"

"Soon. A few more days, I suppose."

"Come by before you go. I'll tell Esperanza to expect you."

"Shalom, Rabbi."

"Shalom, Rabbi."

"SHALOM, RABBI," SAID THE PRETTY, petite, dark-haired woman. "I'm Aliza Weiner."

"Shalom," Ben said. "You're a cryptologist?"

"Cryptanalyst. Chana asked me to look at the notebook you brought her."

"Excuse me, Ms. Weiner, I really don't mean to be rude. I know this isn't your office, but is there a television set somewhere around here?"

Aliza smiled. She was quite lovely. "You follow the soaps?"

"No, no. It's a funeral. Any time now. A police officer—a detective that I knew."

"I saw the YouTube video! Where you put your finger in his neck. He died?"

"A couple of days later."

Aliza got up from her borrowed desk. "I think there's one in the break room," she said, and he followed her down the hall.

The internment was on WNYW: a resplendent cardinal surrounded by a blue phalanx of NYPD brass next to an open grave among a gray huddle of tombstones. Blue-uniformed pallbearers lowering a flag-draped coffin as His Eminence solemnly chanted Canticle Benedictus. The camera panned the assembly, rank upon rank of police officers, pausing briefly at Marko and Chief of Detectives Kleiser. A short, red-haired man in a fedora stood between them.

"He looks like you," Aliza said, "same long-sleeved blue shirt, khaki slacks, blue sports jacket."

"Except I'm not wearing a hat today," Ben said.

"Which one of you was on YouTube? Was that you or the guy on TV now?"

Ben smiled. "Chana can tell you all about it. Now, I've taken too much of your time already. What did you find in the notebook?"

They sat down at a small table, and Aliza laid the notebook next to a yellow pad.

"Before we get to that, there's something else we need to discuss."

She opened the notebook and, with a manicured fingernail, opened a hidden flap in its leather cover, from which she pulled a large photographic negative. Gripping it by the edges, she held it up to the ceiling light so Ben could look through it.

Ben said, "A picture of a mosque?"

"Good! Not just any mosque—the Umayyad, known as the Great Mosque of Damascus."

"Why would have a negative of a landmark stashed in a notebook?"

"Exactly my question. So I had it scanned and spent half an hour looking at it under magnification."

Ben said, "And you found what?"

"Do you see those little specks?"

Ben looked again. "That's just dirt, or imperfections in the emulsion."

Aliza put the film down and shook her head. "Microdots."

"Really?"

"Each of those specks is an instruction manual. Magnify them thirty times and you have a schedule of shortwave frequencies and times, a call sign and authentication table to confirm the identity of a radio transmission, information about making explosives and incendiaries, ways to build and plant various types of bombs: a bomb to kill the occupants of a car, a bomb to put in a car to bring down a building, booby-trapping methods, bombs to bring down a bridge—plans for making all sorts of bombs."

Ben shook his head in amazement. "What language are they in?"

"Russian. Actually, I've seen quite a number of these before: Embedded in different pictures, but the manuals were standard issue for Soviet field agents from about 1930 through the end of the Beria era. After that they used more sophisticated methods."

"That's really amazing. Thanks for finding it and taking the time to look at."

"No problem," she said. "Shall we look at the coded entries?"

"Shoot."

"I matched the letters and numbers to the list of names you gave Chana. From there, it was simple. It's an archaic double transposition or substitution code, where each letter of a name, in Hebrew, becomes a number, and the numerical value following the names was transposed and then becomes letters. The only wrinkle was that the code maker mixed Arabic letters in at random. They're meaningless."

Ben said, "Who would use a code like that?"

"It's old-school. Probably someone trained as a World War II agent, German or Soviet, possibly British. Americans rarely used this system. Our field agents preferred things like one-time pads, where the key is a random sequence of letters and numbers."

She slid the yellow sheet in front of Ben, a column of names, a column of numbers, a third column of mixed numbers and letters. The first name was Gateno, followed by the number 18 followed by the Hebrew words *Parshat Shmini*.

"That's deciphered, but I'm still not sure what it refers to," she said.

Ben said, "This means, I think, that Gateno gave 18 percent of his business for a Torah page that sets out the laws of kashrut, of kosher food. Maybe Gateno was a butcher."

"How interesting!"

"The second name was Labaton, followed by 18, followed by *Parshat Vayera*, which describes the patriarch Abraham's hospitality to strangers. This suggests that Mr. Labaton, who also surrendered 18 percent, had a small hotel or a restaurant. Or perhaps something else entirely, and he was hoping to find hospitable people."

"That doesn't sound like much of a bargain."

"Unless you're superstitious enough to believe that carrying it around with you will increase profits and protect your business from adversity. Then it's a great bargain."

"Who would believe that, Rabbi?"

"Someone raised in an in-bred, medieval society where superstition was as real as YouTube videos or solar-powered homes is to us."

"Thank you for explaining."

"Not at all. Thanks for cracking the code."

"Oh, you're welcome. So you and Chana used to date?"

Ben had to turn his head so Aliza wouldn't see his smile. Chana is giving me the heave-ho, he thought. Trying to salve the bruise by introducing me to someone else whom I might like.

Ben said, "Actually, we're just friends. We had dinner a few times. I'm also consulting for the museum. And, speaking of that, I need to see Dr. Wilson, downstairs."

"You live in Brooklyn now?"

"Cambridge. Near Harvard University."

"Oh. But you often get down here?"

Ben reached across the table and gently took both her hands in his. He looked her in the eye. "Aliza, we need to talk," he said in a low, breathy voice.

"What?"

Still holding her hands, he said, "You're beautiful, sexy, smart, funny, warm and sensitive. You have great fashion sense. You're kind and sweet. I've learned from you, grown as a human being, enjoyed every minute of our time together. It's me, not you."

She jerked her hands away. "What are you doing?"

"Breaking up with you. To save us each a year or two of heartburn. I travel constantly. Before this trip, I hadn't spent a night in New York in three years. I'm going to Pittsburgh next.

Aliza, these long-distance relationships rarely work out. So, my darling, I'm so very sorry if I hurt you, it's been fabulous, but I'm afraid it's over."

Aliza giggled. Ben giggled.

"I'm pretty sure Chana was trying to get us together, bless her heart," he said. "But I really have to go now." He got to his feet and hurried away.

CHAPTER SEVENTY-ONE

_____

M IRYAM ADMIRED THE VIEW OF MIDTOWN FROM her lawyer's office, thinking about all the questions she wanted to ask.

"All the really successful lawyers have offices across the street," said the lawyer, and then placed an exquisite crystal cup filled with ice water on the desk in front of Miryam.

She smiled. "What makes you say that?"

"Because their offices have a view of the Empire State Building," he replied, "while ours merely have a view of the more successful lawyers' offices."

Miryam giggled. The attorney was a graying, overweight man in an expensive suit. The office was richly appointed. Miryam was sure that he made a good living.

The purpose of this meeting, he said, was to get acquainted and to give her a list of documents he needed to get her father's and Shemuel's estates into probate court.

"Am I paying you for this?" Miryam asked, "Because if you're on the clock we should really get to work."

The lawyer snorted. "Many estate lawyers don't bill hours," he said. "Have you ever read Bleak House? Dickens?"

Miryam shook her head, no. "_A Tale of Two Cities, Oliver_

Twist, A Christmas Carol. I started *Great Expectations* but never finished it."

"Spoiler alert: *Bleak House* is a large estate with many heirs and creditors. The case drags on so long that all the assets go to pay the lawyers who worked to settle it."

"Oh. So you'll charge, what, a percentage of the estate?"

"Exactly. The bigger the estate, the smaller my percentage. And the court will have to approve it, anyway. I'll evaluate the assets and liabilities see what's involved, and I'll tell you what I want. So relax. Today, we'll just get to know each other, discuss what you think the estate's major assets are, any problems you see, go over the paperwork."

"Okay. The first problem is I think that the man who just died, the man whom I knew as my father's uncle, was actually a Soviet spy living in Syria who murdered my grandparents and my father's uncle and stole his identity. He didn't want to be a spy anymore, so he kidnapped my father, who was then a little boy, then immigrated to the U.S. on a false passport. Later on, I'm pretty sure that he murdered my father and mother. "

The lawyer stared at Miryam.

"I'm not crazy. Well, maybe a little crazy about my fiancé. He's a rabbi."

"Did your father's uncle have a Social Security number?"

"My father's uncle never set foot in this country. As for the man who stole his identity, the man I believed was my great uncle—not that I've been able to find," she replied.

"Start at the beginning," the lawyer said.

———◦◦◦◦◦———

TWO HOURS LATER, MIRYAM EMERGED into 29th Street and turned right toward Sixth Avenue where, she thought, she'd try to find a coffee shop, call Ben, see whether they could meet somewhere for lunch.

As Miryam turned onto Sixth, she heard the distinctive rattle and screech of skateboard wheels and half-turned to the right, craning her neck to identify the source.

She never saw the muscular man in a Columbia U. T-shirt roll up on her left.

The man who snatched her petite body off the sidewalk.

The man who covered her mouth with his other hand.

The man who shot the skateboard over the curb and into the street.

The man who stopped abruptly as a Yellow Cab's passenger door flew open.

The man who shoved her inside, slammed the door, and sped off on the skateboard.

Inside the taxi, a woman in a Halloween mask pointed a gun at Miryam.

"One sound and I'll blow your face off," she said.

The driver reached over from the front seat and covered Miryam's eyes and mouth with heavy gaffers tape.

CHAPTER SEVENTY-TWO

D^{R. WILSON HAD UNFOLDED AND LAID ALL EIGHTEEN} parchments out on a roll of cotton muslin that covered a long table in his lab. Each page was a study in faded ink and parchment aged to shades from ecru to umber. Ben leaned forward, studying each in turn.

"What do you see, Rabbi?" Wilson asked.

Ben said, "You've made it easy for me. The four in the top row, are all from the same source and appear to be the oldest. The ones in the middle row, eleven pieces, were probably written by the same sopher, but not the same one who did the top row. Those in the bottom row of three were made by still another scribe, and probably by more than one person."

"Go to the head of the class, Rabbi."

Wilson looked up, watching Ben's face. "I believe that carbon dating and further analysis of the parchment and ink will confirm that the four pages in the top row are in fact pages heretofore missing from the Aleppo Codex."

Ben's face lit up. "Wow! That's wonderful."

"The second row was done by a very competent sopher whom I believe had no knowledge of the Codex's scribal style. He employed a calligraphy that was common in Syria about 600 years ago, before the Spanish Expulsion brought Spaniards and their scribes to Aleppo. It's distinctly different from that of the ben Asher family of Masoretes in Tiberius, the team of scribes that wrote the Aleppo Codex."

Ben scratched his head, thinking. "And the third row?"

"One is Polish, probably 17th century, one is Turkish or Kurdish, 18th century, the other is probably German or Austrian, 19th century."

Ben looked at the owners' names, and then consulted the page that Aliza Weiner had prepared for him.

Ben said, "Dr. Wilson, have you been given the background on all this? Do you know how I came by these fragments, and of my suspicions about Shemuel Benkamal?"

"Dr. Kaplan briefed me."

"And have you seen this list?"

"Not until now."

"This was taken from a notebook hidden in Benkamal's office. There were thirty-seven names on the list. Of those, only 14 are represented by a Torah page here. Do you have an opinion or a theory for all this?"

"A theory: The top four are authentic, and Benkamal had nothing to do with them.

"The second eleven pages were done by a contemporary scribe—I mean, a contemporary of Mr. Benkamal—on old parchments that were scraped clean and re-lettered. The ink is modern and was artificially aged. The parchments are from multiple sources, suggesting that the group was produced for fraudulent purposes."

"I agree," Ben said. "The last three are represented by names near the bottom of the notebook list. My theory is that the scribe who produced the eleven in the middle was no longer involved. Benkamal obtained these pages from various sources, perhaps from someone who had an old Torah or who repaired them."

"We are in agreement, Rabbi," Wilson said, offering his hand. "Dr. Kaplan should be here soon, if you'd care to wait."

"I'll be on the cafeteria terrace, while I make some calls," Ben said.

———

BEN'S FIRST CALL WAS TO Miryam's Radio Shack phone, the one he'd given her weeks earlier. The call went straight to voice mail, so he tried her other number.

When that also went to voice mail, he called the landline at her home, which had neither voice mail nor an answering machine. He let it ring for five minutes, in case she was working down in the basement.

There was no answer.

Ben looked up to see Chana waving at him from the cafeteria entrance, and he beckoned her over. After they exchanged perfunctory hugs, she leaned against the rail, lovelier than ever in a sheer summer dress.

Chana said, "So you broke up with Aliza," and laughed.

"I realized that she was just a rebound romance," Ben replied. "After you brushed me off, I needed assurance that I still had all my manly virtues."

Chana pulled a face and touched Ben's arm. "Ben, we really do need to talk."

"I'll make it easy, Chana. You've met someone else, someone who rings your chimes in a very different way, and now that you are truly free to resume your life, you will continue to value our friendship and will always want to keep that part of what we had together."

Chana hissed, "You can really be annoying, do you know that?"

Ben said. "Sometimes. I kind of have to work at it."

"Ben, I haven't met anyone else. And it breaks my heart that I have to say this. But your life is an endless series of YouTube videos."

"That's kind of a new thing, Chana."

"There's actually a story about the videos in this morning's Times! But it's not the video. It's what you do that makes people want to take pictures. One night, you're kicking some sociopath across the room, the next you're fighting three armed men, or you're saving a policeman stabbed by some killer, then you're in a deli rumble with another gunman. How long can this go on before somebody shoots you or stabs you or throws you off a building?"

"A long time, I hope."

"Don't be snide. Ben, I really care about you. I do. But I can't commit to a relationship where I worry every day if you're coming home in one piece or in a box. I just can't do it."

Ben tried to formulate a reasoned response, but couldn't.

"And children," Chana continued. "How could we have children, when first of all you won't be home, you'll be out saving some synagogue or righting some terrible wrong? And then, when our kids grow up they'll get to worry about you too? I just can't do this, Ben. I just can't."

Ben moved forward and took Chana in his arms, a long, chaste, brotherly hug. When she finally stepped back, he said, "I get it, Chana. I do. And don't think I'm not appreciative that you tried to set me up with Aliza Weiner."

"She's actually a little turned on by watching you on video," Chana said. "Maybe more than a little."

"That won't last. Please understand, I never go looking for a fight."

"I know, I know. It's what you do that invites confrontations. It comes with the territory. But that's really who you are, Ben. You like living on the edge. I can't picture you living on a farm in the South of France, a country squire. You'd go crazy."

"You're moving to France, Chana?"

"Just until next spring. It's a lovely place that Mo bought

years ago, and it's part of my settlement. My mother is coming with me."

"When will you leave?"

"Not for a few weeks. I'm taking a year's sabbatical at Fordham, and there's so much to do before I take off."

"We'll talk again, soon."

"Wait," Chana said, again all business. "I haven't been to see Dr. Wilson yet, but I understand that you recovered four pages from the Codex. What else?"

"In a nutshell, the codex that was stolen from the Benka-mal's was not the missing portion of the Aleppo Codex. I'm certain that Shemuel Benkamal, or whoever the hell he really was, never had it. It was all a scam. He created the impression that he had it, he had a sopher stam make phony pages from old parchment, and he traded them for minority shares in small businesses. At some point, the sopher quit, or more likely outlived his usefulness."

"So it was all a giant fraud?"

"There are still plenty of people who think they can buy a place in heaven. People who will spend a fortune for what they think is a sliver from the cross upon which Jesus died, or the rod used by Moses. And don't forget the Mormon Letters. This was just a wrinkle on that ancient con game. Ironically, the *Tanakh* that was recovered, the one stolen from Miryam, might be almost as valuable as the Codex and of great historical importance, but Shemuel apparently had no idea about that. He kept it in a makeup case on his office floor. "The police have it now, as evidence, and when they release it to Miryam, I've suggested that she bring it here for evaluation. Maybe her estate lawyer will suggest that she donate it and take the tax deduction. I think she's going to need one."

"She's in very good hands with that firm," Chana said.

"That reminds me: Do you have his number? She went to

see him this morning, but I haven't been able to reach her since then."

Chana opened her purse, fished around, and handed Ben a card. "That's the firm. The estate guy there is Arthur Sjoberg."

Chana left, and when Ben called Sjoberg's office, his secretary said that Miryam had left before noon, in good spirits.

That was almost three hours ago, Ben thought. A sinking feeling filled his viscera. Something was terribly wrong.

CHAPTER SEVENTY-THREE

BEN LEANED AGAINST THE TERRACE RAIL, THINKING. What could have happened so that Miryam wouldn't answer her phone? Could she have left one phone home and forgotten to charge the other one?

That was possible. He'd done things like that himself.

It was also possible, he realized, that she was in the subway. Only a few of the stations had reliable cell service.

That had to be it, he decided. He'd try to call her again.

Then his phone rang, and Marko said, "Bad news: The D.A. didn't have enough to charge Tobias or Steinberg with murder, so they made bail on the burglary charge."

"When was that?" Ben said.

"Late last night. But get this: The woman who put up both bonds gave her name as Ketsiyah Tabbash."

Ben said, "Kizzy?"

"The same. Where you at? Had lunch? There's a guy you oughta meet."

HE WAS BEING FOLLOWED, BEN realized. A muscular man in his 20s, dark hair chopped into a spiky crew cut; he'd noticed him earlier in the day, when he got on the subway in Bensonhurst. The man was bare-headed, wearing an untucked white, short-sleeved dress shirt over gray slacks.

Three hours later, when Ben left the museum, he'd walked to 77th and Lexington, and then went down into the subway. The guy who got on the train with him wore a Knicks cap with a Hofstra T-shirt and jeans, but Ben was certain that he was the same man.

The last time he was followed, Ben recalled, his pursuers kept changing their appearance. Tobias and Steinberg were out on bail, but this man was younger and bigger, more buff, than either of them.

The last time, he had evaded them. He had called attention to himself. The last time, there was team of two followers, but he'd seen only one at a time. That had led to at least two murders.

Ben decided to ignore the man.

He found the deli on the corner in the East Village where Marko had said it would be, but as he neared the entrance, he was shoved from behind, half-lifted, half-pushed into a brick wall. Something hard and cold was jammed into the back of his neck.

"Just listen," a man's voice said, not much above a hoarse whisper.

"We've got no quarrel with you, Rabbi. We don't really want to hurt your girlfriend. But if you ever want to see her alive, you'll be on the 4:10 Amtrak to Boston."

Something was thrust into his jacket pocket.

"We'll have eyes on you all the way to Boston, so don't even think about staying here. No phone calls. And no cops. Go to the police, and your little Miryam is dead."

Ben said, "What's this about? What do you want?"

"Not your concern. Just be on the 4:10."

Ben felt a hand reach into his left pants pocket and come out with his Radio Shack phone.

The man said, "Now you're going to count to a hundred, and then you can turn around. I don't want to shoot you, but I will. Get on that train."

The gun was removed from his neck. Ben waited.

"I don't hear you counting," said the hoarse voice.

"You didn't say it had to be aloud."

The gun barrel slapped the side of his head, hard. "Start counting, Rabbi."

"One, two, three, four, five ..."

When he got to thirty, Ben turned around. The street was empty.

He reached into his jacket pocket and found a plain white envelope. In it was a one-way Amtrak ticket to Boston and a color picture, the kind printed from a home computer. The picture showed Miryam curled face-up in the trunk of a car, trussed from ankles to shoulders in silver gaffers tape. Her eyes were a silent scream.

He had an hour to get to Penn Station.

CHAPTER SEVENTY-FOUR

ICHAEL TABBASH WATCHED THE LITTLE RED-headed rabbi go into the deli. He'd give him five minutes, he decided. Time enough to use the toilet, if that's what he needed. Michael moved a few feet until he had a clear line of sight to the pay phone in the front of the deli. He'd seen his brother take the rabbi's cell phone. If the guy went to use the phone, he'd call Kizzy and tell her.

He looked at his watch again. Three minutes. Four. Then the door to the deli flew open, and the little redhead came running out, clutching a paper bag.

Sonofabitch, Michael thought. He just got himself something to eat on the train. I should have thought of that.

The redhead loped off, and Michael went after him, stretching out his stride, then jogging, finally running to keep up. By the time Michael reached Astor Place Metro station, he was winded, and his new shirt was stained with sweat.

He followed him down into the station, not too close, waited for the train, watched to make sure his quarry boarded it, and then got on just as the doors were about to close, the way his cousin Gershom had taught him.

He stayed at one end of the car, his back turned, watching the rabbi's reflection in the window. When the little man got off at Times Square and changed to the Broadway local, Michael was right behind him. He followed him upstairs at Penn Central, then to the big board that displayed which train ran on which track.

He watched him board the Amtrak, waited a few seconds, got on the car in front, then moved down the aisle, pushed through the door into the car behind and took a seat two rows behind the little man. He couldn't be sure, but he didn't think he had a chance to use a cell phone, if he'd somehow got one. Anyway, cell service in the station was shitty.

So far, so good. He didn't really want to go to Boston, but Kizzy had insisted. He'd take the next train back and maybe get to the house by midnight.

She hadn't told him much about the man, just that he was a rabbi. He was short and slender, clean-shaven, He sure didn't look like any rabbi he'd ever seen, but Kizzy knew what she was doing. Kizzy was never wrong.

The most important thing, she'd told him, was getting him to Boston and making sure that he didn't call the cops.

He decided to move. The seat across the aisle was occupied by a fat old woman. She gave him a dirty look when he squeezed past her to sit by the window.

Now he could keep an eye on the guy all the way to Boston.

CHAPTER SEVENTY-FIVE

THE TAPES COVERING HER EYES AND MOUTH WERE ripped away, and Miryam was blinded by brilliant light.

"How ya doing? Need some water? A bathroom?" a man's voice said.

"Who are you people? What do you want?"

"Last chance, princess. Water and a bathroom, or back into the dark and piss your pants. Your choice."

Miryam looked around, still half-blinded by what she saw now was a floodlight, considering her answer for a long moment. "Water, please, then the bathroom."

A hand appeared at the side of her head, holding a cup. Miryam sipped a little. It tasted fine, just water. She drained the cup.

"Thank you," she said. "I'd like the bathroom now, please."

"Yeah, there's lots of things I'd like, too. You can use the bathroom later. First, you need to answer some questions."

"If I can."

"Did your uncle, your great-uncle Shemuel, ever mention the name 'Ephraim Tabbash,' or either of those names, by itself?"

"Not that I remember. He never spoke about his business."

"Do you know what his business was?"

"I think he was a partner in several neighborhood shops. But I don't know which ones. Or what they did. He never told me anything."

"How old are you?"

"Twenty-six."

"How long have you lived in his house?"

"My parents disappeared in 1995; I stayed there until I went to Israel for college. I came back a few days before he died. Please, what is it that you want?"

"We want you to answer our questions."

"I really need to use the bathroom."

"Put a cork in it. You start being helpful, you'll get your bathroom."

"Then ask me something I know about."

"Why did your uncle Shemuel kill Ephraim Tabbash? What did he do with his body? Is it in your house?"

Miryam began weep. "I just need to use the bathroom," she said.

Hands came out of the darkness to cover her mouth and eyes with tape. The light winked out. She heard the footsteps of two people receding. A door slammed behind her.

CHAPTER SEVENTY-SIX

F ROM THE MOMENT HE SAW THE PHOTO OF MIRYAM, Ben's mind spun furiously.

Think, he told himself. Ignore the tide of despair rising in your belly and think.

It must have something to do with Shemuel.

Then it probably has something to do with his fake amulet scam.

Then it has something to do with the Torah pages that were made by a sopher.

Shemuel, Daud Khan, David Cohen, must have hired that scribe.

One of the men who broke into the house was the grandson of that scribe.

The scribe's death had ruined his family.

The scribe was supposedly a suicide, but no body was found.

Before that, Shemuel stole the identity of a man who drowned. In a desert.

When Miryam's parents disappeared, Shemuel told two different stories about their supposed deaths. Both involved drowning. No bodies were found.

Was the scribe complicit in Shemuel's amulet scam? Did he

make the fake pages that Shemuel sold as pages from the Keter? Did Shemuel kill the scribe too?

Were the murders of Beneficia and Shemuel, the burglary and the subsequent attempts to break into the house—were they all connected?

Rabbi Silber said the scribe's family name was Tobias, but Rabbi Zeev said that the suicide scribe was named Tabbash or Tabush or Tebele.

Kizzy, one of those who took the safe from the Benkamal house, used the name Ketsiyah Tabbash to post bail for Soper and Steinberg.

Ketsiyah was Hebrew for a kind of edible tree bark. Was Tabbash the Sephardic equivalent of Tobias? Was Kizzy somehow related to Soper?

Ben stopped counting and looked around. He was alone.

Ben burst into the deli, spotted Marko in a corner booth and hurried over.

"There's no time," he began, then stopped.

Seated across from Marko was a short, slender, red-headed man who looked enough like him to be his brother.

"Rabbi Ben, meet Patrolman Daniel McEgan."

Ben slid into the booth and looked at McEgan. "Are you armed?"

"Always," McEgan said.

A waitress put two corned beef sandwiches on the table.

Ben said, "Can you wrap one to go? And can you do it in the next two minutes?"

As the waitress hurried off, Ben took the picture out of his pocket and pushed it across the table to Marko. He handed the Amtrak ticket to McEgan.

"Listen very carefully," he said, "especially you, Officer McEgan."

CHAPTER SEVENTY-SEVEN

M IRYAM HEARD THEM COMING. HEARD THE DOOR
open, then footsteps. Hands on her body, felt herself
lifted.

"You dirty little girl! Pissed your panties, didn't you?" a
man said.

A woman giggled.

She felt herself carried through doors, down steps, over
grass. A door opened. Squeaky hinges announced the opening
of a car trunk. She was pushed out into space, laid roughly in
the trunk. The air compressed around her as the trunk lid
slammed.

The engine was loud, and the muffler under her rattled.
Miryam wondered whether it leaked, whether carbon monoxide
was seeping into the confined space.

Please God, she prayed. Save me. I am young, I want to
live. I want children. I want Ben to save me. Please, God, send
my Ben. Send him soon. Please.

CHAPTER SEVENTY-EIGHT

———————

BEN WATCHED MCEGAN HURRY TOWARD THE DOOR wearing Ben's yarmulke, a paper bag in his hand. "They work in pairs. Look for somebody to follow McEgan," he said.

Marko peeled off his jacket and went toward the door in time to see a young man in a sports coat step out of a doorway across the street and hurry after McEgan.

"Got a good look at his face," Marko said, sliding back into the booth.

He eyed the corned beef sandwich.

Ben said, "There's not much we can do until after dark. Go ahead and eat. I'll try to describe what I think is going down."

Marko said, "Start with why you think the girl was kidnapped."

"Makes more sense if I start at the other end."

Marko took a bite, chewed.

"Some of this is fact; some is guesswork."

"Go ahead." He took another big bite.

"I've been looking at this ass backwards. I thought it was just about a con that morphed into murder, and a gang of greedy thieves. It is that, but it's way more.

"Sometime during, or maybe right after, World War II, the

Russians—the Soviet Union—sent agents into Syria to keep an eye on things or maybe to stir up trouble for the Vichy French, and later for the Free French and the British.

"One of those agents was a young Jewish Chechen who spoke Arabic and was trained as a document forger. That was the guy we know as Shemuel Benkamal."

Marko put his sandwich down. "You know this for sure?"

"I've got his Soviet passport, and three others, and his spy kit: microdot manuals for making bombs, secret communications, all that."

Marko stuffed a French fry into his mouth.

"In 1947, when it looked like there was going to be a Jewish state in Palestine, Syria's Arab masters whipped up mobs in Aleppo, where most of the country's Jews lived. The mobs sacked the main synagogue, killed more than a hundred Jews, burned and looted Jewish homes. That synagogue held the most important Jewish document in the world, the Aleppo Codex, which goes back to the year 920.

"The Codex and other important scrolls and documents disappeared. Some individual Jews and families tried to recover them; most of the Codex turned up in 1958 in Aleppo, where it had been hidden after the 1947 massacre. But most of the Five Books of Moses, about a third of the Codex, remained missing.

"Miryam's grandparents lost their home. They took their son, a toddler, and went to Damascus, where they had family. They asked their cousin, Shemuel Benkamal, to help them leave the country. He found someone to make phony passports and take them to the border with Trans-Jordan."

Marko said, "Whoa. Trans-Jordan? Where's that?"

"The country we now call Jordan, plus what we now call the West Bank, was carved out of the Ottoman Empire after World War One and called Trans-Jordan."

"Got it. Go on."

Ben continued, "They planned to go to Amman, then Jerusalem. They may have had some of the parchments—different things, including Torahs—from the Aleppo synagogue."

Marko finished the sandwich, took a sip of water, and then started on the fries.

"The man guiding them was that same Soviet agent. He took them out into the desert and murdered Miryam's grandparents and her great uncle Shemuel—"

"And stole his identity," Marko put in. "It's starting to make sense. But why?"

"He must have realized that he had no future as a Soviet spy," Ben replied. "He couldn't just quit and go home. He couldn't hide in Syria. He had to have a new identity, and he had to leave the country. But he had no money.

"After killing the parents, he took their baby, Miryam's father Isaac, went to Aleppo, and passed himself off as Shemuel. He made counterfeit passports for a wealthy Jewish family, pretending that he bought them. He got them to pay his way to New York.

"After he got here, he began to hear rumors that some families had smuggled parts of the Aleppo Codex out of Syria. I think a few pages actually came here, one by one, held by superstitious Jews who thought of them as holy protection from evil spirits."

Marko wiped his fingers and mouth on a napkin and sat back. "Finish up."

"Shemuel spread the rumor that he had some or all of the missing Codex pages. He found a sopher stam, a scribe who makes sacred scrolls, such as Torahs, and got him to take old parchment and counterfeit a couple of dozen pages that could pass as pages from the Codex. Shemuel traded these, one by one, in secret, for silent partnerships in small businesses. Before long, he had a steady income. Then he began to expand, by sweetening the deal, trading a fake page along with a little cash, enough to help a struggling startup business, for a bigger piece of it. He did this over and over.

"At some point, the sopher became a problem. Maybe he demanded a bigger cut. Maybe he became a loose end. Either way, that scribe disappeared. They found his shoes, his clothes and a suicide note on the Brooklyn Bridge. But they never found his body.

"A little over nine months later, the sopher's wife gives birth. She was beautiful, she had nice clothes and good jewelry—so the community opinion leaders decide that her husband the scribe had killed himself because she was unfaithful. The woman is shunned; her baby is classified a *mamzer*, a child of a forbidden relationship. He can't marry another Jew; he can't be a sopher stam, the family's traditional occupation. Even worse, his children are considered *mamzers*, and their children, and so on, for ten generations. Some of the local rabbis know this is wrong, but they're cowardly and do nothing to stop it.

"The family was ruined. They left the area, but things were never the same for them. I think their name was Tabbash. Ashkenazi people might pronounce it Tobias."

Marko looked up. "Then Tobias is Soper, the guy you took out in the Italian deli? And Tabbash is the name Kizzy used when she posted his bond."

"Ketsiyah Tabbash. That's Hebrew. Her other names may be aliases. Maybe she married an Armenian—Sarkissian."

"So Soper's what, her brother?"

"Or her cousin."

"Wrap this up. I got calls to make if we're gonna find your girlfriend alive."

"Recall that Kizzy liked to run the Sweetheart Con. I think she got a census job to troll for old guys. The Gypsy con. She found Benkamal and started. Then she realized who he was, his relationship to her late grandfather. Maybe her mom told her. Or a cousin.

"They broke in, looking for valuables, sure, but also anything that would shed light on what had really happened to their grandfather. They wanted to restore their good name. They didn't like being a family of *mamzers.*"

"Say that I buy all that. Now why did they kidnap your girl?"

"To get in her house. They've tried for weeks. Had to stop when you put a security detail across the street. They'll wait for dark and tear the house apart to learn what happened to their grandfather. They'll make her help. That's why they want me out of the way."

"You think they'll find any part of what they're looking for?"

"I think their grandfather, the scribe, along with Miryam's parents, is buried in that house," Ben said. "Yesterday, Miryam found a secret room under the basement. There's a short flight of stairs leading to a cinderblock wall. I'd be amazed if their bodies aren't buried on the other side of that wall."

CHAPTER SEVENTY-NINE

T HEY WERE SIX. THEY CARRIED TOOL BOXES AND Miryam, rolled inside an old blanket, into her house. The youngest, still in his teens, sat on the porch keeping watch, while inside, the others pulled down shades and drew curtains before switching on the lights.

They dropped Miryam on the living room sofa. When the tape was removed from her eyes, she saw four men and a woman, all wearing Lone Ranger masks.

The woman said, "Your rabbi boyfriend went to Boston. No one else knows about this. If you want to live, you'll cooperate."

Miryam didn't believe that Ben would go to Boston without telling her. Why? For something to do with his H.I.V.? Or his DNA test? No, he would have called and called. When he didn't hear from her, he would call Marko. These animals, she realized, will kill her when they finish. Her only chance was to stall until Ben and Marko came.

"What do you want?" Miryam croaked, in a voice cracked with thirst.

"Is there a secret compartment in Shemuel's desk?"

"There always is in those rolltops. I don't know why they even call it secret."

"Where is it?"

"My throat is very dry. May I have some water, please?"

"Maybe later. Where's the secret compartment?

"It's empty. We took everything out."

"Where is it?"

"I'm not sure. Ben moved a bunch of drawers around, took one out, moved another one. Anyway, we took everything out."

"And what did you do with it?"

"It's all at the Jewish Museum."

"What was it?"

"Just family papers. My grandmother's ketubah. Some birth certificates. Some letters in German, Arabic and Hebrew. Old passports."

"The Hebrew ones. What did they say?"

"Nothing much. Family stuff. Little Yossi is getting big, Sara misses you, when are you coming to visit, guess who came to our anniversary party. Stuff."

"What else?"

"I really need water."

The woman looked at one of the men and gestured. He went into the kitchen and returned with a coffee cup half full of water. The woman took it from him.

"What else was in the compartment?"

"Nothing."

"You're totally full of shit. You know what? We don't need your help."

The woman drank the water and dropped the cup on the floor.

"You two, start in the office," she said. "Take the desk apart. Move it aside and look under it."

One man picked up a chain saw. Another hefted his toolbox. They went down the hall and into Shemuel's office.

The woman said, "I'll start on this room, then the basement."

The two remaining men grabbed Miryam and carried her upstairs. "Your uncle's bedroom?" the shorter one asked.

"Water," she said.

"You're just stalling," the taller one replied.

They dragged Miryam into the first room on the right: a girl's room, with pale pink wallpaper, a chenille bedspread and a vanity with a makeup mirror.

They shoved Miriam's bed against the wall and put her on it, face down.

"What's in your closet?" demanded the shorter man.

"My winter clothes. Old suitcases."

"I saw a door in the hallway ceiling. Is that an attic?"

"Just a crawl space," Miryam replied. "Please, may I have some water?"

"We gave you water, and we got nothing in return."

"Sorry. I thought I was talking to a human being."

The tall man picked her up, slammed her down on the bed, and slapped her face, hard, twice. He took out a roll of tape and sealed Miryam's mouth again.

"Find the old man's room," said the shorter man, and his companion took a crow bar out of a toolbox and left.

From downstairs came the sound of hammers and the groan and shriek of tortured wood. The taller man went across the hall to a barely furnished guest room. Ben's suitcases were in an otherwise empty closet.

He went to the next room down the hall, found a bed with a bare mattress and a closet stacked with cleaning gear: a vacuum cleaner, mops, and paper towels.

He went into the last room and found a queen-size bed and full closet.

He tore the bed apart, looked in the hollow brass bedposts and was rewarded with a thick roll of parchment, which he fished out and brought back into Miryam's room to show the shorter man.

He unrolled the parchment to reveal neat lines of Hebrew calligraphy.

"Steinberg, is this anything?" the shorter man asked.

Steinberg, the shorter man, peered at it closely. "It's an old Haggadah with missing pages. The old man probably used it for parchment."

He dropped it on the floor. "Go look some more, Gershom."

A great crash of breaking glass and splintering wood came from below.

In the dining room the woman stepped behind the fallen china cabinet and slowly, carefully, felt the wall, looking for a bump, a ridge, anything.

In Shemuel's office, a man fired up a small chain saw and began cutting chunks from the roll top desk. Sawdust and smoke flew everywhere.

In Shemuel's room, Gershom Tabbash, née Tobias, pulled everything out of the closet, throwing each garment on the floor behind him. Then, standing on tiptoe, he cleared the closet shelf, opening each box and suitcase. He found a shoebox stuffed with cash, then another, and a third. He put them on the bed, then stood on a suitcase and began to probe the wall above the shelf.

In Miryam's room, Steinberg had done the same. Now he took a hammer from his toolbox and began to tap the closet walls, looking for voids.

Downstairs, the woman opened the basement door and flipped the light switch.

When nothing happened, she looked up and saw that the bulb had been removed.

She went into the kitchen, opened a drawer and returned with a flashlight. It didn't work. She dropped it and opened the basement door.

In Shemuel's room, Gershom used a crowbar to pry up a floorboard. Then another. The third time, he was rewarded.

"Hey! Come see this!" he shouted to Steinberg.

Downstairs, the woman slowly descended the wooden basement steps, feeling the wall as she went until she felt concrete beneath her shoe. She felt for the light switch and flipped it on, flooding the basement with light.

When her eyes had adjusted, she saw six cops pointing shotguns at her.

Marko stepped out of the shadows, clamped a big hand across her mouth. Foster grabbed her arms and twisted them behind her, snapped handcuffs into place. "Ketsiyah Tabbash, you're under arrest," he said, very quietly.

Ben appeared from under the stairs. "Where is she?" he whispered.

Upstairs, the office was a shambles. Drawers from the desk were everywhere, their contents strewn across the carpet among drifts of sawdust.

A man ran the saw blade across the desktop, and as it ate wood, the hidden drawer popped up. He shut the saw down and began to work the jammed, ruined drawer out of its compartment.

On the second floor, Steinberg dropped his hammer on Miryam's carpet and went across the hall to find Gershom on his knees.

Gershom had removed four more floorboards to reveal a large, old-fashioned leather briefcase with a brass lock and buckles, standing upright in a compartment.

"Well, open it," Steinberg said, and Gershom fumbled with the lock and the brass fitting for a few minutes, but the lock was jammed and wouldn't open.

"I need a key or something," he said.

Steinberg took out a Buck knife, its eight-inch blade honed to scalpel sharpness. "It's leather. Just pull the damn thing out of there," he said.

Buying in small quantities so as not to arouse suspicion, it had taken Shemuel more than a year to accumulate a kilo of aspirin tablets. He purchased small quantities of sulfuric acid from three mail-order suppliers, and bought potassium nitrate, saltpeter, in New York's Chinatown, where backroom factories turned out illegal firecrackers by the truckload.

He'd crushed and ground the aspirin into a fine powder, dissolved it in warm sulfuric acid, then stirred in the potassium nitrate. The result was trinitrophenol, which gives off toxic fumes and must be stored in glass or aluminum.

Shemuel had removed the wiring from the ceiling light in his office and filled the space in the ceiling with glass jars, each full of rubbery trinitrophenol.

At a rural crossroads general store in Pennsylvania's coal country, a clerk sold him a box of detonators, no questions asked.

Shemuel had never built a bomb before. He followed the microdot instruction manual as closely as he could. The trigger was a pair of electrical contacts on the ends of flexible boards. They were separated by a half-inch, the lower board kept depressed by cast-iron sash weights.

The weights were concealed in the bottom of an old-fashioned leather briefcase.

Gershom Tabbash lifted the briefcase.

The blast blew downward, incinerating everything and everyone in the office below.

It also blew upward into Shemuel's bedroom, incinerating both occupants.

The basement door was blown in. Smoke wafted down the stairwell. The crackle and roar of flames was heard, and the vacant doorway flickered with orange light.

Ben turned to Kizzy. "Where is she?"

Wide-eyed, the woman stared, shocked to silence.

Ben turned to Marko. "Hurry! Get everyone back out through the coal chute. I'm going to find Miryam."

Ben grabbed Kizzy's arm and started dragging her up the stairs.

"She's upstairs!" she yelled. "I'm not going up there!"

Marko said, "We'll take her. I'm coming with you."

"No time," Ben said and dashed up the stairs and into the inferno.

CHAPTER EIGHTY

HE FIRST "YOUTUBE RABBI" FOOTAGE WAS SHOT BY an M.I.T. sophomore and was date-stamped a little before 9:00 pm EDT. Relatively sharp and, considering the lighting, surprisingly clear, the video was shot on an old LG KU990 cell phone, a model not sold in the U.S., with a five-element Schneider Kreuznach glass lens. The digital file was then enhanced with noise-reduction, contrast enhancing and pixel-tightening software created by the student herself.

In stunning slow motion, the video showed a short, compact, red-headed man wearing a yarmulke chasing a much bigger man with a spiky crew cut across the Boston South's Amtrak platform, then bringing him down with a flying tackle, punching him twice, rolling him over on his face and handcuffing his hands behind his back.

The second video was shot with an iPhone 6 and date-stamped less than ten minutes after the first. It was shot by a student at Beth Hatalmud Rabbinical College who had been visiting his girlfriend in Bensonhurst a block from the burning house. A little shaky in places but noticeably sharper than the first video, it clearly showed the left side of the burning home collapsing onto itself.

A few seconds later, the same man shown in that day's

previous YouTube Rabbi footage appears in a second-story window on the right side of the house. He pushes the screen out, lets it fall, and then disappears for a moment. Then one end of a door is shoved through the window and levered until its far end rests atop the wooden pickets of the neighboring fence. The fence is perhaps three feet away but also three feet lower; the door is pitched at a steep angle. The man appears in the open window, crouching, with something, perhaps a big pillow or a laundry bag, clasped in his arms. He dashes across the improvised bridge, leaps off the end and disappears as the house behind him collapses in a fountain of flame.

The door that served as an improvised bridge appears to be suspended in mid-air for an impossibly long time. Finally, it falls into the fire. A few seconds later, the man who crossed the bridge appears on an adjacent sidewalk, carrying what now appears to be a girl or a young woman. Her arms are clasped around his neck.

Both videos got nearly a million hits in the first 72 hours after they were posted, briefly crashing YouTube's servers. Hundreds of viewers posted comments; most addressing the date-stamp time discrepancy: How could a man be in Boston and then eight minutes later appear in New York?

Most posted comments called the first video a fake, contending that it was too crisp, that the slo-mo action was probably shot in a studio, or that the date-time stamp had been altered. These doubters start a petition to make YouTube take it down. YouTube management ignored them: Controversy boosts viewership.

A minority of viewers asserted that the man in the second video, who isn't shown clearly, is not the "YouTube Rabbi" at all, but someone with a superficial resemblance.

Seven viewers post assertions to the effect that it is the same person in both videos, that he is a manifestation of God, an angel. (Two Orthodox Jewish viewers, who believe that the Deity's name is literally "God" and, because writing that name is sacrilege, suggest that the rabbi is a divine being but use G-d instead in their posts.)

Other viewers post sarcastic statements questioning the sanity of the aforementioned seven or ask what they were smoking and where they could get some.

EPILOGUE

ALTHOUGH COMMAND SERGEANT-MAJOR SCOTT MacPherson was one of the Army's youngest and newest sergeants-major, he had been the topkick of his particular infantry battalion more than long enough to know when his commanding officer was pissed.

"This is Mr. Dunleavy from the Department of Agriculture," said Lieutenant Colonel Harry Osborne, in a plummy voice redolent with ridicule.

His face expressionless, a tall, fit man in civilian clothing and carrying a leather messenger bag over his shoulder nodded in MacPherson's direction,

"He'd like to ask you a few questions," Osborne added.

"Privately," Dunleavy said.

Osborne scowled and stepped out of the tent that served as his headquarters.

"What's up, Mr. Dunleavy?" said MacPherson, playing it straight for now.

Dunleavy took a leather pouch from the bag and shook a silver filigreed pin in the shape of an open human hand onto the field table that served the colonel as a desk.

"This is called a hamsa or khomsah, the 'Hand of Fatima.' Ever seen it before?" Dunleavy said.

"Looks like the one I gave my little sister. What about it?"

"Where did you get it?"

"Found it in a cave. In Iraq," MacPherson replied. "About eight or nine years ago."

"There was no mention of it in your after-action report."

"The Department of Agriculture reads Army after-action reports? That's interesting."

Dunleavy allowed himself a thin smile. "Why didn't you report it?"

"I showed everything from the cave to my battalion intelligence officer. He said it was all old and had no intelligence value, so there was no point in writing it up. I kept it as a souvenir. So what?"

"Your report said you also found human remains?"

"Yeah, a pair of mummies. Man and a woman."

"Also in the cave?"

"Yes. When did the Department of Agriculture become interested in human remains?"

"The Department is interested in a great many things, Sergeant Major. Can you show me on a map where you found that cave?"

"All my maps are of Afghanistan."

Dunleavy took an iPad from his bag and brought up a large scale map of Iraq's Western Desert. Using his fingers on the screen, he zoomed in to the border area between Syria and Iraq, near the Syrian town of Abu Kamal.

"That's the area. There's a narrow wadi running southeast into Iraq. It goes under that bridge"—MacPherson stabbed the map symbol on the iPad screen with a grimy index finger. "As I recall, the cave was about ten feet off the wadi floor, in the cliff face. On the western side, between 200 and 300 meters from the bridge. A little hard to find."

Dunleavy closed the iPad case and returned it to his bag.

"A Blackhawk will be here in half an hour to pick us up," Dunleavy said.

"Us? Where are we going?"

"Your colonel has been told what he needs to know. You can take a toothbrush, shaving gear and underwear, but no uniforms except the one you're wearing."

"What the hell is this about, Dunleavy?"

"The US Department of Agriculture believes that there is a fresh-water aquifer close to the surface a few miles southeast of Abu Kamal. We are assisting the Iraqis in finding it by drilling test wells. You're going to help them find a good place to drill."

DEPARTMENT OF AGRICULTURE

Dear President Bar Tzvi,

While assisting our Iraqi colleagues in drilling for water in their Western Desert, one of our Department of Agriculture teams came upon an unmarked grave site containing the remains of what we believe are two Israeli citizens. The remains have been recovered and will be forwarded to Israel through the International Red Cross for identification and re-interment.

Documents found with these remains led us to a U.S. citizen of Syrian ancestry who has reason to believe that the deceased are her grandparents. She will contact your Red Magen David Society to make arrangements for DNA testing to confirm consanguinity.

If there is ever anything else we can do to help the State of Israel, please do not fail to contact us.

(original signed)
Khane L. Herrmann
Undersecretary for International Relations

About the Author

Before his 21st birthday, Marvin J. Wolf had served as a U.S. Army drill instructor, taught hand-to-hand combat to Army officers, ran a weapons squad in cold-war South Korea, sold encyclopedias door-to-door, worked in a junk yard, walked five miles through a blizzard to pay a family debt, and served with distinction as a delicatessen pearl diver. While serving as a combat photographer in Vietnam, Wolf was awarded a battlefield commission, one of only 62 such awards during the decade of that war. Back in civilian clothes, he became a globe-trotting photojournalist; when he regained custody of his adolescent daughter and was forced to choose between frequent travel and single parenthood, he turned to writing. He is the author of more than a dozen nonfiction works and a series of mystery novels. Two of his teleplays, written with Larry Mintz and based on stories from his nonfiction books, were produced as made-for-television movies. Wolf lives in Asheville, NC, with his adult daughter and a pair of ferocious Chihuahuas.